PRAISE FOR

"Krueger's portrait of artists as y[...]
and rebellion—an aesthetic vivisection of the young Victoria[...]
—*The Globe and Mail* on *Mad Richard*

"Krueger's research is evident in every paragraph: from the use of authentic slang to richly sketched portraits of the lives of the era's rich and poor, the book confidently transports the reader to another time."
—*Quill & Quire* on *Mad Richard*

"The knitting together of Charlotte Brontë's and Richard Dadd's different trajectories worked like a dream. I was enthralled."
—Terry Gilliam on *Mad Richard*

"In this remarkable piece of historical fiction, Krueger (*Drink the Sky*) imaginatively delves into the life of Richard Dadd. . . . The two story lines . . . effectively juxtapose Dadd and Brontë, two very different people who travelled in similar circles during the same era and, more importantly, who were both entirely invested in what it means to be an artist. This question anchors the novel, adding depth and dimension to a terrific read."
—*Publishers Weekly* on *Mad Richard*, starred review

"There is much to ponder in this elegant novel about the potentially catastrophic emotional toll of art, the irrational nature of love, the solitude of heartache, and what happens when one life touches another, however briefly."
—*Toronto Star* on *Mad Richard*

By engaging us in two very different lives in a state of transformation, we become engaged in the process of what it means to become an individual, moral human being. It's a powerful story about human strength and frailty. It touches something deep inside."
—*Toronto Star* on *The Corner Garden*

"Lesley Krueger…has perfectly captured the laconic tone of an intelligent teen who can still offer moments of bracing lucidity and keen observation….*The Corner Garden* is an ambitious book. It starts innocently as a contemporary picaresque journey, then delves into a history lesson and the nature of evil."
—*The Globe and Mail* on *The Corner Garden*

"Part carefully-wrought thriller, part eco-excursion into the heart of darkness…a young woman struggles with questions of identity against the backdrop of modern Brazil. Her elegant prose is a pleasure to read, and when Krueger ratchets up the tension, we go with her, hearts in mouth. She has intriguing and serious things to say about human nature and the planet."
—*Quill & Quire* on *Drink the Sky*

"*Drink the Sky* captures both the precise local colour of Rio de Janeiro (where the author lived from 1988 to 1991) and the first-time visitor's wide-eyed wonder. Krueger renders the exotic beauty of Brazil's landscape and wildlife with rhapsodic authenticity….The hidden story emerges piece by piece, as these things do, in a series of coincidences and unsuspected interrelations that weave the book's two parallel plots into a tense finale. As a cleverly plotted mystery, the book succeeds in hooking the reader."
—*Toronto Star* on *Drink the Sky*

TIME
SQUARED

LESLEY KRUEGER

TIME SQUARED

A Novel

ECW

Published by ECW Press
665 Gerrard Street East
Toronto, Ontario, Canada M4M 1Y2
416-694-3348 / info@ecwpress.com

Editor for the Press: Susan Renouf
Cover design: Ingrid Paulson
Author photo: Helen Tansey at Sundari Photography

This is a work of fiction. Names, characters, places, and incidents either are the product of the author's imagination or are used fictitiously, and any resemblance to actual persons, living or dead, business establishments, events, or locales is entirely coincidental.

LIBRARY AND ARCHIVES CANADA CATALOGUING IN PUBLICATION

Title: Time squared : a novel / Lesley Krueger.
Names: Krueger, Lesley, author.
Identifiers: Canadiana (print) 20210176164
Canadiana (ebook) 20210176202
ISBN 978-1-77041-592-8 (softcover)
ISBN 978-1-77305-806-1 (ePub)
ISBN 978-1-77305-807-8 (PDF)
ISBN 978-1-77305-808-5 (Kindle)
Classification: LCC PS8571.R786 T56 2021 | DDC C813/.54—dc23

We acknowledge the support of the Canada Council for the Arts. *Nous remercions le Conseil des arts du Canada de son soutien.* This book is funded in part by the Government of Canada. *Ce livre est financé en partie par le gouvernement du Canada.* We acknowledge the support of the Ontario Arts Council (OAC), an agency of the Government of Ontario, which last year funded 1,965 individual artists and 1,152 organizations in 197 communities across Ontario for a total of $51.9 million. We also acknowledge the support of the Government of Ontario through the Ontario Book Publishing Tax Credit, and through Ontario Creates.

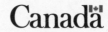

PRINTED AND BOUND IN CANADA   PRINTING: MARQUIS 5 4 3 2 1

For Susan Renouf

I CELEBRATE myself, and sing myself,
And what I assume you shall assume,
For every atom belonging to me as good belongs to you . . .

Do I contradict myself?
Very well, then I contradict myself;
(I am large, I contain multitudes.)

—WALT WHITMAN

1951
Middleford, Connecticut

0

They said the war would be over soon, but they always said that. Not that it was officially a war. A police action, the president said, although the newspapers didn't agree. The Korean War, they called it.

Eleanor was watching the CBS evening news to get the latest updates. General MacArthur was eagle-eying the North Koreans across the mountains, or at least from his hotel in Japan, where he waggled his cigar at the cameras. Millions of communist Chinese soldiers were marching in, thick red arrows on a map tracing their route. It sounded less threatening in print than it looked on her aunt's new television set. They called it black and white, but to Eleanor the picture looked black and blue, the world bruised with crisis. More nuclear tests in the Pacific, too. A mushroom cloud bloomed on the television screen, newsreel footage Eleanor had seen before of the beautiful man-made apocalypse.

She got up to turn off the set. It wasn't just the news; she had a headache. Yet what was going on in the world left her terrified. North Korea invading South Korea, communism fighting capitalism, nuclear weapons always a threat. And her fiancé was in the thick of it, when Eleanor longed for peace and stability after the Second World War. She'd been a child in London during the Blitz, tugged

3

into air-raid shelters, her ears ringing with sirens and wails, learning far too much about fear before she was twelve years old.

She'd also been an adult during the Blitz, and that wasn't a metaphorical description of a girl who had experienced war. It was the impossible literal truth.

Visions. Eleanor had been having visions lately, some of them brief glimpses of other lives, some long vivid dreams, months going by in a night; all of her dreams, no matter how long, complete immersions in different times when she was herself but life was unimaginably different. She had no idea why this was happening, feeling pushed around by a cosmic mystery. She also had a question: Was this the real time she lived in, or was it just another dream?

"You don't have a headache, do you?"

Eleanor turned to find her Aunt Clara coming in from town, taking off her gloves, her enviable coat: a fawn-coloured creation she'd stitched together with salvaged mink for the collar and cuffs. Eleanor hadn't heard the front door close, leaving her no time to prepare for her aunt's worried frown. She'd tried to explain a little of what was going on—a very little—but that had been enough to frighten Aunt Clara. There was mention of psychologists (psychiatrist being too big a word), perhaps the doctor to wrestle down the headaches.

Since they didn't have the money at the moment for, let's say, specialized care, in silent mutual agreement they'd retreated to a diagnosis of migraine and a bottle of Dr. Blyth's little pills.

"I've never had a megrim in my life," her aunt said. "Migraines, as they insist on calling them here. But I'm aware they take many different forms. Lights and colour, all of that."

"You have no idea," Eleanor replied.

1811
Middleford, Yorkshire

1

Eleanor had been dozing, she supposed, and woke cozed against her aunt in the morning room of Goodwood House. A brief moment of disorientation, when she was aware she'd been dreaming but couldn't remember more than an anxious sense she had to get to a party. A woman was urging her to hurry, hurry. They had to get started.

Some girls lingered on their dreams and fancies, thinking it romantic to show the world a poetic face. But Eleanor pushed them away, believing herself to be a practical young lady, perhaps more willful than she ought to be, but happy with the life she'd been given.

"You're back, are you?" Aunt Clara asked.

"I don't know why I dozed," Eleanor said, elbows on her aunt's lap. "I slept very well last night. I always do."

Eleanor lived with Mrs. Crosby at Goodwood, her aunt's estate in Yorkshire. She was an orphan and her rich aunt's ward, her mother having died shortly after she was born and her father when she was fifteen. Dr. Crosby had been the well-loved clergyman of Middleford parish, and his death had been deeply painful to Eleanor. But she'd always been close to her aunt, and after her father died, she had only to move across the park from the parsonage to find a new home.

Eleanor had lived in Middleford all her life, and both loved and chafed at its rural sleepiness.

Yet Middleford was abuzz lately, with the Mowbrays expecting guests. Two brothers: the eldest heir to an estate in Kent, the younger remarkably handsome. Ladies had started calculating their daughters' chances even before they'd learned that Edward Denholm would inherit an estate worth ten thousand pounds a year. Meanwhile his brother, Captain Robert Denholm, had come back a hero from the war against Napoleon. Or if he hadn't, he was very likely to prove a hero when he went.

"Of course," her aunt said, "you wouldn't be so bored if the weather didn't keep away visitors."

Eleanor rolled her eyes. "The Denholms can stay away, as far as I'm concerned."

"When they're actually both rather handsome, my dear?"

"I'm afraid our friends are going to be disappointed. I remember Edward Denholm as thinking too well of himself, while his brother was rather lazy."

"They weren't much more than children when you knew them, Eleanor."

"Well, here's a question for you, Aunt. Do people change? Or do we remain much the same as we age, even if our circumstances alter?"

Her prevailing question. Eleanor was conscious of not quite fitting into Middleford society. She owed a great deal to the education her father had given her, especially since he'd left her nothing else. But it meant she was usually called clever, and among the ladies of the parish, that wasn't so much a description as a complaint. Eleanor was passionately fond of her native county and loved to ride and take long walks. But she was often seen with a book in her hand, and some of the ladies went as far as to call her satirical: a criticism she might have avoided if she hadn't been so pretty.

Eleanor knew she ought to change, teaching herself not to be so impatient. Yet she was happy not to fit in, privately bored by many of the young ladies she'd known all her life and not caring to attract the local heirs: this despite her aunt's wish that she marry well, and soon.

Self-respect was a factor. Eleanor refused to make herself ridiculous to be popular.

"You'll have ample opportunity to decide," Mrs. Crosby said. "At least about the Denholms. Lady Anne Mowbray tells me they're staying for a month."

Goodwood House was Mrs. Crosby's principal residence, and one of the prevailing questions among Middleford ladies was whether she'd leave it to her niece.

Mrs. Crosby's first husband had left her the pleasant but modest estate in Kent where Eleanor had met the Denholm family. Her second husband had left her Goodwood House. They'd never had children, and Eleanor's father would have inherited the estate if he hadn't died a year before his brother. Since there wasn't any entail, nor any other close male relatives, the elder Mr. Crosby had left it entirely to his wife. Despite believing Eleanor to be clever, the parish agreed she ought to inherit Goodwood from her aunt. Eleanor was the last of the local Crosbys. More to the point, she was likely to marry a Middleford son, and whatever reservations they might have had about the girl, the estate was an excellent catch.

Muddying the waters was Mrs. Crosby's daughter from her first marriage. Henrietta lived in the East Indies with her husband, Mr. Whittaker. No one had any idea what Mr. Whittaker had been promised when taking Hetty off her mother's hands, although Middleford took hope from the fact she was likely to succumb to the rigours of life on a tea plantation before she could claim the estate, this despite a series of cheerful letters detailing her excellent health.

It was a dark and heavy morning as they sat by the fire, the solid rain keeping Eleanor indoors. After their talk, Mrs. Crosby turned back to her accounts, while Eleanor reopened her book. Poetry. *The Lady of the Lake.* Reading its rhythmic lines, she might have been sailing a skiff across a choppy pond, especially when rain gusted against the window, rattling the pane.

It wasn't rain. Hoofbeats pounded toward the door, horses coming to a stop outside.

"Who could be calling in weather like this?" she asked, looking up.

"I would think the young gentlemen," her aunt replied. "Arriving early."

Mrs. Crosby closed her accounts and looked at Eleanor complacently. "You've put yourself together well this morning. But then, you always do."

"And you, Aunt," Eleanor teased. "I'm sure they're looking forward to seeing *you*."

"They would have been, twenty-five years ago. My heavens, what happens to time?"

Mrs. Crosby had been a beauty, flaxen-haired with violet eyes, slight but far from helpless. She still looked very pretty, and went to the mirror to adjust a small lace cap that didn't quite contain her curls, which remained improbably blond.

Lemon juice, applied weekly. Her French maid kept Mrs. Crosby young with oils and lemons from the Covent Garden market. Mademoiselle also worked on Eleanor, who had been very blond as a child, but whose hair had begun to darken. Or at least, it was fighting to darken as Mademoiselle fought back, leaving Eleanor's thick straight hair an interesting mixture of shades that served to highlight her pretty brown eyes.

"Hazel," Mrs. Crosby would always correct, convinced that her niece was designed for an unusual fate. Fair hair and hazel eyes, a sweet disposition paired with a good mind. These things didn't often go together, and Mrs. Crosby believed they made her niece compelling to men. To a certain type of man, above the ordinary. If only he could be enticed into noticing.

"In all seriousness, Aunt," Eleanor said, hearing the door blown open downstairs. "I'm sure Mr. Denholm would consider me beneath him, an orphan girl from a provincial family." Interrupting Mrs. Crosby: "You can't object. You know it's true. And I reciprocate by having no interest in either of the Denholms. I'll quite happily cede them to Catherine Mowbray and her sisters—who are, after all, going to all the trouble of hosting them."

"I don't expect you to take an interest in the younger son," her aunt said. "But I expect you to try with Mr. Denholm. Ten thousand a year! That doesn't come knocking very often."

Eleanor was shaking her head when her aunt's housekeeper opened the door to announce the rather damp young gentlemen, Stansfield Mowbray and his friends from Kent. Eleanor had a moment's embarrassment as she wondered whether they'd heard Mrs. Crosby, but decided she didn't care if they had. Besides, the doors in Goodwood House lived up to their name. Oak and thick.

After making her curtsy, she gave a friendly smile to Mr. Mowbray, the heir to his father's baronetcy. Mr. Mowbray was a good-looking young man, his features regular, his hair sandy, his manner bluff and kind. He also had the faintly stunned expression of someone who'd received a blow to the head. Eleanor and he had long ago reached an understanding that they were unsuited, Eleanor privately thinking him dull and Mr. Mowbray, in his heart of hearts, being terrified of her.

"Here I've been proud of an opportunity to introduce my friends to the neighbourhood," he said, "and I find you're long acquainted."

Eleanor had met the Denholm brothers frequently when she'd gone with her aunt to Kent. But the acquaintance had tapered off when the brothers left for school, with Eleanor scarcely ten years old the last time she'd seen them.

"Miss Crosby has grown," Mr. Denholm said, assessing her frankly.

Eleanor did the same, and found that her aunt was right. Mr. Denholm was as handsome as a palace. A rather daunting young man, elegant, commanding, with dark hair and watchful eyes. He was also far too well-dressed, more than a bit of a dandy with his high cravat and tight-cut trousers.

"You've grown as well, sir, from a boy who was rather too proud of his ability to steal eggs from robins' nests. While, Captain," Eleanor said, turning to his brother, "I remember you as a dreamy lad, and sometimes frankly idle. Now, here you are, unpredictably in uniform."

"My apologies," Captain Denholm said, and smiled. "For what, I'm not certain." The captain was taller and seemed more at ease than his brother. He was dashing in his red coat and highly polished boots, but his smile was friendly and his hair a tumble of light-brown curls. Eleanor couldn't see anything particularly wrong with him. But then she didn't have to, her aunt having excused her from tilting at a younger son.

"Please," Mrs. Crosby said, nodding the young men into chairs. If her daughter, Henrietta, had spoken as Eleanor did, she would have intervened. But Eleanor was flirting without knowing it, an underground burble of humour taking the sting out of her words.

"Really, Mr. Mowbray," Eleanor continued, as they sat. "What friends are you bringing among us? Mr. Denholm, I can't imagine there's a gentleman in Middleford who stole eggs as a boy. We have far too many birds; I hear the farmers complain. And Captain," she began, losing her train of thought as she met his amused grey eyes. "I would have thought you'd be a clergyman."

The captain looked aside, and Eleanor was embarrassed to realize she'd struck a nerve. It was left to his brother to answer suavely.

"In fact, it was discussed," he said. "But we're at war and the country needs defending, and my brother has been good enough to offer himself."

"And I'm sure we admire you greatly for it," Mrs. Crosby said.

"I have too much respect for the clergy to join their number," the captain said. "I'm afraid I'd be rather fumbling in the pulpit."

"Far easier to say, 'Steady, aim, fire,'" Mr. Denholm said.

"And perhaps more immediately effective," the captain replied.

Eleanor liked seeing the affection between the two brothers, although they seemed very different. The captain no longer looked lazy, but as dependable as a cavalry officer ought to be. Not that she understood from his insignia whether he was an officer in the cavalry, artillery, or infantry, the young men of Middleford being far too practical-minded to offer themselves to war. Mr. Denholm seemed far more restless, and probably more intelligent than Middleford liked, acute but also distractible, starting as a blast of rain hit the windows.

The rattle reminded Mr. Mowbray to pull a note from his pocket. "I come as a messenger," he said, handing the note to Mrs. Crosby. "My mother hopes you'll be able to dine with us. She wished to invite you herself, of course. But the weather."

"Shall it clear soon, do you think?" Mrs. Crosby asked, scanning the invitation.

"Solid rain riding over," Mr. Mowbray said. "April showers and so forth. Although my father is rather preoccupied with the effect on his crops. The rot, you see."

Few subjects interested Mr. Mowbray more than his father's crops, and he was off on what was admittedly a more suitable topic for a morning call than idleness and eggs. The captain listened politely, although Mr. Denholm grew more restless the longer Stansfield Mowbray's prosing continued, making Eleanor wonder how close the friendship between the young men really was. Mr. Denholm walked over to the window, throwing Mr. Mowbray off his subject.

"I hope we'll have some good weather before your visit ends," Eleanor said, taking advantage of the pause. "We can boast several very pretty walks leading up to the moors."

"I must protest, Miss Crosby," Mr. Denholm said, turning from the window. "You're already speaking of the end of our visit when we've scarcely got here."

"My niece is a great walker," Mrs. Crosby said. "And only wants the weather to clear."

"As does my great friend Miss Catherine Mowbray, I'm sure," Eleanor said. "It's rather painful for us to be kept apart by a celestial waterfall."

"Which one is she?" Mr. Denholm asked, walking back to the fire.

"My little mouse," her brother replied, not a promising description for a potential suitor. Although, unfortunately, accurate.

"Catherine has rare talent," Eleanor said. "I never know whether I like her portraits or her landscapes best. The joint portrait she did recently, Mr. Mowbray, of your younger sisters was a remarkable study in character. Harriet looking sporty, Fanny studious, Cassandra lost in her thoughts. I was particularly struck by Mary Ann watching the artist as the artist watched her. So observant. And Alicia was being..." What was Alicia being? Eleanor tried to remember.

"There *are* rather a lot of them," Mr. Denholm said.

"Although the eldest is very well married," her aunt put in.

"Alicia being very pretty," Eleanor finished firmly.

"It speaks well of your own powers of observation that you can make us see the portrait so clearly," the captain said.

He stood, their call over.

"I'm sure you'll be happy to return to your book," Mr. Denholm said, following his brother toward the door. Eleanor wasn't sure whether that was a barb or an invitation to lament the fact he was leaving.

"In fact, my niece has been helping me with the household accounts," her aunt lied.

Eleanor hoped they would take her blushes as modesty rather than embarrassment that her aunt was so obviously parading her before a young man of means. She wanted to retract the claim but couldn't think how.

"You were going to say, Miss Crosby?" Mr. Denholm asked, pausing at the door.

"My father instructed me, you know," she said. "Of course, my aunt taught me the accounts, but my father instructed me in mathematics. Up to a point."

She was back on her stool in her father's study at the parsonage, with its amply filled bookcase. It was a happy well-lit room, and she always joined her father there for lessons. Her portly, kindly, witty father with his wild eyebrows and bulging lower lip would set her working on geography, French, even some Latin. Her favourites were the sums and problems he would write on her slate, until the day when she was perhaps fourteen and he looked over her answers, telling her, "More or less, more or less. But here I think we've reached our limit."

"Are you tired, Papa?" she'd asked.

"No, but I've been waiting for this," he said, leaning back in his chair and examining her keenly. "The critical point. I instructed my late sister Joan, you know, when she was a girl. She was clever as well, and it's a pity you never knew her. But eventually I found she'd reached the end of her ability to grasp mathematical concepts, hard as we tried to surpass it. The female mind has its limit, my dear, and here it is."

"I didn't like hearing that," Eleanor told the gentlemen, "and asked him to write me an equation beyond what we'd done, and beyond what he thought I could solve. And very fluently, he wrote a series of signs and figures on my slate that I could recognize individually. I could recognize most of them. But I couldn't seem to fit them together, nor could I follow my father when he explained the concepts behind them. It was as if I'd turned the page on a perfectly readable novel and discovered a passage in Aramaic. I tried very hard to understand him, but had to give it up. Written before me were my female limitations, and I felt dreadfully cast down."

Eleanor had been looking into the distance as she spoke, as if seeing her father again out the window, ambling toward the parsonage. When she looked back, she found the gentlemen smiling indulgently. Mr. Denholm wasn't as tall as either his brother or Stansfield Mowbray—not much taller than she was—but all of them seemed to look down at her from a great height, like gods regarding a clever mortal.

"I don't claim it's my only limitation," she said.

"I'm sure you're being modest," replied Mr. Denholm, who seemed inexplicably pleased with her.

"We'll carry your compliments to Miss Catherine," said the captain, and they bowed themselves out the door.

"That didn't go very well," Eleanor told her aunt, as male boots thundered downstairs. "At least not for your purposes."

"You were sweet," her aunt said. "You quite charmed Mr. Denholm, and I continue to hold out hopes of Mr. Mowbray."

"The Denholms were more interesting than I would have predicted," Eleanor said, settling back beside her aunt. "But I wish you'd give up on Stansfield."

"So you *did* like Edward Denholm, my dear?"

Eleanor paused. "He's certainly the heir, isn't he? I found him rather intimidating, although I'd hate for him to know that. He continues to be far too pleased with himself. And I would say he's restless and guess at unreliable—for your purposes, Aunt."

"Not for yours?"

Eleanor remained silent.

"Unlike the captain?"

"I imagine the captain's superiors find him reliable, which is more to the point. I speak with great confidence, of course, after a visit fifteen minutes long."

"You speak with a good degree of penetration."

Eleanor turned staunch. "Not that it has anything to do with me."

"You really don't want your own household, dear?" Her aunt pushed back Eleanor's hair to look in her face. "Husbands are quite pleasant, if properly managed. Not that I want another one."

"I suppose I want the usual thing," Eleanor said. "I don't know what else a young lady is *supposed* to want. But I dislike the manner of getting a husband. I prefer not to be artificial."

"But of course we all are. It's another word for educated."

Her aunt pulled her hair lightly. She was only teasing, but Eleanor got an unpleasant picture of herself as a marionette—it flooded her mind—and she jerked awake that night panting from a nightmare of being manipulated by strings. The classical gods up on Mount Olympus were making her dance, and it wasn't a pretty dance, but a rude Punch-and-Judy twitch and thrust inside a glass-fronted theatre. She was being pulled deep into a theatre that wasn't much bigger than a box, sucked away from Goodwood even as she danced her witless dance, finding she had to struggle hard to pull herself out of, out of—she didn't know what.

Eleanor sat up in bed, willing herself awake, and realized she'd had the same bad dream during her nap. Not the same, but she'd felt a similar sense of being pushed and pulled, an anxious urge to get to the party, get to the party, without knowing what that meant.

They needed her to get started. That sounded faintly ominous. Yet—settling back on her pillows—she supposed what had really started was a competition for the Denholm heir. Even before Mr. Denholm's arrival, the Middleford ladies had reached the obvious conclusion that he was coming here to look for a wife, the parish being known for its marriageable young ladies. A number enjoyed a reputation for beauty, and there were two or three heiresses among them.

Mr. Denholm might believe that Eleanor was one of the heiresses, although she had no more idea what her aunt intended to do with Goodwood than anyone else. Nor did she know how to ask. In any case, she suspected that her aunt hadn't yet made up her mind, waiting to see whether Henrietta Whittaker would give birth to a son, and if she would survive it.

Her aunt would give her something, Eleanor was sure of it, although she might drive an embarrassingly hard bargain with any possible suitor. Middleford had no idea, but Mrs. Crosby was an astute and ambitious merchant. The accounts she'd been balancing that morning involved the importation of her son-in-law Mr. Whittaker's tea. Mrs. Crosby employed a man in London to oversee the warehouse, but she managed the affairs herself—while never, of course, being seen to engage in trade, which would have tainted the fine old Crosby name, and raised awkward questions about where she'd learned to do so.

Middleford wasn't quite certain what Mrs. Crosby had been when she'd met her first husband, the Kentish gentleman with his modest estate. "I was very young when I married Mr. Preston," was all she ever said, and somehow the subject got changed.

Yet during her first marriage, her aunt had acquired a copy of the scandalous Miss Wollstonecraft's *A Vindication of the Rights of Women*, signing it boldly, Clara Preston. Eleanor had stumbled on it in the Goodwood library last year. She'd read it outdoors over the course of the summer, hiding it from Mrs. Crosby for reasons she didn't quite understand, and closing it with the disturbing sense that her aunt must have been a firebrand.

What was the role of a woman, of Woman? Her father had taught her that woman was the helpmeet of man, Eve to generations of Adams. Nor could Eleanor see any alternative, not for a lady. She couldn't imagine herself as a governess. She'd known too many of them, poor threadbare females charged with educating Middleford girls to a middling standard. After being orphaned, Eleanor had been terrified of joining their ranks, and couldn't have felt more grateful to her aunt for rescuing her. Now that Mrs. Crosby expected her to marry, and marry well, Eleanor knew she had to try.

But Miss Wollstonecraft wrote of women *not* being inferior to men, leaving Eleanor with a feeling, an intimation, that the world was changing, the role of women was changing; she had no idea how. A mystery, how her role might change over the course of her lifetime. In a small cool corner of her mind, Eleanor was interested in seeing how her fate would play out. Perhaps this was the real party ahead of her. She was being pushed forward into a changing world. Pulled back by her aunt's ambitions.

What was a woman's role? Perhaps *that* was her prevailing question. It was enough to keep Eleanor awake for half the night.

2

The rain continued to fall heavily the next morning, distant thunder rumbling on the moors. Eleanor sat in a window seat watching puddles spread across the drive. She would rather have been anywhere else, but a walk was impossible, even in the garden.

A blinding flare of lightning . . .

And Eleanor was walking down a deserted London street. The city was empty, the passersby as silent as shadows, so that any one of them might have been Death out for a stroll. There were few carts and no sedan chairs, and she somehow knew that all the better sort had fled or locked themselves indoors. Eleanor found the silence stony and uncaring, and felt frightened by the number of vermin swaggering out in broad daylight. Turning the corner, she found a pair of rats fighting over slops in the middle of Threadneedle Street, shrieking like scraped metal . . .

"Would you like the carriage, my dear?" Mrs. Crosby asked.

Eleanor blinked, pulled back to Goodwood. How odd. Of course, they often went to London, but she couldn't think when she'd wandered down such an uncanny street. Nor had she ever experienced so vivid a memory, a vision, almost a hallucination. Catherine would be intrigued to hear of it. But the Mowbrays' dinner wasn't until Friday, and Eleanor had no hope of seeing her until then.

"The carriage?" Mrs. Crosby prompted.

"Of course," Eleanor said, trying to find her feet. "Would you like to go out? I'd love to see Kitty."

"I'm perfectly happy here," her aunt replied, holding up her sewing. "But you're so actively bored, you're a distraction. Take the carriage and bring Catherine back in time for an early supper, perhaps to stay the night. Tell Lady Anne you'll have her home in the morning. I entertain hopes of the rain lifting."

Glancing at the low clouds, Eleanor didn't see why. But she wasn't going to argue, and was turning from the window when a rattle and splash made her turn back.

"The Mowbray carriage!"

A brief silence from her aunt.

"Of course it is," she replied. "I presume the gentlemen aren't in it."

Eleanor stood on her toes to look down. "Well, it's crowded. But I think there's just Kitty and her sisters. Except," she said, "only Kitty is getting out. Perhaps the rest are going on to visit the Brownes."

"More likely the Morelands," Mrs. Crosby said. "Isn't Alicia the one who's close to the Browne girls? And I don't imagine Alicia is with them."

"I don't think she is," Eleanor said, coming fully back to herself as she understood what her aunt had been planning. She said in mock severity, "You were sending me to visit Mr. Denholm, not Kitty."

"Was I, my dear?"

"And Lady Anne has sent all the girls but Alicia away from the Close."

"While keeping you from visiting. Yes, I should imagine so."

Alicia was the prettiest Mowbray left at home, Catherine's next youngest sister, not quite seventeen but well grown and fair.

"You're playing chess with Lady Anne," Eleanor said, too amused to be annoyed. "The two of you! Moving your pawns around the chessboard."

"One has to do something in such a settled rain."

"Either pawns or puppets. I had a nightmare last night about being a puppet played by the gods. According to my dream, some sort of party is starting, and Mr. Denholm seems to be the honoured guest. Although," Eleanor said, thinking it through, "I don't think Alicia is clever enough to marry him."

"Don't you, my dear?" her aunt asked. "Remember there's a difference between *getting* married to him and *being* married to him. However, I expect you're right. You'd do far better with Mr. Denholm. We'll send a message to Lady Anne to say that Kitty is staying the night, and you can take her home in the morning."

"When the rain clears."

"You can't really think so, my dear."

It was easy for Catherine Mowbray's brother to call her a mouse: she was slight and shy in company. Yet Kitty's masses of brown hair and pale powdery skin made her look soft and sweet to Eleanor's eye, and she was certain her friend would have come off better if there hadn't been so many beauties in Middleford.

Now they leaned toward each other from either side of the fire in Eleanor's sitting room, caught up in discussing the visiting gentlemen. It bothered Eleanor slightly that they were having a gossip instead of discussing a more elevated subject. Her book, perhaps. *The Lady of the Lake.* But Eleanor hadn't cared for it much, and Kitty seldom read poetry.

"Yesterday evening," her friend said, "when we were called for dinner, I passed Mr. Denholm in the hallway. He was openly examining himself in a mirror."

"I told you he was vain!"

"I was prepared to pass him by when he met my eyes in the mirror and said, 'I'm not vain, you know. I don't think all that highly of my looks, not with a brother like mine. But I aspire to harmony in dress, as in life.'"

"He aspires to harmony!" Eleanor cried. "And what did you say?"

"I said I understood," *I understand* being one of Kitty's frequent answers, which she always gave in such a resonant voice it was clear she *understood deeply*. "However, I also understood from the expression on his face that he thought my dress out of fashion."

"No it wasn't. It never is. I'm sure you looked quite perfect."

When Kitty's elder sister Elizabeth had married—very well, to the grandson of a duke—her dresses had been divided up among her sisters. Kitty had made the most of hers, Mrs. Crosby having taught her to sew at the same time she'd taught Eleanor.

"You're right. He's a dandy," Kitty said. "I think he might even be a follower of Beau Brummell. It's not just the trousers and cravat. He's called for pails of hot water each morning for a bath, which looks to be a daily occurrence. He takes hours to dress, then comes downstairs late for breakfast, wanting a fresh chop."

"Your mother must be furious."

"Well . . . ten thousand a year. But given the expense of entertaining an heir, I think the tradesmen will have to wait a little longer than usual to be paid."

Lady Anne was infamous for her overdue bills, even though the Mowbrays were rich. She was a tall, commanding lady, as forthright as Eleanor's aunt was subtle, and as irritable as a mastiff. Of course, the two ladies were the greatest of friends and wouldn't let three days pass without visiting, each intent on finding out what the other was up to.

"Maybe he *would* do for Alicia," Eleanor said. "She's remarkably indulgent."

"I liked his honesty," Kitty said, and smiled. "Just not what he was being honest about."

"Kitty, have you ever met a man you truly admired?"

"I like his brother, although not in that way. The captain is a much more amiable gentleman. He's not at all shy, but he only speaks when he's got something to say."

"A steady aim being more useful than sermons. Yes, we heard. Presumably he's on leave from fighting Napoleon in the Peninsula."

"I heard his brother say that Captain Denholm is aide-de-camp to a general who's been terribly ill of a fever. The general has been home all winter, and Captain Denholm has been with him. But when the general returns to Spain—which will be soon—the captain goes with him."

"And in the meantime he's at loose ends," Eleanor said. "A good time for a young lady to set her cap at him. Although I suppose that's the captain's task, to set his cap at an heiress. Then he can avoid going back to Spain."

"I don't think he wants to avoid it. He seems very brave, as well as being so handsome."

So Kitty *had* met a man she admired. Eleanor raised her eyebrows meaningfully.

"Stop it!" her friend said, blushing her easy blush, and growing so earnest and alarmed as Eleanor kept her eyebrows raised—"You mustn't, Nell, please"—that Eleanor allowed herself to be distracted by the rain.

Yet once she started down the road, Eleanor couldn't help but picture a romance between her friend and the captain. Kitty was right. Captain Denholm was as handsome as a young man ought to be. He had a sense of humour, and didn't appear to think too highly of himself. But from what Kitty said, he thought highly of his profession, and that was an important distinction. Really, they knew very little about him, and in any case, he probably couldn't afford to marry until he was promoted. Yet that was in his favour as well, since a long engagement meant that Kitty wouldn't be taken from her any time soon.

There was also the fact that if Eleanor married the captain's brother, she and Kitty would never be parted. The idea arrived uninvited, and Eleanor rejected it just as quickly. Mr. Denholm was precisely the sort of man she would never marry: self-satisfied and unreliable. Once she and Kitty were tucked into bed, the candle snuffed, Kitty's breathing gone regular, Eleanor pictured Mr. Denholm in the Mowbray mirror, his face half lost in the darkness. His brother seemed a more well-lit figure, honest and open. Eleanor fell asleep planning to put off Mr. Denholm while forwarding his brother's match with Kitty, trying to decide on her first move when they arrived at Mowbray Close in the morning.

They were still at breakfast when the door flew open.

"This weather! Mrs. Crosby, I've saved your coachman!"

Lady Anne burst into the room. She knew, of course, where Mrs. Crosby breakfasted. Knew just as well that she kept later hours than many—herself, for instance—which allowed her to sail toward the table like a frigate, the housekeeper wringing her hands behind her.

"Just a brief stop for Catherine before we fetch the other girls. Kitty, call for your things. Eleanor, I'm desolate. There's no room in the carriage for even so thin a figure as yours. (I'm glad, by the way, to see you making such a good breakfast.)"

"My dear," Mrs. Crosby said, sounding unperturbed. "Have you a moment to take off your cloak?"

"Oh! Scarcely a moment," Lady Anne said, allowing the housekeeper to remove her wrap before throwing herself in a chair. Lady Anne was still a handsome woman, although not dressed with the care of Mrs. Crosby, her clothing usually called countrified (dog hairs), even though she was the daughter of a Navy man and had travelled the world as a girl. She was often described in Middleford by the useful phrase, as jolly as an admiral's daughter, although it failed to take into account the avid curiosity in her dark brown eyes.

"You *must* tell me how you're surviving the deluge," she said, accepting a cup of her friend's tea. "Of course, Kitty will know. But it's always better to get it from the horse's mouth."

"Mama, Mrs. Crosby isn't a horse."

"No, she's a lapdog," her mother said. "I'm the horse. I'd like to say thoroughbred, but Clydesdale is no doubt more accurate. Sir Waldo is a saint to put up with me; anyone will tell you. Of course, I don't deserve him."

Lady Anne squinted into the corner, saying *hmm* and *hum* as she contemplated the perfection of her husband. Sir Waldo had been a close friend of Eleanor's father, a model gentleman with his measured phrases and air of intelligent courtesy. After periwigs and powder grew unfashionable, most men looked less authoritative. But Sir Waldo had taken off his curled white wig to reveal a head of perfectly curled white hair and carried on much as usual.

Eleanor found the Mowbray marriage a mystery. She had no idea why a gentleman like Sir Waldo would marry such an embarrassing wife: embarrassing, certainly, to her daughters. Lady Anne squinted harder at her good fortune, which by now was almost visible in the corner, before shaking her head and ordering Kitty to her feet. These occasional moments of humility endeared her to much of the neighbourhood, and Eleanor exchanged an amused glance with her aunt— which changed, after Lady Anne bustled out, into shared laughter.

"But here it is, Aunt," Eleanor said, as the Mowbray carriage rattled off outside. "I think Kitty quite likes Captain Denholm. She's taken care to listen when he's talked about, and finds him very handsome."

"And what does she report of the heir?"

Eleanor gave her aunt a look, but couldn't resist telling her about Kitty's encounter with Mr. Denholm and the mirror, embellishing the elements of darkness and doubling to paint what she thought was a usefully off-putting picture of Mr. Denholm's vanity, as he "aspired to elegance in fashion as in life."

"Oh, he sounds so young!" her aunt cried, breaking into her surprisingly raucous laugh. "For all his airs—doesn't he sound so charmingly young!"

"It isn't *that* funny!" Eleanor said.

Her aunt made a show of repentance. "Such a very young man, my dear," she added, shaking her head. "I know you can't think so, but to me he sounds like a schoolboy. Young men take themselves so very seriously these days."

"I thought you wanted me to take him seriously."

"Oh, not him, my dear. His money," her aunt said comfortably, and poured herself another cup of her son-in-law's excellent tea.

3

The rain continued for Lady Anne's dinner, although not a soul would have missed it even if Noah had been building an ark on the moor. As the carriage rattled away from Goodwood House, Eleanor felt peculiarly excited, wondering if this was the party she was meant to go to, and whether something was going to start.

She also wondered if her dream meant she'd reached her time to marry. She was being called upon to take up a woman's role—what her father had called Eve's Burden. Maybe part of it was having a dream when your time came. Farm girls tried to, putting fresh ash leaves under their pillows. "Even-ash, even-ash, I pluck thee, this night my own true love to see." Eleanor and Kitty had tried it when they were twelve years old, but Eleanor had enjoyed a dreamless sleep while Kitty claimed to have dreamt of her paints, proving that she'd be an old maid. Perhaps Kitty would dream of the captain if they tried again, but Eleanor shivered at the thought of dreaming about Mr. Denholm.

"I've chosen the wrong cap."

She turned to find Mrs. Crosby frowning at her reflection in the carriage glass.

"You look lovely," Eleanor said, making a minute adjustment to the lace. "I'm only sorry there isn't a handsome widower in the neighbourhood."

"I don't think so, my dear," Mrs. Crosby replied. "He'd want my money, and I'd lose all respect for him when he couldn't get it out of me." Gazing at her reflection, she added dreamily, "An *affair de coeur*. Far preferable for ladies of my condition."

"Would you really?"

"Discreetly. Discretion isn't only the better part of valour, you know, but also a form of intoxication. Hidden meetings, coded letters, the *frisson*. Although for you," her aunt added, shaking herself, "the husband comes first, please."

"What were you like when you were my age?" Eleanor asked.

But Mrs. Crosby was too busy with her cap to answer.

Mowbray Close was a modern house built by Sir Waldo's father on the site of a decrepit manor. Entering the drive, Eleanor saw candles lighting its many windows, while inside the front hall was blazing. Alicia stood at its centre, her pink and white prettiness gleaming like marzipan. She was talking to Mr. Denholm and their parson, Mr. Warfield, who had replaced Eleanor's father. Poor Mr. Warfield had angered Lady Anne by marrying his longtime fiancée after taking up the Middleford living, even though she'd made it clear he was welcome to one of her daughters. Tonight the lady seemed to have forgotten her animus, probably having found she needed Mr. Warfield and his pleasant frizz-haired wife to fill two seats at dinner.

Turning at the bustle, Mr. Denholm saw Eleanor. He brightened so noticeably that Mrs. Crosby pinched the back of Eleanor's arm.

"Lady Anne miscalculated," she whispered. "Keeping him away from you, and in such close contact with Alicia. Clearly she bores him."

"Kitty says he always affects being bored," Eleanor whispered back.

"You're being modest," her aunt replied in a normal voice, as Lady Anne joined them. "I was telling Eleanor that her complexion looks particularly lovely tonight. All these candles throw such a pretty light—don't they?—from her dress to her face."

"*Hmm*," Lady Anne said. "Mr. Denholm had some very flattering things to say about Alicia's dress. Without regard to the lighting."

"Mr. Denholm seems to think a great deal more about dress than a gentleman ought," Eleanor said, making sure that he heard as he walked up. "Mr. Denholm, I was about to accuse you of being a follower of Mr. Brummell."

"Accuse?" he asked.

"Eleanor's way of admiring your cravat," Mrs. Crosby said.

"I doubt it," he replied. "With respect, Mrs. Crosby, I think your niece delights in being hard on us poor gentlemen. Army men like my brother enjoy all the advantages of a uniform. Mr. Brummell only proposes that gentlemen assume their own uniform of simple, well-cut clothes. Surely you can see, Miss Crosby, that this frees up time for other pursuits of which you might actually approve."

Eleanor had to repress a smile when she remembered that he bathed every morning. "I've heard it takes Mr. Brummell five hours to dress."

"As the parson said, 'Do as I say, not as I do.'"

"Surely not our dear Mr. Warfield," Eleanor said. "His actions being every bit as admirable as his sermons."

"*Hmmm*," Lady Anne said again, squinting ferociously at the clergyman before excusing herself to greet more guests. Mrs. Crosby smiled and followed, leaving Eleanor alone with Mr. Denholm.

Her heart beat a little faster, she had to admit. She was blushing, feeling pushed toward Mr. Denholm by her aunt, perhaps by Fate. Although, of course, as a clergyman's daughter, she believed in God rather than in Fate, and surely He couldn't be bothered with Middleford.

"I don't see my friend Catherine," she said.

"In the corner, entertaining my brother," Edward Denholm replied. "It's kind of her, making time for an officer heading off to war. Many ladies speak to him only briefly, as if they don't wish to care about his fate if, God forbid, anything should happen." He gave her a quick glance. "Or perhaps it's his lack of fortune. In which case, they're right. He shan't be able to marry any time soon."

"So I would have thought," Eleanor replied absentmindedly, as if she didn't recognize his warning, continuing to look for Kitty. Finally she nodded, spotting her friend, who was speaking with placid pleasure to the captain.

"I've seen Miss Mowbray's drawings," Mr. Denholm said. "And you're right, she has rare ability."

"Being right about my closest friend!" Eleanor said, turning back. "I wonder how I managed."

"I apologize for my awkward phrasing. But I like Miss Mowbray. I don't imagine the art masters here are any better than the ones we have in Kent. She must have progressed as far as she has on her own, or perhaps with your help." When Eleanor denied it: "Or encouragement. Which is just as important."

None of the local swains would have been capable of making such an observation. But Mr. Denholm was a little too pleased with himself for making it, standing back on his boot heels and looking superior to his company.

"An excellent young lady," he continued. "There's nothing artificial about your friend, nor any degree of pretension." Lowering his voice as he stepped closer: "It's good luck for you to have found each other in, frankly, a rather provincial society."

Eleanor stepped away. "I'm happy here. I like the country."

"And not London?"

"When I'm in London, I'm happy there. I have little cause to be dissatisfied, nor indeed to wish for any particular change in my condition."

Eleanor meant that as a warning as well. But Mr. Denholm didn't seem to hear her, appearing pleased with what she'd said.

"When you're in the country, you're a country mouse. A city mouse in London. Exactly as one should be."

"I don't think I'm a mouse, Mr. Denholm."

"Of course not."

"When I was a schoolgirl, I wanted to be a warrior queen like Boadicea," Eleanor said, smiling as she left, and pleased with herself for having scored a point.

Yet as she walked away, Eleanor felt a little more flustered than she wished to be, especially since she wanted to assess the need for Mr. Denholm's hint. Kitty and the captain were still in the corner, chatting as sedately as brother and sister. Kitty had said she didn't like Captain Denholm "in that way," and showed no sign of doing so, despite her blushes when Eleanor had teased her.

But as far as Eleanor could remember, Kitty had never showed any sign of liking any young man, and wouldn't admit it when teased. And she must have had her preferences. Eleanor had never thought of it before, but now she stopped halfway across the floor, seeing her friend in a new light. Kitty must keep her deepest feelings to herself, guarding her hopes and fears behind a calm opacity: this when Eleanor was entirely open about what she felt.

Eleanor grew increasingly unhappy as she watched them talk, wondering how well she really knew Kitty. Did Catherine like the man or not? If she did, she'd better take more care to show it or she'd lose her chance. Yet maybe she'd been sincere and she only *liked* him. Eleanor realized she had no idea in the world what her closest friend truly felt.

She also felt an obscure need to punish Kitty for failing to confide in her. As Lady Anne sailed past, she touched her arm impulsively.

"You should know about my talk with Mr. Denholm," Eleanor said. "He admires Kitty greatly. 'A young lady of rare ability.' He seems quite struck with her."

"*Kitty?*" Lady Anne cried. She swivelled violently to see Mr. Denholm walk up to his brother and Kitty, greeting her with the rare gentleness of manner her friend was able to call up even in boorish young men. (Of whom, Eleanor had to admit, Mr. Denholm wasn't one.)

"Yes, Kitty," she replied weakly, crushed with shame, blushing as hard as she'd ever blushed. She wanted to unsay every word she'd said. Take it all back. But it was too late.

"Oh!" Lady Anne rumbled, a deeply percussive sound. Such was her energy and resolve that when dinner was called, Kitty was seated beside Mr. Denholm, while Alicia—looking puzzled—was put further down the table beside Mr. Warfield. Eleanor herself was placed beside Stansfield Mowbray, his mother refusing to give up hope of marrying the two estates.

"How are your father's crops faring?" she asked in penance, although with the best will in the world, Eleanor couldn't concentrate on Mr. Mowbray's exhaustive answer. Instead, she watched her friend (her closest friend!) at the top of the table, relieved to see Kitty speaking just as calmly with Mr. Denholm as she had with his brother. She showed no sign of regretting the loss of Captain Denholm's company, and Eleanor gradually relaxed to see her friend agreeably occupied, smiling at the heir's ready wit.

Nothing would come of her meanness. Nothing had happened nor would happen, Eleanor told herself—not seeing the admiring glances that Mr. Denholm cast her way, and failing to register the amused air of Captain Denholm, who didn't miss a thing.

In fact (as only Mrs. Crosby noticed) the captain was enjoying the scene, surprising himself by finding that his tactical training let him recognize manoeuvres in the war between the sexes, fought tonight across Lady Anne's grand expanse of tablecloth, silverware and malice flashing like swords, and misunderstandings cantering among her guests like runaway horses.

"You're enjoying the fish," Sir Waldo observed, nodding at his wife's excellent salmon.

"Indeed, sir," the captain replied. "And the fishing."

The baronet smiled ruefully and shook his head. "Seven daughters," he said.

Hours later, as her aunt's carriage came for them at Mowbray Close, the rain had stopped and a crescent moon shone palely in a smudged black sky. The damp gentleness of the air promised a change of weather, and once they'd said their farewells, Mrs. Crosby spent the drive home planning a series of entertainments. She would trump Mrs. Moreland with a musical evening and squeeze in a tea around the ambitions of the Brownes—asking, by the by, as they turned into the drive at Goodwood, what Eleanor had said to Lady Anne that made her put Kitty beside Mr. Denholm.

Eleanor fell back into blushes. "I wish I hadn't."

Her aunt waited.

"I repeated some silly compliments Mr. Denholm paid her."

"Good work!" Mrs. Crosby said. "Scuppering Alicia, a much more plausible candidate . . ."

"Aunt . . ."

"And recommending Kitty to the brother of a man she admires: two birds with one stone."

"I think the more apt quotation involves 'speaking as a foolish woman speaketh.'"

"One has heard of that, of course," Mrs. Crosby said. "But it's not something I'm familiar with personally."

Eleanor tried to smile, but her renewed mortification was making her feel unwell.

"Surely Lady Anne won't object to a visit tomorrow," her aunt went on. "You and Kitty always meet to discuss a party."

"Maybe we can talk about it in the morning," Eleanor said, as the carriage stopped. "I seem to be getting a headache."

"You don't have a headache. You never get headaches."

Yet Eleanor felt surprisingly ill as she stepped down from the carriage. They said you *fell ill* and she seemed to plummet. Her legs were weak as she went inside and she noticed her knees as she climbed the stairs, and who noticed their knees? That night, she slept restlessly, and found in the morning that someone had been at her throat with daggers. She didn't think it was serious, but knew she couldn't manage breakfast and sent for a cup of tea.

The housemaid must have told Mrs. Crosby. Quick footsteps soon brought her aunt to her room. Feeling Eleanor's forehead, she turned to her housekeeper and cried, "Fever! Send for Mr. Blythe immediately!"

"It's only an ague," Eleanor said. But her Uncle Crosby had ignored an ague and died within a fortnight, leaving her aunt with a terror of fever. Eleanor was afraid the physician wouldn't offer her any reassurance. Mr. Blythe had a tendency to take minor illnesses too seriously, as if to compensate for his name.

It was true Eleanor couldn't help throwing off her covers and pulling them back up, one moment too hot, the next moment shivering. She seemed to be as restless as Mr. Denholm, but it was only an ague. Eleanor didn't need the doctor, although it wasn't long before he stalked into the room in his black coat. Taking her pulse, he frowned and told her aunt, "I'm afraid she's shockingly ill."

"I'm really not, sir," Eleanor insisted, although the doctor shook his head and bled her copiously, her terrified aunt calling for a milksop that Eleanor couldn't eat.

"Perhaps some chocolate, dear?" Mrs. Crosby asked, and Eleanor suspected she was a little more ill than she wanted to believe when she didn't care for chocolate, either.

Mr. Blythe settled himself into a chair, although Eleanor wanted him to leave. Her throat was sore, her limbs ached and soon enough her cough had burrowed so deeply into her chest that each hack hurt her ribs. Outside, the day seemed to be waning. Eleanor couldn't get comfortable, not while being watched like this. She tossed and turned, her joints aching, her legs not quite itching but unable to stay still.

Even worse was the fact that Kitty didn't come. As night passed to day, Eleanor grew certain she was being rebuked for her behaviour at the dinner party, God frowning down at her foolishness. Usually the two of them either suffered through each other's illnesses or shared them. Now her aunt said that Lady Anne had heard about two maids falling ill downstairs—"although mildly, my dear"—and forbidden Kitty to visit, claiming there was contagion in the house.

"There isn't any contagion," the doctor claimed.

"Far too blithely," Eleanor could hear Lady Anne say, and laughed heartily.

"Is something amusing, dear?" her aunt asked.

If Eleanor hadn't mentioned Mr. Denholm's compliment, Kitty would have been allowed to stay at Goodwood. She was being kept at home to pursue ten thousand pounds *per annum* instead of coming over to keep Eleanor company, and Mrs. Crosby was a poor substitute. As another day waned, her aunt fretted Eleanor with cold cloths and warm flannels, leaving Eleanor to silently, deeply long for her father, who had always breathed calm into a sickroom.

"Now, Mrs. Mugwumps, we're not so bad, are we?" he would say, sitting down beside her with a book, and only glancing up occasionally over his spectacles.

He was sitting there now, and Eleanor's heart leapt to see him.

"Papa," she whispered.

A child's voice came out, and it frightened her. So did the way her father raised his eyebrows humorously at being dead.

"Auntie!" she wailed.

"I'm here, darling."

"Poor Papa," she said. "When he was a priest of Bacchus."

Her aunt's account book fell to the floor. As Mrs. Crosby bent to retrieve it, Eleanor realized her aunt was hiding a sob. Why, she loves me, she thought, and her aunt came into minute focus as she picked up her book. A network of fine lines spread out from the corners of her aunt's eyes, looking like cracks in paint. The skin of her neck was beginning to sag and her lips were thinner than they had been. Book in hand, she picked at its cover until, in the nervous pick-pick-picking of her thin fingers, Eleanor recognized her aunt's terror. She also understood that her aunt was her mother, even though she felt Mrs. Crosby's anxiety as a weight on her shoulders, which were already exhausted from carrying the burden of her illness.

That night, Eleanor dreamed a rook flew in the window. When she awoke, Mr. Blythe was beside her and the room was dark, and she heard a hoarse cawing and a sobbing as she fell into—into—Eleanor hardly knew what. It had depth and stars but no end, although as she fell through darkness, she knew she was going to fall through—what on earth was a television?—and exercised every inch of her will to pull herself back to Goodwood.

Eleanor awoke to see the doctor bending over her in sunlight, his soft hand on her forehead. "The crisis passed at four in the morning, my dear," he said. "As so often it does."

Turning to Mrs. Crosby. "A healthy young girl. She'll recover quite quickly."

Eleanor didn't think so. She felt confused by strange words she only half remembered, and had an idea that most young ladies didn't have to suffer so greatly when taking up Eve's Burden. Nor could she manage to shuffle off its weight. As one long day followed another, Eleanor continued to feel weak and tired, increasingly bored but unable to feel any interest in books, or in Kitty's stream of letters, or even in Mrs. Cook's delicate meals.

Then she did. Eleanor woke up one morning feeling perfectly well. Entirely healthy. Absolutely herself. She asked the little maid making her fire to call for bread and butter, jam, boiled eggs, even cheese, although Mrs. Crosby said bread and cheese was vulgar, a servant's food (which never stopped her from tucking into a plate of it herself).

The little maid ran out of the room as if she'd seen a ghost— Eleanor couldn't believe she'd been *that* ill—leaving her to stumble out of bed on her own. Her legs felt absurdly weak but she managed to make it to the window. Looking outside, she felt a stab of joy to see the sun playing on the daffodil lawn. Eleanor wondered how long flowers had been out, and opened the window to breathe in their strong astringent scent, not quite cardamom, maybe a spice from a newly discovered country. She imagined it baked into a biscuit. Her mouth watered.

"Whatever are you doing?" her aunt asked, walking in briskly. "And in bare feet!"

"Don't worry, dear," Eleanor said, going over to her aunt. "I'm better now."

"Then let's keep it that way," her aunt said, and half carried her back to bed.

When Mr. Blythe arrived, he ordered Eleanor to rest for another week. Nor would Lady Anne permit Kitty to visit. From the maids,

Eleanor learned that fever had swatted its way through the servant's hall while she'd been ill, although fortunately no one had died. When Mr. Blythe finally used the word "contagion," Eleanor realized it was selfish to plead for Kitty, no matter how badly she wanted to see her friend.

She also wanted to know what was going on with the Denholms, and called for Kitty's letters, which she'd only skimmed before. Mr. Blythe had allowed her the sofa, at least. Now she lay beneath a warm throw, reading Kitty's description of card games and musical evenings, teas, a dance, even a ride to the ruins of St. Alkeld's Abbey.

Yet despite Kitty's bright prose, she sounded lonely.

"At least *you* would have appreciated ..."

"I had no one to confide that ..."

"I know my darling will join me in believing ..."

Eleanor remembered Mr. Denholm telling her they'd been lucky to find each other in such a provincial society. He thought a little too highly of his own penetration, but she had to admit he was right. She also found herself worrying that she'd lose her friend and be left here alone. Kitty had been spending so much time with the Denholms that she couldn't help picturing the captain down on one knee. (Unlikely.) Mr. Denholm down on one knee. (Even less likely.) Pictured both of them spurning her. (Most likely, but not inevitable.)

Eleanor had no idea what was going to happen, especially to her. So many odd things had occurred lately. A woman's voice calling her to a party. The memory of a London street she couldn't possibly have seen. And a tell-, telly—certainly a *vision*. Eleanor wondered if she'd been sick for several days before the fever had announced itself. It seemed possible. Seemed wise to remain on the sofa as the doctor advised until she regained her strength.

Except that it wasn't. Two hours of restless boredom were enough to teach Eleanor that lying down sapped her strength instead of helping her regain it. In sudden irritation, she threw off her wrap and padded across the floor in stocking feet, kicking a chair aside like a child.

That was a mistake. Goodwood House was a giant ear, everyone monitoring everyone else and all of them whispering about everything, the whispers echoing around the walls and up and down the stairways until it was impossible to sneeze without three dozen people knowing how hard. They'd lock her inside if they knew what she was planning.

Eleanor stood still for long enough to make sure that no one had heard the chair fall, then picked it up gingerly. Opened her wardrobe silently. Made a quiet concession to her aunt by choosing a warm woollen dress over a prettier more springlike one. She found she didn't need stays (she'd lost a shocking amount of weight), but put on a pair of thicker stockings and took her clogs in hand, tiptoeing down the back hall, tripping the switch on Goodwood's hidden staircase, padding down to the ground floor, and putting on her pattens to steal outside.

The cold rain had made for a late spring, but during Eleanor's illness, flowers had burst out like fireworks. Reaching the garden, she hurried down the gravel path between the formal beds of tulips, her skirts raised as she breathed the scent of violets. Ahead was her favourite path up the dale, grassy and blooming with daffodils. She refused to acknowledge any weakness as she opened the gate and continued through the apple orchard, blossoms drifting like pink snow onto her bare head.

As she pushed through a stile, Eleanor felt renewed. A lapwing's high squeezy call sounded at a distance. At the top of the path was a bench looking out at the craggy green hills. Sitting there, she might figure out what was happening to her, and decide what to do about Mr. Denholm, whom she would see again any day.

Her aunt's sheep cropped the new grass around her, their lambs dancing on stick legs. Halfway up, Eleanor paused to catch her breath, hand going to a stitch in her side. The nearest sheep looked up, profoundly uninterested. Eleanor clapped her hands, but even the lambs did little more than glance at her. Walking more slowly now, feeling suddenly and stupidly tired, Eleanor followed the path around an outcrop—and stopped, seeing someone on the bench.

A gentleman sat with his back to her, looking like an angel bent in contemplation. It was an oddly formal pose, and one of eternal sorrow. Eleanor didn't recognize the man and was about to leave when he sensed her and turned. It was Captain Denholm, unfamiliar in a brown wool jacket, and he was weeping.

"I'm sorry," Eleanor said, feeling an intruder. She had a very concrete sense that she wasn't supposed to be here. Wasn't *meant* to be here. Yet something terrible had happened and Eleanor couldn't leave before finding out what.

"Miss Crosby," the captain said, getting to his feet. "Forgive me. You're well. I heard."

"I'm sorry," she repeated, and couldn't help half a smile. "Although perhaps not for being well. I hope that everyone else is. They wouldn't have told me, you see."

The captain looked adrift and distracted. He crumpled a letter he'd been holding into his pocket, fumbling in vain for a handkerchief before wiping his eyes with the back of one hand.

"They wouldn't have told you there's been a great battle," he said, and Eleanor noticed the newspaper lying on the bench. "It was fought outside a village in Spain called Albuera, and my regiment faced Napoleon's Polish hussars. It appears"—glancing at the newspaper—"it appears there's scarcely one officer in ten left standing. And dashed few of the men."

"I'm so terribly sorry," Eleanor said, although she couldn't have been more relieved that no one she knew had died. Unworthy of her, she realized. "There's been a great defeat, then."

"Victory," Captain Denholm said. "They're calling it a victory, since the French seem to have lost even more men than we did, and then run away."

He glanced at the newspaper again but didn't seem to see it.

"Five thousand lost in a day," he said. "A meaningless battle, with Lord Wellington chasing Bonaparte's main army further to the north. But my poor friend Burke . . . Burke fell. He'd been home nursing a fever and was only just back in Spain. I saw him not a month ago. And Herbert. Poor Ensign Chadwick. My good friend Latham, you know. Latham is written up a hero for protecting the regimental colours. His nose and arm cut off by the Poles."

"Oh, how dreadful!" Eleanor said, looking deep into the void that opened at her feet.

"Stupid of me." The captain strode around the bench, grasping her arm as if she might faint. "Boneheaded, when you've been so ill."

"Your friends must be glad you're still in England," she said, looking into his reddened eyes. "Unlike poor Mr. Burke."

"No," he said, dropping her arm. "If I'd been there, my general would have been there. And if he'd been in charge, this wouldn't have happened. The idiot left in command . . ."

He stopped abruptly. "Forgive me."

"Only the lapwings heard." Another cry, the trilling whistle. "And the curlews. They're terrible gossips, of course. But very few people speak curlew."

"It's good of you to try to cheer me up, Miss Crosby."

"*Boneheaded* of me. When my father died, people said the most horrid empty things. And now I'm one of them. At least I understand how inadequate they felt."

Eleanor looked down into the void, the spiralling darkness that had always been there, even though she'd only recently seen it.

"I don't mean to compare the death of one man to such a dreadful calamity," she said. "Even the loss of my father."

"But that's just it, you see," the captain replied. Robert. He'd been called Robin as a boy, and looked half a boy now, a great strapping boy with a mottled tear-streaked face. "Each loss is such a terrible blow. And losing all of them makes it far more difficult to defend Britain. Defend ladies like yourself, you see. Two blows at the same time." A painful half smile. "And scant comfort anywhere."

"I wish I could provide some," she said.

"It's a comfort speaking with you," he replied gently, and Eleanor met his eyes—grey and deep and wounded—and didn't understand what else he said in the warm confusion that overtook her. Oh, it's *him*, she thought, not knowing what she meant.

Yes, she did: it was the man she was going to marry.

Not that Eleanor knew how this could possibly be true, or what Kitty would think about it, or her aunt think about it, or his brother

Mr. Denholm think about it. More to the point, what *he* thought of it. Eleanor couldn't tell, especially since Captain Denholm seemed to be making his excuses—perfectly civilized—and striding back down the dale, his curls catching the breeze. He probably thought nothing of any of this, nothing of her, entirely concerned with the death of his friends, as of course he ought to be.

However, he'd forgotten his newspaper, leaving Eleanor to sit down on the bench and glance at the dense columns of losses broken down by regiment and company. She had no idea which regiment the captain served in. Artillery, infantry, cavalry. Very little idea of anything.

But feelings. Yes, suddenly she had a great many of those.

1840
Yorkshire and Kent

4

The train clattered and swayed toward London, taking them by stages to Kent. Eleanor felt uneasy, not quite over the odd moment at the station this morning when she'd woken from a reverie to find the locomotive rumbling toward her and had no idea what it was.

A huge metal Trojan Horse breathing smoke and cinders.

Eleanor had shrieked like a booby who had never seen a train, and felt strangely certain that she hadn't. Instead she found herself on a deserted street in London with no idea how she'd got there. Found herself in Goodwood House during the long-gone war against Napoleon, Aunt Clara sitting by the fire in one of the dresses now stored in the attic, except that it was new. Found herself most mysteriously in the American state of Connecticut, aware that she was jumping through time and space, and wondering who was doing this to her. A box flickered with moving images, and as she watched a pale hand reached out to do what she knew was called "changing the channel."

Then Eleanor was back in the station where she'd always been, living the life that—surely—she'd always lived, and felt foolish for having shrieked at a train.

"What on earth was that?" her aunt asked, and Eleanor was glad the station was so noisy that she didn't have to answer.

Nerves, she supposed, as she settled into their compartment. A case of nerves, Eleanor's world having tumbled off its axis when she'd met Captain Denholm not a month before on the heights near Goodwood. It had been one of the most important days of her life, despite her odd feeling that she wasn't supposed to be there, not when Robert Denholm was mourning the loss of his friend—and what was his name?—in a meaningless skirmish in northern India. And in brutal fact, it would have been better if she hadn't been, not with her aunt preparing to launch a determined pursuit of the captain's brother.

In some ways, it had been easier to be ill, lying innocently on her sofa. The moment Mr. Blythe had felt sufficiently certain of Eleanor's recovery to end his lucrative visits to Goodwood (or her aunt had), the campaign for Mr. Denholm had begun. The first step had been a party in the Goodwood gardens, which Mrs. Crosby had held to celebrate Eleanor's return to health. Captain Denholm was gone by then, having returned to his regiment almost as soon as he'd left Eleanor on the heights. But Edward Denholm remained in Middleford, and almost immediately, Eleanor had to reproach herself for the way she mishandled his attentions.

A hopeful thought: the position of ladies was changing. In generations past, Mrs. Crosby would have been entirely in charge of Eleanor's marriage, certainly with a rich property like Goodwood at stake. Yet just this past winter, Queen Victoria herself had married for love. For the first time, Eleanor thought she might be allowed some say in choosing her husband, at least if she managed things smartly.

But she'd made a hash of it at the party, hadn't she? Things had gone wrong from the start, when Kitty had arrived early to help set up a tea table under the marquee. Lady Anne had finally permitted her to come to Goodwood, but the long-awaited visit had been unsettling.

"I've spent a great deal of time with Mr. Denholm over the past couple of weeks," Kitty had said, her eyes on the cups she was arranging, "and I think it was largely because he wanted to speak about you. Always asking, 'What would Miss Crosby think?' and 'What does she like?'"

Eleanor thought she heard an edge in Kitty's voice, even a touch of resentment. She wondered if her friend had grown to prefer Mr. Denholm to the captain, and hoped she had. Yet Kitty's irritation might simply be owing to the fact that Mr. Denholm had treated her as a neuter. The young ladies of Middleford knew too much about that, having spent years being pumped by suitors eager for an advantage with Kitty's eldest sister Elizabeth, a great beauty. Did Miss Mowbray prefer puppies, keepsake albums, whist? A puzzle they all tried to solve, at least until Lizzy demonstrated her preferences by marrying the duke's grandson.

It wasn't flattering to be used that way. Nor was Eleanor flattered by Mr. Denholm's interest, especially when Kitty told her he'd asked about her expectations from Mrs. Crosby.

"I had to tell him I didn't know."

"No more do I," Eleanor said. "I'm sorry if he annoyed you."

"He didn't. He's amusing."

Kitty stepped back to examine the table, and smiled.

"Although he's something of a satirist, and not always kind. He's always so elaborately polite to my mother that she suspects him of being insincere. But how can she object?"

"*Hmmm*," Eleanor replied, in Lady Anne's contralto.

"I have to say, I think his father holds the whip hand over him." Kitty gave Eleanor a quick glance. "I shouldn't count on anything, Nell."

"I'm afraid my aunt does," Eleanor answered, and sighed.

It was a fine day for a party. A strong sun, a light breeze, and the trees coming into leaf: that hopeful new green. Yet when Kitty left to find her sisters, Eleanor wanted to be anywhere else. To be a flag flying from the peak of the marquee, her pretty dress blowing in the breeze; what an odd thing to think. To sink imperceptibly into the ground, she decided, when Mr. Denholm walked in wearing a suit of the finest brown wool. Eleanor had a moment to prepare as he looked around. Then his face lit up.

"Miss Crosby!" he cried, hurrying over. "You're blooming! How excellent!"

"If one can bloom when pouring tea, Mr. Denholm," Eleanor said, with bright impersonal efficiency. "I'd offer you a cup, but I believe you prefer coffee."

"You remembered," he said, looking gratified. Then he turned surprisingly gentle. "Although of course I'll take a cup of your tea."

Eleanor hadn't expected that. She blushed and busied herself with the teapot, agreeing disjointedly that she'd recovered, and trying to make sure their fingers didn't brush when she handed him his cup. He seemed prepared to linger, but Eleanor took immediate refuge in the lady waiting behind him.

"Mrs. Warfield. How lovely to see you. May I offer . . ."

Eleanor was in luck. The whole of Middleford had accepted her aunt's invitation, and she served cup after cup of tea. Meanwhile she assured everyone that she was perfectly well in the same polite and meaningless phrases, hoping to bore Mr. Denholm into leaving. Instead, he remained persistently by her side, marvelling at the crowd, the excellent cake, the quality of her aunt's tea. The wretched man stayed beside her even when Lady Anne bulled up.

"Your aunt's cook serves a great deal of cream with her strawberries. Would you like me to speak with her?"

Half an hour passed before Mr. Denholm finally stepped outside. Her duties arguably over, Eleanor beckoned a maid to replace her, slipping out the back of the marquee and heading for the maze. She wanted to lose herself in its twists and turns, hide herself, break away from the wrong Denholm. When she saw the clipped evergreens in the distance, she kicked into a run.

"No wonder, Miss Crosby," Mr. Denholm called, making her stumble. "No wonder you're eager to escape the prosing of society." Coming up, he took her arm as if she needed steadying. "If that's what one calls the good people of Middleford."

"I call them friends," Eleanor said, taking back her arm.

"But you needed a walk. A break."

Eleanor smiled politely and turned away from the maze, not wanting to lead him toward privacy. Instead she took Mr. Denholm down the avenue of plane trees, where other couples sauntered. Not that they were a couple, although it was true Mr. Denholm sauntered, his hands in his pockets and his hat cocked back on his head like a boy.

"A lovely spring," Eleanor said, taking refuge in the weather.

"Now that you're better." A searching look: "You're really not tired?"

"Not in the least. I love a good walk."

"As do I. In fact, I rather fancy a long one."

"A *long* walk. Very well, then. I'll leave you to it."

Eleanor smiled and sat down on a bench. But the unshakeable Mr. Denholm only threw himself down on the grass at her feet. As the wispy clouds flitted overhead, he questioned her need for blankets and shawls. Was she sufficiently warm, over-warm, chilled when the sun went behind a cloud?

"Really, Mr. Denholm," Eleanor finally said, in complete exasperation. "I'm quite capable of asking for anything I need."

He was leaning against the bench, legs crossed in front of him, showing off his beautiful brown trousers, the wool as light as cambric. "I remember that," he said.

"I believe I've made the point several times."

"I mean that whenever I'm mildly ill, I'm quite happy to be fussed over by the eternal mother, in whatever guise she presents herself. But the one time I was really sick—as ill as you've been—I was determined to prove myself a hardy little soldier."

"You had a fever?" Eleanor asked, reluctantly interested.

"Cholera, as a boy. My mother hardly dared say the word. But as you see, I recovered. And no doubt"—glancing up at her—"you're thoroughly relieved."

"Naturally," Eleanor replied, and nodded toward a wander of Mowbrays. "Doesn't Alicia look lovely in her new striped lilac?"

In fact, Eleanor had been deeply struck by what Mr. Denholm had said, although she tried not to show it. He noticed, of course, and looked even more pleased with himself. At the head of the avenue, her aunt looked just as pleased, Mrs. Crosby's gaze having followed Eleanor around the party like a second shadow.

If only they'd known. The truth was, Eleanor had remembered her aunt mentioning the frequent outbreaks of cholera in Kent, the air being particularly unhealthy in the shipyards.

Apparently Mr. Denholm's father hadn't expected to inherit the family estate, being a third son. The first had died unmarried in a carriage accident. The second, a clergyman, had given up his living to take over Ackley Castle and lived there for almost twenty years. He'd married twice and had four daughters, but left no sons when he died. "In a cholera epidemic," her aunt had said. The castle passed next to Mr. Denholm's father, Colonel Denholm, who had resigned his commission to come home from India and start a family.

Marrying an eldest son was no guarantee of riches. Eleanor knew that, of course, but now it struck her forcibly. Fever or accident could easily pick off the most cosseted heir, while a younger brother—even in the military—might well inherit riches.

Eleanor wished no evil to Mr. Denholm. He was an amusing companion, as Kitty said, intelligent and witty. ("Your cook isn't serving sufficient young men to my daughters. Would you like me to speak with her?") He was even gracious enough to give way to the Browne girls when they arrived to chat, perhaps thinking of Alicia Mowbray, and finding it tactical to offer too little of his company rather than too much.

Teas, musical afternoons. The onslaught of sociability continued. The onslaughts from Mr. Denholm, with Eleanor trying time and again to fend him off, and failing. Yet despite her exasperation, she found herself unable to mention his name to Kitty, even when they took their first long walk. She felt oddly tongue-tied as they wound up Goodwood dale, heading for the moors on another beautiful day.

As they reached the top, Eleanor wondered if she could slip into the subject by hinting that something beyond the order of birth

46

ought to be considered when arranging a marriage. Love, she might begin, if only she could have said the word. Affection—yes, *affection* was of far greater importance than it had been when their parents were young. Affection was the motive of the new young queen (exactly their age) who had chosen to marry her handsome cousin, even though no one could pronounce the name of the tiny principality his father ruled, Saxe-Coburg-Something, known mainly for its hyphens.

The prince was a second son, she would say. Preferred to the hyphenated heir by no less than Queen Victoria.

Eleanor knew she was really rehearsing for a talk with her aunt. But she couldn't manage to say it even to Kitty, and only awakened from her reverie when her friend touched her arm.

"Remember?"

They were standing in a field of cowslips. Sharing a smile, they knelt on the grass as they'd knelt when they were children, plucking the yellow flowers in a bleed of white sap and weaving the stems together. Before long, they were laughing like children, ending the morning windblown and happy, running into Goodwood with circlets of cowslips in their hair.

Eleanor flung open the door to her aunt's sitting room to find Mr. Denholm just sitting down. Her joy evaporated as he stood up again with a delighted smile.

"What a lovely picture! I wish I had your talent with a brush, Miss Mowbray. Perhaps we might ask you to capture your friend Miss Crosby and her cowslips."

Eleanor glanced at Kitty, but for whatever reason, her friend seemed unprepared to speak. Eleanor removed her circlet, blushing furiously.

"I'm afraid I'm in no mood to be captured, Mr. Denholm," she said, trying to remain pleasant. "I've just barely been freed from the house. Aunt, perhaps Kitty and I may be excused to prepare ourselves for guests."

"Leave it, my dear. Here's Mr. Denholm stopping by for an instant. He's been summoned back to Ackley Castle, his poor mother being ill."

Kitty seemed ready to sympathize, but Mr. Denholm looked more irritated than worried.

"Again," he said. "I'm afraid my mother's health has never been good, but her physician is excellent and I assume he'll work his magic. However," he said petulantly, "she's written to request my return."

Eleanor put the cowslips on a table, struggling to remember Mr. Denholm's mother. She had been a null figure when Eleanor had visited Kent as a child, compressed into corners even when standing in the middle of a room. Mr. Denholm's irritation suggested she suffered from melancholy, which was known even in practical-minded Middleford.

"I hope you'll have a safe journey," Eleanor said. She took Kitty's hand, asking with a squeeze that she ignore Mrs. Crosby, who was signalling her to leave. Eleanor had no desire for a private conversation with Mr. Denholm, nor did Kitty seem ready to abandon her. Perhaps she *had* grown to like Mr. Denholm instead of his brother. Their stubborn smiles left Mr. Denholm puzzled, until he turned and saw Mrs. Crosby signalling fruitlessly behind him.

"My aunt has a speck in her eye," Eleanor told him blandly.

"I see," Mr. Denholm said, and to his credit, he did. He gave Eleanor a surprisingly cool look and picked up his hat. "I must be off."

"Yes, your poor mother," her aunt said, accompanying him to the door. "Fortunately it's almost time for one of my visits to Kent. You'll see us soon, Mr. Denholm."

"And Kitty, of course," Eleanor said.

"Unfortunately not. I won't say goodbye, Mr. Denholm, but *à bientôt*," Mrs. Crosby said.

The heir bowed himself out, leaving Eleanor entirely relieved.

"Ten thousand a year, Eleanor," Mrs. Crosby said, when the door had scarcely closed.

"My mother says it's not quite eight," Kitty told her.

"I'm afraid, my dear, that this is one of those very rare occasions when your mother is wrong."

Turning to Eleanor. "I wonder when you became so contrary. It doesn't suit you."

"But Aunt. Surely I have some choice . . ."

Without letting her finish, Mrs. Crosby stalked out of the room, looking far angrier than Eleanor had ever seen her.

Over the next week, Mrs. Crosby had refused to speak with Eleanor, saying she was too busy for nonsense. Eleanor hadn't minded, thinking they could talk on the train. But after her odd moment in the station, they climbed on board to find a Yorkshire family taking up most of the carriage, their awful little son already refusing to stay seated, and soon afterwards throwing his book at a tiny overborne governess. When the family left the train at Nottingham, Eleanor hoped for an opening. But a shocking number of thin elderly sisters slid in around them like pipes arranging themselves in an organ. Only when they pulled into Euston Station was she able to manage a hint.

"It's been so long since we've been here. Surely we could stop for a few days?"

"On the way back," Mrs. Crosby replied. "When we order your trousseau."

There was the most extraordinary exhalation from the sisters, a series of squeaks and pips and chirrings that made Eleanor think once again of a pipe organ, this time warming up. She was surrounded by mechanical pipes, each with bulging eyes and a hatchet jaw opened and closed by unseen pedals. Marriage, marriage, they seemed to be piping, and although Eleanor had to smile, there was also a plaintive side to their excitement, a plangency coming from the too-obvious fact that all of them were spinsters. Eleanor was reminded what her aunt was hoping to save her from, and it silenced her for the rest of the day.

Mrs. Crosby's carriage arrived at their inn the next morning, the coachman having set out from Kent before dawn. As they left the yard, Eleanor lifted her handkerchief against the stench of London, unable to remove it until they reached Greenwich and took the road toward Swale. Even then, she and her aunt remained quiet, with Eleanor absorbed in her thoughts. Only as they approached Preston Hall did she rouse herself to say, "You told me once that Colonel Denholm had a brother who died of cholera. I remember you saying he left four daughters. The ladies on the train have made me wonder what became of them."

Her aunt looked surprised but not displeased.

"One went to the bad, I'm afraid, and we needn't dwell on her. Although if we did," she continued happily, "I could tell you that she thought she was eloping with the eldest son of a peer. Of course he had no intention of marrying her. But she was the eldest herself, and the most accustomed to the comforts of Ackley Castle. Living afterwards in a cottage with her mother and sisters proved to be more than her principles could bear."

"What happened to her?" Eleanor asked. "Did she survive?"

"And prosper. She continues with her seducer, never married, several children, a mainstay of London society, at least at a certain level. Julia Holmes, as the family insisted she call herself."

"Mrs. Holmes! Isn't she the mistress of the prime minister? Or"—trying to remember—"the Lord Chancellor?"

"The second of the Denholm sisters managed to marry," Mrs. Crosby said. "She wasn't the prettiest girl, but the most sensible, and she accepted a lawyer. The other two still occupy the cottage."

"So, one marriage among the four."

Mrs. Crosby looked pleased with her mathematics. "Their father, you know, thought he was robbing the estate to secure his daughters' futures. But it turned out his steward was robbing both him and the estate. Colonel Denholm needed years to put things right."

Eleanor remembered being frightened of the colonel as a child, although she couldn't remember why. He was an upright figure whose boots creaked across the entrance hall of Ackley Castle like the wheels of a plague cart. *Creak, click. Creak, click.*

Odd to think of a plague cart. Eleanor had no idea where it came from, but the words echoed in her head like a voice she knew well.

Plague cart. Plague cart.

And suddenly she was breathless, eyes open on darkness as she stood in a London street before dawn. Her back was tight to a damp plaster wall as a *creak-crack, creak-crick* slowly heaved toward her. *Creak, creak, crack.* She didn't want to hear it. Didn't want to see it. Wanted it to pass by and knew that it wouldn't, that it would stop at her house and take . . .

Father! A sob in her mind.

Eleanor pulled herself up sharply. She must have nodded off and dreamt about a novel she'd read. More likely one her father had read her when she was young and suggestible enough that the wall's dampness had insinuated itself into her memory. Yet she couldn't recall a novel like that and felt baffled. Worse: afraid she was growing hysterical at precisely the wrong time, with her entire future being decided.

"Ackley Castle is just ahead," her aunt said. "I wonder how much you'll remember."

Mrs. Crosby rapped on the roof of the carriage and the coachman stopped. When Eleanor leaned out the window, glad of some air, she saw the castle in the distance behind high walls. She remembered the building as immense but not as imposing as it appeared now. The tower at its centre was ancient, the remnants of a fortress still inhabited a thousand years after it was built. On either side were great wings added during the Restoration. Eleanor had the impression of endless windows and chimneys and a lawn sloping down to what must once have been a moat. Sheep wandered across it, erratic clouds on an emerald sky.

"There's a passage in *Pride and Prejudice*," her aunt said, "where Elizabeth Bennet claims that her love of Mr. Darcy came on so gradually, she hardly knew when it began. 'But,' she says, 'I believe it must date from seeing his beautiful grounds at Pemberley.'"

"She was joking."

"The author wasn't. Miss Austen knew very well that it's foolish to marry without money."

Eleanor dared herself to say it. "Just as foolish as to marry without affection. Even the queen . . ."

". . . married one of a small group of princelings sent her way by her uncle, the King of the Belgians. All of them Prussian, unfortunately."

Her aunt rapped the roof and they drove on.

"Nerves, Eleanor," she said. "I don't really blame you. And, frankly, it doesn't hurt Mr. Denholm to understand you're not merely after his money. I'm sure so many girls have thrown themselves at his inheritance that the process has lost its appeal."

"I wonder if that's what made him so vain."

"More likely his mother," her aunt said. "She's always doted on him."

So they were going to have a frank discussion.

"Mr. Denholm was unkind about his mother when last we saw him," Eleanor said.

"He has his faults," her aunt replied. "I wonder who doesn't. But you've made him fall in love with you . . ."

"*I* have!" Eleanor blushed violently. "I'm quite sure I haven't! And that he hasn't, or isn't. We scarcely know one another."

No more than she knew Captain Denholm, honesty reminded her. Eleanor looked aside, lost in the moment she fell into Robert Denholm's deep grey eyes. She didn't have the words to describe the warmth that had spread through her.

"I'm glad you're going to listen to me," her aunt said. "A successful marriage isn't an accident. Nor, I'm afraid, can passion be counted on to last. Mark my words: happiness is a decision one takes, and I can see you and Mr. Denholm taking it. You're alike in any number of ways. I wouldn't ask you to marry a stupid man, no matter how great his fortune. But Edward Denholm is clever, as you're very well aware."

"Must we have this discussion?" Eleanor asked. "What are you telling me? That I *have* to marry him? Surely not. Not anymore. Please tell me you haven't talked about this with Mr. Denholm. Or his father. Even worse."

"It's true he's highly strung," her aunt said, taking her hand. "A restless young man, and an impatient one. But I promise he'll settle if you marry him."

"At least you said *if*."

"I meant when. He's likely to ask you, my dear, and you *will* accept."

"You've been planning this for a long time, haven't you?"

Arguably from birth, when her mother had died. Eleanor took back her hand, feeling caught in the way things had been done for years. For centuries. Back at Goodwood, she'd accused her aunt of playing chess with Lady Anne. She'd been amused at the time but it shocked her now. Generations of young ladies being moved around like pawns, like marionettes. Her nightmare of being caught in strings. Nothing had changed. Not really.

"Permit me to take care of you, my dear," Mrs. Crosby told her. "You're affectionate, and he already fancies himself in love with you—he *does*, Eleanor—and everything else will follow. Especially since I know you're not thinking of anyone else."

It was a question. Eleanor blushed even more deeply, and her aunt's eyes turned as sharp as scalpels. But speaking about Captain Denholm was impossible.

"I think," Eleanor fumbled. "I think perhaps Kitty has grown to . . . that she likes Mr. Denholm. I thought it was his brother at first. But . . . now I think not. I think it's him."

Mrs. Crosby relaxed.

"So that's why she was so firm in her mother's assertion he has *only* eight thousand pounds a year. As if that would give her a better chance. I'm afraid she has no chance at all, my dear. You're being in the way means nothing to her future, and it's sweet of you—lovely—but you needn't bridle yourself. The colonel would never permit his heir to marry a girl of small fortune. Nor, I'm afraid, would Edward Denholm even speak to Kitty if she wasn't your friend."

Finally hearing her aunt, Eleanor realized that she was going to marry Edward Denholm, not his brother—and now, in modern times, despite the happy choice made by their queen. The party had started and Eleanor couldn't leave, incapable of running away like Julia Holmes, mistress of whomever.

"How much do you plan to give them with me?" she asked, feeling shockingly bitter.

"It depends how much the colonel requires."

Her aunt pushed back a strand of Eleanor's hair.

"Isn't my daughter happily married to Mr. Whittaker?"

"Yes," Eleanor whispered.

"Of course, you might prefer Stansfield Mowbray."

"You said you wouldn't marry me to a stupid man."

"He's not stupid, he's dull," her aunt said, trying to coax a smile before turning more serious. "I actually think more highly of Stansfield than you do. He may be a bit slow to come to a conclusion, but he gets there eventually. He also likes to do the right thing, which is an excellent quality in a husband. As long as one behaves oneself."

It was another question, and Eleanor nodded mutely. Of course she'd behave. Her father had given her principles.

Seeing her capitulate, Mrs. Crosby moved away, letting her breathe.

"Once you're engaged to Mr. Denholm," she said companionably, "Stansfield will have to follow the same program of impinging on his acquaintance to find a wife. There's really no one suitable in the neighbourhood. Except Kitty, of course. It's a pity about incest. They're actually rather well-suited."

"Aunt!"

But Mrs. Crosby only smiled again, not seeming to notice the abrupt lurch of the carriage. Or perhaps it hadn't lurched. It was only Eleanor's world spinning further off its axis. When she looked outside, everything was the way it had always been. To her left was a high brick wall. Gateposts lay not far ahead. Beyond them was Mrs. Crosby's estate.

5

Preston Hall had begun life as the ancient manor of a small Kentish lord. Her father had told her it would have been a loud, smoky, rumbustious place, the lord and his retainers cooking and sleeping among the livestock, horses stabled inside, chickens laying eggs in the corners, the great hall as much a barn as a palace.

Most medieval manors had disappeared centuries ago, burned down in chimney fires and raids. The central hall at Preston was a rare survivor, protected by a warren of rooms added over generations. Eleanor liked the way the rooms rambled one from the other, giving the house an eccentric but pleasing aspect, like a kindly old gentleman. An ancient gentleman, born before the *Domesday Book* was written.

Maybe even earlier. A year ago, Mrs. Crosby's new steward had been repairing the cellars when a workman had dug up a small hoard of Roman coins. Digging deeper, the men had uncovered a lovely mosaic floor showing that the Hall had been built on a Roman site fifteen hundred years old.

Eleanor hadn't seen the mosaic until now, standing on a scaffolding looking down at the pebbled portrait of a dark-haired lady, her bust shown against a pale circular background. The colours were still astonishingly vivid after fifteen hundred years. Glossy red apples floated around the dark-haired lady, each with a pair of green leaves fluting from its stem. Apples! Her aunt's orchard was full of apples this very minute, new green fruit the size of a baby's fist. According to her aunt's steward, the Romans had brought them here from Syria.

"The house is a palimpsest," Mr. Denholm said, standing beside her.

Eleanor kept her eyes on the apples. "I don't know what that means."

"It refers to an old vellum manuscript from which the writing has been erased and written over. Except that traces of the original writing remain."

An intelligent man, it was true. Eleanor looked up.

"I often think of the way each second of our lives is erased as time flows forward," she told him. "But of course what happens remains written on each of us. I suppose we're like palimpsests ourselves."

"Miss Crosby, you're far too clever for me," Mr. Denholm said, turning to his brother. "Isn't she?"

Captain Denholm was the great surprise of Eleanor's arrival. The two brothers had ridden over that morning with an invitation to an informal supper at Ackley Castle. When the captain had walked into her aunt's sitting room, Eleanor felt her heart explode.

"Captain?" she'd said so stupidly that the brothers had laughed. It looked like a set joke, one they'd played on other neighbours. As they sat, Eleanor was relieved that her surprise had covered up her embarrassment at meeting Mr. Denholm, which was just as genuine as her shock at seeing the captain. She hardly knew what unsettled her more, meeting the brother she was supposed to marry or the one she wanted to.

Yet as they exchanged the usual civilities—their mother's health, the Yorkshire hunt—Mr. Denholm proved to be in an odd mood. He paid more attention to his immaculate cuffs than he did to her aunt's conversation, his smile an absentminded tic he called up when silences demanded it. He soon got up restlessly to stand by the window, only reluctantly accepting Mrs. Crosby's suggestion that Eleanor show them the mosaic.

Now he'd called her far too clever. Far too clever *for me*. Eleanor didn't miss the emphasis.

"I wonder if any of us can be too clever," the captain said, looking embarrassed for his brother. "Not with life so unpredictable."

"Yours, in any event," Mr. Denholm replied.

"My brother refers to the fact I'm going to India," the captain told Eleanor. "A few days' leave and then I'm off."

"India!" she cried, feeling caught in another explosion.

"I consider myself lucky. Our father served there for a decade . . ."

"A decade!"

". . . an ensign when he sailed out with Lord Wellington—Colonel Wellesley, as he was then—and a colonel himself when he came back to fight Napoleon."

"And he would have made general had he not inherited Ackley Castle," Mr. Denholm said impatiently. "As he will no doubt tell you at supper."

The mosaic lay in a deep cellar lit by flickering candles. Eleanor was happy it obscured her repeated shock. Yet when she caught the pained expression on Mr. Denholm's face, she thought she understood, at least, the reason for his mood.

"You'll miss your brother," she said gently. "Although no doubt it's a fine chance for the captain."

"Thank you for enlightening me about my feelings," Mr. Denholm replied.

"The posting is a bit of a surprise," the captain said, stepping in, and shooting his brother a look. "Although a happy one, as you say."

"I hope so. Given your long sacrifice. I mean of home."

Mr. Denholm only grunted. So much for Mrs. Crosby's bold prediction that he'd ask for her hand. Eleanor didn't believe he loved her, and doubted he'd been hurt by her coolness when he'd left Yorkshire. More likely she'd wounded his vanity, and she didn't care about anyone's vanity. If it was inflated, it deserved to be punctured. But that didn't make the visit any easier.

"My aunt plans to dig out the cellar," she went on, not knowing what else to say. "Her steward says he can rebuild the exterior wall down to Roman level, and put in a row of high windows up there, you see, at ground level, to let in some light. Then she'll hold a ball, and we can dance on floors that haven't been trod in more than a millennium."

"Ruining them," Mr. Denholm said, with an unexpected tremor of feeling.

Eleanor felt out of her depth. "Why don't we go back upstairs," she said, "where it isn't quite so gloomy? The lady's used to being alone. I don't think she'll miss us."

"The goddess," Mr. Denholm said, as he led the way back up the stairs. "She's likely a domestic goddess. That's why they covered her with dirt, getting rid of her when the family converted to Christianity."

"And you speak of me being too clever," Eleanor said.

"Is this the way to the garden?" Mr. Denholm asked, opening a door at the top of the stairs. Without waiting for an answer, he walked outside.

It was a still day, warm for the season, and the humid air seemed to inhale the scent of the spring flowers; inhale and diffuse it so the air was indistinguishable from their perfume. Showing her aunt's gardens, Eleanor thought this heaviness might be another reason for the odd tenor of their meeting. She was surprised to find the brothers in no hurry to leave, although they didn't seem to want to be there, either. Even the captain seemed apathetic, and Eleanor fought faintness when she wasn't a young lady who fainted. It was the strangest morning she'd ever spent.

"Are you well, Miss Crosby?" the observant Captain Denholm asked, walking beside her.

"It's only the heat," she said, pulling herself up. "It was cool when we left Yorkshire, and here the scent of flowers seems a bit loud."

"Loud flowers," Mr. Denholm said from behind her. "Are you secretly a poet, Miss Crosby?"

"I'm actually rather practical-minded," Eleanor replied, aware that she never used to keep secrets from anyone. "You've seen my friend Catherine's drawings, but as I think we've established, I only do accounts. Rather neatly; I will say that for myself."

"It's too bad your father didn't push a little harder," the captain said. "I can't see any reason why ladies can't become proficient at higher mathematics, at least the most clever among them." He gave her a friendly smile. "It's an elegant science."

"Not loud?" his brother asked.

"Eight is a loud number," Eleanor said. "Seven rather proud of itself."

"And six a bit of a vixen," Mr. Denholm said. "Rather like you."

"Really, Mr. Denholm," Eleanor said, turning on him. "I've been attempting to account for your rudeness, but quite honestly, I can't."

He had the grace to blush. Or perhaps he was flushing with anger. For a brief moment, Mr. Denholm met her eye and seemed ready to say something. Then he bowed abruptly and left, striding toward the stables for his horse, leaving Eleanor alone with the captain. That might have been her goal if she'd been capable of forming one.

"You'll meet our father at supper," Captain Denholm said, gazing after his brother. "Or renew the acquaintance. It's not easy being his heir. I drew the long stick, being the second, and inclined toward the military." After hesitating a moment, he said, "Perhaps you'll show me the rest of the gardens, and I'll have another corner of Kent to think about in the Punjab."

With a little flutter, Eleanor wondered if he meant he'd think of her. She led the captain into Mrs. Crosby's white garden, which she'd planted as a bride. Most of the plants remained green this early in the season. But there were beds of sweet white hyacinths, and the air was thick with their delicious caramelized scent.

"I was mistaken when you arrived in Yorkshire," Eleanor said. "I believe I said that I thought you'd be a clergyman." They exchanged a smile at her pertness. "But now you imply you've always been inclined toward the military."

"From the time I was a lad," he said. "Wishing to defend not so much my country as its quite exasperating people. Meaning my family, I suppose, but also the nation. Of course I speak affectionately."

"Exasperating, are we?"

The captain—Robert, Robin—gave his easy companionable smile. He showed none of his brother's vanity, or his readiness to take offense. He was dressed again in his thick brown coat, the wool far more practical than the elegant weave favoured by Mr. Denholm.

"I don't mean to interrupt," she said.

He shook his head. "What happened, you see, is that my father heard about a letter the Duke of Wellington wrote to a nephew. The duke had advised him to get a university education before entering the army. He said the nephew would learn soldiering when he got his commission, but at Cambridge he would, and I believe I've got the exact words, 'get that education both of learning and of habit which you will never get again.'"

They left the gardens to follow a path around the fish pond, dammed from a creek with grilles placed at either end to contain the fish. The path continued at the far side under an archway of freshly greened trees, their shade still blooming with bluebells. All was silent save for the mutter and splash of the creek beside them. The birds were resting as it approached midday and the buzz of insects was muted. It was peaceful with Mr. Denholm gone. His brother was a far more restful companion, humorous and attentive, and handsome despite his casual clothes, not because of them.

"So I went to Cambridge," the captain said, "and surprised myself with a growing inclination toward the church. I must be outdoors, and the life of a country parson began to appeal. Collecting specimens, you see."

He shot her an amused glance, seeming to say, Can you picture me as a parson? Pausing on a small bridge, Eleanor decided that she could, in precisely these rustic clothes and precisely this gentle country. She tried to remember what the local parsonage looked like, and pictured herself as a clergyman's wife. That was what her father had prepared her for, knowing that she needed to be outdoors and active, just like the captain. As they stood together amiably, Eleanor felt rueful at the loss of a peaceful life, the loss of a possibility, a dream—nostalgic for what she wouldn't have, now that she was the ward of an ambitious aunt.

"In the end, my father pulled me out of Cambridge and arranged a commission. I resented it at the time, but it was the right decision."

"And here I've always thought young ladies were the pawns moved around by their parents. And their guardians," Eleanor added, and met his eye candidly, acknowledging what neither of them could say. "But of course another of the pieces on the board is a knight."

"Old men sending young men off to war," the captain agreed. He smiled and shook his head again, continuing along the path toward the farmyard. Its funk reached a distance, and soon they heard the chatter and grunt of sociable animals. Rounding the stables, they walked among Mrs. Crosby's flock of prize chickens pecking away at the straw and muck—pecking into the pigpen, and through the open stable doors—one rooster shaking his green tail feathers, a gleam of aged bronze.

Struck by something, the captain bent to pick up a chicken, cradling its hastiness against his tweed jacket, the bird's head darting this way and that.

"They've got five toes."

"Dorkings," Eleanor told him. "They've always had the breed at Preston Hall. They're good layers and the meat is superior. Lately my aunt has learned from her steward that they were probably introduced into Britain by the Romans. Like mosaics and apples, I suppose."

He looked entirely charming: those eyes, those curls, that warm smile, holding the chicken expertly. Court me with chickens, Eleanor thought. Then she heard voices and saw her aunt coming from the house with her steward, Mr. Stickley. Mrs. Crosby halted, putting her hand on her voluble steward's arm to silence him.

"Here you are," she called, walking over. "And Mr. Denholm?"

"Gone home. As I must," the captain said, stooping to release the chicken. Mr. Stickley signalled a stable boy to fetch the captain's horse, a fine buckskin stallion. Scarcely a moment passed before he legged it up into the saddle.

"Until this evening," he said, and rode off.

"Explanation," her aunt demanded, having waited until they reached her sitting room.

"I'm afraid I'm rather hungry," Eleanor said, throwing herself on the sofa and unlacing her boots. "After such a morning."

Her aunt didn't ring the bell.

"Mr. Denholm was unbearably rude," Eleanor said, tossing her boots aside and flexing her toes. "His brother is going to India, and I think he's upset about the captain leaving. But when I said as much—and sympathetically, Aunt—he thanked me for enlightening him about his feelings. A few more jabs and he left. The captain was embarrassed, and hinted at some unpleasantness with their father, although of course he couldn't say what."

Mrs. Crosby rang the bell, not quite looking at Eleanor as she spoke. "I wonder if your indifference when he left Yorkshire might also be a factor."

"I thought of that, too," Eleanor said. "But I imagine a mild flirtation—on his side, I mean—can dwindle very easily to nothing."

"Mr. Denholm needs to marry."

"I don't see why. He can't be six-and-twenty."

"It's true he seems young for his age, but his father insists." Seeing Eleanor's frown, her aunt added, "No, I haven't spoken to the colonel. Lady Anne got it from her son, and you know very well she can't keep anything quiet." Mrs. Crosby checked herself. "I speak, of course, as her very close friend."

"'Love your enemies' the Bible says."

"I have no enemies."

"'And do good to them that hate you.'"

Her aunt paused to consider this. "At least to their faces," she agreed. "Behind their backs one can be more resourceful."

When Eleanor laughed, Mrs. Crosby said, "I imagine the colonel has known for some time that the captain is bound for India. Of course he's anxious for a grandson."

"And yet," Eleanor said. "I remember you saying the colonel was a third son himself. The two eldest died in Kent, while the colonel survived two decades of war abroad."

Her aunt started nodding, then halted and looked at her coolly.

"I see," was all she said, and they were silent until the housekeeper opened the door.

As they drove toward Ackley Castle, Eleanor felt as if she were nailed inside a coffin. The cloudy evening light seemed thin and she felt breathless, trapped, the future pressing in on her, a darkness at the edge of her field of vision. This is dread, she thought. She dreaded seeing Mr. Denholm, suspecting he was capable of being even ruder than he'd been that morning.

The colonel would be worse. Eleanor pictured a martinet, as thin as a knife, bullying his heir and poor overborne Mrs. Denholm, who had retreated into melancholy. Hypochondria, that useful new word. Her aunt had told Eleanor that Mrs. Denholm's illness recurred unpredictably. She would wake up one morning unable to walk and only rediscover her legs some weeks later, rising from her chair like a phoenix. Most physicians felt that such a wandering illness was hysteric in origin. Melancholic, hypochondriac. Imagined, really.

Eleanor couldn't see herself succumbing to imaginary ills, but perhaps marriage to Mr. Denholm would wear her down. It struck her that marriage might not just be Eve's Burden but God's Test. Eleanor was facing a test; that's what had started. Although her father had disliked the thought of a God more judgemental than loving. It was a sour and depressing belief, he said, that cast a pall over far too many lives.

Just as dispiriting to picture were the marriage negotiations: the colonel asking not just for the inheritance of Goodwood but for such a grand dowry that Mrs. Crosby hesitated, bargained, and chipped him down until they reached an acceptable compromise. Acceptable, that is, to the older generation. In the end, Eleanor would be truly trapped, and Mr. Denholm ordered by his father to accept what he obviously no longer wanted, once he'd thought it through.

What he neither wanted nor needed, Eleanor thought, glimpsing the richness of Ackley Castle through the trees. Soon they turned down the drive, crossing the old moat on a gravelled dike. Inside the walls, she was surprised to see the family waiting courteously outside the great wooden doors to the tower. Mrs. Denholm was in an invalid's Bath chair and her husband was standing behind her: a tall, thin upright man. A knife, as Eleanor had suspected.

Yet his expression was welcoming and Mrs. Denholm seemed far from oppressed. As they stepped down from the carriage, Mrs. Denholm gave them a lovely smile. Eleanor saw no sign of fretfulness, and the colonel nodded courteously as he walked toward them. Certainly he was commanding. Used to being in charge. But that was hardly surprising in a senior army officer tested in years of war.

"Mrs. Crosby. Miss Crosby," he said. "It's been far too long." With his strong handsome features, he looked like Captain Denholm. Or rather, his son—hanging back near the entrance—took after the colonel. Mr. Denholm looked far more like his delicate dark-haired mother, who would have been a beauty when young and healthy.

"My dears," Mrs. Denholm said warmly, and took Mrs. Crosby's hand.

Eleanor found it a puzzle. She couldn't imagine that the happy-tempered lady in the chair had peevishly called her son back from Yorkshire, and wondered if Mr. Denholm had used a letter from his mother as an excuse to escape a flirtation that was getting out of hand. He was so mercurial, Eleanor had no idea. Now, walking forward, bowing, saying her name quietly, he looked much different than he had in the morning, subdued and apologetic, with a downward tilt to his head like a well-trained dog that had misbehaved and knew it.

"I was told you'd grown, Miss Crosby," the colonel said, walking them toward the castle. "Which is just as well, since you must have been all of ten years old when I last saw you."

"I believe I was rather a spindly little girl," she replied. "My father used to call me his crane fly."

"Your excellent father," Mrs. Denholm said, entirely unperturbed as two footmen carried her chair up the steps. "I *do* remember you as being rather skittish. Blond curls and such dark eyes."

"Hazel," her aunt said. Apparently one was supposed to ignore the chair. "In some ways, my niece hasn't changed."

"An innocent," the colonel surprised her by saying.

"Perhaps we should say genuine," Mrs. Denholm said. "To your credit, Miss Crosby." The footmen put her chair down inside the door, one of them moving smoothly behind it to push her.

"I'm more often accused of being blunt," Eleanor said, following Mrs. Denholm into the castle. "I'm surprised your sons didn't mention that."

Captain Denholm looked amused; his brother as if he agreed with her. Yet Eleanor was distracted as she walked further into the tower and her eyes adjusted to the penumbral light. To every side were suits of armour and weapons hung on the ancient walls. Swords hung above their scabbards and pikes with long oiled shafts. A wide wood staircase curved toward a higher floor, and behind it were stained glass windows with scenes from the Garden of Eden: Eve with her hand on the head of a lamb, a lion lain down, his yawn lordly in the sombre evening.

As Eleanor craned to look up at them, the low sun emerged from the clouds and splintered through the windows. Fragments of rich-hewed light struck the armour, the colours breaking into shards of yellow and crimson and indigo as they fell into fragments on the grey stone floor.

"Oh! How wonderful!" Eleanor cried. "It's like being inside a kaleidoscope."

She turned a slow circle, clasping her hands in delight at the riven colours, there for just a moment before they fled, the sun disappearing again behind the clouds.

"I couldn't have been here before at this hour," she said, coming to rest. "I would have remembered this. How extraordinary!"

Eleanor realized the others were watching her indulgently, and wondered why people always looked at her that way. The brothers had smiled at her just as complaisantly when they'd first met in Yorkshire, gazing down at her like gods on a clever young mortal.

There was another time in London, she couldn't think quite when, but she'd found herself alone in a street. "You shouldna be here," a tiny ragged Scotswoman had said, taking Eleanor's elbow to lead her away. They didn't do it with others and she had no idea why they did it with her.

"You certainly aren't shy any longer," the colonel said. "Not a timid gel. When Mrs. Denholm got up a simple family supper to make sure you were comfortable."

"That's so kind," Eleanor said, following Mrs. Denholm's wheeled progress through a series of grand chambers. They didn't pause. Mrs. Denholm didn't play chatelaine, showing off her domain. But they went slowly enough for Eleanor to admire the high frescoed ceilings, the great carved mantles, the devout and bloody paintings on the red flocked walls.

Mr. Denholm walked beside her silently, his brother a few steps behind with her aunt. Mrs. Crosby hadn't fussed Eleanor with instructions, and she was determined to try to treat the Denholms naturally. Yet as the magnificence continued, one room opening into another, Eleanor began to understand what it meant to be heir to ten thousand pounds a year—what it might mean to be his wife—and grew terrified.

Finally they reached a pleasant sitting room where the Denholms obviously spent much of their time. The scent of flowers blew through the open French doors and the latest books were stacked on tables, with sheet music scattered on a new pianoforte. A magazine caught Eleanor's eye. She grasped it like a lifebuoy.

"Mr. Dickens's new maga," she said, leafing through it. "He said he planned to start another novel this month. It seems he has."

"Perhaps my father can read it for us after supper," Mr. Denholm said, a hint of treacle in his voice. Eleanor didn't like it, but remembered what his brother had said about the difficulties of being their father's heir.

"As the ladies wish," the colonel replied with model courtesy.

"It *would* be a treat," Eleanor said. "It used to be, at home. My father read so beautifully."

"Mrs. Denholm is right, as she always is," the colonel replied. "Your father was an excellent man. Precisely the sort of clergyman one wishes to seed throughout England. My wife knows, Miss Crosby, that I'm in favour of a national initiative to civilize the British native, sending out a cadre of well-trained missionaries. The usual lackadaisical clergy have led England into a sorry state. I don't know which is worse in a backwater like Yorkshire. The peasantry, the yeomanry, or the aristocracy."

Eleanor bristled, but her aunt touched the back of her arm and she reined herself in, only meeting the colonel's eye. He was looking at her keenly, and she realized he didn't mean a word he'd said.

When the time came for supper—the doors closed and the fire crackling—two footmen wheeled in a round table already set with silverware and flowers. They positioned it close to the fire, lighting the candles and pulling up chairs to the butler's silent instructions.

"If you wish to be seated," the colonel said, inflexibly correct.

Afterward, the footmen wheeled in savoury courses on a succession of carts as the butler almost invisibly served, appearing like a shadow at their elbows.

Yet Mrs. Denholm began to fidget, apologizing, unable to make herself comfortable. Her cushion irked her, and the angle of the back of her chair. A note of petulance entered her voice ("I am *cramped!*") and for the first time, Eleanor could imagine Mrs. Denholm writing to demand her son come home. As she wheeled herself restlessly back and forth, the ticking of her bath chair and the constant rolling of laden carts made the room resonant with wheels. Eleanor could almost hear the old drawbridge rising outside, the creak of ancient winches and pulleys, the dull echoed thump of wood meeting wood as the bridge locked itself in place.

She started feeling trapped again, unable to think of anything to say to Mr. Denholm, who sat to her right. He couldn't seem to think of anything to say to her either, concentrating on his supper, while on Eleanor's other side his mother grew more and more petulant, finally shoving her dish aside irritably, her fork clattering to the floor.

"Mrs. Denholm got up a simple family supper to make you feel comfortable." Perhaps not. A long formal dinner would have been excruciating for the poor lady, although when Eleanor gave her a sympathetic smile, Mrs. Denholm looked fierce.

"Well," the colonel said, seeing this and standing, taking the role of the wife signalling withdrawal of the ladies from the dining table. "I've been extorted of a reading from Dickens. Perhaps we can join you later in the library."

Turning to Eleanor. "You will, of course, excuse our unconventional ways."

Eleanor smiled reflexively and rose, giving a brief regretful glance at her half-eaten chicken. They were only partway through the meal and she was still hungry, always suffering from a healthy appetite which required bowls of porridge or bread and cheese when they arrived home from more fashionable dinner parties, where young ladies were supposed to subsist on two peas and a prawn. Fortunately, when she and her aunt came into the library, they found plates of sweetmeats and bowls of fruit on a table, the footmen ready to serve, the shadowy butler directing the staff with almost imperceptible nods of his head.

Eleanor hadn't managed to talk to her aunt. The moment they'd left the room, they'd been surrounded by busy aproned housemaids frantic to lead them to closets and help them to everything they might require, from pitchers of hot water to soap to (whispered) rags should this be your time, miss. If Goodwood was a great echoing ear, then Ackley Castle was an anthill, an untold number of soft-footed servants moving ceaselessly through its rooms and corridors, answering needs before they were expressed and preventing talk by their presence.

Aunt, she might have said. This is dreadful. How would I breathe here?

How *will* I breathe here?

Mrs. Denholm didn't join them in the library and no mention was made of her absence. When the gentlemen came in, the captain managed to catch Eleanor's eye and smile apologetically. She fell into his sympathy, and for a brief moment felt warm and happy. Then she remembered that she shouldn't, or couldn't, and in some confusion she looked around for his brother, finding Mr. Denholm leaning against a window sash staring moodily into the darkness.

Edward Denholm clearly wanted nothing more than to slip outside and disappear. But his father was already standing before the fire, magazine in hand, waiting for them to settle. When all were ready save his son, a sharp, impatient, nearly invisible clench of the colonel's fist brought Mr. Denholm immediately back to himself. He hurried toward some chairs, which had been set out in a theatrical line, as if this were a box at Covent Garden and the colonel occupied the stage. Throwing himself in the nearest chair, Mr. Denholm looked around with ill-concealed annoyance, and a footman brought him a plate of fruit directly.

"The old curiosity shop," Colonel Denholm remarked, and Eleanor smiled at the description of his household, before realizing it was the title of Mr. Dickens's new number.

"'Night is generally my time for walking,'" the colonel read, still sounding conversational, as if he were the one who liked walking. "'In the summer I often leave home early in the morning, and roam about fields and lanes all day, or even escape for days or weeks together, but saving in the country I seldom go out until after dark, though, Heaven be thanked, I love its light and feel the cheerfulness it sheds upon the earth, as much as any creature living.

"'I have fallen insensibly into this habit both because it favours my infirmity'"—and here Eleanor felt jolted, for rather than having any infirmity, Colonel Denholm seemed as fit as a much younger man. Then she remembered that this was Mr. Dickens speaking—or rather, his narrator—and felt fooled and foolish and amused at herself.

"'Because it favours my infirmity,'" the colonel repeated, as if he'd caught her mistake, "'and because it affords me greater opportunity of speculating on the characters and occupations of those who fill the streets. The glare and hurry of broad noon are not adapted to idle pursuits like mine; a glimpse of passing faces caught by the light of a street lamp or a shop window is often better for my purpose than their full revelation in the daylight.'"

Perhaps this wasn't the narrator, then, but Mr. Dickens himself describing the way he found his stories. This time, he or his narrator encountered a pretty little girl named Nell out very late on an errand. She'd lost her road and needed help getting home, although what she was doing out so late, she said, "'I must not tell.'"

A mystery. Eleanor sighed with pleasure.

"Are you called Nell?" the colonel asked, looking up from the magazine.

"My father did sometimes," Eleanor replied, wishing he would continue.

"And is the reading up to his standard?"

"Yes. Conversational. Thank you, sir. Telling a story rather than indulging in the melodrama of bad actors. I dislike that sort of reading, although some find it clever."

"So you have good taste, Miss Crosby."

"Because I enjoy your reading, sir?" she asked.

"Perhaps because I want you to have it. Knowing that, like Little Nell, you hope to inherit a fortune."

"Leave it, Father," Mr. Denholm said.

"I beg your pardon."

"Don't tease her, sir, on top of everything else. She's asked for none of this."

Mr. Denholm got up abruptly and left the room. Eleanor caught a quiet mutter: "Making her feel like a pawn." She blushed heartily to find that the brothers talked to one another (of course they did), having never meant Mr. Denholm to hear what she'd said.

"Please go on, Colonel," her aunt told him imperturbably.

"I think not," Colonel Denholm replied, making to flip the magazine aside before controlling himself and putting it carefully onto the mantle.

"I think so," her aunt said, to Eleanor's surprise.

The colonel glanced at her with shocking dislike, then picked up the maga and read on.

As the colonel finished the story, his wife wheeled into the library. Once again she didn't apologize, but wanted, she said, to bid them farewell. Deeply relieved at their dismissal, Eleanor stood quickly, having to restrain herself from running for the door. Instead she was forced to keep pace with the lady's slow-moving chair. Mrs. Denholm spoke to her pleasantly, failing to mention her elder son's absence as they retreated through the extravagant rooms, each lit now by candelabra. Housemaids held them high, their faces turned to the walls, one a little scrubs whose tired arms shook, making her candles cast unreliable shadows. The resonant art appeared even bloodier in the flickering light, and the hulking ancient furniture looked as if Mr. Dickens had written it into reality.

The tower felt barbaric. It was lit by rush torches, and in the hissing circle of light, Eleanor pictured the coats of armour awakening from their long slumber. Spectral knights would creak and groan, sensing their weapons and leaping, flying high onto the castle walls to grasp the ancient swords. Skeletal horses would burst through the doors, and the ghostly party gallop off into the night, crying out hoarsely for Might and Right and the Holy Grail.

In fact, it was the colonel who spoke, stepping behind Eleanor to say, "You'll do," in a voice so low she scarcely heard it.

Did she hear it? Certainly, outside, she heard her aunt's coachman apologizing for a delay. The traces had snapped and were being mended. Behind her, she could also hear the older ladies disagree politely about whether Mrs. Denholm should step inside (hastily corrected) *go* inside to avoid the night air, and whether Mrs. Crosby ought join her. Eleanor had no intention of going back inside the castle. She drifted away, heading for a chestnut tree just coming into bloom. Even from a distance, its flowers smelled ecstatic.

A man stepped out from under the tree. Eleanor's hand went to her throat.

"I mean you no harm," Mr. Denholm said.

She couldn't see him: nothing more than a man's form, no moon to light his face.

"You startled me!"

She couldn't go on.

"I owe you an apology," Mr. Denholm said.

"You'll do," his father had said. *You'll do.* Eleanor could feel inexorable wheels bearing her forward and wanted nothing more in the world than to run away.

Yet an unexplored corner of her mind lit up with the knowledge that it would be wise to appease the man she was bound to marry. She never used to have secrets, nor had she ever been calculating. Now she knew she needed to charm Mr. Denholm if she was going to live her life with him. Unless, Hope chattered inside her, Edward Denholm ran off like his cousin Mrs. Julia Holmes, mistress of whomever.

He was no more likely to run off than she was. At least, not very far. It was surprising how well she knew Mr. Denholm after such a short time.

"Since no one can hear us," Eleanor said, "I'll agree the evening was awful. I *do* feel a pawn. One wishes to have at least the pretence of a choice. I'm sure you must feel that, too."

"I know something about it," Mr. Denholm said wryly, before his voice changed. "But you see, I care for you, and I *would* like it if you'd marry me. Even though I'm afraid you don't like me very much. In fact, I've grown really rather certain that you don't."

"But I do," Eleanor said, her voice a scratch. "Like you."

She felt rather than saw or heard his delight. But the carriage was arriving. Her aunt called her, and without saying anything else, Eleanor turned and ran back to the entrance, telling them she was here.

Afterwards, in the carriage, her aunt asked, "What were you saying to Mr. Denholm?"

Eleanor was surprised she'd seen them and didn't know what to say.

"Perhaps I should ask instead what he said to you," her aunt persisted.

There was no way to avoid it. "I think he asked me to marry him."

Her aunt waited.

"And I think I said yes. But aunt," Eleanor added hastily, "from what I know—from reading novels, not Mr. Dickens's novels, bad novels that Kitty and I laugh at"—because how could she take this entirely seriously, or completely tamp down her hysteria?—"he didn't say enough that you can have a breach of promise suit if he withdraws. I couldn't testify to that. Nor did anyone hear us. And nothing was put in writing. Obviously."

"It shall be," her aunt said comfortably, as the carriage wheeled them home.

6

The next morning, Mrs. Crosby set off again for Ackley Castle, saying she was going to pay a morning call on Mrs. Denholm. Eleanor had no idea why her aunt insisted on the fiction. It was so obvious what was happening that the words might well have been written on the walls, clipped into the hedge outside, painted on the front door.

"The colonel and I shall be negotiating the terms of your marriage to Mr. Denholm. (And, by the way, the captain is lost to you forever, since even if you're widowed by a Kentish carriage accident or the shipyard cholera, widows are forbidden to marry their brothers-in-law by statute and by God.)"

Eleanor couldn't stay inside. The sky was clouded over but the air felt dry and likely to stay so. She didn't burden herself with an umbrella as she left the Hall, setting off quickly for the fields, climbing over a wooden stile and punishing herself on the worn uneven pathway beside the grain, avoiding the road and its prying eyes.

At first she headed west, not consciously aiming for Ackley Castle and surprising herself when she glimpsed it through the trees. Her feet had chosen to go there on their own. Almost on their own, since her heart wanted nothing more than to chance upon the captain the way she'd done at the lookout bench in Yorkshire.

Meeting Robert Denholm would be a disaster and Eleanor knew it. Her heart would burst and she would tell him what she felt. She wouldn't be able to help it and he wouldn't be happy. He was a fond brother and a good and sensible man. Speaking would put him in a terrible position, her words like rocks thrown in a pond, the ripples lapping toward a future in which he would be her brother. With a wrenching exercise of will, Eleanor swivelled away from the castle, heading for a public footpath leading north toward the Medway.

The river was many leagues distant. Eleanor wouldn't walk anywhere near that far, but she kept to the path, needing the release of exercise even while disliking the low rolling farmland she'd thought gentle only yesterday. Now it seemed monotonous, one field after another tamed and lamed by its hedges, all so different from the free high moors of Yorkshire. The gods still walked the moors, she was certain. While they buried their goddesses in Kent.

Eventually Eleanor reached a spiked ha-ha at the bottom of a hill that left her no choice but to take the path left toward a nearby road. Clambering over the final stile, she jumped onto a potholed roadway that must have jarred the farmers' carts as it led up what couldn't be called a hill. A rise, perhaps. As she walked up it, the air was dusty and the poppies in the hedgerows had no scent. She didn't want to be here anymore than she wanted to be at the Hall, but she didn't know what else to do.

Reaching the top of the rise, Eleanor stopped for a moment to orient herself. In the distance she spied a moving figure, a horseman taking the high road to London. Telling herself it must be Captain Denholm, Eleanor felt grateful for the opportunity to bid a silent farewell to his amused grey eyes, to his sympathy, his solidity and depth, and to her hopes of happiness.

She also knew very well that it wasn't the captain, the horse not a fine brisk buckskin stallion but a farmer's workaday nag. Of the rider, she could tell only that he was young, meaning he was probably a farmer's son out on an errand so unimportant he would be unlikely to remember it tomorrow, and probably didn't want to be doing it now.

Feeling as sardonic as her soon-to-be husband, Eleanor reminded herself that most people spent much of their lives doing what they didn't want to do. Rather than being a tragic heroine crying farewell to her knight, she was an ordinary girl who would soon join in the common fate, dutifully—pragmatically—trying to make the best of it, just like everybody else.

Feeling deflated and ironic, her feet aching, Eleanor turned back toward Preston Hall.

She found it in a bustle. A kitchen maid hurried across the narrow entrance, a basket of sandwiches in her hand. Crossing her path was the steward, Mr. Stickley, who carried one of her aunt's boxes. When Eleanor walked inside, both moved past her like water flowing around an obstacle, keeping their eyes averted. They were packing for a journey, although Eleanor couldn't imagine why.

Quick steps, and she turned to see her aunt's housekeeper hurry out of the sitting room, carrying a vase of flowers.

"Mrs. McBee. What on earth?"

"Your aunt is in her bedroom," the housekeeper said, casting a searching glance at her before continuing on her way.

Puzzled, not knowing what to expect, Eleanor went upstairs and knocked on her aunt's door, opening it without waiting for an answer.

"We're leaving?" she asked.

Mrs. Crosby stood by the bed, an open case on a bench at its foot, her shifts and stockings already packed and a lacy chemise in her hand. She looked as if she'd been working quickly, but now she stopped and deliberately folded the chemise before placing it gently in the box.

"Mademoiselle is packing your trunk," she said.

"But why?"

"Because Colonel Denholm is an impossible man, and vulgar," Mrs. Crosby said, picking up another dainty. She looked at it blankly, then balled it into her fist and threw it at the floor, where it fell limply.

"So there's no marriage?" Eleanor asked.

"If I thought you had any feeling for Mr. Denholm, I should be very sorry."

With an angry hiss, her aunt resumed packing, hurrying back and forth to the wardrobe as she spoke, bundling up clothes and shoving them any which way into the trunk.

"The colonel is absurd," she said. "Starting out by asking a ridiculous sum as dowry on top, eventually, of Goodwood. Which of course I expected, and he *did* bargain down, although perhaps not as much as I would have preferred. However, Ackley is a rich property, fair is fair, and he understood without *too* much pushing that Preston Hall is for my daughter."

Mrs. Crosby paused, nodding abstractly at her trunk as she thought back through the negotiations. Then she remembered her anger and resumed packing.

"Yet after we reached a bargain, the impossible man had the gall to announce himself head of the family and begin to dictate my actions. My steward Mr. Stickley sent away . . ."

"Mr. Stickley?" Eleanor asked.

". . . when I've been entirely discreet, and am, besides, *demonstrably* a widow—who by-the-by earned my money, *especially* this Hall. Anyone who knew Mr. Preston could tell you that, including the colonel. Should I therefore happen to divert myself . . ."

"*Mr. Stickley?*" Eleanor asked.

". . . it's nobody's business, not when we've been so discreet. And how the colonel found out without bribing the servants I have no idea. Nor should the man encourage gossip, considering his relations with Mrs. Ormsby. That great friend of his niece, Julia Holmes."

"But Aunt," Eleanor said. "You're saying he wished you to end an *affair de coeur* . . ."

"Plainly. When it has nothing to do with anything. But you don't like Mr. Denholm, so it's of no matter, really."

Her aunt sat down abruptly, and Eleanor sat next to her on the bed. The room felt unstable, even as its furniture stayed stolidly in its place, although it was true the open wardrobe gaped at them.

"It's too bad about Captain Denholm," her aunt said, taking her hand. Eleanor was so unmoored she couldn't even blush. "I talked with him over dinner last night. He's a good young man, intelligent and modest, with a far easier temper than his brother. It will be a great joke if he comes back from India so rich a nabob that he can marry whomever he pleases. Of course he's head over heels in love with you. As you very well know."

Eleanor felt helpless. "I don't seem to know anything."

"However, he'll be gone for years. He rode off this morning, and I'm sorry to say, we really can't expect him back."

"Aunt . . ."

But Mrs. Crosby only gave herself a shake, standing up and adjusting her cap in the mirror. After a series of gentle, nearly imperceptible tugs, she paused and smiled happily at what she saw.

"Of course," she said, meeting Eleanor's eyes in the mirror, "having two young men fall so rapidly in love with you does rather suggest it won't be any trouble finding you a husband."

"Oh, please, Aunt," Eleanor said. "Surely it proves the opposite. I'm no more engaged than I was six months ago."

Mrs. Crosby ignored her, walking over to the wardrobe and taking out a dress.

"We'll go back to Goodwood and prepare your clothes," she said, putting the dress on the bed and folding it expertly. "You needn't worry about Stansfield Mowbray; we can do better. There's still time to go to London for the end of the Season. I'd forgotten about the eldest son of the Earl of Grimsby."

"No!" Eleanor said, leaping to her feet. "Aunt? Really? *Please stop!*"

Her aunt turned around and gave her a nod. "I know. Too early. Go help Mademoiselle pack your things. Or rather"—looking at the trunk—"send her to me. I've made a hash."

Eleanor walked to the door, reaching for the knob. But she couldn't help walking back toward her aunt.

"Mr. Stickley? My entire life turns on a steward?"

"Don't be a snob, Eleanor. He has attributes." Her aunt smiled privately. "I did consider taking him back with me to Goodwood, but I think I'll leave him here to rub the colonel's nose in it."

"But if you were so keen on the match, couldn't you have stopped . . . I mean, for a while."

"You *are* practical-minded," her aunt said, with some satisfaction, brushing back Eleanor's hair. "However, it was far from just Stickley. The colonel seems caught up in this wretched modern *morality* and self-righteousness. Evangelism. Methodism, for all his supposed allegiance to the established church. One hopes it's a short-lived fad, and that we return to the much more forgiving manners of my youth."

Her aunt paused to smile back at the ramshackle Regency.

"But I doubt it," she said, giving herself a shake. "If you'd married his son, that dreadful colonel would have been after me for the rest of my days. Do this. Don't do that. I wouldn't have been able to lift an eyebrow without him interfering, complaining, ordering. Did he honestly think I was going to give him Goodwood for *that*?"

"I might have died young and freed you," Eleanor said.

"Don't even joke about it. Do you know what else he said? That I might want to go to India for an extended visit with my daughter."

Mrs. Crosby paused in astonishment, as if the colonel had just said it.

"Of course," she added, raising an eyebrow at Eleanor, "I'll have to come to Kent fairly frequently to oversee the mosaic. However, you needn't join me and risk meeting the lovelorn Mr. Denholm."

Eleanor lingered, doubting she could possibly have heard any of this.

Her aunt clapped her hands. "Go, go, go."

And soon enough, they were gone.

1857
London

7

Nothing was happening the way it was supposed to. Pushing *The Times* aside, Eleanor felt disturbed and unsettled, and it wasn't just her. All England had been horrified by the news out of India that British officers and their families had been massacred in a rebellion by sepoys, Indian troops supposedly loyal to the Crown.

Sitting in her aunt's breakfast room in London, Eleanor was trying to make sense of news from half a world away. Some said the massacre had occurred when the sepoys were forced to bite off bullet casings greased with pig and cow fat, contrary to their religion. Others that the sepoys were rebelling against the brutal rule of the East India Company, and against the equally misguided attempt by missionaries to convert them to Christianity. Benjamin Disraeli had stood up in the House of Commons to scold the missionaries. This wasn't an isolated incident, he warned, but a deep-seated rebellion that was likely to spread, leaving Eleanor frightened—terrified—for Robert Denholm.

The strength of her feelings shook her. Sometimes Eleanor woke up certain that she was in Kent, sometimes at Goodwood. But no, she was in London, settled into her aunt's townhouse for the last of the

Social Season. It was exactly as Aunt Clara had promised. Yet it also wasn't, and that was proving to be a problem.

For one thing, her aunt had told her she'd forget about Captain Denholm, and Eleanor knew she ought to. Robert Denholm would be gone for years, and he would be changed when he got back, presuming he did. Physically he resembled his father so closely that Eleanor could imagine him becoming like the colonel in other ways. He probably wouldn't become as satirical, and she couldn't imagine Robert Denholm losing his underlying kindness. But he might well become as brisk and demanding as his father, having grown identically used to both danger and command.

Despite this, Eleanor thought of him constantly. She knew that Robert Denholm wouldn't have arrived in India before the massacre. Taking the modern route through Egypt and a steamer across the gulf meant a journey of at least eight weeks. If he'd sailed around the Cape Colonies, he wouldn't be there for months. But she knew he would dutifully march toward danger the moment he landed, and shuddered to picture what might happen.

"You have rather a mania for India at the moment," Mrs. Crosby said.

Eleanor looked up to find her aunt watching her keenly.

"Aren't you worried about Hetty?" she asked.

"My son-in-law's tea plantation is as far from the rebellion in Meerut as we are from Italy," her aunt replied, regarding her coolly. "We agree the captain is an excellent young man, my dear, but you know very well that it's time to look elsewhere."

"I *do* know that," Eleanor said. "And I'm trying. But it's not working, is it?"

Her aunt grimaced. Because here was the other problem: they were being snubbed. Chins were raised as they walked down the street. Fans flicked open at the opera, and just this past Sunday, one of the town's famously bankrupt lords had smirked at her in church instead of pursuing her dowry. Eleanor had begun to worry that she might never marry, and she had no idea why else she was here. By which she didn't mean Londinium.

London. (How odd.)

She also had no idea why they were being snubbed, although she couldn't help wondering if her aunt's financial situation had recently deteriorated. Mrs. Crosby's grimace said she knew precisely what was going on. But she refused to talk about it, saying only that society was fickle and opinion would change again soon. Eleanor felt as if she were living inside a mystery. Which was an excellent thing when you were reading Mr. Dickens, or Colonel Denholm was reading Mr. Dickens, but not when you had to live through it.

The visit to London had started off very differently. Brilliantly, in fact. Mrs. Crosby had originally planned an informal visit, dipping a toe into the social waters. Then came Queen Victoria's surprising decision. The queen had withdrawn from society in late winter to await the birth of her ninth child, and she'd been expected to remain secluded for the rest of the year. Yet after Princess Beatrice had been born, the Lord Chamberlain made it known that the queen would return to town in the summer, allowing eligible young ladies to be presented at court.

Mrs. Crosby had leapt at the opportunity. Her own rank wasn't high enough to sponsor Eleanor, but she'd persuaded Lady Anne to write the chamberlain for a place, the trade-off being no trade-off at all: that Kitty would join them in London so she could be presented as well.

They'd made their curtseys a month later, a debut both glittering and sombre. Eleanor remembered every detail of her slow petrified walk toward her monarch, and could still feel her shock at discovering that Queen Victoria was as tiny and round as a robin. Her aunt, who was exactly Victoria's age, had told Eleanor that the queen had been a very pretty girl, slender and fond of dancing, with flawless skin and large blue eyes. But that was nine children ago.

Prince Albert stood behind her. Mrs. Crosby said he'd been handsome when he was young, as pale as porcelain with a well-turned leg. Theirs was a love match and they might have led an easy, happy court. But Albert had proved to be a swotter, that useful new word: a German missionary come to England intent on reformation. He promoted the concept of *deserving*, her aunt said, thumping as hard as a preacher on the idea of the deserving poor and creating, by implication, the undeserving, when poverty had once been considered a matter of God's will or bad luck; take your pick and toss them a penny.

As Eleanor backed away from the royal couple, she'd been alive to Mrs. Crosby's picture of Prince Albert as evangelism incarnate. But all she'd seen was a paunchy balding man, looking as exhausted as if he'd been the one to deliver his ninth child instead of the hardy-looking little queen; overburdened, perhaps, by his expectations of their jolly, corrupt, recalcitrant country.

Afterward, they began a delightful Season. Even as she mourned the loss of Robert Denholm's company, Eleanor had loved the change from quiet Middleford, life suddenly blared through a bullhorn. They spent the freshest hours of the morning riding their horses through Hyde Park with other fashionable young ladies. In the afternoon, they either waited at home for callers or called on her aunt's intimate friends. Eleanor particularly enjoyed Lady Georgiana, the Countess of Wigan, a fabulously tall dowager who presided over a grand salon with her doddering earl.

"I knew Beau Brummel, my dear," she told Eleanor. "Took him five hours to dress."

Poking at her stays. "How long to tighten 'em? What's your waist?"

Afternoons were spent at formal teas, evenings at the assembly rooms or at private dinners and balls. Eleanor and Kitty had partners for every dance, although Mrs. Crosby was so displeased with the young gentlemen on offer that Eleanor was relieved to find she wasn't required to take them seriously.

The heir to the Earl of Grimsby, the Hon. Mr. Newton-Pye, had proved to be a walrus, his eyes small crescents in enormous cheeks, his nose a pockmarked snout. When they were introduced at the countess's dinner, he bellowed, "How do you *dooo*?" raising his spherical head above the waves as if trying to decide if Eleanor were edible.

"I'm not making this up," she told her aunt the next morning.

"No, of course not, my dear," Mrs. Crosby replied. "Speak to Mr. Stickley about the problems of breeding, and not just of hounds. The Countess of Grimsby has an enviable pedigree but almost nothing in the way of eyes."

A month's happiness (despite the captain's absence), cakes, riding, waltzes. Then came the baffling freeze. Backs suddenly turned. Invitations failing to arrive. Kitty was relieved, saying that being so incessantly paraded had made her feel like a circus lion forced to jump through hoops. Too many candles, too much noise, expectations resounding like whips. But the snubs left Eleanor increasingly puzzled, and it was only when Kitty's eldest sister, Elizabeth, came to town—The Hon. Mrs. Charles Mortlake—that she finally learned what was going on.

After recovering from the birth of her second son, Elizabeth Mortlake was joining her husband in London for the end of the parliamentary session, where he sat on the Whig front bench. Lizzy led a witty salon at the highest levels of society, and Eleanor hadn't expected to see her until after she'd called on all of Society. But Eleanor and Kitty received a summons to the Mortlake townhouse on Lizzy's second day in town, the butler showing them into a morning room filled with vases of heavily scented white roses.

As Lizzy stood, smiling affectionately, Eleanor saw that motherhood suited her. Elizabeth had blue eyes and reddish gold hair coupled most unusually with a skin of unblemished ivory. Her beauty had seemed glacial when she was younger, but now a slight maternal plumpness softened her face as she glided toward them.

"Oh! Haven't I missed you!" she cried, embracing Kitty.

Turning to Eleanor, her smile remained entirely benign, but her gaze turned more penetrating. Despite her otherworldly looks,

Elizabeth was as sharp as her mother, although her discernment was smoothed—camouflaged—by an airy, laughing manner.

"And here's poor Nell," she said, taking one of Eleanor's hands in both of hers. "I've heard what's going on. A pox on Colonel Denholm for being so indiscreet."

"Is that what it is?" Eleanor asked, flustered yet relieved to know. "I had no idea. Although I don't think Kitty was unhappy when the invitations fell off."

"It's rotten of the colonel," Lizzy said, gesturing them into chairs, and taking a seat herself. "You really didn't know, Nell? I'm afraid he's put about stories that he called off your marriage when he learned of your aunt's indiscretions with, well, a steward."

Eleanor's cheeks burned, but she detected at the edge of Elizabeth's directness an intention to help. She hadn't wasted much time getting to the point, and if she'd simply wanted to gossip, she would have summoned Kitty alone. The one thing that had always surprised Eleanor about Lizzy—the great beauty, the social success—was her underlying kindness.

"My aunt was the one who called it off," Eleanor said. "And the colonel seems to have known about Mr. Stickley for a while. He told Aunt Clara to sack him and go to India. You can imagine how well that was received."

"Impossible man," Elizabeth said, with a burble of amusement. "'Do as I say, not as I do.' I refer to his friend Mrs. Ormsby, whom of course we won't mention. The colonel isn't much liked, you know, which would perhaps have allowed Society to disbelieve his claims, since they're rather inconvenient. You're felt to be sweet. As well you ought to be." She ignored Eleanor's blush and went on seriously, "But it also wafted out of Kent that your aunt was an actress before her first marriage, and that takes us rather beyond the pale."

The thought had never entered Eleanor's head. An actress? Yet it seemed so obvious now that she could only stammer, "I didn't know."

"Because it isn't true. I'm not saying Mama wouldn't be friends if it were. They were born in a different time. But I've always rather invisibly known that your aunt comes from a perfectly respectable family, and that the break with her father wasn't her fault.

"Not," she added, seeing the question on Eleanor's face, "that I know who they are or what caused it. Nor does it particularly concern us, since even if she were to let it be known—well, in the current mood, she wouldn't be believed. In any case, one doesn't make excuses."

Eleanor felt dazed. She'd never stopped to think about having a good reputation, but she could see with wretched clarity what it would be like to have a bad one. It would never go away, not entirely, certainly not among ladies who lived to gossip (and had marriageable daughters). She's a sweet girl, but. She felt helplessly angry at the colonel's pettiness.

"Kitty should come stay with you," Eleanor said, "so she isn't tainted by association."

"I won't do that," Kitty told her.

"No, she won't do that. It would seem an admission of guilt," Elizabeth said, and smiled even more beautifully. "I mean to throw a ball to mark the end of the Season, and everybody must come. New dresses for all of us. And my husband will force Edward Denholm to be there."

Edward Denholm. Eleanor had seen him occasionally in the distance, like one of those floating bodies in the corner of one's eye, a smudge on the light. But Mr. Denholm didn't seem to be in town very often. She would spot him riding in Hyde Park one day and at the opera the next, then he'd disappear for a fortnight. Eleanor had been wonderfully relieved.

"I'm not sure I want to see Mr. Denholm," she said.

"I'm afraid you're going to have to, Nell," Lizzy told her. "You need to be seen speaking with him, and pleasantly, as if the whole story has been got wrong. And since my mother thinks you didn't much care for him, it shouldn't be too difficult. Unless he decides to be contrary."

It was a question. A glance at Catherine showed she wasn't prepared to answer, still unwilling to reveal her true feelings about the Denholm brothers.

"My aunt calls him young for his age. I would say unpredictable."
Unable to resist: "What do you think, Kitty?"

"I agree with you," Kitty said. "And I don't want to go to another ball, Lizzy."

"What we'll do, then, for both your sakes," Elizabeth said, "is decline the more malicious invitations. I'll make it clear that I need you with me. We'll be busy getting new dresses. My treat. I've also heard of an new art master we can try. I want to take more lessons, so I can better draw my children."

"*Do you?*" Catherine asked, in the same deep tone as her invariable, *I understand.*

"No," Elizabeth said, burbling. "But I know you've had a miserable time here, and you deserve to do something you like."

Kitty's pleasure was so great it was almost painful to see. Eleanor asked, "Lizzy, don't you have any faults?"

Elizabeth laughed as if it were a compliment, a rhetorical question, when Eleanor wanted to know. Perhaps Lizzy's fault was to have no faults. Or rather, to study to have no faults and believe that she succeeded. Eleanor knew it was hateful of her, but as she took in Elizabeth's beauty and kindness—her kindness illuminating her beauty—she found her inhuman, a goddess come down from Mount Olympus to solve their problems. Deigning to solve them.

She also wondered if Kitty had already been tainted by their friendship. Perhaps the entire Mowbray family was at risk of being tainted because of their long association with Mrs. Crosby, meaning that Elizabeth intended to pull them firmly back into the good graces of society in order to secure her own family's position.

Entirely hateful of Eleanor. Yet she disliked being an object of charity, even now, when she wanted nothing more than to ask Edward Denholm about his brother, and Elizabeth was giving her a chance.

8

Charles Mortlake was the younger of two grandsons of the Duke of Brixton, not quite heir to the title, but within a couple of convenient deaths of succeeding. In the meantime, he and Elizabeth occupied a rich estate in Hampshire he'd inherited through his mother. Now three-and-thirty, he was neither a tall man nor a handsome one, although he had what Eleanor's father had called a good face, lively and expressive, with quick dark eyes and a thatch of hair he habitually pushed back from his forehead.

When she'd first met him, Eleanor had thought Charles was wrong for Elizabeth, too active and sometimes abrupt. But on the night of their ball, as they stood greeting guests at the bottom of their grand staircase, they looked inevitable. Walking carefully down the stairs, Eleanor found it hard to picture Elizabeth beside any of the handsomer men who'd courted her. They would have looked like a pair of actors hired for the occasion. Nor could she imagine Charles Mortlake being satisfied with anything less than perfection.

"Mrs. Crosby, you're so very welcome. Darling Eleanor," Elizabeth said, taking both her hands in hers. "Doesn't Nell look lovely?" she asked her husband. "Do you know that when we were choosing our dresses, she showed the most exquisite taste."

"Mrs. Crosby, Miss Crosby," Charles Mortlake said. "I'm grateful to you for occupying my wife while I've been over-occupied myself. Of course, you've known her so long, you realize she needs an object. It's most kind of you to supply one."

Behind them, guests were backing up on the stairs, craning to see who was absorbing their hosts. Important people, no doubt. Elizabeth continued to burble about their dresses and their art lessons (which she hadn't attended) until Eleanor grew embarrassed, eager to get away from the eyes and impatience of the other guests. It was only a minute or two before Charles bowed them off, but it felt like an eternity.

"She certainly does it up in bows," her aunt said as they walked off. Then she brightened. "Sir Waldo! Lady Anne! Kitty, in your beautiful new dress!"

Lizzy had said she wanted Kitty to stay overnight, but hadn't mentioned the arrival of her parents. Now Elizabeth smiled across the room, enjoying her surprise, and nodding approval as the Mowbrays made a point of greeting Mrs. Crosby and Eleanor warmly. Lady Anne put a proprietary hand under Mrs. Crosby's elbow, while Sir Waldo leaned in to tell Eleanor, "If your father was still with us, none of this would have happened."

Turning to a passing gentleman, he said, "Lord Cobble"— bowing—"I was speaking of my great friend, the late Reverend Dr. Crosby, whom I'm sure you'll remember . . ."

Turning to Kitty, Eleanor saw a young man bearing toward them. It had started: the gentlemen freed by the Mortlakes were arriving to sign their dance cards. Then she realized it was Mr. Crawley, a copper-headed young man from Gloucester who had shown such a marked interest in Kitty he would have asked anyway.

Eleanor had no idea of Kitty's feelings about her not-quite-suitor, but as he eagerly signed Catherine's card, and courteously signed Eleanor's, she felt like a mama seeking out his hidden advantages. Murdo Crawley was a rather plain, freckled young man who had been blinded in one eye during a childhood accident. But rather than bowing to the injury, he'd turned sporty, going in for pugilism and long hikes, even mountaineering in Switzerland, and surely it counted in his favour that he collected art during his travels. Despite the smallness of his estate, Mr. Crawley was ambitious, and liked to move among significant men.

After Mr. Crawley came a flood of young gentlemen, some of whom Eleanor assumed were sent by the Mortlakes and some by Sir Waldo, who was touring the room with the dignity of a schooner. The men signing her card weren't anything like suitors. But Eleanor knew that wasn't Lizzy's point, which was to send her back to Yorkshire cleansed.

When the dances were due to begin, Eleanor took her first partner's arm and joined a milling crowd on the dance floor. Up in the balcony, the conductor surveyed his small orchestra, baton raised. Then he dropped it, and Eleanor entered the happy whirl around the ballroom. Two dozen couples circled each other like gears in a watch, always turning, the ladies' brilliant gowns billowing. As they passed, Eleanor whispered to Kitty, "Your impossible mother hasn't left my aunt's side."

"Isn't she *dreadful?*" Kitty asked affectionately, and twirled away.

The schottische came next, then a polka. As she danced, Eleanor saw all of Society. The Duke and Duchess of Brixton were drinking punch. The Countess of Wigan was showing off her new rubies. ("The pleasure of bankrupting one's heir, my dear.") The only person Eleanor didn't see was Edward Denholm, when she'd thought that was the point.

Then the polka ended, and as her partner bowed himself away, she saw Mr. Denholm walk into the ballroom wearing one of his beautiful suits. Eleanor had been looking forward to a rest. But as she reached the punch table, he started toward her, Charles Mortlake standing in the background as if Edward Denholm was a toddler he'd set wobbling down a garden path.

"What a delightful coincidence, Mr. Denholm," she said as he arrived, aware that everyone near them was watching.

"Miss Crosby," he replied, not meeting her eye. "I'm told I need to offer you an apology on behalf of my family."

"That would be nice," Eleanor said. "My aunt wasn't an actress, you know."

Mr. Denholm gave her a quick glance. "She seems the type who might have been. And my father has an objection to deceit."

"I wonder whether it's a sincere one," Eleanor said.

Edward Denholm remembered to force a smile. "She's certainly never provided any particulars about her family. And my parents have known her for years."

"So have the Mowbrays," Eleanor said, smiling back. "And they believe her family to be entirely respectable. We wouldn't be here otherwise, would we?"

"I wonder who they are."

He spoke so aggressively that Eleanor had to pause.

"I don't know," she admitted. "I've only been told there was a breach between my aunt and her father. I think it must have been painful, she's kept it so quiet."

"And what is one to make of that? Truthfully."

Mr. Denholm finally looked her in the eye.

"Truthfully?" Eleanor asked, looking back. "I would imagine my aunt's background is rather banal. Knowing Aunt Clara, she would probably prefer to be thought an actress than be known for what she is.

"*Truthfully*," she continued, "I think my aunt is probably the daughter of a gentleman with a large family and a modest estate. Or a perfectly respectable physician at one of the spas, or a solicitor, or a naval officer who captained a small ship during the last war. Any one of them might have forced her to marry Mr. Preston, which I suspect is the cause of the breach. I believe your parents knew the unpleasant Mr. Preston fairly well."

Mr. Denholm examined his boots, but nodded, seeming to agree this made sense.

"Of course that wasn't my father's only objection," he said. "Although perhaps we should leave it at that."

"Better not speak about stewards, you mean," Eleanor said. "Or of bribing servants, and certainly not of women named Julia Holmes or Mrs. Ormsby."

"Gentlemen require more latitude than ladies," Mr. Denholm began.

"And have never heard that pots shouldn't call kettles black."

Mr. Denholm smiled faintly, looking more like himself.

"In my experience, pots can be quite convinced of their right to boil whenever they see fit. Not that I always agree with them."

Eleanor pictured the family sitting room at Ackley Castle, his father ordering Mr. Denholm to be seated with a quick clench of his fist.

"I wish we could be friends," she said impulsively, offering her hand. "Can't we try?"

"Miss Crosby, I find this very painful," he replied. Taking her hand like a suitor, Mr. Denholm slowly and minutely examined her calfskin glove, smoothing a wrinkle with his thumb. "My father sees an insuperable objection to our . . ."

"Be friends and not talk about it," Eleanor interrupted, resisting the temptation to snatch her hand away. Too many guests were watching, as if she and Mr. Denholm were performing a play for their benefit, as of course they were. She knew she couldn't do anything hasty, but managed to take back her hand with a vague unpromising smile. Afterward, they stood together awkwardly. Eleanor knew she needed to find a way to end this, but couldn't resist.

"I wonder if you've heard from your brother," she asked. "I think it's probably too early, but I hope in any case he's well."

It might have sounded as if she were ending things with a polite query. She hoped so.

"Thank you. He managed to send a letter when they docked at Karachi. He's well, at least so far. Although it seems dire there, frankly. And of course he's off to the thick of it."

Eleanor caught her breath. Or tried to. She'd imagined this; she'd known it. But she found she could only take in shallow breaths like an overheated dog. The ballroom was warm. The gaslight, the press of bodies made it far too warm. Yet she tried to nod calmly at Mr. Denholm as if she were no more than ordinarily concerned.

"He only had time to scrawl a quick note," Mr. Denholm went on. "But from the sounds of it, the entire Bengal Army is in revolt.

They'd received reports the sepoys had occupied Delhi after leaving Meerut. Massacres, I'm afraid. Ladies and children. English ladies, the wives of officers, suffering the unspeakable."

He glanced at Eleanor, then did a double take, knowing that he shouldn't have said that.

"The Bengal Army," she replied, picturing the captain up against a rebellious army, and panting harder as she tried to speak. She could see, as if seeing herself from a distance, that her concern appeared exaggerated. "My cousin is in Bengal," she began, certain that Hetty was fine. "Perhaps not close. I hope she's not close. But if the whole Bengal Army . . ."

She felt herself tottering, and a firm arm passed around her waist, holding her up. It wasn't Mr. Denholm, who was still facing her, looking miserable.

Charles Mortlake. Charles Mortlake was supporting her, asking if she were ill.

"I asked," she said, trying to sound conversational, "I asked Mr. Denholm. About his brother. And he tells me, the Bengal, the entire Bengal Army is . . . in revolt." She was dizzy, feeling only lightly tethered to the room. "And my cousin, my cousin Henrietta is in Bengal. And he says, they've done"—gasping—"the *unspeakable* to ladies."

Distant murmurs of horror. Looking down a narrow tunnel, Eleanor saw an older lady staring at her calmly. The lady seemed to be thinking, This is interesting. I believe I'll watch.

"Poor show, Denholm," Charles Mortlake said, the words reverberating through the bone of Eleanor's stays. His voice was low but carried like an orator's, which of course he was, on the Whig front bench in the Commons.

"First you spread lies about the girl's family and now this. Revenge taken cold, is it?"

"Revenge for what?" She thought she heard a whisper.

"She turned him down," came a voice Eleanor might not have heard.

"Miss Crosby! Are you . . ."

Eleanor never fainted. But suddenly she was lying on a sofa in a quiet room, Lizzy Mortlake holding salts to her nose, her aunt hovering, Kitty and Lady Anne behind them. Removing the salts, Elizabeth daubed a lace handkerchief as thin as air against her forehead.

"I could throttle that man," her aunt said.

"She's perfectly all right. She's always been strong, and she doesn't faint. Really, Nell," Lizzy said, pushing back her hair. "Some might accuse you of taking it to extremes. But perhaps I shan't, since you've certainly dispatched the Denholms."

"My stays are too tight," Eleanor said.

Elizabeth burbled with laughter. "A thousand ships launched over Helen's pretty face. The Denholms dispatched because your stays are too tight. Small particulars leading to such grand results." Carolling: "And my ball is the success of the Season."

In her darkened carriage, not much later, Mrs. Crosby sounded bitter.

"I dislike the modern age," she said. "Such hypocrisy, and so much of it directed at ladies. Things are getting worse; our lives getting worse. It's fashionable to claim that we're far more fragile than we are, and Nell"—turning to her—"be careful not to give yourself over to it. It's very easy to fall into doing what Society expects even when it's very much against one's interests. When I was young, we were able to observe the dictates of Society while dancing around them, observing the formalities while privately doing very much as we wished."

Eleanor had no answer, nor did Mrs. Crosby seem to expect one.

"Now they're refusing to let us get away with anything. Even the queen was criticized for using chloroform for the birth of her last child, when it sounds a marvellous invention. She's supposed to have ducked 'the pain of Eve.' Poor bloody Eve."

Eleanor started at her aunt's coarseness, and wondered uneasily if she *had* been an actress. Perhaps it was something that couldn't be proved, so Lizzy felt able to deny it.

"Instead we're expected to behave like Mr. Dickens's wretched Little Nell," her aunt said, "when it's very clear Mr. Dickens believes that women are born to serve men. I greatly prefer Miss Austen, who wrote her male characters into subservience."

"You tried to make me marry Mr. Denholm."

"I did," her aunt agreed. "It was rather old-fashioned of me, but the marriage would have been a success, especially with his brother unlikely to come home. Please don't faint again."

"Kitty loosened my stays."

"Edward Denholm is very much in love with you and he was humiliated tonight. His father deserved it, but he didn't. Whatever were the Mortlakes thinking?"

"They were protecting their good name. And yours. And mine."

"'Good name.' Names used to be good when they were bold. Now it means conforming. They were making the Denholms conform."

"Out of fondness . . ."

"Because they like intrigue," her aunt said. "And because they can."

Mrs. Crosby paused.

"I was under the impression that Colonel Denholm had managed to overcome the financial mess left by his brother. Apparently he didn't. Lady Anne told me tonight his debts are large and the Ackley estate is under a considerable mortgage. Charles Mortlake looked into it, and what he found makes sense. The colonel arrived home from India at the start of the Hungry Forties. Of course, there's a financial panic every decade or so and most of us survive them. He could have settled his brother's affairs before things got too bad and been one of the survivors. I thought he had. But now it seems he didn't and the estate is in difficulties. We were fortunate to have avoided a marriage. It's just too bad that poor Edward Denholm has been doubly injured."

Her aunt paused to think.

"Possibly trebly," she said. "The news out of India is dire. Mr. Denholm was right: there have been massacres. Ladies raped and thrown down wells. Their children thrown down wells, and quite possibly raped beforehand."

"Good God!" Eleanor cried.

"We have to hope Captain Denholm is spared," her aunt went on. "But frankly, I'm more concerned about you. Life will grow even more constrained when the unspeakable starts to be spoken about. 'Ladies need to be protected.' From rebellious sepoys, thousands of miles away. More likely because men enjoy exerting control, and now they have a new excuse to do it. So for you to go fainting at even the merest mention of cruelty—which is rife in this world, my dear, and must be borne—surely, *surely* you can see that it reinforces a view of womanhood one simply can't support. Not as a thinking creature."

The carriage stopped. They'd arrived at her aunt's townhouse. Eleanor knew she ought to drop it. But she was unsettled by her aunt's outburst, which came straight from the ramshackle past.

"I'm surprised you can be so complacent," she said, "with your daughter in India."

Mrs. Crosby grasped her arm, holding it so tightly that when the footman opened the door, he stepped back, surprised to find them locked together.

"We've established that Hetty is far from the fighting," Mrs. Crosby said. "My daughter will be perfectly fine, even with her husband in Cape Town."

"He's in Africa?" Eleanor asked. For the first time, she felt concerned for her cousin.

Her aunt enunciated each word: "He has to sell his tea." Eleanor could almost hear her say, You're concerned because she's without a husband to protect her? Do you think I need a husband to protect me?

Eleanor thought she'd rather like a husband's protection, or at least Captain Denholm's protection. She was prepared to argue the point, when Mrs. Crosby dropped her arm and left the carriage, staying silent until they stood in the foyer and the housekeeper took their wraps.

"Hetty's always been so good with animals," she said mildly, surprising Eleanor with her change of tone. "Dogs. Horses. You must remember that incontinent hedgehog she brought home, which drove me mad. Now I like to picture her in the Himalayas, with tigers guarding the plantation and elephants protecting the house. Monkeys on patrol to warn of trouble. Not that they'll find any, *since Hetty is almost as far from the fighting as we are.*"

Eleanor pictured the stained glass windows at Ackley Castle, Eve and the peaceable lion, the light breaking through them into kaleidoscopic fragments. It was astonishing to find her aunt taking solace in such a romantic vision.

"What harm is there?" Mrs. Crosby asked, as if reading Eleanor's thoughts. "I can't do anything to stop whatever happens, so I might as well picture her happy."

"A pretty picture, mum," agreed the amenable Mrs. McBee.

Robert Denholm was good with animals. Eleanor remembered him holding her aunt's chicken against his coat, its head darting, and tried to picture him in India holding—what?—a spitting mongoose in place of a sword?

"I dislike the modern age," Mrs. Crosby said. "Everything so much more hidebound and earnest than when I was young. Mark my words, the middle class aims to take control, and they've got their dreary prince behind them. Trends are always exaggerated in London. Life can be better here, but also worse. Tomorrow we pack. Our Season is over and we're going home."

1900
Middleford, Yorkshire

9

Eleanor raised her arm. When she dropped it, she and Kitty lifted their feet from the pedals, squealing with laughter as they hurtled downhill. The bumps, the dust, the threat of spills—they were nothing against the speed of their bicycles. Speed was modern and they were modern, although Kitty wouldn't go as far as wearing bloomers, as Eleanor threatened. Being a suffragist, Mrs. Crosby would take it in her stride. But they loved to imagine Lady Anne's horror.

Reaching the bottom, stopping on a little wooden bridge, they caught their breath and looked at each other and laughed again. It was a beautiful October afternoon and they were free. The brutal war in Africa was a shadow behind every tree as the casualty lists grew longer and longer. But for the moment, their heaviest burdens were their painting boxes and collecting gear. Also a letter from Robert Denholm, which crinkled secretly in Eleanor's pocket.

Her fears that she would never marry might prove premature. Not that her aunt would agree that the purpose of a young lady's life was to marry. Times were changing and young ladies had far more choices than they used to, although her aunt had been known to imply that marriage would still do very well for Eleanor.

Eleanor tended to agree, at least now that Robert Denholm had written.

"Will this do, or would you like to go further?" she asked Kitty.

"We're fine here," Kitty replied. "I can use the little upstream clearing. And you'll be able to murder some insects to impress Arden."

Their art master, David Arden. For some reason, Kitty used only his last name. His lessons had been the success of their London season, and Lady Anne had not only engaged him to teach her girls in Yorkshire, she'd lined up several other Middleford households to employ him, making a northern stay worth his while, and getting a discount on her fee.

David Arden was an excellent teacher. When he'd first arrived at Elizabeth's London townhouse, Eleanor had come into the old schoolroom with a book in hand, proposing to read aloud during Kitty's lesson. Mrs. Gaskell's biography of Charlotte Brontë. She'd found it in Charles Mortlake's library, and opened it at random to find the story of Miss Brontë having been a governess. A boy had thrown a book at her, which inspired a scene in *Jane Eyre*.

Eleanor just barely remembered a boy on a train throwing a book at a tiny overborne governess. The dates didn't add up. Charlotte Brontë had died before Eleanor was born. But she was intrigued and took the biography, thinking she might as well be occupied during the lesson, even though her real role was to act as Kitty's chaperone.

"I didn't know this was a reading lesson," David Arden told her, his dark eyes bright. He was a Welshman, short and broad-shouldered, a powerful-looking man with miners not far in his background.

"I can't draw. I've tried," Eleanor said. "And concluded a long time ago that if I worked very, very hard, I would be very, very mediocre. Kitty is far better worth your effort."

"Do you like dancing?" he asked.

"Very much."

"I do, too, but my sisters tell me I'm a bear at it. That doesn't diminish my pleasure."

"Actually, you look as if you might be quite a good dancer," Eleanor said, not flirting, although girls often mashed on their art masters, who tended toward Arden's sort of workingman virility. "I'm not exaggerating. I have no artistic talent whatsoever. Fortunately, Kitty is brilliant."

"I am not! Please stop saying that, Nellie."

David Arden kept his eyes on Eleanor. "Is there nothing you've ever drawn that's given you pleasure?"

She remembered sitting with her father as he drew his insect specimens. Despite being a clergyman, her father was a devotee of Mr. Darwin's theory of natural selection, *On the Origin of Species* a well-thumbed volume in his library. Eleanor had often sat beside him drawing a child's version of the dragonflies and nymphs he collected. She usually did better with the plants they landed on, but she'd got off a good housefly once. The bulging kaleidoscopic eyes.

She also remembered Robert Denholm saying he'd thought of being a clergyman after catching the collecting bug at Cambridge. She had no intention of mentioning Robert Denholm, but told Mr. Arden about her father.

"Well, here," he said, breaking a frond off a fern in the window. Eleanor turned it over to look at the spores on the underside.

"That's a good way to start," he said, and switched his attention to Catherine.

Now they were at the brook, where Arden had assigned Kitty to paint motion. Opening her collecting box, Eleanor wondered if the assignment came from the challenge posed to art by the new craze for moving pictures, but Kitty said not. Painters had always worked to suggest the work of wind and the movement of water. Perhaps the human figure just turning aside. Didn't Eleanor try to capture the vibration of her dragonflies' wings?

"I chloroform them," she said.

"Poor dragonflies," Kitty replied, throwing a blanket on the grass by the stream. "Isn't it a lovely day? So beautifully warm. I may not stir for a while."

She plumped down on the blanket and lay back, crossing her ankles and clasping her hands behind her head in contentment. Kitty had blossomed since the start of their lessons, seizing the opportunity to study with a real artist instead of the provincial amateurs she'd suffered in the past. Her laugh was freer and her dedication to her work was humbling. She'd struggle for hours to get the angle of an arm right, most of the time spent staring at her paper. Kitty had always seemed boxed up tight, but something inside her was loosening, allowing her to lounge on sofas or throw herself on the grass in sunny freedom.

Eleanor didn't feel like joining her, not right now. She wanted to move, to circle the clearing, using her net as an excuse as she chased an impatient-sounding wasp, but really trying to work out what to do. Robert Denholm had written to apologize for the behaviour of his family. His letter had arrived from South Africa, where he'd taken up the fight against the Boer. She couldn't mention his letter to her aunt, and if she was going to discuss it with Kitty, she had to learn her friend's true feelings about the Denholm brothers. She didn't want to cause her pain.

A dragonfly lit on a Michaelmas daisy, its four transparent wings veined like stained glass windows, its body red and narrow. With a quick stab of her net, Eleanor caught it and balled the net closed with one fist, trapping the creature, planning to kill it and draw it. She'd left her chloroform bottle by the blanket, although as she walked toward it, Eleanor halted, losing her taste for killing.

"Poor dragonfly," she said, letting it go, although its wings were tattered from the net and it flew off unevenly.

"Kitty?" she said, throwing herself on the blanket.

"It really *is* a beautiful day. Thank you for sparing the poor bug."

"I've wanted to ask."

Eleanor left a silence, which Kitty didn't break. They both stared up at the fluffy white clouds tumbling across the sky.

"When the Denholms came to stay with you, I thought at first you liked the captain. But then I thought you liked his brother. And then I didn't know."

Kitty smiled. "That was a long time ago."

"Bear with me?"

Kitty sat up, clasping her knees and looking at the stream splashing happily down the hill. "I did think I liked Edward Denholm for a bit. He's charming. Witty. Also very handsome, and I *do* like a handsome man."

"Then why not the captain?" Eleanor asked.

"I think that was you."

After an indecisive pause, Eleanor drew the letter from her pocket and thrust it at Kitty. There was no reason anyone couldn't read it. It was one neatly handwritten page: a simple, straightforward apology for his father's behaviour and his brother's indelicate conversation at Elizabeth's ball, which Edward Denholm must have confessed. Robert was sorry they had caused her pain, and sent his very best wishes.

Implicit, Eleanor thought, was his knowledge that she hadn't wanted to marry his brother. He didn't allude to any significant loss she might have suffered, nor indeed to any feeling of loss on his brother's part. She wondered if this implied that Edward had freed Robert to contact her.

"He must have withdrawn or the captain wouldn't have written," Kitty said. "How did you get it?"

"Enclosed in a letter from my cousin Henrietta. She recently joined Mr. Whittaker in South Africa, helping him find new markets for his tea. I have no idea how they came across Captain Denholm, or vice versa. The country is large and there's a war on."

"It would be nice to know how the captain persuaded the Whittakers to send it. He obviously knew he shouldn't send you a letter without your aunt's permission."

"You've never spent much time with Mr. Whittaker. He's a *big* personality, and probably a very good salesman for his tea. I imagine both he and Hetty would consider it a lark to send me a letter in secret. What do *you* think? Of what he says."

"Surely the content is less important than the fact he sent it at all."

Nodding, Eleanor took back the letter and smoothed its wrinkles. The return address was the captain's regimental headquarters. She didn't know if he was posted there or if headquarters was a letter drop. Nor could she guess where else he might be, despite her obsessive reading of *The Times*. She only knew he'd arrived in Africa several months ago and must have seen battle by now. Perhaps his experiences had shaken him and he'd wanted to send her a token before going back into danger. Think of me, he was saying.

As if an hour went by when she didn't, or a week when she didn't spend a night tossing and turning until she was exhausted into sleep, borne down by the casualty reports and bolting awake with nightmares—this, even before receiving her letter, when she'd had no right to care.

Ladysmith, Mafeking, Kimberley. With the speed of the telegraph these days, they received reports from the battlefield almost as soon as the bullets stopped flying. The Boer War was different than past wars not so much in its savagery—Eleanor couldn't imagine a war being anything less than savage—but in its speed and immediacy. When Robert's father had gone to India to fight in the Sepoy Rebellion, it had taken six weeks for reports to reach London. Soldiers were long buried before their families knew they were dead. Now photographs showed their bodies still warm, killed by fast-moving Boer fighters.

During the ten years the elder Denholm had spent in India, the railroads and telegraph had pushed forward with the power of juggernauts. With the arrogance of the elder Denholm himself. Robert said his father had gone out an ensign under Colonel Wellesley . . .

Wrong name, how odd. Colonel Wellesley had become the Duke of Wellington, dead these fifty years. Eleanor couldn't remember the real colonel's name, and felt on the verge of—what?—before pulling herself back, deciding that it didn't matter. The Denholms' father had gone out an ensign under a famous colonel and come home a colonel himself, and might have made general if he hadn't inherited Ackley Castle.

So much was changing. From what Eleanor heard, Edward Denholm was pursuing an heiress this autumn in a concerted attempt to hold onto the Ackley estate. Maybe he liked the heiress, and that was why he'd been gracious enough to withdraw. She was an American, although whether her family was in steel or railroads Eleanor had no idea. By now, however, everyone knew the Denholms were on their uppers. Perhaps an American heiress wouldn't care. She'd get a castle for her money along with a handsome husband. Kitty was right; Edward Denholm was handsome. Eleanor had always thought so, although she'd looked at his beauty from one remove, as if he were a statue in a gallery.

"You don't think Captain Denholm is handsome?" she asked.

"I like dark-haired men," Kitty said. "Fortunately for our friendship. Shall you write the captain back?"

"I think so," Eleanor said, before daring a final push. "Murdo Crawley is fair."

Catherine's suitor, recently acknowledged, at least by her parents. Kitty picked up her paintbox, closing back in on herself.

"He's a ginger."

"I'll write to the captain," Eleanor said, enough being enough for one day. "Although I have no idea what to say."

In the schoolroom two days later, David Arden got the younger Mowbray girls busy with their pencils and turned his attention to Eleanor. She'd drawn a wasp on a sprig of Michaelmas daisies, tinting it afterwards with watercolours, and was absurdly proud of her efforts. It had been impossible to get the dragonfly she'd seen in the clearing proportionate to the daisies, and she'd had a moment of inspiration, putting an elegant little wasp in its place.

"You're growing deft with your pencil," Mr. Arden told her, his black eyes in busy conversation with the paper. "This is an excellent botanical study. What happens if you add movement? Does it want to become art?"

"I know you've been talking about that with Kitty."

"Was there a wind?"

Eleanor didn't remember.

"From the west," Kitty said, glancing over from her study. She'd graduated to an easel and oils.

"You're picturing it," Eleanor told her. "I don't remember physical details as well as you do. I wouldn't even know that people remember things differently if I hadn't seen you at work."

"So my lessons are of some value after all," Mr. Arden said.

That slight readiness to take offense. A little chip on his shoulder. Their exemplary teacher was a workingman in other ways than his accent.

When Eleanor had said that once to Kitty, she'd told her, "Don't be a snob, Nellie."

Mr. Arden left her with instructions to redraw her composition as if a west wind were blowing, and headed over to see Kitty's study of the clearing, an oil on board. As they discussed it, Eleanor heard the same defensiveness in Mr. Arden's tone, as if Kitty were progressing beyond his ability to teach. Sometimes lately he would pick up a pencil and draw over a composition as if to show he could still outdo her. Often his appreciation sounded ironic. He might have been saying, You have talent on top of a rich family. A little unfair, isn't it?

"You're a Frenchwoman at heart," he said. "An Impressionist."

"I wish I were."

More thoughtfully: "With an excellent colour sense."

That sounded honestly appreciative, the proud teacher in him at war with the prickly and competitive artist. Eleanor didn't make much progress on her windblown daisies as she watched them pick apart the study, Kitty being more critical than Mr. Arden. Of course, the Mowbrays—all of Middleford—would be far more critical still. Horrified, actually. Kitty's painting of the clearing was done with big active brush strokes that captured the movement of the grass and trees. The splashing little creek was a slash across the board while Eleanor (she'd been surprised to find) sat slightly off-centre, motion-less, her back toward the artist, her hat and blouse and bunched-up skirt a focus in the tossing sea of ripened grass.

Mrs. Crosby would like it. Mrs. Crosby had been freed by modern times, she said, finally let loose from a lifetime of being stifled by society. Her aunt could set up an invisible platform in her sitting room and harangue Eleanor about suffragism. She'd come of age in a prescriptive society, she said, self-righteous and preening, which had looked down on her for battling conformity, its funereal tone set by a queen who made herself secondary; who continued to make women secondary by mourning her fusty hyphenated husband almost forty years after his death.

Her aunt was exactly the same age as Queen Victoria's ninth and last child, Princess Beatrice. Eleanor felt young—and was very pleased to be young—but there were also moments when she felt older than her aunt. Mrs. Crosby had purchased her own bicycle and insisted on going for rides with her and Kitty, which was embarrassing in a lady of forty-two. She'd even beg rides in Stansfield Mowbray's new motor car.

"I was born in a different time," she said. "And I'm exceedingly glad to get quits of it."

Of course, Mrs. Crosby wanted to have it both ways: reviling the past while having tried to marry Eleanor off to a man she didn't love. At least the old-style Mowbrays weren't being hypocritical as they tried to broker a marriage between Kitty and Murdo Crawley.

Yet Eleanor thought they might get a surprise. Kitty's artistic flowering had made her more assertive. As David Arden traced one finger just above the barely dried paint of her study, she was not only able to accept his criticism (as she'd always done too easily) but also to reject it, contradicting Arden at times with a quiet, "But, you see, I was trying to . . ." Eleanor could imagine a day, dawning soon, when she'd even be able to stand up to Lady Anne.

Then Eleanor got a surprise. As Kitty spoke with David Arden, she said something that lit up his face with a quite unnecessary degree of admiration. Kitty saw it and turned away, as well she ought. With a secretive smile, though.

Eleanor felt—what did she feel? Jealous of their teacher's very male, proprietary interest in her friend: a jealousy she never felt about Murdo Crawley. More than that. A sense that Arden's admiration was unwise and ought to be discouraged, especially since Kitty seemed to like it. When they went silent for a moment, looking over the study, Eleanor walked over to join them, pretending boredom with her drawing.

"Kitty surprised me, you know, by putting me in her painting," she told Arden, making a point of looking it over. "Although I can see the need for something central in the composition. A cow might have done, of course. Or a flowering shrub, maybe with insects. Then she could have used me as a studio apprentice to draw in some dragonflies. Critics in five hundred years would be able to say, *Pyrrhosoma nymphula*, anatomically correct but artistically static. The wings don't vibrate. One can easily see they've got none of the panache of Catherine da Vinci Mowbray."

Kitty blushed as Eleanor spoke, while David Arden listened with dark Welsh amusement and (she was certain) a degree of resentment that she had broken into their private conversation.

"You'll have to take some boards to Gloucester," she told Kitty, before turning back to Arden. "A friend of Catherine's brother has invited us for a visit. Mr. Murdo Crawley. We go in a couple of weeks, and perhaps the weather will hold. I always find a certain tenuousness to November that might be interesting for Kitty to paint. Although, of course, it might just rain."

"I'm not sure it's a set engagement," Catherine said.

"I think it is."

"In any case, I have no plans to go," Kitty said abruptly, and the atmosphere turned strained enough that David Arden found it necessary to walk over to Mary Ann Mowbray, checking her still life.

"What are you doing, Nellie?" Kitty whispered.

"What are *you* doing? Or more to the point, what's *he* doing?"

"After all the fuss about Edward Denholm."

"It's not the same."

"Don't you think I feel the same about Murdo Crawley?"

Eleanor knew the illogic of her position. Nor would she dream of marrying a man as touchy as Murdo Crawley. She also knew it was wrong to believe in a very small corner of her mind that, despite her love for Kitty, and her admiration for her sweet smile and masses of light-brown hair, her dearest friend was not over-whelmingly attractive to men. More important, she was penniless. Kitty would be lucky to land a husband, especially one who would support her painting the way the art-collecting Murdo Crawley surely would.

Eleanor was a snob; they were right.

"I'm sorry," she whispered. "It's just . . ."

"Just what?" Kitty asked aggressively, speaking in her normal voice.

Eleanor took her arm and led her to the far side of the schoolroom. Making sure her back was to the others, Eleanor said in an urgent whisper, "Don't ruin your chances, Kitty. The artist admires your talents. But he also resents them, and he flirts shamelessly with his other pupils, Agnes Moreland especially. You've seen that, surely. But he's very aware of his wallet and isn't going to . . ."

"He's standing right there," Kitty hissed.

"Then we'll talk about it later."

"You sound like your aunt," Kitty said, turning on her heel and going back to her easel, and that was that. Nor did Eleanor know how to repair it, and only stayed a short while longer before finding (unconvincingly) that she was needed at home.

In bed that night, Eleanor felt restless and unhappy. She was afraid of Kitty rejecting Murdo Crawley because of an impossible mash on their art master. But she also disliked her own bossy attempts at intervention. Throwing back the covers, she got up and lit the gas lamp in the wall beside her dressing table. Its light was harsh and unflattering, which her aunt thought was a good idea. Not to discourage vanity but to get the hair done right. Eleanor had taken out paper and ink earlier that evening to answer Robert Denholm, but she'd found herself unable to write a word.

Now, not knowing what else to do, she dipped her pen in the inkwell and scratched out, "My dear Captain Denholm." Looking at it, she scored out *my* before balling it up and tossing the paper into the fireplace, where the embers set it on fire. The small conflagration floated for a moment, as if trying to fly out to Africa, then fell and crumbled to ash.

"Dear Captain Denholm," she tried again. That was better. "I hate myself."

Scratch. Crumple. Ash. "Dear Captain. You're right. Your family is impossible and my aunt is worse." Scratch. Crumple. Ash. Ash. Ash. Eleanor wasted half a forest of paper before deciding to get it right.

Dear Captain Denholm,

I'm in receipt of your letter and wish that we could talk instead of write.

That was a serviceable start, although she couldn't think of anything else to say. Except the truth, of course, which was impossible.

I was glad to receive the apology, but it's not necessary. I like your brother, as I've told him, and I've always hoped we could be friends. Any closer connection was never my idea. Nor does any of the gossip you allude to seem to have stuck, either to my aunt or to me, although her suffragism is controversial, at least in Middleford. (I'm not sure anyone else has noticed.)

In any case, what's more important to me is your good opinion. I think you know that. When I got your letter, I wondered what you really wished to say, and it's presumptuous of me, but I thought you meant that you're a soldier facing battle, and you were asking, Think kindly of me. Please understand that I do. I do very much indeed. I send you all my good wishes, and my prayers that we'll meet again before too long, and in this earthly vale of tears. Or at least in Middleford, which is too practical to have vales.

Eleanor bit her pen, trying to think how to finish a letter she would never send.

Anything I might add would be redundant. But please write back, at least if you'd care to. I would like very much to know that you're well.

Sincerely? Best wishes? Yours?

> Yours <u>most</u> sincerely,
> Eleanor Crosby.

At breakfast the next morning, her aunt asked, "What were you writing last night?" When Eleanor hesitated, she added, "The fireplace was littered with scraps of paper."

Eleanor put her tea down carefully. "You say you're in favour of the rights of women. But apparently I have none, including the right to privacy."

Her aunt waited.

"I was answering a letter from Robert Denholm. It was enclosed in the one from Hetty, since I know you're going to ask."

Her aunt held out a hand for the letter.

"It's mine. He sent it to me. And he sent it from a war, which has to be respected. Not that it contains anything Hetty and Mr. Whittaker couldn't read, and probably read. You haven't anything to worry about."

Her aunt's hand didn't move.

"Kitty found the content inconsequential. The important point is that he wrote at all."

A mistake. Her aunt's expression said, So Catherine Mowbray can read it and I can't?

"Didn't you have friends when you were young?"

Eleanor went and got the letter, which her aunt read quickly.

"And your response?" Mrs. Crosby asked.

It was on the tip of Eleanor's tongue to say she'd only written a draft, which was true. But she couldn't resist handing it over, waiting for her aunt to reach the line about suffragists. When she did, Mrs. Crosby gave Eleanor a cool look over the top of the page, but finished reading before she spoke.

"We're letting the genie out of the bottle," she said. "Women are owed their rights, but now everyone will be claiming them, including children. They *are* claiming them, when they used to love and obey their elders. Or at least obey them."

"I'm going to be twenty-one in December."

"Ancient as stones," her aunt said, leaning back to look Eleanor over.

"It's an effective letter," she said finally. "Not a mash note, which wouldn't have done, but exactly the letter a well-brought-up girl would write, and Robert Denholm will like it.

"However. I thought you read the newspapers. We're still feeling consequences of the American panic of '93. Everyone felt it. Britain felt it. I'm still feeling it seven years later."

Eleanor didn't understand.

"Manufacturing recovered from the crash far more quickly," her aunt said. "Now it's siphoning off the labour that estates like Goodwood depend on. It's also raising wages. Large estates like this one are getting very expensive to maintain. You must have noticed that I'm having a harder time finding servants as well as labourers for the fields. Preston Hall is small enough to survive. But it might make sense to gradually combine the estates of Goodwood and Mowbray Close into a large mechanized operation—tractors, you know—and rent out one of the houses, probably to an American wanting to play gentleman. Not immediately, not even soon, but eventually."

"Of course, that's your decision," Eleanor said, crossing her arms.

"Stansfield Mowbray will make a good farmer, and he's quite a sturdy young man. He's also bought an excellent motor car."

"I won't, Aunt. You agreed."

Mrs. Crosby didn't push it, although she seemed to be working up to something else.

"There's a family living near Murdo Crawley's estate in Gloucester," she began, and Eleanor tossed her napkin aside, ready to leave.

"Once upon a time," her aunt said, stopping her, "a man arrived in the mills of Manchester who was much more clever than his master. Such was his luck and his master's lack of it that this man ended up owning the factory. From there, his family rose until they became rich manufacturers. Not long ago, in the third generation, the heir bought an estate in Gloucester, where he's done the opposite of the Mowbrays. One daughter and five handsome sons."

Eleanor tried to interrupt, but Mrs. Crosby kept speaking. "Three of them old enough to marry. And it's a fairy tale because the name is Darcy."

Eleanor rolled her eyes.

"The original man was a Huguenot weaver by the name of D'Arcy. But he lost the apostrophe, which Oscar Wilde would say was careless of him. The eldest son of the current Mr. Darcy will inherit millions, and the others will be well taken care of. You wanted a choice."

"It sounds far too complicated."

"You like Robert Denholm because he isn't complicated?"

Eleanor felt the sting, but replied, "I feel one could count on Captain Denholm. Not on his brother. Edward Denholm is far more complicated. And you're right. I didn't like that about him."

Her aunt looked at her for a long time. Eleanor bore it, not having anything else to say. Finally Mrs. Crosby sighed.

"Send your letter. It never hurts to have a fallback. I may fail in whatever panic comes next, and we'll be glad to have a soldier. There will always be another war."

Eleanor dawdled on her way back from posting her letter. She hadn't changed it, only added a postscript saying that her aunt knew she was writing and he could send her an answer directly if he wished. Eleanor felt a sense of accomplishment. She'd thrown the dice, arguably for the first time. First her father and then her aunt had organized her life, but she'd done this on her own and felt giddy with independence. Giddy to picture the captain receiving her letter in a faraway continent. Breathless to imagine his large capable hands touching the envelope she'd touched. Terrified to think he might not survive to receive it.

She was still lost in her thoughts when she turned a corner and saw Kitty waiting. Eleanor hesitated, wondering if her friend was still angry with her. But Kitty stepped forward and said, "Your aunt told me you'd gone to post a letter. I couldn't bear for us to fight any longer."

"I can't, either," Eleanor said, and embraced her.

Holding hands, they went to sit on an old drystone wall where they'd sat ever since they were children. Yet as they took their usual places, smiling in shared remembrance, Eleanor saw how much older they'd grown. They no longer kicked and dangled their legs, but sat calmly and sensibly. She might not have seen that if they'd just stood and talked.

"I never want anything to come between us," Kitty said.

Not Kitty. Not a kitten any longer, but a self-contained cat. She wasn't talkative but she was observant, talented, shy, maybe a little stubborn. Grown.

"You were posting your letter to Robert Denholm," she said.

"I told my aunt. She said it's just as well I have a fallback. Now she's proposing a family of Darcies, of all things."

They laughed. The odd giddiness of the afternoon. Soon Kitty— Catherine—slipped down from the wall and picked up a small parcel she'd been carrying. After untying the string, she held out her study of the clearing. But she'd worked it up, improved it into a finished painting. An eye opened onto the world.

"I'm rather proud of it," Catherine said. "I think I got you. So hopeful and blithe."

Eleanor wondered if she was really like that. "It's wonderful."

"It's yours. I want you to have it. But"—Catherine said, holding it back as Eleanor reached—"if you take it, you have to promise never to get angry with me again. I hated that. I didn't sleep at all last night."

Eleanor nodded her solemn promise, mysteriously ready to cry.

"I won't marry Mr. Crawley," Catherine warned.

"I know, darling."

Catherine gave her the painting, and after they'd looked at it for a while, she neatly rewrapped it. It was time for tea, and they took the path together until it branched and they embraced again, knowing they'd be friends forever.

10

Eleanor was in her room two days later when she heard a bawl downstairs. It was extraordinary. It was also her name.

"*El-an-or!*" Lady Anne was bawling like a cow who'd lost her calf. Hearing her, Eleanor knew immediately that Catherine had run off with David Arden. She was utterly shocked but not the least surprised. She also knew she'd better not let on she'd had even the faintest suspicion or Lady Anne would never forgive her. All this came to Eleanor in two turbulent seconds before she gathered herself and ran downstairs to find Lady Anne battling her wrap. Mrs. McBee was trying to remove it but Lady Anne was engaged in pugilism, trapped in the fabric and trying to fight free.

"*El-an* . . ." Then she saw her and went limp, so Mrs. McBee was able to remove the wrap.

"I presume you know all about this," Lady Anne said.

Better not to speak. To raise her empty hands.

"That Catherine has run off with the artist to South Africa. I need to know where."

South Africa? With a war on? Eleanor sat down abruptly on one of the chairs at the wall, feeling completely unmoored.

"The girl obviously had no idea," said Sir Waldo, appearing behind his wife.

"Clearly," her aunt said, coming in from the library.

"Shall I get the salts, madam?" asked Mrs. McBee.

"I don't faint," Eleanor said. "It's just, Catherine wouldn't leave me without saying goodbye."

Then she realized that Catherine's painting had been her goodbye and let out a horrified full-throated sob. She sounded like a goose honking, making such a vulgar noise that she ended by giggling hysterically.

"Leave *you*!" Lady Anne was huffing underneath. "I'm not sure the point is leaving *you*."

The lady squinted at Mrs. McBee, and the housemaids gathering to dust the stairs, and the coachman meticulously examining the horses' bridles outside the open door.

"Of course, this has to be hushed up so my husband can fix it."

Sir Waldo groaned.

In the library, Mrs. Crosby offered whiskey even though it was eleven o'clock in the morning. They learned Catherine had left a letter on her pillow, having slipped off in the middle of the night. She said Mr. Arden had secured a position as an artist for a newspaper; she didn't say which one. They were getting married and travelling to South Africa so he could return dispatches from the war. Her parents needn't worry. She would stay well away from the fighting and paint portraits for a living. These things were done.

"And you had no idea, Eleanor," Lady Anne said, her pupils like cactus spines. "Despite having spoken to her privately in the school-room the other day."

Of course: the other Mowbray girls had been there. Alicia wouldn't have noticed anything. As far as she was concerned, they were all having a ripping time and everyone was lovely. Harriet, at fourteen, was mainly interested in horses and had been intent on drawing horses, while the smallest, Cassandra, was a dreamy child of seven who would often while away their lessons singing to herself. *Good-Bye, Dolly, I Must Leave You*, with words she couldn't possibly understand.

But Mary Ann Mowbray was a clever and observant child just turned eleven. She would have heard every word and repeated them all to her mother, intent on making sure she got things right. Mary Ann wasn't the least malicious, just helpful and precise. She was the one who reminded Eleanor of herself.

"I did speak to her," Eleanor said hesitantly, trying to make sure she repeated everything Mary Ann would have heard. "I'd mentioned something about needing more supplies to go to Gloucester. More boards, I believe. And she said something about the invitation not being firm, and I said it was, and she said that she had no intention of going. This wasn't the first time she'd expressed some disinclination toward, frankly, Mr. Crawley, and I spoke with her about that."

"Having felt no inclination toward Mr. Edward Denholm yourself," Lady Anne said testily, "and advising her to stand firm in her opposition."

Eleanor wondered if she would ever get past Edward Denholm.

"I told her not to be foolish," she said. "I don't know Mr. Crawley well, but he got over his accident in ways other young men wouldn't. He's determined, I've thought. It struck me that he was likely to support Kitty's painting, and I'm not sure every young man would."

"That's a good point," Sir Waldo said, trying to smooth things over. "She told you nothing about the artist?"

"You saw *nothing*?" Lady Anne asked.

Eleanor paused, a species of answer she knew she'd have to back away from.

"I thought she might have admired him. But it's a fad among his pupils to admire Mr. Arden, and I would have said he had too great a concern for his wallet to leave with anyone. It makes no sense to me.

If he's got a new position as an illustrator, I don't see why he'd burden himself with a wife."

"I can only hope they *will* marry," the baronet said. "And that his choice isn't mercenary. Surely he knows Catherine hasn't any money."

"The demand hasn't come in yet," Lady Anne said, and stood. "It might be waiting when we get back. As we should. This is useless. Miss Eleanor is being far from candid."

Eleanor felt wounded and must have looked it.

"She knows nothing, my dear," said good Sir Waldo. Although she did, and didn't, and Lady Anne was still glaring at her as they left.

"Well. Drama," her aunt said afterwards, as they sat back down. "What weren't you saying?"

When Eleanor bristled, Mrs. Crosby said, "There's always something one holds back. I imagine you were trying to keep Lady Anne from blaming you. Catherine did, perhaps, confess a weakness for the artist, but you didn't take her seriously."

"It was a look. He looked at her warmly, and she quite properly turned away. Then she smiled like the Cheshire Cat. And Aunt," Eleanor said, relieved to speak. "I'm worried. I think Catherine is far more talented than we've realized. And Mr. Arden's feelings strike me as very mixed. He seems to me both proprietary and envious of her talent."

Mrs. Crosby considered this before saying, "Sir Waldo is right. There's not much chance of a marriage. Mr. Arden is of an age to have a Mrs. Arden hidden away somewhere in Wales, probably with several Ardettes. It's possible he decided to do a flit, and thought he might as well take Catherine with him."

Eleanor couldn't begin to imagine.

"I may be wrong," Mrs. Crosby said. "But in any case, Catherine has followed him into some degree of danger. I imagine they've gone to the Cape Colony. It's largely peaceful there, but if this ends unhappily, and it could, Lady Anne will certainly blame you. She has to blame someone besides herself." Her aunt looked rueful. "So much for Gloucester. Lady Anne hadn't quite secured our invitation, and now she won't."

"Surely the Mowbrays won't go, either."

"Mr. Crawley was planning to invite a large party. By the time it convenes, she'll have a better idea where Catherine has gone and be glad of an opportunity to paper it all over."

"I can't imagine Murdo Crawley will want them to come."

Mrs. Crosby seemed to calculate the chances, nodding her head back and forth—he'll say, then Lady Anne will say—before speaking in an American accent.

"Bet you a dollar," she said.

The telegram arrived a week later.

"You promised you wouldn't be angry. Mrs. David Arden."

Eleanor's eyes filled with tears. So Catherine was married, and presumably on her way to South Africa. Eleanor read the news standing at the front door of Goodwood House, having heard the messenger's bicycle skid up the drive. She'd run downstairs to meet him, snatching the envelope and tearing it open. A shilling in her pocket—an absurd tip. The boy lifted his bike around quickly and raced off before she could change her mind.

I'll bet you a dollar, her aunt had said. Now Eleanor would be out both a dollar and a shilling. Lady Anne would be furious, and this would put paid to any remaining chance of visiting Gloucester (not that Eleanor wanted to) while the Mowbrays would go there themselves to paper it over. Knocking on Mrs. Crosby's bedroom door, she found her aunt bent over the household accounts with Mrs. McBee. Eleanor handed over the telegram, describing her last meeting with Catherine.

"I suppose I'll have to show it to Lady Anne."

"This is Middleford," her aunt replied, laying down her pen. "She already knows you've got it, and quite possibly what it says. Of course we'll have to take it over. People are very fond of hearing what they already know."

Mrs. McBee murmured gently, "Two daughters married. One husband the grandson of a duke, the other of a miner. Both in their own ways quite notable men."

Her aunt had always trusted Mrs. McBee utterly, but it occurred to Eleanor now that they were friends, both intelligent and watchful women. How absurd—how snobbish—that it had taken her this long to notice.

"But will he make Catherine happy?" Eleanor asked.

"I think you've probably described their marriage," her aunt said. "Two artists, one of them competitive. But, my dear, to look on their inevitable problems as exceptional is to believe in such a thing as the perfect marriage. I speak as someone who was happily married to your uncle for longer than I care to admit, at least among people who can add. Of course they're going to have problems. Everyone has problems. But I've no doubt they're happy right this minute, and good for them."

Her aunt seemed ready to say something more, but shook her head.

"Lady Anne," Mrs. McBee said, sounding as if her voice had been caught in a downdraft. "Will not be pleased."

They arrived at Mowbray Close to find that the Mowbrays had received a telegram of their own. Like Eleanor's, it had arrived from Liverpool, presumably sent from the docks five minutes before Catherine sailed for South Africa. Raging around her sitting room, Lady Anne insisted that Eleanor must have known. Why would Catherine have made Eleanor promise not to be angry if she hadn't been planning to elope? And if she'd been making plans, Eleanor *knew.*

"Last spring," Eleanor began. Lady Anne growled an objection, as if spring couldn't be trusted, either. (And this being Yorkshire, it couldn't.)

"Last spring," she insisted, "when the Denholms arrived, I thought at first that Catherine liked Captain Denholm. Then I thought she liked his brother. But I couldn't tell, and I realized the extent to which

Catherine guards her feelings. I hadn't known that before. She's always been my very dearest friend, and she always will be, but I'm not sure I realized before that there's a very private side to her nature."

"*Hmmm.*" Lady Anne's squint was at its most narrow. Then she collapsed into a chair.

"At least he married her," she said quietly. "At least we have that."

"A moment to mourn," Mrs. Crosby said gently, touching her shoulder. "Then we make the best of it."

Lady Anne shook her off irritably. "Don't you ever stop?"

"One can't," her aunt said simply.

But Lady Anne didn't like hearing that. She lumbered to her feet, turning in an odd splay-foot circle until she spotted Eleanor and fixed her with a wounded glare.

"She's ruined herself and you could have stopped it."

Lady Anne lurched out, calling for her maid, leaving Eleanor feeling gutted.

A small voice said, "I'm sorry."

Alicia rose from a chair by the window. Amazing how such a pretty girl could be in the room without anyone having noticed.

"It's not your fault, Nellie," she said. "I'm sure you miss her awfully. We all do already."

Eleanor surprised herself by letting out a sob. Alicia embraced her, and as Eleanor lay her head on Alicia's shoulder, she found it astonishing that a seventeen-year-old girl could be so maternal—that her embrace could feel so warm and accepting. Eleanor sensed her lost mother's presence, and felt what she couldn't really have felt as a child, not when her mother had died when she was only a few months old. Her mother was safety. She'd felt safe. And seventeen-year-old Alicia made her feel safe, too. How odd.

11

November. That bleak month. Eleanor was finally and completely alone, the Mowbrays departure for Gloucester having ended even Lady Anne's hectoring visits. Eleanor felt in danger of rattling apart, and decided to set up a program of study to fill her days. She'd done it before and had soon trailed off, but this time she was determined to make a go of it.

Eleanor had just finished reading *The Portrait of a Lady*, in which Mr. Henry James created an ambitious heroine in Isabel Archer, introducing her by saying that she would be an easy target of criticism, then spending several hundred pages criticizing her. She could imagine Mr. James being even more withering about the ambitions of an obscure girl in Yorkshire, a casually educated young lady who hoped for a purpose in life, for self-improvement, or at least for consolation. Others would think her absurd—the properly educated, certainly Middleford, everyone aside from Catherine—but she couldn't think of anything else to do, especially with the weather so bad.

In her empty sitting room, Eleanor blocked in an hour each day to translate from the Greek. Her father had drilled her beyond the rudiments and she enjoyed translation in the same way she enjoyed piecing together a puzzle, finding the right fit for a Greek word in

English. βίος, a man's *bios* meant his trade or his living, she remembered, so a soldier's *bios* was war. Death was his living. But the word also meant life itself, "life" and "work" being interchangeable in classical Greek.

Yet they also weren't, and Eleanor would need to decide which puzzle piece of meaning best fit a given sentence. She thought *The Odyssey* would do for a start, with Mr. Butler's translation at hand as a crib. Robert Denholm must have read *The Odyssey*. And if she was going to spend half her waking hours brooding on war, it would do her good to spend time on the story of a soldier finally coming home.

Another hour she'd dedicate to her botanical drawings, not worrying about the west wind, about vibration or the difficult matter of *art*. A white orchid had just bloomed in the greenhouse, its petals the colour of risen cream, and if she made a good job of it, she might frame it as a wedding present for Catherine. She'd read *The Times* at breakfast and turn to novels in the evening; no change there, but daydreams would no longer be tolerated. Otherwise: sewing, arranging flowers for Mr. Warfield's church (war, war; it was everywhere), and either walking or riding in the afternoon when the weather permitted.

The one remaining subject was mathematics, which Robert Denholm had thought she might give another bash. Eleanor didn't know where to start, but that was solved when her aunt was called into Kent, by what (or whom) she didn't say. Eleanor usually stayed with the Mowbrays, but this time Mr. and Mrs. Warfield took her into her father's old parsonage. Mr. Warfield's parsonage, as it had been for six years. Eleanor hadn't slept there since her father had died, but girded herself by remembering that Mr. Warfield had read maths at Oxford.

As her boxes disappeared around the back, a new girl led Eleanor in the front door of the parsonage. The Warfields always had a new girl, the household having become disorganized since their arrival, or at least since they'd begun to populate it with children, four at last count. As she waited in her dear old parlour, Eleanor saw that whatever financial arrangements her aunt had made for her stay were badly needed. In her father's time, the parlour had been proud of itself. Now the carpet was soiled and the sofas stood skew-whiff, one of them missing a leg and propped up on a pile of old books.

"Here you are," Mrs. Warfield cried, walking in rapidly. She was a brisk, round-faced, good-humoured lady with food stains on her bodice and hair that frizzed in the heat.

"It's very kind of you to have me," Eleanor said, shaking Mrs. Warfield's sticky hand. (Four and a half children, she saw.)

"Nonsense. We're delighted," the lady replied, taking a chair. "I only hope it isn't too difficult. I'm putting you in what must have been your old bedroom."

"It might be a little affecting, but only at first," Eleanor replied, sitting down gingerly. Lady Anne's insistence that she wasn't telling the truth about Catherine had left Eleanor intent on speaking nothing but.

"If you'd prefer another room," Mrs. Warfield began dubiously.

Eleanor knew there wasn't one. "I can miss my father anywhere. And the worst of it doesn't come back as often anymore."

Mrs. Warfield gave a sympathetic wince. "I'm sure it feels just as horrid when it does."

Like being kicked in the head by a horse. There was a family story about Eleanor being kicked by a horse when she was young. She didn't remember it, but after her father died, she'd recognized the sudden overwhelming nausea, the dizziness, the sense of floating free of time as something she'd experienced before. These days it could come at her from several directions, as she mourned not only her father but also the loss of Catherine. Not to mention the silence from Robert Denholm, who must have received her letter by now, if he was living, and hadn't replied.

If he was living. βίος, she thought again. Death and life so close for a soldier. Lately she only felt partway tethered to life herself.

"However," she said, "I admit, I come with a project to occupy myself. I wonder if I can ask Mr. Warfield's advice. My father taught me some mathematics, and I thought this might be a good time to go on with it, if Mr. Warfield would be kind enough to recommend some primers."

"Earnest girl," she would hear one of the Warfields whisper to the other that night. It said much about their marriage that Eleanor wasn't sure who had spoken. But Mr. Warfield not only agreed to lend her some books, he offered lessons, a promise he fulfilled meticulously whenever too many Middleford ladies called in a row and he needed an excuse to retire.

Greek. Drawing. Taking the older parsonage children outside for a much-needed ramble. Sewing. A restless sleep. Then one day the mail came late, while they were at luncheon. Mr. Warfield raised his eyebrows at something on the tray, making Eleanor's heart turn over at the prospect of a letter, probably from her aunt, possibly from Catherine, but just maybe from the captain. My aunt allows the correspondence, she would say. She'd been so thoroughly truthful that surely they'd accept her assurances and not keep the letter back for an agonizing couple of days until Mrs. Crosby had written her approval.

Mr. Warfield passed her the envelope without comment. Eleanor was surprised to find it thick and creamy, and sent from not far away. She was at a loss until she recognized the writing.

"Elizabeth Mortlake?"

Eleanor couldn't imagine why Lizzy had written, and opened the letter terrified that it contained bad news.

Relief as she read. Her aunt's hand would have gone out as soon as she'd finished, and Eleanor would have had no reason to hold it back, although she might have. But the Warfields were so absentmindedly concentrating on their ham and pickle, she told them, "Elizabeth writes from Gloucester. She and Mr. Mortlake are staying with a colleague of his in Parliament, a manufacturer named Mr. Darcy. His estate is close to Murdo Crawley's, where the Mowbrays have gone. Her mother has told Elizabeth she blames me for Catherine's elopement. Lady Anne believes I knew of their plan and didn't warn her."

Meeting her minister's eyes, she said, "I suspected she admired him but knew nothing of their plans, and now Elizabeth is kind enough to take any blame on herself. She says she's reminded her mother that she was the one to first employ Mr. Arden in London.

"'Although I'm not sure this is a matter for blame,' she writes, 'not because I'm avoiding it, but because this might prove a good marriage for Catherine. We're not all the same person, and mark me, Eleanor, we need to take our own paths.'"

Eleanor stopped, feeling self-conscious, not having suspected before that Elizabeth might be referring to the captain. The Warfields didn't notice, too busy nodding.

"With seven daughters," said Mrs. Warfield, who had three, "Lady Anne can't expect all of them to marry as handsomely as Mrs. Mortlake. At least one probably won't marry at all. And although we have to pray not, there's a good chance of a disaster. A misstep, better said."

"Not Arden," Mr. Warfield said.

"Not David Arden," Mrs. Warfield agreed.

"He may be a radical," Mr. Warfield said matter-of-factly, which would have made Sir Waldo choke on his biscuit. "A nonconformist, of course, being Welsh. But he's hardworking and intelligent, his mind a compendium of odd facts, the way one often finds among self-educated men. I can't speak to his artistic abilities, but Mrs. Warfield admires his painting."

"He got himself to France," she said. "And trained there."

"I didn't realize you knew him more than casually," Eleanor said, conscious of not having read them the end of Elizabeth's letter.

"He liked playing with the children," Mrs. Warfield said.

Eleanor hesitated. "Perhaps having some of his own in Wales."

"We wondered about that," was all Mr. Warfield replied.

Whether he thought Arden was a widower, a bigamist, or the father of a tumble of illegitimate children, he was too discrete to say. Eleanor folded her letter and put it back in its creamy envelope, the ending hers alone.

In any case, *Elizabeth had written*, developments here in Gloucester are such that you needn't worry about my mother anymore. You'll be forgiven for something you didn't do, while Alicia will be lauded for something she isn't responsible for, her looks coming from our father.

So Alicia was going to marry one of the Mr. Darcies, perhaps the heir. Eleanor was happy for her and hoped her Mr. Darcy was indeed a fairy-tale prince. Putting the letter aside, she finished her luncheon, and after Mr. Warfield had taken up his shabby umbrella and left for a parish council meeting, she excused herself to tackle mathematics upstairs.

Trigonometry. On some days Eleanor understood it, or at least glimpsed the possibility of understanding it, but today the equations looked like the markings on the backs of her father's collection of poisonous spiders. Throwing her maths aside, she took Mr. James's *The Turn of the Screw* to her fire, where she failed to understand that, either. Did ghosts really appear in the story or was the heroine only imagining them, going half mad from being too much alone?

A blast of half-frozen rain hit the window, watery ice trickling down the panes. Eleanor could easily imagine ghosts and gods coming in from the moors on a day like this so they could haunt a warm corner. Not that she believed in ghosts, and she'd found her one attempt at table turning to be silly. Last year, the Moreland girls had hosted an evening with a medium in billowing scarves who painted lines around her eyes like the Roman lady in her aunt's mosaic. The medium had told each of the girls what they wanted to hear, either romance or money or a flawless complexion. (Poor spotty Lilian Browne.) Eleanor had found it funny, and the medium had picked up on that, turning to her and saying, "The spirits don't care to speak with you."

Yet this morning Eleanor was bored and restless, and the weather made it impossible to go outside. On impulse, she sat down at the dressing table. Pushing aside her brushes, she lay her hands flat on the mahogany as the medium had done, laughing silently to herself and planning to ask about Robert Denholm. The candle flame wavered slightly as the wind gasped through the drafty old window, the curtains fluttering, her eyes in the mirror impressively dark and mystical.

Eleanor tried to clear her mind the way the medium had advised. But focusing inside only made her conscious of her everyday thoughts, fragments of "time better spent mending" and "Mr. James is sly," which she heard at a slight remove. Most of it was embarrassingly banal. Yet as she listened to her internal chatter, Eleanor also recognized it as a haphazardly woven blanket thrown over her horror of being alone; of being abandoned again as she'd been abandoned by her mother and father.

"Stop feeling sorry for yourself," came Elizabeth's amused voice. "Catherine's letter will arrive tomorrow."

Eleanor's lids flew open, and she glimpsed a disturbance at the corner of her eye like the flounce of a lady's skirt as she left. Swivelling, she saw nothing. Not surprisingly, since nothing was there. Yet she'd heard Elizabeth as clearly as if she'd been in the room. Eleanor had no idea what was happening and shivered violently. Then the wind moaned through the loose pane and she leapt up in terror, running out of the room. Turning one way and the other in the hallway, she had no idea where to go. Finally she took a deep breath and decided on the nursery—yes, the nursery—where there was a baby who probably needed soothing.

When Catherine's letter arrived the next morning, Eleanor decided she'd fallen asleep at the table and dreamed, that was all. The letter was a coincidence, for the obvious reason that it couldn't be anything else. There was no such thing as ghosts, and in any case, Elizabeth was alive and well in Gloucester, staying with a man named Darcy who wasn't the least bit a prince, but an industrialist so economical he'd dropped the apostrophe from his name.

With any luck, his son would make Alicia happy.

My darling, *Catherine wrote*, here we are in Cape Town, where I find myself warm and married, the two conditions inextricable. This is only a short note to assure you of my health, and of my husband's health. I will write more presently. At the moment, we're busy inhabiting a tiny cottage that is our first home, with roses growing up it! The conventional fighting part of the war seems largely to have ended, although the Boer commandos continue to execute raids on British forces, particularly on troops in the blockhouses from which the Army controls the countryside. Still there is a great deal for Arden to do in the Cape Colony to fulfill his new responsibilities with *The Illustrated London News*. Not far from Cape Town are some of those dreadful modern inventions called concentration camps where Boer women and children are housed in tents and starved and Africans face the same. The plan is part of the Scorched Earth policy in which the Army attempts to starve out the Boer commandos by burning their farms and salting their wells as well as placing their wives and children in camps. My husband is at one camp today and it's my thought to join him presently. I am far from a professional artist and have neither the intention nor the possibility of placing my attempts in newspapers, but I can draw the children. And indeed, seeing my husband's preliminary work, my original plan to earn my way by offering myself to do portraits of ladies in Cape Town seems fatuous. In Britain we have lived without war on our green and pleasant land these many hundreds of years but now that I see it close, I see differently, as my husband predicted. You must always remember your promise not to be angry with me! For <u>anything</u>. Even though I imagine you now live in the shadow of a newly risen volcano at Mowbray Close, known as my mother, who no doubt erupts regularly, and I do apologize for that. Speaking of apologies I haven't seen Captain D. or heard of him although I will keep my eyes open. Indeed my eyes are wide open.

Write to me soon.
Love, Kate (as my husband calls me)

P.S. Mr. and Mrs. Whittaker have returned to India, leaving a name for jollity behind and a number of trifling debts, which Mr. W. in his expansiveness forgot to pay.

A letter from Robert Denholm arrived two days later.

"My dear Miss Crosby," he wrote, and Eleanor cherished the *my*, tracing it with her finger until she grew afraid of tearing the paper.

My dear Miss Crosby,

Thank you for answering my letter. You divined my meaning and I'm glad you weren't displeased. I was afraid you might be. However, I should tell you that we're not facing battle in the conventional sense. With the arrival of two hundred thousand of our troops, the Boer is firmly outnumbered and no longer able to engage in traditional pitched battle, nor lay the sieges he did at Ladysmith and Mafeking. Instead he has reconstituted himself as a force of light infantry, assuming the new name of Kommando, a word from the Afrikaans. He rides in small units, well armed and well mounted, striking rapidly across land he knows intimately to destroy railway lines and our defensive blockhouses. His immediate motive seems to be not victory but revenge for our victories. Ultimately, I believe, he hopes to tire us into leaving Africa, but we will not.

I write from the countryside: for it is against the Kommando I am fighting. He is unnerving, arriving from everywhere and nowhere. In a sense, we are fighting modernity; fighting speed and craft. This is not the front because there is no front. Instead, my particular tariff takes me far afield with my scouts, trustworthy Africans who hate the Boer for taking their land. I should say they hate the Boer marginally more than they hate us, knowing that Britain has its eye on African land as well, particularly in the Witwatersrand, with its gold.

The time we spoke in Kent, you asked why I had chosen a military life. I told you that it permitted me a role in protecting Britain. Protecting you, if I may say so. That remains true. But on the ground, one can see that the Boer is fighting to protect his land and the African his, while Britain would like all of it, thank you, and things get muddy. Forgive me; the nights are dark and the hyenas chatter outside our ring of fire.

I like to think of your aunt's garden in Kent, with its five-toed Roman chickens, and the mosaic that came to light after fifteen hundred years. The domestic goddess, with her look of amusement, reminds me of you. I do indeed hope that you find time to think of me, as loveable as you are, while in my isolation I think of you.

Yours most warmly, Robert Denholm.

It was written in copperplate, looking as if it had been copied from a draft. But scrawled across the bottom was, "Please write. I'd like it awfully. Robin."

Eleanor walked out with her letter into a grey cold day as beautiful as summer. We all take our own paths, Elizabeth Mortlake had said, and Eleanor could see hers rising from the moors like a Roman road building itself ahead of her. She ran along it, the invisible cobbles leading her toward the crest of the hill where she and Robin Denholm had first talked. He had been weeping for friends killed in a battle disastrously executed by its commanding officer. Which one? It might have been the Battle of Magersfontein, remembered in the soldier's verse: "Dearly we paid for the blunder/A drawing-room General's mistake."

She was bad with names, and there were so many battles. But Eleanor had looked in Robin's grey eyes and known she was going to marry him, even though she hadn't known him at all. She still didn't, but he was a good man; she held on to that certainty. She would learn more about Robert now that they were writing, hopefully none of it unpleasant, since she could hardly stop writing to a lonely officer. She also couldn't imagine him being anything less than honourable.

Reaching their bench, she found the wind whistling shrilly across the rocky hilltop. Looking into someone's eyes in weather like this would have been a trick. Her own were tearing up, and she realized that the hard north wind was going to tumble her over unless she got out of there.

Kicking off, Eleanor ran downhill, elated despite the coming storm and the ever-present shadow of war. (Or maybe just slightly because of them.) She curved down the dale, the grass still green and springy. Finally she stopped out of breath under a crooked oak, tracing with a finger the runnels in its bark. In summer she wouldn't stop here in dire weather, but it was too cold for lightning and she paused to look at the road, calculating whether she could make it back to the parsonage before it poured.

In the distance, a carriage came around the bend. A horseless carriage. She wondered who else had got one, then realized Stansfield Mowbray was at the wheel. Stansfield had brought Middleford's first motor carriage back from Paris. Eleanor had stumbled on it parked in the drive at Mowbray Close, its two pairs of huge spoked wheels suspending a metal box between them. Stansfield had been shyly proud of himself in a beige dustcoat like the one gardeners wore, a pair of driving goggles pushed onto his forehead. It was the first time in his life he'd surprised her.

Now he was back from Gloucester and driving three others she could just barely make out. Friends must have returned with the Mowbrays, and Stansfield couldn't wait to take them for a spin. A girl who was probably Alicia sat in the rear-facing seat, but Eleanor didn't recognize the others. One was a gentleman sitting too close to Alicia, perhaps Mr. Darcy. Hoping for a lift, Eleanor ran downhill to intercept them, wishing as she squeezed through a drystone stile— her hair windblown and skirt tearing on a sharp white rock—that she could meet Mr. Darcy under more elegant circumstances. Not that it made any difference, certainly not anymore.

The motor carriage slowed as it approached, Stansfield pulling back on the brake. Now that she was close, Eleanor saw that the gentleman sitting close to Alicia wasn't a possible Mr. Darcy but a very definite Murdo Crawley, and that both of them looked remarkably pleased with themselves. In shock, she turned to Stansfield in the driver's seat. Beside him was a proud and prissy-looking young lady with curly black hair piled under an enormously fashionable hat. Both she and Stansfield appeared every bit as pleased with themselves as Alicia and Murdo.

"Miss Crosby!" Stansfield cried. "Out for an old-fashioned walk?"

"Walks are ripping," Alicia called. "You know Mr. Crawley. He's a great walker!"

From his seat, Stansfield said, "We're here with Miss Darcy," and the curly headed lady gave her a supercilious bow. Eleanor smiled through the introductions but disliked Margaret Darcy on sight. Judging from her sharp brown eyes, Miss Darcy returned the favour.

"You'll want a lift," Stansfield called, and Miss Darcy smiled up at him proudly.

It wasn't pride. Closer to adoration, as if Stansfield was a hero just back from conquering a recalcitrant country. Maybe Margaret was the recalcitrant country. Lady Anne must be ecstatic; there would be money. Yet as Eleanor scrambled on board, she saw Miss Darcy use the moment to put a small hand in Stansfield's great one, and a look of true affection passed between them.

How complicated the world became when your oldest friends attached themselves to people you didn't like and did it very happily. Not that Eleanor disliked David Arden. She mistrusted him.

Once they were settled, Stansfield sounded his klaxon at no one in particular, and they motored off, running hard before the coming storm. Two new couples. Three, counting Eleanor and the letter in her pocket. Sitting beside them, she wondered what Mr. Crawley saw in the seventeen-year-old Alicia Mowbray. But she also knew.

October 1914
Middleford, Yorkshire

12

The flowers had bloomed beautifully all summer, as if in consolation for the war. As she wandered through the autumn gardens, Eleanor felt as if they'd been blooming forever, and she'd been wandering here since Odysseus sailed off to fight the Trojans, a soldier's girl, her boy gone off to war. The Trojan War, the Napoleonic Wars, the Boer War—it could have been any of them, and she was eternally left behind, unable to find any more purpose in her life than girls ever found in wartime.

Now the Goodwood gardens were drooping, their scant blossoms limp on weak stems, the banks of pelargonium gone all elbows. Eleanor paused when she saw cutworm on a rose bush, semicircles bitten out of the leaves as if they'd been machine-gunned. It could have been any war, but in brutal fact they were fighting a modern war against the Germans, and it wouldn't be a short one.

Everyone insisted the fighting would be over by Christmas, but in his letters, Robert said not. She was sure he was right, but it was hard to read about a long war and the part he expected to play in it. Eleanor had to anchor herself in the banal. Cutworms. Roses. Pelargoniums.

Not that Robert told her many details, leaving Eleanor to parse his letters as minutely as if she were trying to break a code. Censorship, of course. Everyone grappled with it. In his first long letter home, a mention of working with local scouts had suggested that Robert was being sent out on reconnaissance, perhaps taking a look at the German armies as they massed inside their own borders. Eleanor had been relieved when he next wrote from headquarters, where he'd missed the opening battles of the war. Maybe his general found him too useful to send directly against the Germans. She hoped so.

Then his letters had stopped at the beginning of September. Eleanor didn't jump to thinking that Robert had been injured. Instead she'd assumed he was back on reconnaissance, proud of herself for intuiting this much, and with Robert for playing such a crucial role.

Yet his continued silence quickly became half-heard wheels, distant traffic; something else she'd known forever. As it rumbled on and on, Eleanor still hadn't been afraid he'd been injured. Stupidly, in retrospect. Instead she'd worried that he was backing away from their increasing intimacy. They'd grown far closer in letters than they'd ever been in person, confiding in each other, developing jokes.

"Dear Nora," he'd started writing. Eleanor had become Ibsen's Nora living in a doll's house, Goodwood having shrunk to insignificance beside the tiny shabby requisitioned rooms where Robert wrote her early in the morning or late at night. Maybe he'd begun to doubt she was capable of understanding him. A case of second thoughts.

Then she'd read about the Battle of the Marne. At first, Eleanor had insisted on believing that Robert was still back at headquarters. The casualty lists in *The Times* were horrific but he wasn't anywhere near the fighting. Leafing through the papers, day after day, she'd pictured him busy at a field desk writing dispatches.

Until she'd read that two million men were massed at the Marne River. *Two million men.* Eleanor had realized that Robert must be among them, and her sick understanding made her bolt from the breakfast table, not really hearing her aunt's alarm.

Rushing down the hallway, she'd grown intensely conscious of her body, the prickling of the hair on her arms as she passed an open window, the clumsy slap-slap of her heels on the carpet. Nothing could be more fragile than the human body. Her small frantic beating heart was the size of a fist. Her skin was paper to a bullet. When she reached the door, wanting to lose herself outside, her knees knocked together so hard she crumpled to the floor and sobbed.

Finally this morning, six days after the victory on the Marne, a stained envelope had appeared on the butler's tray at breakfast. Such laughable incongruity, mud presented on silver. She'd grabbed it and run into the garden, where she'd torn it open savagely.

My dear Nora.

Let me first of all assure you that I am well and uninjured. I knew you would wonder when I couldn't write, or hoped you would, and perhaps we should have a code word to signal imminent battle, one that could get past the CO. I have to censor the men's letters, as you mustn't say, and we're to leave ours open for the CO to read as he chooses. The new one seems intent on it, more set on protocol than Col. Marsby, who believed that a gentlemen doesn't read another man's mail, and look how far that got him. However the new CO is closeted with the major as I write, so we'll sneak this one through and perhaps agree on "chickens" as a code word, memorializing your aunt's five-toed wonders. What were they called? Dorsets? Dovers?

"Dorkings," Eleanor said aloud, making a gardener look up.

In any case, it's filed under D in my mental pigeonholes, which I admit fatigue has made fall in on themselves like shell craters. There's an awful breathless exhilaration in being tested in battle, they're right, but mainly after making it through, and somewhat to my surprise I seem to have made it, left with only slight damage to the mental pigeonhole containing the names of chickens. But please don't let anybody say that God was on my side, since if God was present at the Marne, he is <u>harrowing</u>, and I'm not sure I want him anywhere near.

Robert was alone in his cynicism. Everyone else Eleanor knew had been inspired by the allied victory, young men growing hectic with the wish to prove themselves in battle. Or at least, not to be called cowards. Most of the boys she grew up with were trying to get over to France, angling for commissions. Eleanor figured this was half the reason her aunt had approved of her correspondence.

There were also the hints Eleanor had picked up here and there about her aunt's financial problems. She was becoming as stretched as everyone else. Robert was a bird in the hand as the bailiffs knocked discretely at the door.

Old bailiffs, too doddery to sign up.

The new letter was long and Eleanor read it circling the garden, growing increasingly unsettled by what Robert had written. His brother, Edward, was manoeuvring to get into the Royal Flying Corps, bucking their father—already back in uniform—who wanted Edward to join him in the Buffs. Meanwhile, Robert called the volunteers flooding across the Channel "toy soldiers," leaving Eleanor frightened for the boys she knew, Stansfield Mowbray chief among them. Stansfield had been angling for a commission in the Lancasters, although a promising letter from the colonel had left him looking less like a toy soldier than an eager dog bounding around the parish. A large and joyous dog, his tongue hanging out, a golden retriever receiving permission to roll around in the mud.

All the men she knew were on the move. The Ardens had recently returned from David's assignment in Africa, and Kate wrote that he was quitting his job at the *News* to sign up as a private. He planned to draw the reality of war, she said, a modern disciple of Goya, although Eleanor couldn't make out from Kate's headlong prose whether this was despite David's pacifism or because of it. Even Murdo Crawley had given it a bash at a couple of regiments, although he'd fooled no one with his blind eye and had begun to talk about running for Parliament.

"I'm damned if I'll let them make me useless."

Murdo had looked almost bitter lately, even with his wedding only a few days off. It would be a double wedding, the same ceremony doing for Murdo and Alicia as for Stansfield and Margaret Darcy. Eleanor wished them all very well and felt particular sympathy for Murdo, longing to be useful herself. She was alone too much and tended to fall into circular thinking: If Robert is at headquarters, then he's safe. But if he's safe, he'll feel a coward and try to get into action, where he'll want to prove himself by being far too brave. Her studies hadn't helped. Her Greek and the fraying elegance of mathematics had become resolutions she couldn't fulfill: And wouldn't Henry James laugh?

(What on earth did Henry James have to do with it?)

Eleanor had realized earlier this autumn that she needed to get out of the house. When the Red Cross had posted a bill offering first aid classes, she'd jumped at the chance, running upstairs in the Middleford Arms on the appointed day. There she'd joined a covey of young ladies in a dusty high-ceilinged room normally used for amateur theatricals. Mrs. Browne had been in charge, the daughter of a physician, as she hadn't always cared to be reminded.

"Young ladies," she'd carolled, rapping the podium. "Young *patriotic* ladies."

Soon afterward, Eleanor had found herself modelling the patient, lying on an ancient canvas stretcher while the unpleasant Agnes Moreland bound her foot too tightly. A toy patient on a symbolic stretcher that would rip apart if anyone tried to lift it: Eleanor's enthusiasm had dissipated rapidly. Speaking above her, Mrs. Browne said that if they passed the first aid exam, they'd get a certificate that would allow them to roll bandages at the local Red Cross depot.

Not to nurse, not to clerk for the army. Roll bandages. Her aunt's suffragism was on hold for the duration, the leaders wanting to prove female support for the war. Yet with her foot bound like a Chinese wife's, Eleanor had finally found herself sympathizing with the fight for women's rights.

Her aunt had brightened when she'd told her. "I knew you'd get there eventually."

"I'd rather go to France. Not that I have any idea how to help."

After a pause, her aunt had replied, "You're quite a good shot. Maybe we can cut off your hair and send you over as a sniper. Even better: cut off one of your breasts so you can volunteer as an Amazon. If you think the army is so greatly in need of your help."

"I don't think I've ever heard you so savage."

"Then you haven't been listening, my dear."

Turning on her heel, Eleanor ran out of the garden, angling up the dales toward the old oak below the bench where she and Robert had first talked. She'd already read the letter four or five times. But when she got there, she took it out and read it again, the writing deteriorating badly toward the end as Robert raced to get all his thoughts on paper before bottling himself back up again for duty.

> I'll send this off later today. But for now it's very early, and I'm enjoying the beauty of the dawn. I'm not artistic like Kate, but you'll know what I mean when I say the pinks and oranges are deep as wells. I look out the window aware that I'm not so much looking up at the sky as looking down from our small warring planet; down through the thin skin of atmosphere into the depths of eternity.
>
> On other mornings lately, I've stood among the men as they craned back their necks to watch the sunrise, congregating in the middle of the trench we're ordered to dig, some of them sitting on sandbags, knowing better than to take so much as a glance over the trench's edge. German snipers await the fool who lifts his head. As a young chap at Sandhurst, I studied troop formations during the Napoleonic Wars, Waterloo back to Albuera then back again as far as the Romans. Past editions of your faithful officer would order the infantry into position, the artillery, the cavalry into position, until the battle order was given, the bugle sounded and the carnage began. There was a comprehensible beginning to the fighting and a definite end, orders to withdraw from

engagement serving the same function as factory whistles at the close of day, the surviving men flooding off the field as if clocking out of one of Blake's dark satanic mills.

Here it never ends. Snipers fire whenever the mood takes them and shells fall randomly behind our lines. Even stretcher-bearers entering the field can be picked off as they evacuate the wounded. In Napoleonic times, I remember reading, the field would be eerily silent after battle, if busy with camp followers, wives (some of them officers' wives) searching for their dead and wounded husbands, looters picking over the bodies, some chap getting himself a new sword. Now, at the front, one is constantly at war, unable to risk a moment's inattention, making sure not to lift one's head to enjoy the sunrise or a beautiful smoky sunset amid the ever-present smell of never-you-mind. I'm already walking in a stoop, having quickly lost the pattern officer's proud erect carriage.

"Hardly sporting," the old men say, sending horses out to be machine-gunned, insisting on fighting the war in the way Wellington fought a hundred years ago, when the enemy now is two hundred yards away and modern and mechanized and planning.

She would soon have this one by heart, as she had all the others. Yet something went different, and Eleanor looked up with a prickling sense of expectancy. It wasn't the letter. Instead she knew that something was about to happen. Someone was going to come around the corner below, although the road was empty, a slash on the landscape. This wasn't déjà vu. The word *glimpse* came to mind. Something was about to happen that had happened here earlier and would happen again in the future. It was going to be ephemeral; nothing important. She felt ephemeral, a breath on the landscape, barely tethered to the earth. The hill was eternal and she was transparent, a will-o'-the-wisp.

When Stansfield Mowbray motored around the corner, Eleanor remembered him appearing the same way earlier this year. But this was more than a memory; beyond anything she'd experienced before. She was back there. Stansfield had been driving his new Rolls-Royce with Miss Darcy beside him and Alicia and Murdo Crawley in the rear. Now, the motor carriage looked populated with the same four figures, yet she could also see that Stansfield was the only one in it. She was living in both times at once, and there was a third time crowding in that she sensed but failed to make out when a Rolls-Royce drove around the corner faster than she easily could make out. She felt disembodied, unable to move, so panicked she couldn't breathe. A breath that couldn't breathe.

Then the Rolls-Royce lurched with a delayed pop and her weird displacement ended. Stansfield had a puncture. He stopped and got out to look at the tyre, leaving Eleanor to put her letter back in its envelope and pause a moment to gather herself before starting down-hill. She walked slowly on the rocky old path, feeling anxious, hugging herself until she reached flat ground and angled sideways through the squeeze stile by the road. She'd torn her skirt the last time she'd seen Stansfield here and hadn't been able to repair it afterwards, not so one couldn't tell. Her hair was in a tumble. Stansfield wouldn't care, but without quite thinking about it, she decided to cut it all off.

"Hullo!" she cried. Stansfield was already removing his spare tyre from the side of the car. "I don't suppose I can help?"

"S'all right," he said companionably, jacket, off, shirt sleeves rolled to his elbows as he loosened a bolt. "It happens often enough that I've got a method."

Eleanor sat down on a large stone at the side of the road, remembering that she hadn't had much for breakfast. She was hungry, that was all. Hungry and getting a headache, even though she never got headaches. She watched Stansfield unscrew more bolts and remove the tyre, then throw himself down on the ground to pump the car up on a jack.

Stansfield always looked happier when he had a job to do. When he was asked to be sociable and idle, he got his vacant blow-to-the-head look. He needed to move, and Eleanor imagined he'd make an exemplary officer. He would be efficient and capable and considerate with his men, a noble chap. It was possible to like and even admire Stansfield once the threat of marriage was past.

Unbolting the flat tyre, he asked, "Have you heard from Kitty?" Lady Anne still wouldn't allow a letter from Catherine to enter the house, making Eleanor the conduit to her siblings.

"Kate?" she replied. "As we're to call her. She's well and painting. They're in London. Her husband signed up."

"Husband," Stansfield said dubiously, frowning at the bolt in his large greasy hand.

"My aunt wonders about the marriage. Whether there's an earlier Mrs. Arden hidden away in Wales." Stansfield cocked an eyebrow but didn't seem surprised. "I don't see Kate going into that knowingly, and she's far too clever not to know. What do you think?"

Stansfield paused for a while before shaking his head. "Kitty's deep," he said, and corrected himself humorously. "Kate."

Going back to work, he rolled the blown tyre aside and crouched to bolt on the spare, his strong arms working, muscles admirable. When he was finished, Stansfield dropped from his crouch to sit back against the car, legs bent like a boy, greasy hands clasped in front of him. They enjoyed a pleasant undemanding silence on the windless day, having known each other forever.

"Look here," he said after a time. "I know you and Margaret took against each other. But when I'm off, she'll be living at the Close. I'd consider it a great favour if you'd give it a try. Being friends, you know. Mother isn't the easiest row, is she?"

Eleanor hesitated. She didn't want to lie to Stansfield but couldn't see the two of them getting along. If she were able to define what she didn't like about Margaret Darcy, she might be able to talk herself out of it. But what could she do about something as intangible as the angle of Margaret's chin? Her superior air, which wasn't unusual and was clearly defensive, a girl from trade meeting her fiancé's county family and his oldest friends. (It was true. Eleanor was a snob.)

"All right. I'll give it a try."

Stansfield looked pleased. "She's solid, you know. One can count on Margaret. I shall. For life, you know."

For Stansfield, that stood as eloquence. Eleanor was touched.

"Give us a lift home?" she asked, getting up and brushing the chalk off the back of her skirt. Stansfield held the door open for her.

"Hear you've got a beau," he said shyly, as she got in.

"I don't know if he thinks of it that way, but we write. Robert Denholm. Captain Denholm." Settling herself, she added, "Maybe you'll see him over there."

"Good job if I do," he said, and shut the door.

13

The next afternoon, Eleanor paused at the top of the garden as she arrived at the Mowbray's annual fête. She was pleased with her dress, the ruched bodice in the light greyish green that suited her better than any other colour. The slim skirt was done in a darker striped cambric. Even her fashionable aunt approved: the perfect afternoon dress, exactly what was wanted. Yet Eleanor had paused not to show it off (as Agnes Moreland was whispering to Margaret Darcy) but to take a good look around.

Under a pale blue sky, the usual marquees dotted the lawn, serving the usual tea and cakes. Down the hill, the games were being played where they'd always been played. The thwack of a distant cricket bat, the applause. Everywhere she saw the faces she'd always known. No one in Middleford would miss the Mowbray's fête nor, she suspected, particularly enjoy it. They were too conscious of being on their best behaviour, the wives worried about what their husbands might say, the husbands wanting a beer.

But here was the difference this year: khaki. The dressmaker's son stood outside the nearest marquee worrying his neck under the scratchy woollen collar of his Red Cross uniform. Bob Flodden was an asthmatic refused for military service, but his mother had told Eleanor he was going out as an ambulance driver. A gaggle of four other young men showed off the uniform of the British Expeditionary Force, three farmers' sons and the baker's boy, all of them looking so thoroughly impressed with themselves that they almost managed to look unimpressed by the baronet's park. Lean poplars above, lean boys below. Walking shadows, Eleanor thought, and shivered.

Practical-minded Middleford was surprising itself by sending its sons off to war, overtaken by a patriotic need to thrash the Kaiser before he crossed the Channel. The fête was timed to celebrate the Mowbray marriages, especially the heir's marriage, but also to let Sir Waldo beam approval on the local war effort. Doing errands in town beforehand—her new dress, a stunner of a hat—Eleanor had heard mothers talk as if they were sending their sons off on short-term loan, like books going out from the lending library. Mrs. Flodden, pinning a sleeve: "Our Bob's not a shirker. He'll do his bit, even with the asthma. Have some fun with the *parley-vous* and be home in time for Christmas pudding."

Watching Mrs. Flodden bobbing around her in the mirror, Eleanor had decided against playing Cassandra and repeating what Robert had written. Mrs. Flodden had to know she was repeating a superstition anyway, like saluting a magpie to ward off sorrow.

"Good morning, Mr. Magpie. How's your lady wife today?"

"The boys'll be home by Christmas."

Not much difference and Mrs. Flodden knew it, a tiny shrewd brave woman, supporting five children on her meagre earnings, the ones her husband didn't drink.

Eleanor was about to step into the fête when someone spoke behind her.

"Look at you. You've cut your hair."

Eleanor turned to find Margaret Darcy, who brushed a surprising kiss on her cheek.

"That's the only way you'd notice, from behind," Eleanor said. "The effect is rather spoiled in front by one's hat. I hope you're well. Not too over-burdened by the preparations."

Margaret simpered, there was no other word. But Stansfield must have been after her as well. She was obviously making an effort.

"I hope you know how delighted we all are. I can't remember not knowing Stansfield. He's always been such an inevitable part of my life, like the Mowbrays' great oak. They must have introduced you. It dates to the time of Elizabeth."

"I hardly think Stansie's a tree," Margaret said, her voice going as thin as her smile.

"You've cut your hair?" Agnes Moreland asked, joining them. "Your beautiful hair, Eleanor. It's going to take forever to grow it out. When surely it's only a fleeting fashion. In France."

Mademoiselle had cut it that morning *à la garçonne*, approving for once of Eleanor's fashion choice, which she usually found too British. The only problem was her stunning new hat, which had been made to sit on top of a large coil of hair. When she'd tried it on afterwards, it had flopped down into her eyes as if she were a child playing dress-up. Eleanor had to borrow one from Mrs. Crosby and spend half the morning transferring the red silk poppy trim.

"My aunt launched one of her bon mots," she said. "'The only reason one pays attention to fashion is to stay ahead of it.'"

"Your aunt or Oscar Wilde?" Agnes replied. Margaret tried to hide it but she liked the dig, and gave a significant eyebrow raise to Agnes.

"It's as good as one of Mr. Wilde's, isn't it?" Eleanor replied blandly. It was obvious Margaret and Agnes were going to be friends and that she needn't bother. I tried, Stansie, she said silently, and after Agnes sweetly savaged her dress—"Is that meant to be a military colour?"—Eleanor excused herself to circulate.

Mrs. Browne, resplendent in a new Red Cross uniform, wanted her back in the first aid class. Some of the girls were signing on after the course as Voluntary Aid Detachment nurses, helping with the injured lads sent to Middleford's small hospital. "Finding a role," she said pointedly before leaving. Eleanor stood wondering whether she ought to go back when there was a sudden tug on her bodice. Mrs. Flodden was behind her, straightening a seam. Eleanor had no idea why people kept doing that, as if she were a public concern, like an orphan (she *was* an orphan) or perhaps a clogged pump.

"Doesn't Bob look handsome in his uniform?" Eleanor asked over her shoulder.

"Doesn't his mother think so?" Mrs. Flodden replied, giving a final tug and going for cake. Afterward, Eleanor saw her aunt in animated conversation with a manufacturer—a recently widowed manufacturer—and was wondering whether to join them when she saw Lady Anne bearing down on her. Despite Elizabeth Mortlake's promise, Lady Anne still hadn't entirely forgiven her for Kate's marriage. She often felt relegated to the fate of the Rev. Mr. Warfield, still a source of disappointment five children after failing to marry one of her daughters.

Lady Anne arrived already talking. "I was happy to see you with Margaret. I do so hope it continues." Squinting hard: "I would like that."

"Stansfield asked me to be friends," Eleanor replied.

"*Hmmm.*" Lady Anne craned her neck until she spotted Margaret, who was strolling with Agnes, deep in a good gossip. Probably about her, Eleanor realized.

"Agnes Moreland," Lady Anne said, with surprising venom. "It often happened at Girton. The least popular girl oozing up to the latest arrival and attaching herself like a leech. Dreadful creatures, leeches. I don't know what the Morelands were thinking, not drowning the child at birth."

Eleanor couldn't help smiling. "I didn't know you went to Girton. I wonder why I haven't heard that before."

"Well, they had to do *something* with me," Lady Anne said, holding out her arms and turning a circle to show herself off.

Eleanor wasn't sure what to say. She'd never had a chummy conversation with Lady Anne. It seemed an oxymoron.

"Were you at Cambridge the same time as my father?" she asked.

"With your uncle. Your father came up later. More to the point, Sir Waldo was at King's College. Which put paid to any thought of *education.*" Lady Anne looked triumphant. Turning back to Margaret and Agnes, she frowned more thoughtfully.

"She's a bitter girl, Agnes Moreland. I don't want Margaret falling under the influence. She's a little too proud already. Hard to take without Stansfield calming her down."

Entirely thrown, Eleanor could only say, "Of course the boys will be home by Christmas."

"You can't believe that. Robert Denholm knows what he's about, and must have said. I always told your aunt, 'Send her after the younger brother, not the elder. More sense and far less sensibility, as our friend Miss Austen would say.'"

Lady Anne paused to nod slowly, growing pleased with herself. "I said that even before we knew the Denholms own precisely one stone of that drafty old castle, and that one likely to fall off. Oh! Those places! Impossible to heat! A hundred years from now Ackley Castle will be another ruin. You watch. We'll go there for picnics."

In a century? It struck Eleanor as oddly possible. "That would be nice."

"*All* of us," Lady Anne insisted. "Stansfield *will* come back."

"Of course he shall."

"There's no 'of course' about it. But he's resourceful and he's lucky. He'll make it through."

With a final nod, Lady Anne sailed off to greet other guests, her arm raised in a wave.

"Good morning, Mr. Magpie. How's your lady wife today?"

"They'll be home by Christmas."

"Stansfield is lucky."

Superstition as balm on anticipated wounds. Eleanor looked around without seeing anyone else she particularly cared to speak with. Elizabeth and Charles Mortlake were coming for the wedding but didn't seem to have arrived yet, and the engaged couples were busy talking with Agnes Moreland. Yet Eleanor hadn't been here long enough to leave, and in any case, her aunt was now surrounded by so many admiring gentlemen it would be impossible to pry her away. Instead, Eleanor thought of the oak. When she and Kate had grown bored at other fêtes, they used to climb the old oak, Queen Elizabeth's tree. They had a favourite place along one low branch, which looked for all the world like an extended arm with a slightly crooked elbow.

Walking over, Eleanor leaned against the ancient bark, which smelled faintly like marshland: earth and damp and mushrooms. Rumour said Elizabeth had touched it with her redhead's long pale fingers. Of course, rumour had her touching every old oak in England and half the noblemen, which couldn't have left her much time to defeat the Spanish Armada.

Smiling, Eleanor wondered what it had been like at the rude court of Good Queen Bess, the hooped skirts and gentlemen's capes and Shakespeare performing his own plays in front of the groundlings. She could half hear their coarse whoops coming from the games down the hill, where grown men jeered and howled.

And with a strange dizzy jolt, Eleanor was back there, walking into a dark room, a tavern crouched under wide oak beams. It smelled of smoke and hops and charred meat, dust motes tumbling through a nearby circle of candlelight. She heard the word *glimpse* and didn't know what it meant. She was just a girl fetching her father. Looking around the crowded tables, she grew worried when she couldn't see him amid the roaring drunken jollity, and turned when Kit Marley raised his tankard to recite . . .

An acorn hit her shoulder. Another memory. Not that Christopher Marlowe was a memory, but a dream that must have grown out of one of his plays, even though she hadn't been asleep. The acorn was a memory, Eleanor told herself firmly. She'd pegged down acorns from the old oak throughout her childhood, sometimes gathering them out of season from Mowbray Wood with a backup store of pebbles and conkers. When another acorn flicked onto her hat, she began to smile. A dream of acorns. Ghostly acorns.

Giggles from above, far from ghostly. Coming back to herself, Eleanor looked up to see Mary Ann and Cassandra Mowbray sitting exactly where she and Kate used to sit, legs dangling from the long crooked branch. Cassandra waved at her sweetly and Eleanor felt knocked through with nostalgia.

Tossing down her hat, she climbed the burls the way her feet remembered, grabbing onto the bough and swinging up inelegantly to join the little girls.

"You can't come here," Mary Ann told her. "You're an adult."

"How awful for me," Eleanor said. "Am I an adult? Surely not."

She nudged Mary Ann further along, and Cassandra clambered over her to sit close to the trunk, hooking one arm securely around it, a thumb going to her mouth. Such a sweet vague little girl, her skin soft as whipped egg whites. Not for the first time, Eleanor wondered if Lady Anne had run out of names by the time she got to her seventh daughter.

"Well, if you're going to be here," Mary Ann said, "you can tell us who that gentleman is. We think it's Edward Denholm, but we weren't expecting him."

Eleanor didn't think it could be Edward, and was surprised to see him walking back from the cricket match down the hill.

"You're right, it's Mr. Denholm," Eleanor replied. "I thought he was in London trying to get a commission. Maybe he's come to ask Stansfield for help."

"He had a row with Elizabeth this morning."

"Oh, has Elizabeth arrived?"

"But they made up. Now he likes her. There! She's just come down from the nursery."

When Mary Ann pointed, Eleanor saw Elizabeth in a lovely blue dress and a hat trimmed with full-blown living white roses. She was on her own, marvellously erect, surveying the party. A movement at the corner of her eye, and Eleanor saw Edward Denholm see her, too. He lit up the way he'd once lit up for her and motored smartly across the lawn.

As Edward got close, Elizabeth heard him call and smiled happily. Their greeting was flirtatious, no other word, and Eleanor didn't like it. Not because of Edward Denholm; he could do what he wanted. But Elizabeth Mortlake was married with two children. Eleanor didn't care to see her listening with such amusement as Edward launched into a long and animated story. It seemed to involve the cricket match. He mimed bowling, and Elizabeth put one hand flat to her breast as she listened, burbling with laughter.

"She oughtn't be so very friendly, ought she?" asked Mary Ann. Eleanor didn't know what to say, and Mary Ann persisted. "Ought she?"

"Elizabeth is so beautiful, men can't help behaving like that," Eleanor said, supposing that Elizabeth couldn't help it, either. It must be such a temptation, great beauty. Not using it was like Leonardo da Vinci refusing to paint.

"Do you think she's beautiful? We do, but she's our sister."

"I'm quite sure there are goddesses less beautiful than Elizabeth."

A giggle from Cassandra. Glancing over, Eleanor saw that her thumb was out of her mouth and she was pegging down another acorn. A small pause, then a pebble. A new target must have arrived under the tree. Craning over, Eleanor was embarrassed to see Charles Mortlake. He couldn't have heard what they'd said about Elizabeth. Surely not.

"Cassandra! Stop!" she whispered.

But Charles Mortlake looked up, and when he saw them—saw Eleanor sitting with the children, her legs dangling—he looked every bit as amused as Elizabeth. He jumped to grab the branch where they sat and monkeyed up the trunk to join them, not caring for his fine wool trousers. Once settled, he took Cassandra in his lap.

"Hullo there. Excellent view," he said, and looked directly at Elizabeth and Edward Denholm. Eleanor tried to think how to distract him and couldn't.

"Lizzy's a goddess," Cassandra said.

"Yes, she is," Charles replied. "And amusing herself with a mortal, from the looks of it."

Most men would be jealous, but Eleanor didn't see a tick of it in Charles Mortlake. Smiling, nonchalant, he was the definition of indulgence, every bit the grandson of a duke, his sophistication, she realized, far beyond her. Eleanor remembered the ball in London, how Elizabeth and Charles had used Edward to restore her reputation, and her aunt's reputation, and more to the point, the Mowbrays' reputations.

How, she realized, they had used her.

"Poor Eleanor, I've shocked you," Charles said. "Should you prefer me to make a scene? When Elizabeth will grow bored with Mr. Denholm in five minutes, and send him off to help Margaret Darcy find her lost apostrophe."

That sounded right. She hoped it was. "I suppose I'm too earnest," Eleanor said. "I've been accused of it."

"Earnest. By whom?"

"The Warfields," Eleanor said. "Observing my attempts at self-education. Doing mathematics and reading Mr. James's novels, where he takes aim at girls far more worldly than me."

Charles paused and smiled. "You always surprise me, Miss Nora. Tell me how Robert Denholm is."

"No doubt in danger. While we're at this absurd party. Up a tree."

"I thought it was rather a nice party."

"Miss Darcy lost her apostrophe," Cassandra said. "Poor Miss Darcy."

"Oh, it's all right," Charles said. "She can get another if she wants."

"*Can she?*" Cassandra asked, immensely impressed. "What's an apostrophe?"

Charles took out his handkerchief rolled it into a tube that he hooked at the end, and it was exactly an apostrophe. Then he tossed it lightly into the air and it hung there, and hung, and hung suspended, Cassandra clapping her hands and Mary Ann oohing and aahing, staying there so long it looked uncanny. Eleanor hated magic tricks. She wanted to know how they did it and could never figure it out.

"For your next trick, you can stop the war," she said.

Charles met her eye. His were an extraordinarily deep brown and even more amused. She realized he didn't want the war to end, not yet, not with men wanting to prove themselves, filthy with it, Charles first among them as he waited to enter the war cabinet. She heard Robert saying, "Old men sending young men off to war," and while Charles Mortlake wasn't old, in this moment he looked ancient.

We're really in for it, she thought. This is what they want, what they've always wanted. Her aunt's voice arising from deep in her memory. "There will always be another war."

May 1915
Sussex, England

14

Eleanor could hear the big guns booming across the Channel. Not precisely hear them, not during the day. That was a phenomenon of night, of changes in the atmosphere, and last evening as they'd had a drink in the library, they'd heard a deep cannonade from the battle-field. Now, getting ready for breakfast, she felt a thud in her eardrums that wasn't quite a sound but a change in the air pressure. The next moment, there was a quiver coming up her elbow as she leaned on the dressing table, as if a small earthquake was rattling the chalk of Sussex.

They were staying at South Farm, one of the Mortlakes' smaller residences, a short rail trip down from London near the Channel. Elizabeth had given her a room facing east, lit by the white rays of the morning sun. They'd gathered in Sussex for one of Lizzy's schemes: forcing the Mowbrays to acknowledge Kate's marriage. More to the point, forcing Lady Anne. In accepting the invitation, Eleanor hadn't expected to find herself reminded so audibly of the carnage on the western front.

Not that she needed a reminder, not with the names of the dead and injured filling column after column in the newspapers. The war wasn't going well, although no one said that. Or said it without being howled down. Robert had made it uninjured through the latest round of fighting in the Ypres salient but thousands had not. Many of his men had not. Yet now he was getting leave, and after spending most of the week with his mother in Kent, he would meet her in London, where they would see each other for the first time since the war began. Eleanor would go up to London after Elizabeth's attempt at a reunion.

Lizzy's scheme had raised its head after David Arden was offered a gallery show in London. Poor David had been injured in February after only four months in uniform, losing his right arm below the elbow and collecting shrapnel in his left leg. Blighties, they called wounds like that, which sent a soldier home not hopelessly damaged. Blighties were highly sought-after, Robert wrote. Seldom achieved. Fortunately David was left-handed, although the phantom pain in the missing arm was bad and he could still scarcely bend his left knee. He was on medical leave while being treated in London, and he'd been allowed to live with Kate in their Bloomsbury flat instead of taking up a hospital bed. Eventually he would go before a board that would determine his future, although going back on active duty was clearly not an option. Meanwhile he'd been painting with his one arm, rapidly securing the show, and Elizabeth wanted the family to reconcile so they could support him.

What is Elizabeth thinking? *Kate wrote.* It will be hard enough to get Mother to speak to me much less Arden—but she's also scheming to throw both Mother and Father together with pacifists? Roger Fry and the Bells are invited to the opening and probably they'll come since they got him the show, or Roger did, partly because of artistic infighting I won't bore you with and partly because Arden is painting THE HORRORS OF WAR. Masked, of course, because there's a fine line to walk with the Army refusing to let him paint the wounded and dying except when they're being saved by heroic medical officers, of whom fortunately (says his wife) there are many. Wounded trees and houses are all right, which gives him an out. Not that he always takes it. Those won't be exhibited, not with the Ministry at the show checking him up.

Eleanor was grateful that the opening gave Robert an excuse to say goodbye to his mother before the end of his leave. Mrs. Denholm was ill again, back in a wheelchair, unable to find her legs. With her husband and both her sons in uniform, a case of nerves was hardly surprising. Edward had finally got into the flying corps, piloting what amounted to a motorized kite, fighting off Germany's fleet of lumbering Zeppelins before they could drop their bombs on London. Where had such an improvised rackety war come from, and so suddenly? She almost didn't know.

Eleanor lay her hands flat on the table to feel the vibrations, remembering the time she'd done that at the parsonage and been certain she'd heard Elizabeth's voice. This spring, she'd been diagnosed with megrim headaches, and had decided that the strange displaced dreams she'd been having lately, her weird glimpses of other times, were a precursor to the headaches, a more elaborate version of the kaleidoscopic colours she often saw before the first eye-gouging pain.

The Americans said migraines. Her aunt had taken her to London to see Mr. Blythe, who had moved south as a neurological consultant and spent most of his time working with head wounds. They'd gone to the hospital to see him, the consultation a favour to her aunt. Mr. Blythe had told her that twenty-one was a common age for girls' megrims to start, and filled her in on the history and etymology of her headaches, a very thorough session in which he'd neglected to do anything to stop them. Not severe enough to risk ergot, he'd said, and medicine hadn't another gun in its arsenal. Why not a cold cloth and a dark room?

They used to joke about Mr. Blythe over-treating mild ailments, but now he made it clear he thought she was being hysterical, and Eleanor could see why. An orderly wheeled a soldier into the lift as they were leaving, the top of his head covered like a mummy. Only one eye was left visible, and the soldier had winked at her quite merrily.

Mrs. Denholm's wheelchair. The Tommy's wheelchair. The creak of wheels echoing from the past. Eleanor's mind could circle endlessly these days, and hours go by. Leaning on her flat hands, she levered herself up, going downstairs to find Elizabeth alone at the table.

"There you are! Did you sleep well?" Elizabeth asked.

She seemed to sleep admirably herself, always looking rested. But then, Charles was in the war cabinet, not in uniform, having something to do with logistics. Supplies. Weapons, from the sounds of it. And there had been happy news in the Mowbray family, when so many faced sadness. Margaret and Stansfield were expecting their first child in July, nine months to the dot after their wedding. Eleanor was supposed to be ignorant of the process, girls being light and airy angels, but with Mrs. Crosby as her aunt, she'd been educated.

She also dreamt about Robert. Fragmented dreams, often nightmares. But sometimes her dreams had an otherworldly beauty that she tried to hold onto after waking. Last night they'd had their arms around each other as they walked through tall sunlit golden grass. She knew this was an African savannah and that Robert had been there for a while and she had come to join him. They walked forward as slowly as if they were walking through water. She could feel him beside her, the strength of his bones and the pliability of muscle. He was wearing a clean white shirt, the sleeves rolled up. Peaceable lions yawned nearby and flamingos preened in the river. There was no danger. Never-ending love. It was such a luxurious dream that Eleanor had woken feeling comforted and humid, no other word, and knowing more than Mrs. Crosby had taught her.

"I don't think you're awake quite yet," Elizabeth said with a burble.

"The bed's extremely comfortable," Eleanor answered, rousing herself. "And they forwarded a letter from Yorkshire yesterday saying that Robert is already back from the front. He'll be crossing the Channel in a couple of days. I refuse to think about German torpedoes, but in any case, he's safe for the moment. So, yes, I slept quite well, thank you."

"But you've lost weight. I'm going to have to worry about you, Robin's Nora. Cocoa?"

Lizzy poured a cup before Eleanor could answer and smiled when passing it.

Eleanor bent over the cup for a thick rich breath. "Where did you get such good cocoa?"

"One can't live without chocolate," Elizabeth said. "The only thing we truly needed from the New World. The Spaniards should have collected the seeds and left. I'm sure they could have grown it somewhere. Spain is big enough, and the valleys can get quite muggy. I don't feel the same about tomatoes, I'm afraid. I've never liked tomatoes." With a burble: "Or Americans particularly."

"Robert says the Canadian troops fought very bravely at Ypres."

Elizabeth stopped burbling, her knife suspended over her toast. "Nora, you're at risk of becoming boring. Not everything need refer to the war. You have a role to play, you know. The men need to have something to fight for, and come home to. Robin Denholm does. I wonder what he'll say in London, whether he'll ask himself what happened to the sweet little girl he met, with her delicious sense of humour."

Eleanor winced. She often asked herself the same thing, what had happened to her youth, whether they'd taken it permanently. She was only twenty-one and she didn't want the war to change her. She wasn't a pacifist like Kate and David. She assumed the war had to be fought, the German juggernaut halted. But she didn't know how *not* to think about it, or how to lose the permanent knot in her stomach. If the sun were in eclipse, surely you wouldn't look at the ground and say, How prettily the chickweed grows.

"I want him to like me," she said. "I want to like myself. I'm not sure we actually know each other very well. Or really, what there is to know about me. I've done so little in my life when he's done so much already. But I don't think that's a recommendation, Lizzy. I don't want to be a delicious young girl. I'd like to have more purpose and substance." Hearing herself sound earnest, she added, "But I'm afraid I haven't found the lovely little shop where they sell it."

Elizabeth looked indulgent, ready to say more when Lady Anne and Sir Waldo came down the hallway and into the room.

"Oh! Such a day!" Lady Anne cried when she saw them. "We went for a morning stroll, and Elizabeth, your garden is so much ahead of ours. The wisteria! We dawdled under the trellis, if you can imagine *me* dawdling. However do you get it to bloom so magnificently?"

"Pruning and guano," Lizzy said.

"Pruning and . . ." Lady Anne threw herself in a chair. "My *dear*. Is that cocoa? I could eat a second breakfast. It's a terrible habit to take one's breakfast in bed, Eleanor. You mustn't start, should she, Sir Waldo? Scaring off the gentlemen with *podge*."

But Sir Waldo had gone still, looking over his wife's head. When Eleanor turned, she saw Kate framed in the doorway, and the look on Sir Waldo's face made Eleanor think, Oh, Elizabeth, you didn't tell them.

Lit from behind, her face half in shadow, Kate wore one of her artistic outfits, a simple dress in a broad blue-and-yellow plaid. She'd cropped her hair and looked perfect. Gamine. Sir Waldo opened his arms and said, "There's my dear girl."

Kate ran into her father's embrace. Eleanor relaxed, thinking that Elizabeth had arranged things beautifully. Reconciliation was simple. Time had to pass, that was all. But Lady Anne hadn't spoken, and when she did, it was an explosion.

"Elizabeth! What were you thinking?"

"Now, Anne," Sir Waldo cautioned.

She didn't seem to hear him and wouldn't acknowledge Kate. Getting to her feet, looking clumsy and ill, Lady Anne tacked crookedly out of the room.

A moment's consternation. Elizabeth's schemes were usually successful, and a rare pettishness constricted her lovely mouth. The horses in her merry-go-round had pranced onto the grass and the calliope music gone all jangled. Kate gave her sister a cynical glance. This was the new Kate, infused with the modern assumption that things wouldn't work out. As other classes of society had known forever.

"Nora, you'd better go after her," Elizabeth said. "Until your aunt comes down."

Eleanor found one hand going to her breast. *Me?*

Lizzy nodded. Such was the power she exerted (how?) that Eleanor left the room, her job presumably being to tamp down Lady Anne's fury (*how?*) or at least keep her from uprooting the wisteria, trampling the blossoms, and wrenching down the iron trellis, each stake a weapon.

Eleanor wandered the garden, amusing herself with irrelevancies, no doubt from an unconscious wish not to find Lady Anne. (Dr. Freud was on everyone's lips.) Only when she walked out the front drive did Eleanor find her sitting on a bench with a view of the downs. The Mortlakes' house was built on an escarpment above miles of sloping pasturage, so the bench looked down a long vista of hill and vale as England folded toward the coast. The pastures were bordered by dark green trees and the footpaths wandering through them white and deeply cut, taking ancient routes across hillsides where cattle browsed unheeding. At an angle in the distance, a raw chalk cliff gently eroded. Behind it was the Channel, the beaches and inlets guarded by coils of barbed wire.

Eleanor walked over to the bench and sat down beside Lady Anne.

"Elizabeth suggested I keep you company until my aunt comes downstairs."

"Late as usual," the lady replied. "Does your aunt think Mademoiselle's regimen is going to get her a third husband? When men her age can marry girls scarcely out of the nursery. Surely she's read the casualty figures." Eleanor was about to speak when Lady Anne added, "Not that suitability has always concerned your aunt. Lieutenant Stickley, isn't he now? Her steward? A temporary gentleman."

"I wonder if you know that David Arden won the Military Cross for his actions when he was wounded."

Lady Anne looked straight ahead, not blinking, only a slight flaring of her nostrils saying that she was listening. Kate had told Eleanor about it in London. She'd been there several times lately, not just for the headaches but so Mrs. Crosby could meet with the

Ministry, having offered Goodwood for use as a hospital. Eleanor didn't think her aunt wanted to marry again, although if she couldn't get Goodwood off her hands, marriage might prove a fallback.

But just last week the Ministry had decided that the Middleford was air bracing, soldiers recovering well at the town's small hospital. The army would use Goodwood as an infectious-diseases facility, erecting ranks of barrack-like tents on the grounds and housing officers in the residence itself, freeing her aunt from addressing the mortgage until after the war. Not that Eleanor was going to tell Lady Anne that she was about to lose her closest friend, if that was the right word. They would be moving to Kent.

Kate had met them at Euston Station. Mrs. Crosby had taken their baggage off in a trap, planning to check into their hotel before going to the Ministry. David wasn't long out of hospital, and Eleanor agreed to walk with Kate to his new studio in one of the enormous and shabby Victorian warehouses along the canal. Whenever she took the train to London, Eleanor looked out at the brick monstrosities and wondered what on earth went on in there. Hundreds, maybe thousands of windows, all of them too filthy to see through.

As they left the station, Kate told her that David had taken a room on a sixth floor, despite his painful leg, wanting something high enough to look over the other old buildings. They'd cleaned the windows, and afterwards he'd told Kate that the light off the greasy canal had the same jaundiced phosphorescence as the light in No Man's Land. He was pleased. His nightmares got worse. Kate said it was like that now.

She led Eleanor into a warren of streets behind the station. Little sunlight made it to the ground, and the cobbles were green in the gutters, pond scum hanging from the metal sewerage grates. The whole area stank of wet horses and algae and mouldy bread. Sometimes when they passed an open door, there was a fugitive smell of hot metal. The streets were empty, although once a gang of workmen jostled around a corner and chaffed them—"Eh, luv, you lookin' for summut, luv, lookin' for me, luv . . ."—even though they were grandfathers or weedy lads, too old or young to serve.

Kate's route was intricate, sometimes taking them through alleys barely wide enough for a single file of workmen to pass. Eleanor was uneasily aware she could never find her way out on her own. Turning a corner, they came across a solitary man leaning against a wall, who sang out in a fine tenor when he saw them, "There's a rose that grows in No Man's Land, and it's beautiful to see."

The singer was a uniformed soldier smoking a cigarette, his legs crossed, a wound badge visible. Eleanor smiled, but the soldier grabbed himself and thrust a handful at her, asking if she wanted some, the army had the rest. They hurried off, although Kate insisted that the men were harmless, ignore them, and remained intent on explaining Arden's war and what he was painting before they got to the studio.

"They were ordered over the top of the trench," Eleanor told Lady Anne. "There was a major offensive along the front, but something went terribly wrong. I can't begin to know what it was, but it was misty and smoky, and apparently their platoon ran off in the wrong direction. Kate says this isn't mentioned in the citation, but everything that happened was a mistake."

"A royal cock-up," she'd said, her vocabulary cruder since her marriage. Modern.

"They ran through a wood and ended up in a field, although it had been fought over until it was all muck and shell holes, and the few remaining trees were skeletons. David remembers a horse's ribcage and"—a foot so black and leathery he'd thought it was a boot, Kate said, with the suggestion that she was holding back, as David had probably held back—"and they were strafed with machine-gun fire. Very suddenly. No backup, no cover, the mist or smoke or miasma limiting their vision.

"Many of the men were killed right away and others badly injured, including the lieutenant who was the senior officer present.

A good number ran off. David was one of the injured ones, suffering a wound to his forearm, making his right arm useless. But he managed to get the remaining men into a pair of shell holes, craters, maybe a dozen boys. He was the eldest, you see. He got one of them to tie a tourniquet on his arm torn from a, well, from the uniform of someone in the crater who'd been there for a while"—a skeletal German—"and strapped the arm against himself."

Lady Anne gave no sign of listening and stared out at the downs.

"Apparently in No Man's Land, one waits until dark to move, although David came under fire that morning when he pulled one painfully injured soldier into the crater—his cries were terrible, you see—but the poor boy died."

Still no acknowledgement.

"When it was dark, David got every half-fit man to support another, or carry another, the remnants of their platoon crawling from one crater to the next, David carrying the badly wounded lieutenant over his shoulder."

Kate had been scathing about the lieutenant, one of Robin's tin soldiers whose stupidity had led the men astray. Or his youth, or bad luck, or bad orders. David had refused to saddle any other man with the lieutenant and Kate said he'd been tempted to leave him behind, not out of spite but because his injuries were grave. Shot in the shoulder with a head wound for good measure. He'd mostly been conscious and hadn't complained, so there was that.

"I think it's a very long story of crawling through mud. He had to guess at the right direction. They eventually stumbled on a pair of stretcher-bearers, who took out the ones they figured would survive, and the lieutenant. David stayed with the more gravely wounded, and the stretcher-bearers came back more than once, heroic men—conchies, in fact, Quakers—with David insisting on being the last one out, exhausted by then, staggering as he carried the final man as it was coming on morning, almost daybreak, and they were shelled.

"Kate says he doesn't speak about that, but the poor young man was killed and David was injured for a second time in his leg, although he still carried the boy's body out. So, the Military Cross for valour."

It was his concern for the other men that had kept him going, Kate said, not martial fervour. Improbably, the lieutenant had survived, at least so far, the bullet just that inch high enough to have missed his vital organs, although the head wound was keeping him in hospital in London.

"David has a hooked prosthesis now for his right forearm."

Eleanor wondered what else to say, but decided she had nothing left. There was a long silence, which Lady Anne finally ended by saying, "I wonder if you know that he's married. Not to Catherine."

"Most people don't," her aunt said.

Eleanor had been conscious of her aunt standing behind them for some time. Now she came around the bench to sit on the other side of Lady Anne.

"A few of us know, and Eleanor does now, although of course we don't say anything."

Eleanor gave her aunt an indignant glance. Of course she wouldn't say anything. But Mrs. Crosby was intent on Lady Anne.

"David Arden is an admirable man," she said.

"Is that your word for it?"

"A very promising artist, according to the critics."

"And does that excuse his morals?" Lady Anne asked. "You imply that it's supposed to. Artists seem to think they can do whatever they want, but I don't excuse it. He's a scoundrel, and while scoundrels may, may *blossom* in war, capable of doing the unconventional, the *admirable*, whatever you want to call it—fine. Give them their medals. But what about after the war, when a scoundrel out of uniform returns to being a shabby little man who abandoned his wife and children. He's got my daughter, Clara."

"I think you know there aren't any simple answers to questions like that."

Lady Anne was silent. It was an active silence now. Brooding.

"He married very young, Anne."

Lady Anne snorted.

Mrs. Crosby paused for a long time before saying, "I married my first husband when I was far too young. You know that. But let's be honest for a moment and admit it was my own miscalculation. Implying that it was my poor father's fault can be useful but perhaps we shan't hide behind that any longer. Henry Preston could be very charming, and I wanted Preston Hall. I think I've always liked houses better than men. They're what men ought to be, solid and silent, although I think we can agree they share a tendency to groan."

Mrs. Crosby couldn't make Lady Anne smile.

"Of course I learned soon enough that Harry Preston was a bully, and I think it was embarrassment that kept me there afterwards, and the fact I was expecting Hetty. I would have left him after she was born, and I would have been justified, no matter what the church says. But I spent months wanting *so fiercely* for him to die that I blamed myself when his horse actually trampled him. I'd sent out psychic emanations, you see. I know it sounds odd, but after listening to what they're saying these days, I think I was suffering from marital shell shock. I also think the stable boy did something to the horseshoes, Preston having beaten him almost as badly as he beat me. But that's another question."

"There's no parallel, Clara."

"I think there is. David Arden married because he thought he'd got as far as he could, teaching school in Wales. Painting shopkeepers' portraits. Being a good father to his children. You've said yourself he hasn't enough money to support Catherine because he sends most of what he earns back to the children. As well he ought. But he managed to get out of Wales and make himself an artist. He had to take his chance, and not only for his own sake. If he'd stayed there, he might have become another Henry Preston."

Another long silence, and Lady Anne brushed her eyes wearily.

"The world's coming to an end," she said.

"Shall we go inside and see Kate?"

The simple physical embrace. Kate came up to her mother and put a hand on her shoulder. Grudgingly, Lady Anne put an arm around her, and they stood together for a long time.

Afterwards, they spent a silent afternoon in the library. Eleanor wanted to be anywhere else, but it had started raining solidly. She took a book from the shelf and pretended to read, wondering what she would do if she found out Robert was already married, and whether Kate had learned about David's marriage before or after they ran off. That would make a difference in Eleanor's opinion of David. Not of Kate.

A bell pull, and everyone froze. It was probably nothing, but telegrams were a threat these days. Elizabeth got up and went into the front hall, and they heard a brief discussion with the housekeeper, a few murmurs and a delay. Probably nothing, Eleanor told herself, and in any case, no one would send her a telegram about Robert, not here. It could only be Charles, but he wasn't fighting. He was in charge of supplies. Weapons, probably.

When Elizabeth came back to the library, she held a telegram.

"Oh!" Lady Anne cried, half rising.

"A telegram from Charles," Elizabeth said, and Lady Anne sank back down. "I don't know how to tell you that Stansfield . . ."

"No!" cried Lady Anne.

"Stansfield has been killed."

15

Eleanor and her aunt arrived at the station well before Robert's train was due to arrive. They'd been in London ever since the Mowbrays had rushed off to Yorkshire with no plans to return for David's show. Lady Anne was frantic about Margaret, afraid the shock would make her deliver the baby too early and they'd lose him, too. She was sure it was a boy.

Kate would come to London, of course. She wrote that Margaret was holding on so far, controlling herself admirably. Staunch: the word came to Eleanor as she read Kate's letter, along with Stansfield's well-known voice. "One can count on Margaret. I shall. For life, you know." Irony wherever you turned these days. The gods may have retreated to Mount Olympus but they sat there raining down mockery.

"There he is," her aunt said, touching Eleanor's arm. An officer was striding into the station through the same entrance they'd taken from the street. A brief clench of the heart, yet Eleanor chiefly felt puzzled. She knew it was Robert but didn't recognize him, or have any idea why he would be arriving from the street. He wore a weary battle-stained overcoat that drew approving glances from the few scattered families on the platform. And while the overcoat looked large, Robert didn't seem as tall or as muscular as Eleanor remembered. Tall enough, but slimmer, and as he got closer, she saw that he'd changed.

His face was thin now, the cheekbones sharper, his grey eyes deeper with a smudge of exhaustion beneath them, despite having been home for six days. Nor had she noticed before that he had such a pretty mouth. His upper lip lacked the double peak that most people had. It was as smooth and almost as full as his lower lip, which had a slight look of stubbornness.

She focused on the lips, unable to meet his eyes. Robert was greeting them, his mouth moving, but Eleanor couldn't take in a word. Nor did she know what she felt. Mainly fear, aware that he could be torpedoed tomorrow when he shipped back across the Channel. Daring a glance, she met his grey eyes with such a jolt that they both blushed and looked aside.

"Did you get here on an earlier train?" her aunt asked, easy and pleasant, valiantly covering the confusion.

"I walked."

"From Kent?" her aunt asked. "When on earth did you set out? Have you had any sleep?"

"Slept rough last night," Robert said. "I knew it would be warm enough, with the clouds. Bunking down on the good clean dirt of England."

It wasn't only the gods raining irony. They turned as they heard a train approach the station, its chuff and pump amplified as it drove under the Himalayan ceiling, a hollow echo bouncing back from girders lined with roosting pigeons. The screech of brakes as it pulled in scattered hundreds of birds. Such a flapping confusion of wings. Eleanor wondered if pigeons were clever enough to remember that the scatter would be repeated when a new train pulled in five minutes later.

Mrs. Crosby led them out of the station before the flood of passengers got out. She walked at a surprising clip. They soon reached the cab ranks and she told a driver to take them to the Savoy, where she liked one of the restaurants. She expected Robert was hungry—"rather famished," he agreed—and established that his mother was well enough, back to walking, and that while of course as Eleanor's aunt she was their chaperone "in society's eyes," the demand of unspecified errands meant she would leave them at the Savoy, seeing them again at David Arden's opening.

Robert sat beside her aunt in the cab, Eleanor across from them, looking at her folded hands. She felt panicked by the thought of Mrs. Crosby leaving them alone. So far, she hadn't been able to manage more than a few words, and while Robert answered each of her aunt's questions thoroughly, probably too thoroughly, he had no real conversation, either. Something about enclosed spaces took away Eleanor's breath. Enclosed spaces that rattled. She preferred walking and riding, and understood why Robert had walked from Kent. Eleanor would happily leap from the cab this minute and walk all the way to Yorkshire.

"Here you are, then," Mrs. Crosby said, and Eleanor realized that the horses had stopped. A man in the Savoy uniform was opening the door, beaming approval at the handsome captain getting out and giving his hand to a fashionably dressed girl. (The grey-green afternoon dress and a new stunner of a hat. Eleanor *did* like hats.) But the doorman's approval made her feel an object in the public eye, and she found herself clinging to the open door as her aunt said goodbye, a panicked appeal in her eyes that only made Mrs. Crosby flick her wrist below the level of the window. *Off with you.*

It was a marvellous change from the days when her aunt had tried to make her marry Edward Denholm. Instead, fully sanctioned by Mrs. Crosby—and without a chaperone—Eleanor found herself walking into the Savoy on Robert's arm. In the bustle of luggage and elderly bellboys, she grew conscious of the hundreds of anonymous rooms hired out above. Of the *beds*. No mother would have left her there, although it would be just like her aunt to silently raise an issue and expect Eleanor to finesse it, coming back engaged.

They couldn't see the restaurant Mrs. Crosby had recommended. Robert had to hive over to the concierge to ask for directions, but turned the wrong way as soon as they left the counter. Eleanor knew it was the wrong way but couldn't manage to tell him. When they reached the lifts, Robert turned back in some confusion, still not seeing the restaurant and heading off in another wrong direction. A faint slick of perspiration rose on his handsome upper lip, and Eleanor felt like a croquet ball pocked around a lawn. Alice in Wonderland's game of croquet, the hoops made of doubled-over soldiers.

Finally, a bellboy took them in hand. The restaurant proved to be a vast field of tables. Underneath a high tent-like ceiling, it was loud with prosperous gentlemen and matrons, the ladies showing off the latest fashions as if they'd never heard of the war, their husbands probably running it. At a table by himself, half hidden by a palm tree, Eleanor saw a member of the war cabinet, she couldn't remember whom, eating his soup through mustachios he used as a sieve. She thought of the Hon. Lieutenant Newton-Pye, heir to the Earl of Grimsby, human walrus, killed this spring in France.

Robert looked thoroughly overheated by now and took off his overcoat as they stood in the entrance, drawing notice to his tunic. There was a perceptible silence, the handsome captain making people look up from their meals, the notice swiftly followed by approval, either murmurs or significant nods or doting silence from the matrons. A thin woman raised her hands, prepared to clap if anyone else did.

"I hope you don't mind," Robert said. Still holding his overcoat, he turned on his heel and strode out of the restaurant, forcing Eleanor to sprint to keep up with him, out of the hotel and into the Strand, where he finally stopped, taking off his hat and pushing back his hair with the heel of one hand. He gave her a look of surprising distress. "I'm sorry. I simply didn't like the look of the place."

"I didn't like them liking the look of you," she said. Robert gave her a glance that dissolved into amusement, becoming more like himself. Himself as he had been.

"If you really don't mind," he said. "There might be something better ..." He gestured east along the Strand and started walking, overcoat over one arm, not offering her the other one, walking a bit more slowly but still forcing her to keep up her pace to stay beside him.

They reached Fleet Street without Robert seeing anything suitable. Not that he seemed to be looking, his eyes focused down the road. He turned north along Chancery Lane, still not seeming to see anything, soon angling northeast toward Holborn, workmen and carts and horses taking the place of the motor cars chuffing along the Strand, the smell more rural despite the brick offices crowding in on either side.

Eleanor realized Robert had forgotten about eating and probably about her. She was seeing panic, Robert a piece of shrapnel flung out of France. If any of the workmen had spoken to her as rudely as the men near Arden's studio, Robert would have punched him. Eleanor had no idea what to do until he stopped abruptly, as if waking up, looking around and noticing a low eatery across the road with a grimy small-paned Dickensian window, the glass as thick as old bottles.

"What about that one?" he asked, entirely reasonably, as if they'd been talking all the while, considering one restaurant after the other and rejecting others before now.

"If you like," she said, and he gave a considered nod before crossing the road and opening the door.

Cooked onions. Grease, at least not rancid. Looking around, Eleanor had an idea she'd been here before. She couldn't imagine when, although the long low narrow wood-partitioned room probably predated Dickens, likely an ancient tavern, meaning she could have strolled in any time over the past fifteen hundred years. Set Mr. Stickley digging in the basement and he'd find a Roman goddess five feet under. (Lieutenant Stickley.) The proprietor edged forward crablike to meet them. He was busy with a cloth, wiping one finger after the other, doing it slowly enough to make it clear that he had no use for the likes of them.

"Yes, hofficer, how can I 'elp?" he asked, his half-dozen customers either ignoring them or staring belligerently at Robert's tunic. Eleanor wondered if this was a warren of conchies, then heard the exaggerated "hofficer" and realized that this was about rank and class. The proprietor could have said "captain" and spoken better English. Everyone recognized pips these days.

"If you've got a table free?" Robert asked, when obviously there were plenty.

"My boy's over there," the proprietor said. "And 'e don't half like what's going on. No more do I."

"No more do any of us," Robert said. "But we get on with it, don't we?"

The clientele liked that, nods and murmurs, Robert passing a test. After his own slow nod, the proprietor flexed his chin at a table, where Robert took a seat with his back against the wall. The eatery wasn't Dickensian, Eleanor realized, sitting down across from him. It was a trench, and now Robert was safe.

The proprietor hovered, waiting for their order. Robert said casually, "Whatever you've got, and plenty of it."

The man liked that, too. "And the lidy?"

"I've eaten, thank you. But some coffee would be nice."

The proprietor leaned in confidentially. "The coffee ain't up to much," he said, as if speaking about someone else's establishment.

"If it's hot?" Eleanor asked, another acceptable answer. Two mugs quickly appeared and he was right; it was dreadful. Cooked grounds. But sipping it provided another excuse not to talk, and so did the plate their proprietor soon slung in front of Robert. A fry-up, she thought it was called. Only when Robert had devoured most of it and got to the kidneys did he stop. A fastidious expression passed over his face at the sight of the kidneys and he pushed his plate away.

"I'm sorry about Stansfield," he said, and Eleanor couldn't help recoiling. She had to force herself to meet his eyes.

"Yes," she said.

Something about his sister being her closest friend and they must have known each other since they were children. He sounded insincere, and Eleanor wondered if he'd seen so much death that one more didn't matter.

"We've lost, Middleford has lost quite a few boys," she said. Poor Mrs. Flodden, hoping that being in the Red Cross would get her Bob through. "But I knew Stansfield all my life, and it's difficult. Far worse for his family, of course. His poor mother. Although Stansfield's commanding officer was kind enough to write. Apparently he died instantly of a head wound."

The faintest movement of Robert's handsome mouth, although he nodded gravely. Eleanor couldn't have felt more naïve. The mother of every boy killed on the western front was probably told he'd died of a head wound, without pain, instantly, or perhaps with a final prayer on his lips that would take him directly ...

"What really happened? Do you know?"

Robert sat back, clearly sorry he'd brought it up, not wanting to have this conversation. But there was a core honesty about him, and he had to tell her, "I heard he'd been killed not long before I left France, and I knew my brother would want me to look into it. They'd gone to school together, as I'm sure you remember."

"I don't think I ever knew how they'd met. They seemed unlikely friends."

"Mowbray was someone to count on. My brother always thought of himself as someone who wasn't. Each supplied what the other lacked." A brief glance. "That might have changed. In Edward, I mean."

Eleanor didn't want to talk about Edward. "I remember thinking that Stansfield would make an excellent officer. He needed to be active."

"Not always advisable," Robert said, before checking himself. "I'm sure he was, but I'm afraid that's no guarantee of getting through. I think we should find another subject, if you don't mind."

He tried to come up with something and couldn't. Eleanor waited him out, not sure she wanted to hear it any more than he wanted to say it.

"He was wounded leading an assault on a machine gun position," Robert said finally, giving in and resenting it. "It wasn't a head wound. Abdomen. They aim for that. Bigger target. We do the same. But the stretcher-bearers got him out alive, and he was in an ambulance on his way to hospital when the ambulance had a smash-up. The driver thought he could skirt a shell hole in the road, or thought it wasn't all that deep. The water covers that up, you see. So in he went, and Mowbray wasn't in good enough shape to escape a second ... insult, I believe the medical types call it. Not that he was likely to have made it anyway."

When Eleanor was silent, fighting tears, Robert said aggressively, "You wanted to know."

"Did *you?*" Eleanor asked. "I imagine you've seen far worse. But I mean, when you decided to go in for the army, did you want to know these things?" Finding her handkerchief but only able to crush it. "That's a serious question."

"Do you mean am I a damned bloodthirsty . . ."

"*No.* But do men, going off to war, do, do, they think it's going to be edifying? Do they want to *know?* Find their purpose in life? Their role? That's a *serious question.* I remember you writing after the Marne about the exhilaration of being tested in battle."

"Do I look exhilarated, Eleanor?"

Eleanor, not Nora. He spoke gently, but there was dislike in his eyes, not necessarily directed at her, or not all of it. She allowed herself a moment.

"You're not there," she said. "You're back home, and I can see that we must strike you as naïve. Absurdly so. People keep telling me"—doing an exaggerated Elizabeth Mortlake—"'The boys want sweet little girls to, to, come home to.'" Blushing, but determined to go on. "You told me once yourself that in fighting for England, you felt you were fighting for people like me. You felt a need to protect us. But I wonder when it comes down to it if we're irrelevant, if not *awfully* boring or, or as repulsive as you found the Savoy. What's important is the exhilaration you feel facing the ultimate. To *know.* The very height of life. I keep wondering if that's what men really want. If it's why you keep agreeing to fight, generation after generation after . . . Stansfield *rushing* to learn."

"If that's what you've come up with, I wouldn't call you naïve."

Robert stood up abruptly, throwing some money on the table and taking his hat and his overcoat. Eleanor wondered if he was going to leave her here. He seemed capable of it.

"I don't imagine you want any more coffee," he said.

Eleanor stood up, still wearing a hat that suddenly struck her as ridiculous, and Robert offered his arm to walk her past the crab-like proprietor and out of the trench, leaving her unable to predict anything that was going to happen between them.

Robert stopped outside the eatery. Without Mrs. Crosby, neither of them had any idea what to do next. Eleanor got stuck when she remembered she needed new stockings, unable to get the stockings out of her head, and the fact it was impossible to take Robert shopping. They shuffled in place, darting glances at each other like schoolchildren with a mutually embarrassing pash.

Just at the edge of Eleanor's understanding was what soldiers wanted when left so improperly alone with their girls, if that's who she was; what mothers warned they wanted; what Robert might have had in mind all along without, she half suspected, knowing how to get it from someone like her, even in a hotel, or especially in a hotel, which had panicked him. It simply wasn't *done* with a respectable girl, trusted by her aunt; certainly not with a girl who didn't know how to go about helping him even if she could work out whether she wanted to or not.

She wanted to. Robert would be back at the front in days, where he could die in an instant. Eleanor felt half inside her dream of the African savannah, wading through the waist-high grass, Robert beside her, arm around her, bending down to kiss her, his steady grey eyes reflecting back the golden grass and sun. Gold and grey, colours that spoke to each other. A yawning lion. Humidity that drenched her.

Not that she could have answered if someone had asked whether she loved Robert. If they asked who he was. Who *she* was and what on earth she was doing here.

Yes, she loved him. She didn't know why but she did and it terrified her. What she might lose without ever having it. What she might be better off losing before she learned the value of what she'd lost.

"I wonder if we might try the National Gallery?" she asked in a panic. "I thought . . . since we're having an artistic day."

"Are we?" Robert asked humorously, in his eyes an acknowledgment of all this. Regret? And something else you saw in men's eyes, more elemental. But he didn't push, although she wished he had, instead turning and setting off. It was a long walk to Trafalgar Square and maybe that was the attraction. Ahead he marched, keeping his eye on the invisible horizon. Eleanor knew now that he was marching. Not even when they turned the corner around St. Martin's in the Field did he pause to glance up at the clock—near 2 p.m.—and wonder, as she did, how they were going to fill the remaining three hours until David's opening. How to fill them without ruining everything.

Fortunately, the National Gallery proved to be a network of trenches, at least once you started seeing things in that light. Long narrow galleries, few windows, a heavy protection of ceiling and—what seemed important to Robert—working men who tipped their caps. Maybe he needed Tommies around so he could keep on being an officer. In the gallery, the guards even wore uniforms.

They strolled past the paintings, not really looking, but finally able to talk about ordinary things. Robert's mother wanted to move out of Ackley Castle into a more comfortable house, but his father wouldn't hear of it. His brother had been part of the aerial photography initiative over Neuve Chapelle. Got a battering from the winds, and she was right, they flew motorized kites. But for the first time, they'd mapped an enemy position, giving the old men a leg up on planning the offensive that soon followed. Modern warfare. Too bad about the old-fashioned weather, the torrential rains that were half the reason (but only half) for that particular defeat. Eleanor told Robert that the Hon. Walrus had died at Neuve Chapelle and he said he was sorry, although he didn't sound it.

Their conversation wasn't ordinary. Even a year ago, Eleanor would have been stunned by the death of so many boys she knew, by the number of young widows and bereft fiancées; at the sight of all the wounded lads shuffling through the streets like an army of old men. Zeppelin raids on Vauxhall Bridge, conchies beaten while handing out pamphlets, girls thrusting white feathers at men not in uniform. And Goodwood going to be a hospital, she said. Some Middleford girls were already working as VADs but her aunt wouldn't hear of Eleanor training, not even for Goodwood hospital.

"Quite right," Robert said.

"Please don't say that. I'd like to have a purpose, some role. Lately I seem to be of little more use than a hat stand. And you haven't even noticed my hat."

Robert gave her an amused glance but kept walking. "I think it's up here," he said, having claimed to be looking for a painting. She thought he'd forgotten, but now he stopped in front of a Renaissance work, *The Raising of Lazarus*, Christ on the left lifting one flat palm to Heaven while pointing his other index finger at Lazarus, as if he were gathering electricity from the heavens to spark Lazarus back from the dead. To the right of the canvas was an incredulous-looking Lazarus removing his graveclothes as spectators gaped with shock.

"When my brother and I first saw the picture, we were little horrors. Lazarus, of course, having been dead for four days, and the two of us very well aware of the state of birds and animals dead for half that time, especially in hot weather. Yet there he is, looking ready for a bout of wrestling, and likely to win it."

Robert half smiled, although he didn't seem to see the painting, or was seeing it with Edward.

"Mockery being an effort to cover up fear, of course. I had nightmares after seeing it, Dr. Frankenstein's monster coming after me, the sewn-together body parts. Since here"—knocking his knuckle against the picture frame—"the putrification of the body is made unmistakable by being so emphatically denied.

"You asked why I went into the military," he said, still looking at the painting. "To confront one's fears? Or find some meaning before we become dead meat? Of which, believe me, I've seen sufficient lately."

Robert shrugged. "Probably a little bit of this and a little bit of that, like Mrs. Cook making her cake. But when you get over there, none of it matters. You're there because you're there, just as we're here because we're here. Is there any purpose or meaning?"

Eleanor waited for him to answer his question. When she realized he wasn't going to, she said, "I was thinking lately about the gods retreating to Mount Olympus, but still raining down mockery. If you're right, and mockery is meant to cover up fear, then the gods are afraid of us. Maybe they should be."

Robert blew out his breath, seeming to agree.

"I *do* like your hat," he said, tweaking its brim. Eleanor slipped her arm through his, leaning against him ever so slightly. They walked on silently, not looking at any more art than before, but afterwards finding a place for tea.

David Arden's paintings were of No Man's Land. Not quite the same as the religious works in the National Gallery, but this time Robert was looking at them, circling the gallery. They mostly showed the front from a distance, an indistinct and featureless moonscape of craters and slumped and slumping earth, all of it made wispy by fog or smoke. The canvases were pale, the cloudy light yellow and jaundiced, as Kate had said, something like a pea-souper. The only colour came from a few muted figures in the medium distance holding weapons and sometimes wearing red crosses. They were painted off-centre: slightly abstracted men behaving heroically.

Eleanor walked beside Robert, stopping at one canvas that showed stretcher-bearers carrying a wounded Tommy. Robert kept moving, and after a brief look, she followed him to an image of ambulances moved away from the viewer, ant-like men marching beside them. The next showed ruined houses that on closer examination were functioning as billets with clothes hung out the windows, or maybe blown out the windows, or maybe those weren't just clothes. Here was David returning to all that in his paintings. It made her think of Odysseus visiting the underworld, the ghost of Tiresias appearing and saying, "Why, poor man, have you left the light of day and come down to visit the dead in this sad place?"

Kate had met them at the door. "Don't ask about home. I have to get through this." She'd leaned against Eleanor as Robert nodded and went directly to the paintings, not speaking to anyone else. The images had pulled him, she supposed. There were plenty of other people in the square gas-lit gallery. One was a solitary lurking man whom Eleanor thought must be an official from the Ministry, keeping an eye on things, but most were gathered into fluid talkative groups that broke apart and re-formed—artistic types wearing exaggerated versions of Kate's clothes. Eleanor particularly noticed two tall women, a beautiful one they called Vanessa and an eccentric named Ottoline with hair coloured the same scarlet as the macaws in the London zoo. They intimidated Eleanor, and she didn't know any of the others. On top of which, her aunt was late. Eleanor had soon joined Robert in looking at the paintings.

The final one halted her: a tent of wounded men in rows of beds with nurses working among them. It was as faded as the depictions of No Man's Land and bore more than a slight resemblance to a graveyard with its rows of oblong stones. She looked at Robert, but he didn't want to talk, and began circling the paintings again. Eleanor decided that she'd had enough and turned to look again for her aunt. She still wasn't here, but David Arden had left the other artists to stand on his own. He was wearing his uniform, the wound patch redundant given his hook, and he was watching Robert examine his paintings with something like hunger. At that moment, Robert turned and saw him, and there was an exchange of salutes, not unironical. Each knew who the other must be, although Kate hurried over to introduce them, freeing Robert from a spell.

"Would you like one in your library, sir?" David asked.

"I'll be back there in a couple of days," Robert said.

"I've been trying to figure out a way to get back myself. But they don't seem to want me," David replied, raising his hook. "Despite my cleverly curved bayonet."

Eleanor could see these simple sentences were as laden with meaning as poetry, a code she didn't have the key to. The whiff of discord was enough to draw the artists over, and soon Eleanor found herself surrounded by a discussion of art that sounded equally coded. David's work apparently stood in contrast to an exhibition across town by a group of artists disliked by the talkative man who had arranged David's show, Roger Fry. He was scathing in his criticism of the other artists, who called themselves the Vorticists and portrayed modern life as a machine. Good on David for rejecting the vortical blast, Fry said, taking a stand for impressionism with his fine exploration of light.

Eleanor had no idea what any of this meant. She slipped away to look at the paintings again, not seeing any other option with her aunt so late. Kate's word *jaundice jaundice jaundice* beat in her head, and this time she saw the Flanders of David's paintings as being sickened by war. Following one of the walls around a corner, she was surprised to walk into a small anteroom, and even more surprised to see three canvases with Kate's signature, portraits rather than landscapes, two brightly slashed visions of women and a little boy.

She thought this might be work Kate had done in South Africa when David had gone there for the *Illustrated London News*. She'd written about painting Boer families left without a man by the last war. The boy was elfin and the women were thin, the women's angularity not quite beautiful but striking, challenging the viewer as they stared out from the canvases. Eleanor thought about the literal sense of *striking*. The intensity in the women's eyes struck a blow at viewers. Others might have seen their lives as dun and restricted, as washed-out as David's No Man's Land, but Kate had painted them in colours both raw and intense. Umber. Indigo. Chinese red. The muted grey-green that Eleanor loved.

"She's better than he is, isn't she?" a woman asked.

Turning, Eleanor saw the macaw at her elbow, the tall odd-looking woman. The tall odd-looking *lady*, she corrected herself, registering her more fully.

"I like them," Eleanor said. "But I'm her friend. I don't know what a critic would say."

"She's a woman. They don't say anything."

If they could have talked as openly as the lady seemed to wish, Eleanor would have asked about Roger Fry's motives in getting David an exhibition. Whether he'd done it less to help David than to take a stand against the artists he disliked, the mechanical ones. But the woman's batty imperiousness frightened Eleanor a little and she couldn't seem to frame an intelligent question.

"So you think she ought to be satisfied exhibiting three paintings in a closet?" the lady asked, mistaking Eleanor's silence. "Through the charity of her husband?"

"Not at all."

"So you *dislike* the position of women? When we're rather taunted with just a hint of respect these days. An atom of it, held just out of reach."

The tall lady held her hand up with surprising grace, dangling an invisible something, as if she were holding a sprig of mistletoe. Eleanor was tall herself but the woman had long arms and loomed over her oddly, casting a scythe-like shadow in the anteroom. I'd like to be useful, Eleanor wanted to say, but didn't want to sound naïve.

"So how does one avoid exhibiting in closets?" Eleanor asked.

"Of course, one can't hold it against him."

"Against whom?" Eleanor asked, not quite picking up the thread.

"Against whom are you holding something?" the woman asked. She seemed to want to play with her, even flirt, and feeling slightly panicked, Eleanor excused herself and left.

Mrs. Crosby had arrived. Back in the main gallery, Eleanor found her aunt standing with Robert.

"I seem to have got here just in time to leave," Mrs. Crosby said. "Robert tells me we ought to get to the station. Just let me put down my guinea for one of the paintings. The townscape with laundry, I believe. If that's laundry. Of course, once it's our painting, we can decide for ourselves."

"If," Eleanor said, taking her aunt's arm as she turned, "you don't mind putting down something for me as well, for one of Kate's paintings? The one of the little boy."

A brief hiatus as they went to look at Kate's work, crowding silently into the anteroom.

"You'll notice my niece is loyal," Mrs. Crosby told Robert, embarrassing Eleanor with her insistent matchmaking. "And expensive," she added, taking out her purse.

Robert had stored his kit at Victoria Station, planning to catch the late train to Folkestone. He'd spend the night there before picking up an early morning transport across the Channel. Her aunt had kept a cab waiting outside the gallery and they set off immediately. Eleanor found herself back to monosyllables in Mrs. Crosby's company and Robert was worse, brooding and silent. The streets were empty and coloured a strange medicinal blue by the covered street lamps as anti-aircraft guns boomed from the Heath. The weird desertion of central London meant the trip went quickly but seemed long and fraught. Eleanor was conscious of her last minutes with Robert ticking away. Her last for now, she corrected herself. At least when they arrived at Victoria, Mrs. Crosby said she would wait in the cab.

"I won't say goodbye, Captain Denholm, but *à bientôt*," her aunt said, an odd echo of something that Eleanor couldn't quite remember, one of so many echoes lately.

Inside the station, Eleanor hurried behind Robert as he marched to collect his kit from Left Luggage. He had to elbow a path through a crowd heavy with khaki, many home leaves ending, boys heading south to cross the Channel. Afterwards, burdened with his kit, he elbowed another path to the platform. They stood together awkwardly, not as close as Eleanor would have liked. The train was already in the station and the platform milling with families and sweethearts saying goodbye. Eleanor found the other figures as faint as the soldiers in David's paintings, not quite in focus and oddly silent despite the hubbub, which seemed to mutter above her head. She badly wanted to say something but didn't know what. Robert didn't seem able to speak, either. Finally Eleanor dared herself to put a hand on his chest, feeling the rough wool of his tunic on her palm.

"That painting of Kate's," she said, insisting on meeting his eyes. "I see the little boy as being . . . ours. The son we haven't had, not yet. And if things go as badly as they can, the one we might never have. Because you see, I'll always have him, to think of you, and this day with you. But I would . . . I'd like it terribly," she said, trying not to cry, "if you'd come back."

His arms flew around her and they kissed. Eleanor hadn't known it was like this, but she also did. She felt nothing but his warmth as the train started up beside them: the chuff of steam, a mechanical screech, the flight of panicked pigeons from the rafters. There was a rush to board and jocular comments—"All right, me lad, leave us through"—until Robin finally pulled away. They met each other's eyes and held them until the last minute, when he lifted his kit and jumped onto the train as it was pulling out, standing in the open door to wave goodbye. Eleanor couldn't make herself run after him as some girls ran after their beaus, instead watching him until he, too, was a figure from one of David's paintings: distant, half obscured by clouds of smoke and steam, disappearing, tiny, gone.

1940
Preston Hall, Kent

16

Edward Denholm was the first to telegraph his imminent arrival in Kent, having got his leave in record time after his father's fatal heart attack. Eleanor supposed the Royal Air Force was used to coping with the sudden disappearance of its pilots, the mortality rate for air crews being what it was. And he only had to find his way down from Yorkshire, which Eleanor knew he could do fairly easily, more traffic heading up the trunk line (replacement crews) than came back down.

Eleanor's job in the Ministry involved transportation, and she was used to deflecting questions by claiming it was too boring to talk about, and it was. But the reason she'd signed the Official Secrets Act was that anyone looking into the manifests she filed could figure out the size and location of armed forces bases that the Ministry—not to mention the entire bombed-half-to-pieces country—would rather the Nazis not find out. Edward's base didn't seem to be large, but she had an idea it was important. Robin's most recent letters from a remote corner of Scotland left her pretty sure he was training as a commando, having proved himself so admirably at Dunkirk in the early days of the war. Quite primitive equipment was sent up to Scotland. They seemed to need a lot of rope.

"Education?" the man from the Ministry had asked. Charles Mortlake had been the one to give into her entreaties and set up a job interview. Eleanor had no idea how senior the man was. His name sounded made up. Norfolk. Of course, there were the dukes of Norfolk, but the family name was Howard.

"I was privately educated," Eleanor replied. "My father was a vicar."

Norfolk perked up. Perhaps this was the last place, the last job, where this sort of thing was not only acceptable but preferred. The decayed gentry. Her ancestral home of Goodwood had been half ruined during the last war by being used as an infectious diseases hospital. Its ruin would be completed by this one, the army having requisitioned the poor old girl again, the air healthy and the location remote enough not to distress the citizenry with the sight of the burns cases they planned to send there.

"Can you type?" Norfolk asked.

"No, but I imagine it's not too difficult to learn. And I *do* learn quickly."

"Quite right. But I presume you can spell."

"And add. Maths skills, I suppose. I like words and numbers."

"Crossword puzzles?" he asked, which Eleanor later understood to be a feint toward her suitability for intelligence work, code breaking, which she would probably have enjoyed and been reasonably good at. But that was as far as it went, something she half regretted. Her ideal would be an interesting job and a settled personal life. But given the over-interesting lives they were leading during the Blitz, she was happy to have a routine job busy enough to leave her with little time to think. She was a cog, but (she hoped) a useful cog.

She could also get an idea what was going on, and of course one of the hardest parts of life these days was the constant uncertainty. Picking up information might not have been the best way to get to sleep, but with the nightly bombing raids, the Blitz, no one slept anyway. And she liked it. There was this unpredictable thing: when one did something, when a woman got a job, she was no longer the subject of decisions but played a part in making them. Most women had known that forever, of course. Maids, market women, farm women, factory workers—even though they had only a small part to play in deciding how their lives would go. A miniscule part. But at least Eleanor had that now, too.

On the day Edward was due in, she and her aunt set off on foot to Ackley Castle, petrol being too precious to use when they could walk.

"I was born in a different time," her aunt said, not sounding as if she regretted it. Glancing over, Eleanor saw lines dug more deeply around her aunt's mouth, the stress and time she spent outdoors telling on her. She called herself a farmer now, a steward, with poor Lieutenant Stickley in hospital, although she remained obstinately chic. Their family hadn't quite gone with the wind, no evening dresses made out of curtains, not yet. But she'd had trunks shipped down from Goodwood and rummaged through the attics of Preston Hall, harvesting the clothing of centuries to be remade at night behind their blackout blinds. She and Mrs. McBee sewed determinedly as German planes droned overhead, schools of airborne sharks ready to dive down and sink their teeth into London.

Men's jackets from the last century were particularly useful. Good thick wool. Her aunt was wearing a cut-down jacket with a tweed skirt and a silk scarf that Eleanor suspected had once danced its way around the ballrooms of Yorkshire, having spent its previous life as a panel in the gown of a Crosby miss. Eleanor's own prized overcoat was a handsome chocolate brown lined with grey-green silk and padded with a quilting of old cotton. It had raised envy throughout the Ministry, the other girls twittering. Even Murdo Crawley had stopped her in the street one day to rub the wool between his fingers. "Your aunt?"

Murdo Crawley, MP, who had recently positioned himself on the far right of the Conservative Party, perhaps seeking to distinguish himself in a way he couldn't overseas, if "distinguish" was the right word. He made speeches that were shockingly non-anti-Hitler.

"How *is* poor Alicia?" Eleanor had asked.

"She's not poorly," Murdo had replied, looking confused.

"Holding up. Good soldier," Eleanor said.

"There's Edward."

Aunt Clara nodded across the dishevelled back garden of the castle to the terrace where Edward Denholm stood smoking a cigarette. His mother lived in one corner of the ground floor, a bedroom made beside her sitting room against those times a flare-up in her multiple sclerosis left her unable to walk. These were frequent lately, stress being a trigger. Eleanor expected her to be back in her wheelchair, but she was standing behind the closed French doors, pulling herself up straighter when she saw them.

"I'll speak to him briefly then go to his mother," her aunt said. "You might as well get it over with." Pausing, a hand going to Eleanor's arm. "Oh, my. He does pout beautifully, doesn't he?"

Her aunt sailed toward Edward, leaving Eleanor to follow reluctantly. She hadn't seen him since the Mortlakes' last dance before the war, when Robin was already with his regiment. Everything had gone so badly she didn't really remember it, or at least she didn't want to. Now she was his brother's girl. As her aunt gave Edward her sympathies in a low murmuring burr, Eleanor scuffed the stone with the toe of her boot like a schoolgirl. The ancestral shoes wouldn't do as replacements. She'd bought a pair of sturdy brogues just before the war, a brand favoured by the jolly daughters of admirals, which had never been fashionable but would outlast Armageddon.

Once her aunt was gone, and Eleanor blurted, "My sympathies as well. Of course."

"No one's really sorry though, are they?" He didn't quite look at her. "Including me."

"I'm sure you are, though."

"Life's too short to be stupid about it."

Edward glanced over. She'd forgotten that his eyes were so dark, nearly black. Of course he was handsome; she'd always thought he was handsome, academically, from a distance, while finding Robin far more physically stirring. Edward threw down his cigarette and stubbed it with a well-polished shoe. He was much leaner now. They were all thin these days from the stress and rationing and shortages. Her aunt spoke of Londoners as being unexpectedly elegant amid the smouldering ruins of the Blitz, so many podgy Britons slimmed to actors, cheekbones prominent, their movements gone feral as war returned after centuries to England's green and pleasant land. Beautiful hard-edged young women, their nails sharpened to talons. Dangerous-looking men. The children were minks sliding through the fallen bricks, the ancient stones, the gargoyles tumbled from old churches to grimace at the cobbles.

"In fact, I'm devastated," Edward said.

"I lost my father when I was fifteen. You know that, of course. I really am sorry."

She wanted to go inside but knew she had to stay until he signalled willing. Which he wouldn't, pulling out his packet of American cigarettes and offering one. When she shook her head, Edward began knocking out another cigarette before pausing and flicking it back in. His nerves were excruciating.

"Every happiness to you and Robin, of course," he said, still looking at the packet. "Best man at your wedding, I suppose, if any of us make it." Darting another glance at her. "I presume there's going to be a wedding."

"Nothing official," she replied, and figured she ought to add, "I've told him he'd better get through it, though. I only plan do this once."

"You know what he's training for."

Not officially, either. She shrugged. If you avoided gossip, conversations were half silences these days. "I might be the one not to make it," she said. "My aunt's townhouse hasn't been touched, nor the Ministry, and that can't last."

"So why in God's name don't you stay down here?" He looked around at the dilapidated grounds as if they were perfectly groomed. His inheritance, of course.

Eleanor chaffed him: "A pilot asking me that."

Their eyes met and they smiled, both mordantly amused, shaking their heads. It always came to this. She *liked* Edward. He was quick off the mark. Intelligent. Undependable, although that might have changed. Vain, which probably hadn't. He looked good in his uniform, which hadn't come off the rack.

"You'll have to take me up flying after the war."

"Steal you away?"

She'd thought he was past that. Some American girl. But she was probably long gone.

"You can't be like that anymore, Edward. Can we agree?"

"In that case, you're going to have to find me someone."

"Oh, for God's sake." She was aware of never having said that before, not in quite that way. Everyone was engaged. The Moreland twins. The Browne girl, because why not? All of them could lose everything at any moment, including Kate. David Arden had finally got himself accredited as a war photographer, and if there was an offensive—either side—he could be killed taking pictures. So could Kate, of course, obstinately painting in London, the east-end children central to her sketches, foxes, minks, the babies curled like hedgehogs, wildlife taking over the ruins as the Germans bombed, destroying the city so Hitler could claim his *Lebensraum*, his new territory. Already taken, thank you very much.

"Any objection to widows?" she asked Edward.

"I thought you only planned one go."

"Edward, I'm serious," she said. "Don't."

Robin arrived two days later, bringing his father home for burial in the family vault. Only a senior officer would have been awarded the privilege of transport, even though he hadn't been far away, stationed at Aldershot. Eleanor went to meet Robin at the train station, his mother having ceded the claim. She stood half-hidden by the ticket counter as the train pulled in and watched him jump down even before it stopped.

Robin strode quickly back to the baggage compartment in the rear, talking to the conductor and afterwards turning impatiently to look for someone from the castle. Eleanor signalled behind her and the two old men his mother had sent creaked themselves up from their cart and laboriously wheeled it up the incline toward the station. She'd always hated that sound.

"They're coming," she called, and Robin paused as if electrified before seeing the ancient cart turn the corner and labour onto the platform. When the conductor registered the retainers' age, he helped Edward heft a plain wooden coffin to the edge of the carriage, not that he was a sprig himself. The four of them slid it onto the cart, Eleanor praying for no mishap, and when it was settled and tied into place, the conductor hopped back aboard and signalled the engineer. Without sounding its whistle, the train trundled off.

Eleanor passed the old men on her way into the station. When she reached Robin, he folded her into a long exhausted embrace she never wanted to end.

"I'm so sorry," she murmured into his tunic.

"How's my mother?"

"With your brother," she said, pulling away, "I think in a way she's relieved. She said he couldn't have stood a long illness like hers. Just as well to go quickly, one way or another."

She nestled back against him and they kissed. This time Robin was the one to pull away, still as restless as he was on his last leave.

"I've only got a few days," he said. "We should go."

They found the others in Mrs. Denholm's sitting room, with its tottering piles of books and sheet music and the inadequate fire. Edward sat close to his mother but rose to greet Robin with that brotherly cordiality that Jane Austen called the true English style, burying his real attachment under a calm façade that looked like indifference when they would have done anything for each other.

Burying their attachment and what looked like Edward Denholm's equally cordial wish to murder Robin for snapping her up. Eleanor imagined that had also been part of brotherhood since Cain and Abel, although Jane didn't get into that, or at least not so far. She was reading Austen's novel *Emma* in the cellar at night, enjoying the mismatch between Emma's Highbury and the loud bone-rattling Blitz above. Kate, a firm atheist, was reading the Bible.

"Wherefore, thus sayeth the LORD God: O woe be unto that bloodthirsty city, for whom I will prepare a heap of wood."

"It was a delightful visit, perfect is being much too short."

They couldn't agree on who was more savage, Jane Austen or God.

Mrs. Denholm clung to Robin, and his answering embrace was gentle and patient, even though she held him for a long time, leaning on his tunic, her head barely reaching his chin. Eleanor was surprised: she'd thought Edward was the favourite.

"It's a terrible reason for us all to be together," Mrs. Denholm said, finally pulling away. "Nor would your father have liked it much, taking such a passive role in the proceedings."

Another surprise, her irony as clear as her fondness.

"I'll be leaving the castle for a house in the village," she said, and they all sat down. "We might as well get it out all at once. This is yours now, Teddy." Another ironic look around. "Or it shall be, yours and the creditors', after years of paperwork. I doubt inheritance is at the top of the government list. I have no idea what you'll do with it."

"Speak to my gunner about shooting down a Messerschmitt, I suppose, once you're safely in the village." Edward sat with his hands jammed in his pockets and his legs out toward the fire. "Bit of a challenge to get the angle right, but I imagine we could bring it down directly on the tower. I doubt my latest man's ever played billiards, but his night vision's off the charts. A Canadian." Chewing on this. "You'll take the billiards table with you, I hope."

"One is desolated, really," Mrs. Denholm said. They sat silently for a moment, before she gave herself a shake. "And you, Eleanor, the great heiress, slowly losing Goodwood."

Sting and sympathy. Mrs. Denholm scarcely used to say a memorable word.

"I've never thought of myself that way," Eleanor replied. "It's a pity, though, isn't it? All these lovely old houses that no one can afford to keep up anymore. The past disintegrating behind us. But I suppose that means we can be modern, if this ever ends."

"Not such a fan of that," Robin said. He seemed to be the only one.

"It's barely started," Edward said.

The funeral was the next morning, a hasty wartime affair, although Mrs. Denholm had made sure to have the dean down from the Cathedral, an old school friend of her husband. The surrounding farmers and villagers all came to the service at the small flint-walled local church, making a surprisingly good show of filling the cramped pews.

Taking her seat at the front, Eleanor figured that in olden times the ornate censer-swinging ceremony would have been half an entertainment for the local people, solemnity breaking the usual drudgery of their days. But they all faced enough drama lately and it must have been duty that brought them, or habit, maybe respect for a senior army officer whose experience, they might have hoped, would have kept them from having to fight on the beaches, fight on the landing grounds, in the fields and in the streets, as the prime minister had recently promised; fight in the hills of Kent, which were only a mild impediment between London and the southern coast, where the Nazis might land any day.

The dean spoke and she didn't listen. A good and faithful knight, he said, and then they were singing a hymn, "Oh God our help in ages past." Not so much in this one. Eleanor was mainly conscious of Robin's thigh against hers. The casket lay on a trestle in front, the lid closed despite the colonel's natural passing. Mrs. Denholm had kept the utilitarian coffin but had draped an ancient flat-weave tapestry of St. George defeating the dragon on top. There must have been embalming but it wasn't quite adequate, and the church smelled faintly as London did these days, the overworked wardens unable to shovel up every remnant of flesh, not when houses were tottering, façades poised to tumble into the street, floors to pancake, the wardens under orders (often ignored) not to put themselves at risk of becoming casualties themselves.

It wasn't entirely like London. There was incense in the church, not the smell of cordite. No waft of burnt paper, no stink of sewerage from the not-infrequent times bombs plummeted into the old Victorian sanitary tunnels and blasted up unclean geysers. The smell here was a reminder of ordinary death, not of chaos and battle. Mrs. Denholm gently wept and Robin sat with his head bowed and eyebrows raised, sucking on his handsome mouth as if thinking, He can't really be dead, can he? My father?

After they laid the colonel in the family vault, Eleanor and Robin walked back to the house together. He looked distracted, distant, finally slowing his pace deliberately to let the others get ahead of them. They were soon alone in the overgrown yew walk and he stopped her with a hand on her arm.

"I was thinking we might beg a lift with the dean to Rochester, then pick up a local to London," he said, not quite looking at her. "If you'd like. That would give us a couple of days on our own before your leave ends and I have to get back."

Her heart lurched. Here it was. She felt an impossible mixture of desire and panic, her voice becoming a scratch.

"We're more likely to survive a couple of days in Kent. I can't describe the Blitz when you haven't seen it and, and . . . my aunt can be tactful." Risking a glance at him. "I know that's hard to believe."

"All the damn parental considerations," he said. Half a pout: "It's bloody intrusive."

Something seemed off about his plan, and it occurred to her to ask, "Would the dean really give a lift to an unmarried couple planning a few days in London?"

"I suppose that's my cue."

Robin looked around humorously to make sure they had the privacy for him to kneel.

"No!" she cried, and Robin's surprise looked ready to turn into hurt. "Not like this. Not a vulgar speeded-up wartime . . . I told you I'm only going to do this once, and I don't have a dress. Or flowers."

He seemed to be trying to work out whether this was an excuse.

"It's not an excuse. The dean won't drive us without a dreadful little ceremony. And in fact, once I think about it, I can tell you we likely can't just hop a local to London, even with your uniform. Or I can't. I've already booked a ticket for a couple of days down the line, knowing something about it from the Ministry. My job being . . ." She stopped. "We can walk."

"Nora, that's quite mad."

"You walked to London on your last leave."

"Yes, but I dossed down for a sleep . . ."

"It's getting warmer." Her voice sounded tinny, faintly panicked. She tried to control it. "The wind's turned; have you noticed? Blowing in from the south. Just before the war—I'm quite proud of myself, actually—I bought some tremendously practical footwear at Robert Lewis, including a pair of boots that I've been meaning to take up to London. You need good footwear to make it through the streets these days. Especially when they're not visibly streets." Blocking her throat was an absurd virginal sob. She'd had no idea that sobs could be virginal.

"It's what I'd like," she said, trying again to control herself. "We're both great walkers, I think. It could well be the last normal thing we'll ever be able to do. The Blitz is real, Robin."

A moment's consideration. "All right."

They decided he would say his farewells to his family, telling them only that he was going up to London for a couple of days. No need to mention Eleanor. She would speak with her aunt, who would likely give her a knapsack of farm provisions, but she wouldn't have much else to carry.

Of course, no one was fooled when Robin explained his plan at luncheon, including the rather lugubrious dean, who seemed to spend a moment considering whether to interfere before deciding the matter was beneath him (hierarchically rather than spiritually) and taking more fish. Nor did her aunt try to stop Eleanor when they returned to the Hall. On the old deal table in the kitchen, she packed some Durex into Eleanor's knapsack along with the eggs and cabbages and bacon, giving an embarrassingly explicit demonstration of how to use them. (She was also packing a cucumber.)

"You can have the box. I don't need any at the moment, do I?" An allusion to poor Mr. Stickley that made Eleanor pick up her knapsack and flee for their meeting place in the orchard, finding Robin already pacing and waiting, eating a windfall apple. Then they were off.

17

It was late afternoon, and the day was unusually warm for October. Robin threw down his sour apple as they took the public footpath leading from the orchard into the cornfields. As the south wind continued to blow, the trees bordering the fields rustled with memories of summer. Tendrils of hair blew onto Eleanor's lips, which were damp even though she and Robin weren't talking much. Their plan was to keep off the roads near to the Hall and castle, not being secretive but not wanting to be noticed, either. At every moment, Eleanor was conscious of what was going to happen that night. It gave her a feeling of imminence. No other word.

Robin walked briskly, keeping a step ahead of her. He'd spent his childhood wandering the countryside here and knew every inch. They hopped stiles and crossed cattle guards, and after an hour or so the footpath turned abruptly downhill, where it met a sunken wooded lane Eleanor had never seen before. Robin turned her up the lane, which wasn't much wider than the footpath and had been walked so long it was dug down deeply below the fields on either side. The overhanging trees made the light around them look humid and weedy as a river.

"Like a river, or being in a glass house," Eleanor said.

"Ours is long out of commission."

"The grandparents must have led beautiful lives."

"You don't?"

"A file clerk. They would be horrified. But I'm not."

Robin led her over a stile onto a new footpath that took them up a hilly field where they startled some pheasants that whirred up like fireworks. He said it would soon meet an old road to London once used for driving cattle to the Smithfield market, which she remembered vaguely having heard about and pictured as narrow and rutted. Yet when they reached the road, it proved to be macadamized, still narrow and closely bordered with hedges but smooth enough that after jumping a fence they could pick up the pace.

"Not tired?" Robin asked, as if he hoped she might want a rest.

"It's not even dark," she said.

But the sun was rapidly sinking. Soon they were walking into a peach-coloured sunset that turned the air that rare dusky rose. It picked out berries in the hedgerows, each twig ending in a cluster of jewels, a broach of burgundy pearls, a drift of glass rounded by the sea. The air smelled of woodsmoke and well-tended animals. Robin took her hand, and Eleanor realized she was perfectly happy. Surely you were allowed that once in your life.

Before long, the rose colour faded and the wild animals came out, nosing into the unexpected warmth. Robin dropped her hand to point out a hedgehog trundling along under the hedge. I love hedgehogs, she told him. Not such good eating. Oh, do stop, Robin. Around the next bend, an owl flew in front of them, its big wings flapping like carpet beaters. And there on the hill, two hares leapt joyously up a pasture into the last light of day.

Maybe not so joyously. A fox undulated behind them, looking debonair with his anticipatory swish of tail. Old England. A peaceable kingdom. It wasn't, of course; alive with prey and predators. But it also wasn't war.

At a quiet crossroads, Robin stopped and offered his canteen.

"Not yet, thanks."

"Neither thirsty nor tired." Robin took a swig.

"I'm actually quite fit, despite the city." The growing darkness helped her say it. "I've thought, sometimes, we don't actually know each other very well. I'm the type who needs to be active."

"Some things are pretty obvious, surely."

"What a bore, to be so obvious."

He smiled, leaning close enough that she could see him looking possessive. She was glad he was so pleased with her. Pleased with *them*. Well, she was, too, despite the flutters.

"I *will* have a drink, actually."

He handed her the canteen. Cool water. It must have been icy when he ran it in. The click of cold metal on her teeth fell somewhere between surprising and unpleasant.

"You wanted something stronger?"

She shook her head as they walked on. "Edward would have packed brandy, wouldn't he? The two of you are so different, I'm quite fascinated. Being an only child, I suppose. I have Kate, but I don't think it's anything near the same when you haven't got the same parents."

"I'm not sure anyone has quite the same parents. My father was far easier on me than he was on Ted."

"Does that mean you miss him more?"

"Rather less, probably. I'm afraid my brother minds everything too much."

"I hate to say it, but I find him a little exhausting. Although I do like him."

"I like Kate, for what it's worth. Her husband . . . better in small doses."

"I'm not sure he's coming back." A feeling she had, which meant nothing.

"Because he doesn't care if he does? But there's something thwarted about Arden, don't you think?"

"What a fate. Not wanting to come back and you do." She shook off her earnestness. "So we've settled *him*."

It was almost dark now, although the moon wasn't far past full and would cast a good light. As they walked on, Eleanor felt the hair prickle on her arms, but for a new reason. The Luftwaffe would fly in soon. She hadn't kept track consciously, but since the Blitz had started in early September, she'd been trained like Pavlov's dog. She looked up but there weren't any bombers, and of course she would have heard them first anyway. Nor did they always fly in over Kent. Wind speed and direction, she supposed, cloud cover, weather—fortunately it had often stormed in September—and an attempt to confuse the anti-aircraft gunners. But they would be here soon, and across the country, the AA gunners would be in their positions and even more twitchy than she was. The whole of London would be listening for sirens.

Eleanor looked back over her shoulder to see the stars coming out in the east. There, the sky was already clear and black, while a rich navy lingered in the west. A couple of years ago, London would have cast a light bright enough to cloud the heavens, even though it lay below the horizon. Now, everybody's blackout curtains would be drawn, the watch committees knocking up anyone who left a crack. Finally, busybodies had found a justification. Eleanor suspected the watch of being made up of the same ones, the same type, who centuries ago had denounced their neighbours as witches. Night must have looked like this when the witch-hunters went out hunting, lit only from above, the windmills and hayricks and trees casting giant uneasy articulated shadows under the waning moon.

"What are you thinking?" Robin said. When she paused, he turned amused. "You so audibly *think*," he said.

"How flattering to be paid such attention." Eleanor flounced a little and smiled. "If you give me a penny, maybe I'll tell you I was thinking about the blackout. How nobody likes it, although of course we all know we need it. I was wondering if it's largely because it gives nosy neighbours an excuse to spy."

Eleanor held out her hand, and Robin made a show of fumbling in his pockets for a penny.

"Only shillings, I'm afraid." The shillings in his palm caught the moon and glinted. She took one.

"Now I can add to my art collection."

"Art collection."

"It's a story," she said, as they continued on, the road winding uphill. "It starts with the time my aunt took me to an art opening when I was eight or nine. I was leaned over by an immensely tall woman with scarlet hair. My aunt told me later it was Lady Ottoline Morrell. She apparently said something apposite, although I can't remember what. Mainly she scared me."

"Didn't she die a couple of years ago?"

Eleanor thought so. "It ended up a family joke, how I told my aunt I should like one of the paintings, please. A little boy by Vanessa Bell, Virginia Woolf's sister. My aunt bought it and dunned my father. Who was amused, fortunately. That was the start of my collection, which is my aunt's term. I've also got a couple of Kate's, and some photographs of my parents, Elliot & Frye, and I managed to get a red chalk sketch I wanted out of Goodwood. Praying hands. That's where I might need my shilling. I had to buy the sketch at one of the content auctions. My patrimony. Cost: eight shillings. The creditors wouldn't let me just take it. Nor will they in the final auction, I fear."

"They wanted your shillings?" When she nodded: "I suppose we'll come to that."

They reached the top of the hill and paused. The moon was bright but the valley below had disappeared into mist, which had risen as evenly as cream in a bowl. They could see a short distance into the valley and then there was nothing, a greyish blank, until the moonlit road emerged up the next hillside.

"Ghostly," Eleanor said, and as they descended into the valley, the cool humidity clung to her like a spectral child. The muffling of their footsteps was beautiful, echoing behind them as if they were four, so they sounded like a family of padding animals. There must have been sheep in pastures to their right, the beasts shifting uneasily as they passed. They could only see a few feet ahead, even though Robin had out his flashlight, but he was confident they were still on the old road to London. Nor had they seen any traffic since the mist descended, although as they started uphill again beside a low stone wall, a brief

203

flare of light behind it marked the opened and quickly closed door of an invisible house. A man holding his own flashlight walked out of the fog and onto the road. Farmer, from the looks of him.

"That will be His Majesty's uniform," he said belligerently. "And who's him wearin' it?"

"From Ackley Castle, my friend. I'm Denholm," Robin said. "Glad to see you're keeping an eye out."

The man wavered. "Who's your father then?"

"We just lost him. You can stand down. I'm on my way back from leave."

Unacknowledged by either Robin or the farmer, Eleanor felt herself turning to mist. This is what it's like to be inconvenient, she thought. Robin angled himself half in front of her, even though the farmer refused to see her anyway, because what did she signify? If not a German spy, then a girl freebooting it at night. Freedom was fine for Robin but not for her. When the farmer stood down (as Captain Denholm had ordered) it was still without a glance at her. Grumbling, "Ow right, then," he stomped off into another flare of light and slammed the door.

Eleanor couldn't help giggling into Robin's overcoat. "The invisible woman. Or Mata Hari. I'm not sure which he thought me. Is this woman's role? I should capitalize: Woman's Role. Men either don't see us or can't bear to see us in case we contaminate them. I'd like to think we're advancing, but . . ."

"It would be better to stay off the road. Though we easily could go wrong in the fog."

"Since you're travelling with a seductive spy, that *is* of course a danger."

Then she remembered the Durex and blushed, glad he couldn't see it. In silent agreement, they picked up the pace, Robin soon falling into a march. It was forty-five miles from Preston Hall to London and they couldn't have made a dozen so far. That was lucky given the farmer; people around here knew Ackley Castle. But fame had its limits, and Eleanor was glad when the road began winding through less populated country, hilly country, parts of it wooded. In one long climb after another, they found the heights clear of mist but the valleys so shrouded and humid they half swam through them. Occasional drivers or riders or passersby stopped to challenge them, not thinking for a moment they might be challenged themselves, too rooted in the land and their own rightness upon it.

"And what happens if *we* encounter German spies?" Eleanor asked. They'd just waved on a truck with only its sidelights lit, driven, she was certain, by a black marketeer running meat into London.

"It's all right," Robin told her. "I've got a pistol, too."

"You mean he did?"

"Never took his left hand off it."

"Well, this *is* an adventure," Eleanor said merrily.

"You're still not tired?"

"I shouldn't have boasted quite so thoroughly about my new boots. But I'm fine."

"Up the next hill is a dry old wood," Robin said. Well, here we are, Eleanor thought, and grew conscious of breathing rapidly.

When they reached the heights, Robin led the way over a low wood fence into a stand of trees. It was still unusually warm in the dry heights when they were out of the mist. A humid summer night: how odd for October. The moon was high now and the wood open enough for a silvery light to find its way down to the bracken covering the floor. Its dry fronds rustled against their legs as they took a narrow animal path away from the road. The first leaves had fallen onto the bracken and where the moonlight caught them they glowed like old gold, like fool's gold, like veins of fire to light the path.

Before long, they passed a huge old yew tree surrounded by a crumbling metal picket fence. Ahead Eleanor could make out an even more ancient oak that looked as if it had been building its boles since Elizabethan times. The night was alive with small invisible scurrying creatures, or maybe they were sprites called out by the summery warmth to dance around the toadstools. Pixies, she thought, the word coming to her out of nowhere. She wanted fireflies, but looked up and saw a brilliant watch of stars and that was enough.

Then they reached the oak and there were fireflies, too. Just a few of them, woken to flit up into the branches like newborn stars. "Surely this can't happen," she said, feeling under a spell. There was an owl here, too, on a lower branch, its alert ears visible in the moonlight. The land sloped down again beyond the oak, and Eleanor could see wisps of mist wandering up the hillside to infiltrate the trees. Not see it precisely, but sense a change in the air that turned the more distant trees woolly, so they might have been embroidered on the tapestry of night.

"Here?" Robin said, spreading a blanket from his knapsack under the oak. He seemed determined and eager and slightly nervous, which had the surprising effect of calming Eleanor. She trusted him, and was surprised to realize how deeply she loved him. When they sat down, and lay down in what might as well have been a savannah, she helped him with her clothes, slowly at first. If they survived the war they would marry and have children. If they didn't survive, at least they would have had this.

They were awakened by a rumble. Eleanor bolted upright, finding that mist had risen and shrouded the hilltop, leaving them in complete darkness. No stars. No moon. Robin clicked on his flashlight and aimed it at the forest floor, which let them see each other and a few feet of bracken. They couldn't make out what was approaching from the south, but knew it was the Luftwaffe coming for London. The fleet was still far away and high enough it seemed like the grumble of a distant storm. Nor could Eleanor make out the ack-ack guns and tracers and searchlights that must already be targeting them.

"That isn't . . . ?" Robin asked, knowing that it was but still slightly muzzy from sleep. "Not sure what to do."

"Some people don't bother with shelters, figuring that when their time's up, it's up." Eleanor paused, wondering how much gossip he'd heard about the past month's horrors; the ones that didn't make the newspapers or BBC. "Especially after a bomb gets down the Underground, where people have been told to go to be safe. Although we try to keep news of incidents like that from getting out."

He noticed the unconscious slightly nervous *we.*

"I'm in transportation at the Ministry. It's rather boring. But one hears things."

"How do you cope with the bombs?"

"We've fixed up the cellars, Kate and I. Cots and candles. They're quite deep." Eleanor heard her voice shaking. "You mean now? If the artillery gets off a lucky shot, they might bring a plane down on top of us—or the castle, for that matter, if Edward's gunner is up there."

Robin didn't seem to find it any more likely than she did.

"Sometimes they discharge their bombs randomly on their way back home, whether to 'sow terror,' as the newspapers have it, or because there's been a cock-up in their bomb bay over London. I think a cock-up is far more likely."

"So we're just as likely to get hit . . ."

". . . here, there or anywhere. Unless you know of a cave."

"Bit claustrophobic," Robin admitted, surprising Eleanor. So they shared that, too.

Going silent, they leaned back against the tree and let the bombers approach, which was harder than she would have thought. Her mouth was dry and she was scared—terrified—wanting to run but knowing it was a chicken-with-its-head-cut-off sort of thing. (She had no idea why the thought of chickens frightened her.) The Luftwaffe could have been approaching from the west or east, since Eleanor knew the ears were easily fooled, but it sounded as if the bombers were coming directly toward them, the droning hum of the engines growing louder.

Ack-ack fire blasted from the lee slope of the next hill. Who knew they had artillery there? Bright lights speared into the sky like beacons muzzied by the fog. Then the first bombers were above them, frighteningly loud now, their hum both demanding and insinuating. In two minutes, the first of them would reach London, losing their bombs on the dockyards, on factories in Dagenham. What was left of them. Six straight weeks of bombing, forty-five days and nights of solid vicious *blitzkrieg.* Nights, lately. Every single night, each of them carnage.

The bombers came in endlessly, the anti-aircraft fire a continuous series of shocks in the ground and the air. Eleanor huddled into Robin's arms. The planes were still high up but the drone of their engines was pervasive, a loud industrial chorus from Hitler's Wagner: bass notes and tenor and the occasional soprano scream of descent, all of it blending into an oratorio that went on and on and on and on and on and on. On and on, no end to it, both of them too cowed now to even think of running, transfixed by the power, unable to believe there was so much machinery in the world, so much metal, so much ingenuity and evil and such dreadful, dreadful waste.

We could solve all the problems in the world if we threw half this much effort into it, Eleanor thought.

"So many?" Robin asked.

"They must think they're winning," Eleanor replied. "I don't think so. They might."

One night last month, 185 German bombers were shot down. This was in *one night*, and clearly they'd only got a fraction. The radio said the RAF had lost twenty-five fighters, and read between the lines: Britain was relying on ground fire. The RAF wasn't nearly as well supplied as the Luftwaffe, which, six weeks into the Blitz, was able to throw hundreds of bombers at London again tonight.

"One Messerschmitt came down on Victoria Station last month. That wasn't just a rumour; I saw it. No idea what happened to the crew. Parachutes and POWs maybe. If the crowd got them, they would have been lynched. They don't publish the casualty figures, but there must be thousands dead in London alone, and then there are the Midlands."

From far away, they could sense rather than hear the bombs falling, invisible concussions carried through the air and the rock and soil of the hilltop. Dogfights had started up, the RAF coming in from the north, bringing with it distant fire and the occasional whine of a crashing plane. Nothing close.

"My brother," Robin said. "Usually."

"No," she replied, surprising him. He'd turned off his light but they could see flashes of each other's faces in the weird light-streaked foggy darkness. "I think he drops spies into Europe. I saw the manifest. They send French clothes and shoes to his base."

She shouldn't have said that, but they might be killed at any moment. They probably wouldn't be, but if Edward didn't make it through his next mission, Robin might find solace in knowing how it really happened.

"I sometimes think back in London," Eleanor said, as the noise diminished slightly, the fleet now scattered over the city, the estuary, some perhaps making for Manchester or Liverpool. "Maybe the terror would be greater if it wasn't so regular. But every night: time for tea, finish work, go home. Oh, there go the sirens. Into the shelter. Random strikes might be harder to take psychologically. As it is, people are bearing up."

"I didn't know. I've wondered."

Eleanor imagined pulling back the fog like a curtain to show him a panorama of London in the flaring light of ack-ack fire and searchlights and incendiary bombs, the great city illuminated by man-made lightning that flashed on and off to reveal miles of offices and houses and the snake of a river curving through it. Toy bombers would be banking above it and dropping their lozenge-sized bombs. Puffs of smoke on the ground as the artillery fought them off. Each small volcanic burst of fire would reveal the route of an old Roman road or medieval cow path; reveal the ragged craters of past and present strikes.

It was giving her a headache, but she insisted on picturing the domes of churches, St. Paul's still improbably standing. Looking inside it, they would see fire-watchers hunkered in the rafters, waiting to save history. Looking further down, they would see ARP wardens drinking tea in their makeshift posts, preparing for the moment when local strikes would call them into action. Below them was a layer of families and strangers huddled into their basements, maybe forgiving each other for old mistakes but probably not, and further down in the Underground were people who didn't have their own shelters, or who had been caught outdoors, or who were living in makeshift tents in the Underground stations after being bombed out of their houses, and below even them were the forgotten graves of the plague dead, whose skeletons shimmied at each new strike. Dante's many layers of hell were twenty miles away, a battlefield screaming carnage. With luck, Kate was sitting safely in their cellar reading her unbeliever's bible by candlelight. O woe be unto their city, being blasted into a heap of brick and wood.

Her headache was bad now, pain spearing her right eye. Eleanor could no longer tell what part of the clamour was overhead and what was echoing in her skull. Noise beat inside and out. She held a hand over her eyes, and the next time she took it away she saw a line of shadowy figures passing through the trees. Beyond surprise, she thought they must be elves and fairies in solemn procession. Urging them along was Queen Mab, a long-legged armoured sovereign who strode beside them, light glowing from her braided hair.

A longer look and Eleanor realized they weren't fairies but ancient people robed in linen and broaches: Britons following Boadicea in her fight to save the country. They didn't seem to see Eleanor but trudged along stoically, a long-dead company mustered out of the past to help fight the Nazis. As Boadicea strode past, she turned her long neck and gave Eleanor a look of sorrow and compassion, as if wishing she didn't have to live through this. Her face was the face of Eleanor's mother in her scavenged photograph.

No, it was someone else.

Eleanor slept.

Morning sounds. Bird calls. Eleanor stirred on Robin's shoulder, if that's when she was. She meant *where* she was. Sitting up, hugging herself, feeling cold and stiff, Eleanor found that the night's bombardment was over. It was coming on dawn, and the only remaining sign of the bombers was the distant smell of smoke on a cooler wind. Foul industrial smoke as if a factory had burned. As several no doubt had.

Robin sat up after her, shrugging his shoulders. "Here you are. You fell asleep during the raid. How on earth did you manage?"

"I dreamt that Elizabeth Mortlake was Boadicea come back to save us from Hitler."

Robin barked out a healthy laugh. No better start to the day than bird calls and laughter. As she came fully awake, Eleanor felt amused at herself as well. Another of her glimpses, this one more droll than most. Robin kissed her hair and tried to pull her closer, but it was daylight and anyone might arrive at any minute. She shrugged him away and unbuckled her knapsack, tearing off a loose buckle and shoving it inside.

"My aunt packed us some hardboiled eggs for breakfast."

As she got them out, Eleanor remembered the Durex. Not that she'd ever forgotten it, although she'd been too embarrassed to say anything last night. Seeing it now, her stomach clenched, although she told herself it was unlikely she'd get pregnant the first time, surely. The first two times. And if she did, they would marry?

"A picnic," she said, having to clear her throat because it came out wrong. "A picnic," she repeated more clearly.

"She didn't pack a thermos?" Robin asked, and no, there wasn't any coffee. But they were famished and wolfed down bread and eggs and pickle. After one long pleased look at each other and a longer kiss, they brushed themselves off, Eleanor picking dried bracken off Robin's coat before they got back on the road. And she was right; the world was stirring. As they clambered over the fence at the edge of the wood, a farmer crested the rise with his horse and cart, startled to see them and pulling the dray to a stop.

"Can I help you, Captain?" he asked, making it clear he had no suspicions they were spies but was quite certain about everything else.

"Quite all right. Carry on," Robin said, sounding the very pattern of English manhood, as Eleanor could now attest he was. The farmer saluted him ironically and drove on, leaving Eleanor to take Robin's arm as they hiked the last twenty miles into London, slowing down in Greenwich to marvel at the damage: the knocked-down houses and offices and an upended still-smoking lorry from last night, a steel-helmeted bobby directing traffic around it, one of the heavy rescue crews working on a collapsed naval office where they must have thought there were survivors, a street glittering with shards of newly broken glass like drafts of unmelted hail; all this, and surrounding it, block after block of intact buildings that bustled with ordinary life.

A store with a queue out front where a shrill woman complained about rising prices. Several homeless families dossed down in the tunnel under the river, a ropy old grandfather looking senile and lost, five or six children kicking a can up and down the tunnel with a hollow echoing rattle. When they reached the west end, playbills advertised reviews outside theatres, and a doorman touched his cap as they walked by his hotel, a shallow crater still sending a thin plume of smoke into the road. London was a patchwork, a motley, a mosaic. The destruction was terrible but life went on.

They found her aunt's townhouse still undamaged and a note from Kate on the front table. She'd gone to the hospital, having got permission to draw children in the casualty ward, and would doss down there for the rest of the week. Reading her scribble, Eleanor wondered if Kate had received a telegram from her aunt suggesting she arrange to be away or whether this was a coincidence. In either case, she and Robin would have two days completely alone before she was due back at the Ministry and Robin had to carry on north.

"So this is what it's like these days," he said, looking around the dark sitting room, where she and Kate had stacked mattresses against the windows and upended the dining table to hold them in place. Eleanor turned on the light to show him that the room was otherwise cozy with chintz armchairs, her aunt's well-polished occasional tables, and the family portraits they'd salvaged from Goodwood smiling dustily from the walls.

"Two days," she said, knowing that two days could be forever.

18

The townhouse would be destroyed six weeks later when the terrace block took a direct hit from an incendiary. Eleanor and Kate would be safe, having been caught out shopping and forced to take shelter in the Underground. Four days later, Edward would be reported missing in action, and they would have an anxious eleven-day wait before news finally arrived from the Red Cross that he was a prisoner of war in France.

Of course, Eleanor knew about none of this during her two days with Robin, when they used up the box of Durex and ate everything in the knapsack but the broken buckle. Yet she also half knew or suspected it. Maybe it was just that she was expecting it, although it seemed to be more than that. With Nazi bombs excavating London, Eleanor was conscious of living inside a palimpsest of past, present, and future. Boadicea, the Blitz, the ruined townhouses, the brutalist modern terrace that would replace them. (What on earth was brutalism?) Anything could happen, and would, and did. She was increasingly subject to headaches, which made her feel as weak as a pebble washed to and fro by waves beating ashore. That had always been a woman's role, to be to-and-fro'd by more powerful forces (men), but Eleanor had hoped that was changing.

After Robin left, she tried to talk about this with Kate. But Kate was working obsessively, painting the children of the Blitz. David's children, really, Eleanor thought. Nor could she find a moment to speak with her aunt when she came to town to see what remained of the townhouse. Three proved to be a crowd, the third being her aunt's old friend the Countess of Wigan, George Wiggins, the female impersonator. Instead of joining Eleanor and Kate in their new Bloomsbury flat, Aunt Clara was staying in the countess's recherché walk-up in Soho, and her friend came along everywhere.

Dinner at the Café Royal, a brief silent inspection of the new flat in Bloomsbury followed by a quick walk back to Soho, where they made plans to meet at the townhouse the next morning. The countess proved impossible to shed: an immensely tall pigeon-fronted dowager who had taken to staying in character as if her corset were a portable shelter. They all had their Blitz ticks, the irreligious crossing themselves, the unsuperstitious leaving their houses right foot first. The countess always wore her coifed blond wig, her stage name having as many layers of puns as London did history. A constant presence—a Presence—and curiously intent, she seemed to know that Eleanor had something to say and wanted to hear her say it.

When Eleanor arrived at the ruined townhouse the next morning, she found her aunt already outside with the countess, who was wearing a caped greatcoat from the Goodwood trunks that had survived the moths, most of them, since the age of Beau Brummell. Eleanor was already fighting a headache when she saw that the block of houses in the terrace was reduced to a line of ground-floor façades. All that was left of her aunt's graceful two-hundred-year-old residence was a pair of open arches that had once been windows and a gaping doorway opening onto a litter of bricks and charred timber. The chintz and tables and ancestral portraits from Goodwood had been reduced to ash, while Eleanor's small art collection, whatever was left of it, lay underneath tons of debris. Sheer chance that she and Kate weren't with it.

As they stared at the ruin, a dusty old man in a cloth cap ambled up and sat down on the front steps, opening his thermos and pouring himself a beaker of tea. He didn't seem to see them, or wasn't concerned that they were watching, or maybe he was in shock from his own losses.

A long silence before her aunt finally said, "Fortunately the lease is almost up. Ninety-nine years in the family. Now it's the Duke of Westminster's problem. Part of his problem. He owns half of London."

"The strength of arches," the countess said, still intent on the façade. "An engineering marvel. How unfortunate that my own have fallen so disastrously."

Six weeks earlier, on their single foray out of the townhouse, Eleanor and Robin had stumbled on a playbill advertising a matinee by the countess in a Soho club.

"My aunt's friend," Eleanor had said. "Oh *let's*."

Her aunt's friend? Robin had trouble grasping this.

"The countess told me recently that your father was right," Eleanor said. "After her first husband died, my aunt went onstage as an actress. There was some sort of delay in getting Preston Hall, legal problems and so on, and she had to support my cousin Hetty."

Touching his arm. "Our secret. She hates anyone knowing. Although I don't think the problem is that she went onstage. More that she was dreadful. 'I couldn't help myself. I *simpered*.' In any case, she met my uncle at the stage door, and I hope they were happy. I think they were."

"I don't mind for myself," Robin said, still looking at the playbill. "But I wonder if you know who's going to be down there."

Eleanor's look got him through the door. They had to stop at the bottom of the stairs for their eyes to adjust, the club being as dim as a wine cellar and just as well-stocked. Glasses littered the small round tables, half-filled with spirits or recently emptied, the ice cubes still not melted. Soldiers of all ranks sat crammed together with their girls on the main floor, while a few steps up around the edges of the room were longer rectangular tables of homosexuals, fairies (as her aunt said she wasn't to call them). Whistles and blown kisses greeted Robin as he led the way toward an empty table.

"Oh, I see," Eleanor said, as he held out a chair. "You mind being here because of *me*."

"I went to Eton," he said, sitting down across from her. "The bullies were the ones I disliked, actually."

The club lights dimmed, a single spotlight flipping on to light the bar stool onstage. The countess came on casually to applause and whistles, sitting down, making a point of shielding her eyes from the spotlight to look around the club, nodding at one or two men and pausing for a second of barely perceptible surprise when she spotted Eleanor, who waved gaily. She'd always liked the countess, whom she had once thought was a real countess, an amusing throwback, born in a different time. In fact, she was as sharp as a knife and as modern as—whatever the fashion was lately. Short skirts and bravery.

"The Blitz," the countess began, and waited for the hubbub to settle. "The Blitz. These days we talk about nothing but the Blitz. But have you noticed that the Luftwaffe is as unreliable as *men*. Discharging its load"—pausing to raise her eyebrows—"either too early"—the first guffaws—"or far too late, long after a lady has lost interest. Lying in the shelter thinking, Oh, *do* get this over with. I'd much rather paint my nails. Or pump some water from the well. *Pump* the well. Pump, pump, well, Clark Gable. As Herr Hitler pounds away, heil, heil, heil, no more able to get us off—stage, my dears—than a decidedly unmagical frog . . ."

Laughing, shocked, and enjoying it, Eleanor looked around the room and was startled to see Mr. Stickley at a rectangular table, Lieutenant Stickley out of uniform and (obviously) out of hospital, sitting with a group of homosexual men, with whom he looked at home. The Stick had been hospitalized for breaking up under pressure. The penny dropped, half-heard comments about a chap he was fond of being killed, poor Stick going mute, Charles Mortlake having to pull strings. The unused Durex.

Oh, that's it, Eleanor thought. Funny old world.

At the bombed-out townhouse, the countess held Eleanor back as her aunt went up the steps for a closer look.

"You won't tell Clara about seeing Gordon Stickley at my show."

She'd been so limpet-like because she'd thought Eleanor was planning to. "But surely she must know. I mean about . . ."

"She doesn't want you to know. Her innocent flower."

"My aunt gave her innocent flower a box of Durex."

"If you expect people to be logical, my dear, your life will be one nasty surprise after another."

"I like surprises," Eleanor said. "Especially the most recent."

She meant surviving the bomb, but the Durex was on the table, wasn't it? The countess arched an eyebrow and Eleanor couldn't help smiling, giggling despite her headache, making the countess titter until they met each other's eye and broke into roars of laughter. The house gone, the ancestors gone, her art collection buried, her life barely saved, but sex, and well, glorious sex.

Aunt Clara called irritably, "Surely you can't find this amusing."

"Mustn't succumb," the countess called back. "As my old friend Mae West likes to say, usually before doing so."

"You know Mae West?" Eleanor asked, feeling giddy from her headache. "As well as Beau Brummel?"

Even the old man on the steps was staring at her.

"Just a little joke," she said weakly.

1951
Middleford, Connecticut

19

Eleanor's headache was dreadful, worse than any she'd ever had. Her life was supposed to be moving forward like everyone else's, but this recent cascade of migraines kept throwing her back into the past. Boadicea, the Blitz, the Sepoy Mutiny written up in the newspaper, *today's* newspaper, poor Stansfield Mowbray driving a Rolls-Royce around the corner again and again and again.

Eleanor had always seen odd things. Yes, she had, even during the Regency. But lately so many images crowded in that she slept fitfully and spent her days dreading another attack. Doctors had become a threat, the world crazed with cracks she could fall into—places, time, other lives—as if something kept breaking the screen of her aunt's television set and sucking her through it.

She turned it on. The CBS evening news, a report on the House Un-American Activities Committee. Murdo Crawley was there in the background, trying to reach the foreground. Congressman Murdo Crawley, who had positioned himself on the far right of the Republican Party. Her headache was so bad that Eleanor couldn't remember how she'd met him, but the name was unforgettable and she knew he was married to Kate's sister Alicia.

Who was Kate?

Eleanor turned off the television and paced the room. She had no idea who any of them were—Kate, Alicia—but told herself that her name was Eleanor Crosby. She'd done this lately during her headaches, holding onto herself by her fingernails. My name is Eleanor Crosby and I live at One Goodwood Road, Middleford, Connecticut, U.S.A.

The World, she'd written in school notebooks. The Solar System, the Galaxy, the Universe.

"Which universe?" said a voice in her head. She had to fight it off.

"Eleanor Crosby," she repeated.

She lived with her Aunt Clara (Goodwood Road, Middleford) having been back home since finishing college two years ago. Aunt *Clara Crosby*, she insisted, who had moved here from England after the war, sailing over to claim this old clapboard house left to her by her second husband. It had once been his family home, then a private hospital, but the poor old girl had been abandoned for years, haunted, they said, by more than one ghost.

Some might claim the ghosts were the root of Eleanor's problem, but she didn't think so. She didn't remember seeing one, although she clearly remembered her aunt setting up a dressmaking shop in the parlour and calling herself a couturier. Aunt Clara had taste and Eleanor did the books, and she told the voice, the ghosts—which weren't there—that she would do them until Robin got back from Korea and they got married.

A sob at the thought of Robin, serving at the front. Captain Robert Denholm, U.S. Marine Corps. His brother, Teddy Denholm, was a pilot shot down not long after the start of the war (police action, according to the president). He was a prisoner of war, and Robin had to fight to get his brother back.

I am . . . she thought, and had trouble continuing. I am, I was, Eleanor, born in England, as was my aunt.

So was Kate. Where was Kate? Who was Kate?

Eleanor couldn't go on. She was too dizzy, on the verge of another blackout. (They laced my stays too tight!) When she told the doctor what was happening, or part of it, he said she was suffering from stress, from nerves. He warned her to slow down, take care of herself, stop being so intense or . . . she stopped pacing to consider it. The implied threat of hospital. Of one of *those* hospitals, which her aunt couldn't afford, not a good one. All of which Eleanor found unfair because whatever was wrong didn't feel internal but imposed from outside.

Not ghosts, no connection to the television, and her aunt didn't believe the theory Hetty sent from India that it was reincarnation gone wrong. Maybe it was a case of radiation from the nuclear tests disrupting her mental ganglia, if that's what they were called. Eleanor had liked biology but had been distracted in class by sharing a lab bench with Margaret Darcy, whom she'd disliked; she couldn't remember why.

"It comes from outside, not inside," she'd told her aunt. Last night?

"You can't say that to the doctors. They won't like it." Hand on her forehead, feeling for a temperature. "Promise me, Ellen. I'm trying to keep you at home."

But now a fissure opened in the air and without moving, Eleanor was through it. She felt breathless this time, her eyes open on darkness, aware of standing in a London street before dawn. Her back was tight to a damp plaster wall as a *creak-crack, creak-crick* slowly heaved toward her. *Creak, creak, crack.* She didn't want to hear it. Didn't want to see it. Wanted it to pass by and knew that it wouldn't, that it would stop at her house and take . . .

Father!

1665
London

20

Sickness was abroad, plague ransacking the city. They had stayed in London so her father could minister to his parishioners at a time when it was difficult for them to understand God's purpose and they cursed Him in their grief and their pain. Eleanor could have left with her uncle and aunt, who had secured permission to take their household to her aunt's estate in Kent. But her father had insisted on staying and Eleanor had stayed with him, having refused her aunt's entreaties to come away.

"Now see here, Nell," her father had said three weeks ago, as her aunt packed up noisily, shouting at the servants, shouting at her father to make the girl see sense. He had called Eleanor to his room, where she had turned briefly to look at his rich tapestry of Eve offering Adam an apple. Turning back, she found her father sitting at his table in front of the big diamond-paned window that overlooked the garden. It was a good place to read, the river at the garden's end reflecting bright watery light onto the paper. Her father was a man of light, at least these past few years; a broad substantial figure in a parson's coat and breeches who beamed goodwill like a big soft evening cloud with the sun just behind it. That glow about the edges. The warm grace. She had no intention of leaving him.

"See here," her father repeated. "Your aunt wants you in Kent, and you'd better go."

"I will if you come with us."

"Nell, listen to me." Her father paused a moment and surprised her with a change in his manner, leaning forward and clasping his hands on his table, his expression strangely rueful. "I can't go."

"You mean you won't."

He shook his head. Another pause, then he gave a small smile. "There comes a time in a man's life, Nell, when he is called upon to serve his penance. Or do his duty. The two are often interchangeable. When, in essence, God wants him to do what he doesn't particularly care to do. I have prayed on this."

He didn't seem to be speaking to her, then checked himself and met her eye.

"Many don't do their duty. What do we think of them?"

"That they ought?"

"That they are human and fallible, and to be pitied. I don't particularly like to be pitied, Nell."

She didn't understand him when he talked like this.

"Duty, penance, and pride are a powerful combination, and when one adds love of God, one's course is clear."

"And love of one's fellow man," she felt compelled to say, to show she understood this much, at least.

"I've been less good about that. Amusement I can manage, God help me." He sat back in his chair and clasped his hands on his paunch, watching her closely. "I'm speaking of finding a purpose and embracing it. I must stay here, and I wish you to understand my reasons."

Her father had never spoken so seriously to her. He was usually attentive and fond and satirical, as if he was forever in the middle of telling a joke. It came to Eleanor that he was speaking as if it were the last time they would see each other, and that this was the message he wanted to leave her with. It only made her feel more stubborn.

"You," her father said, "have no penance to pay, having had little opportunity to sin. Only a few small occasions of disobedience, as

I recall. You haven't had time to do worse, have you? Your aunt has brought you up well, has she not?"

"I'm very grateful to my uncle and aunt."

"Who wish you to accompany them to Kent. As things stand, one of your sons will be your uncle's heir. Fifteen is young to marry, but circumstances oblige you to take a husband early. Your aunt has thoughts."

Eleanor's cheeks blazed. She wanted to marry a man like her father and hadn't yet met one.

Maybe not exactly like her father. She knew in her heart he would be quieter. Taller. More reliable: a thought she pushed aside.

"Here is your purpose in God's eye," her father said. "You'll spend your life as a wife and a mother. A helpmeet, as the daughters of Eve are asked to be. That is your duty, and it will be your pride. I hope it isn't your penance, although I know your aunt will choose well."

"But I'm not yet married, is it true, Father?"

"Eh, what?" he said, recognizing the start of one of their debates, amusement igniting his eyes. He had trained her in logic, in Latin and a little Greek, and had given her a glimpse of mathematics. He liked to spar with her, saying (as she had heard him say to her uncle) that it was like being attacked by a determined little sparrow.

"I'm not yet married. Is it true?"

"I humbly agree."

"And therefore my duty is to my father. My purpose is to serve him. My pride is in making him comfortable so that he may serve God."

Her father chuckled, but seemed moved. She went to him, winding an arm around his neck and kissing his cheek. "If God wants me, he can take me as easily in Kent as he can here."

Her father had no answer to this. It was what people said when they chose to stay, or if they had no prospect of leaving, as was the case among the great body of the poor. Those who had started fleeing—the king and his court to Salisbury, the peers riding off to their estates, wealthy commoners like her uncle and aunt packing up for their houses in the country—preferred to say that God helped those who helped themselves. Resignation was suspiciously close to the religion of the Pope and antithetical to the muscularity of the Protestant faith.

Eleanor had overheard her father say precisely this to her uncle: God can take me here in London or in Kent or while I'm riding a unicorn across Hy-Brasil if he prefers. I'm more concerned with whether he will like what he sees when he does.

"My poor child," he said, kissing her hair.

When her aunt learned that Eleanor was staying, she passed her in the hall with a fierce hiss and slammed into her father's room. Eleanor followed on soft feet, intending to listen at the door. But her aunt's French maid loomed over her when she got close, yanking her away by one arm. They began a silent tug-of-war, the maid under orders to keep her from eavesdropping, Eleanor trying to escape, until finally she managed to break free and slap the maid's cheek.

Really, the Frenchwoman wanted to hear as badly as she did, and having obeyed her mistress as nearly as she could, she signalled truce so they could lean their ears against the door together. Inside was an argument about God's will: whether he was testing them with the pestilence or whether the plague was the work of the devil. Her father and her aunt couldn't agree, although Eleanor heard her aunt say very clearly, "Whether or not he's testing us, William, I wonder whether in staying here, and keeping her here most pridefully, you mean to test God."

The next morning, her aunt and uncle joined a flood of refugees jostling toward the city gates, swearing when they jammed at corners, cartwheels clattering together. The great bulk of gentle London had concluded on the same day that it was time to flee in a crowd Eleanor recognized without ever having seen it before.

Her uncle planned to cross the river at London Bridge so they could turn south, and Eleanor and her father walked beside their carriage toward the bridge, Eleanor holding tight to her father's hand. She felt sorry for the poor whipped horses, the lost urchins, and discarded servants crying piteously to be taken. Her aunt was more benign than many, taking most of the household and leaving principally those who refused to go, Cook chief among them. Cook had survived the plague before and said she intended to do so again. Among the rest were guards charged with protecting her uncle's property, uneasy men well armed.

Eleanor was afraid her aunt and uncle would try to snatch her at the bridge, but the way was so packed that her aunt had no hope of even opening the carriage door, and her uncle sat high on the box with his coachman. As the crowd pushed them back, her aunt could only turn her face from the window while her bullish uncle called down, "William," as if saying her father's name would pin him to the world.

Elbowing back through the crowd, they soon reached home, where her father shooed her inside before leaving to meet his sexton. After barring the doors, Eleanor faced the desolate hall and looked terror in the eye. Her heart beat like a rabbit's and her breath panted in and out until her chest hurt. Propelled into a run, she clattered downstairs to the kitchen, where she found their squint-eyed cook sitting by the fire.

"So yuh didn't scarper," Cook said. "Stubborn, you are."

A cat sat on Cook's lap, one of her pride of watchful beasts. They were half the reason she wouldn't leave, rumour having it that the Lord Mayor planned to kill the city's cats and dogs to halt the spread of plague. "And mine a healthy breed," she'd told Eleanor's aunt, having improved the race like a pigeon fancier, drowning runts and mating the better mousers. Her cats were now smarter than dogs, she claimed, and famous for keeping her storerooms free of vermin.

"Hullo, Pisser." Eleanor tried to hide her panic by patting a big tom. "Want your ears scratched, do you?"

"You're not expecting to eat?" Cook asked.

"When my father gets home."

"Not feeling sick, are ye?"

Shaking her head, she forced herself to sound casual. "I'm going to bring my book and sewing down here, so you'd better get used to it."

"Put you to work peeling tatties."

"No, you shall not."

She loved their old cook and gave her a kiss before skittering upstairs for her things and running back down, scraping a bench toward the fire.

"You won't go out," her father had said at the door, and there wasn't any chance of that. Nor did Eleanor have to, the gardens yielding well in the mockingly fine weather, the chickens laying and the piggery grunting with piglets just as the household diminished. It wasn't only loyalty to her uncle or father that made her uncle's men protect his walls, chasing out known shifters and priggers and former soldiers limping home from the Dutch war, which continued as heedlessly as the sun kept rising.

Eleanor tried to distract herself, sewing and reading to pass her days while her father was out. With neither maids nor friends in town, she was left with few companions. But her disposition was active, and before a week had passed, Eleanor found herself walking in circles around the empty house as if it were a cathedral and she was doing stations to plead for God's mercy.

Then came a day, after rain, when Eleanor lingered at the door as her father girded himself to go out. ("The poor souls. It's a miserable death.") After closing and barring the door, she leaned against it, everything as usual except that her fear had invisibly dissipated and she realized she was bored. Grabbing her cloak, Eleanor put her head outside to make sure her father had turned the corner. Then she slipped out, her pattens pattering on the cobbles, wanting to learn what was going on.

The city was empty, the few passersby as silent as shadows, hoods drawn, hands up their sleeves, so any one of them might have been Death out walking. Few carts, no sedan chairs. Eleanor found the silence stony and uncaring, and more than once had to start away from vermin swaggering out in broad daylight. A pair of rats fought over slops in the middle of Threadneedle Street, shrieking like scraped metal.

Beyond them, she saw a cobbler they often used walking toward her. She was about to greet him when she saw the ravage of his face. She realized that his walk was a shamble and told herself, He's walking to his grave. She pictured him lurching to the churchyard and unfastening the gate and finding a vacant hole to fall into.

A tug on her arm. Startled, Eleanor found a beggar woman at her elbow.

"Please, good young lady. My children are starving. For my children, young lady."

"Away with you," said an old voice behind her.

A look of panic on her face, the beggarwoman scrambled off.

Eleanor turned to find the Scotswoman watching her, the Widow McBee: tiny, tattered, her hands wrapped in rags. She was far from terrifying, but Eleanor's father had got her appointed as a searcher of the dead, one of two old women in the parish whose job it was to inspect bodies and name the cause of their dying. Not even a beggar wanted to breathe the same air as a searcher. Her father said the power of naming was too potent. "In the beginning was the Word, and the Word was with God, and the Word was God."

"Sacrilege, that," he'd said. "I'd ask you not to repeat it if there was anyone left who might understand."

"You shouldna be out," the widow told her.

"I wanted to see," Eleanor said.

"Well, you've seen, and now you'll be off home."

The bundle of rags took her elbow, but Eleanor snatched it back.

"I can go on my own, widow," she said, although she was conscious at each step that the tiny tattered Scotswoman was following her to her uncle's house and making sure she went inside.

They were lucky: their household was healthy. Her father looked tired and pale when his cheeks had always been a bright cheerful red. But despite his exhaustion he showed no more sign of plague than the rest of them, as the city died. Bells tolled endlessly, mournfully, each set in doleful harmony with the others. When the bells of one church went silent, it meant no end to the dying but was a sign that the ringer had died, or the sexton, or the priest—maybe all of them. No one dug graves anymore. Instead, they hacked trenches outside the city walls so the plague carts could tip in their loads and go back for more.

"Nell," her father said one afternoon. He'd called her to his room, and the river light danced across his walls. "My child, it's time to go. Tomorrow I have a chance to speak to the Lord Mayor about getting a certificate of health. Then it's off to Kent."

"We're going?" Unspeakable relief.

"You're going," her father said.

"No, Father!" There might not have been as much conviction in her voice as there had been the first time. "No, Father," she repeated more firmly.

He stood, ready to order her, and staggered. Wheezing, her father put a hand on his table to brace himself. Eleanor had never heard that sound but knew it was wrong. She ran around the table and managed to get her arms around his bulk as he went down, able at least to cushion the blow. She knew she was calling for help although the world went as silent as if God had folded it within a cloth. Her father's lips were moving but no sound came out of them. Eleanor leaned close to try to hear but heard nothing. When she leaned back to look in her father's face, he was staring over her shoulder with an expression she couldn't decipher. Then his pupils widened in great surprise and he sat up in her arms before collapsing dead.

Commotion as Cook rushed into her father's room, followed by her father's men. The men stopped fearfully but Cook ran up and yanked her father's garments over his head to find his underarms free of buboes. The guards stood down. Not the plague. And here was her father's chest as hairless and innocent as a boy's.

"He worked himself to death," Cook said. "A saint, he were. A ministering angel."

Cook elbowed Eleanor out of the way and got the men to lift her father onto his table, papers shoved by rude elbows onto the floor. There was a great deal Eleanor didn't grasp or later remember, although Cook permitted her to help wash her father, and that she would never forget.

The Widow McBee was there. Eleanor didn't know when she arrived nor understand why she was arguing with Cook when they seemed to agree. Cook said it was an apoplexy and the Widow McBee said it were, and Cook said she wouldn't get more nor her groat she was owed for telling *Them* it weren't the plague. Because it weren't, she insisted, and the Widow agreed it weren't, and said she wouldn't take more than she were owed, not from his reverence. Nor indeed would the puir good minister go to his own grave, she told the cook, Eleanor crying out in shock but the widow saying the sexton and the gravediggers were dead, all dead. A funny look on Cook's face when she said that then *They* didn't have to know it were Himself gone, just a man from the household. They could all stay safely here, could they not, and the widow agreed once more, turning down the extra groat Cook now offered, a refined expression on her dirty face.

Then Eleanor was standing outside her uncle's house before dawn. Her back was tight to the damp plaster wall as a *creak-crack, creak-crick* slowly heaved toward her. *Creak, creak, crack.* She didn't want to hear it. Didn't want to see it. Wanted it to pass by and knew that it wouldn't.

The door opened behind her and the men carried her father to the plague cart wrapped in his winding sheet. The Widow McBee was still there, first of all murmuring to the men on the plague cart and then saying to Eleanor, "Come now."

"We're to go with them?"

Cook gave her a basket and embraced her for a long time. When Eleanor was free, she found the cart creaking up the street while the Widow McBee tugged her in the opposite direction.

"Come now. We're for the stairs."

"Why for the stairs?"

"A Scotsman with a punt there to take us cross the river, ur-en't there?"

Eleanor didn't understand. The widow kept tugging at her arm.

"To get you to your uncle in Kent."

"But I don't know how to get there."

"Wull who's going to take you, isn't she?"

"But if you know a way out of the city, why didn't you leave before?"

"Dudn't have where to go, dud I?" A crow of triumph from the widow: "But won't they be glad to see me now, and what I bring!"

Eleanor's legs were saplings with thin roots bursting through her boots. They snaked out of her, wormed out of her to insinuate themselves under the cobbles in search of good soil. They were stealing all the vigour out of her and pulling her into the ground, under the ground like her . . .

"I can't!"

"Come, little mistress," the tiny ragged widow said, urging her onward. "Come on now. Come, my sweet. We'll get you safe. We'll get you home."

1589
London

21

"Right now!" her aunt cried. "He's disgracing the family, raising a cup with godless rogues."

Eleanor kicked the rushes on the floor, having no intention of obeying her. She was eleven years old and didn't like being ordered around like this, not anymore.

"I said . . ."

"Now, Clara, don't be a scold."

Her uncle spoke mildly as he looked into the hall, making her aunt droop in dismay. Eleanor's uncle was the arbiter, taller than her father, more muscular, hawk nosed and masterful. Her aunt still looked at him as if they were sweethearts. Lady Anne Mowbray had once called her craven. "He walks this earth like the rest of us, Clara, and not an inch above it."

"I only mean to say," Aunt Clara said, "the girl can bring your brother back from the tavern when no one else can."

He thought about this. "Then you'd better go," he told Eleanor, and she ran.

It was still light as Eleanor dodged through the streets, wanting to make good use of the last of the sun. She darted first into the Hart, already knowing that he wasn't there. Afterward she ran breakneck to the Boar's Head, where she'd dreamed he was drinking, which made it true. The Head was dark when she clattered inside, the room crouched under oak beams and smelling of smoke and hops and roasted mutton, dust motes tumbling through the circles of candlelight.

Eleanor stopped just inside the door, letting her eyes adjust until she could look around the crowded room, waiting for a glimpse. She didn't really know what *glimpse* meant, but the word had come to her as words sometimes did. The Boar's Head was a jolly place, home to a club of players. They were always raucous, and today they were joined by a complement of sailors, rude men who had brought exaggerations home from their war against the Armada, so her father said. She couldn't see her father, even though she knew he was there, the Head halfway to being his hearth and home—this despite the fact he was a minister of the Protestant religion. (Recently, it was true, without a church).

At the longest table, Eleanor saw her father's friend Kit Marley standing with his tankard raised. He was reciting something she couldn't hear above the hubbub, a poem or a ditty, maybe even a speech from the play he'd written, which her father said had made a what-ho-ho on the stage. Marley was enjoying himself, twisting this way and that, toasting his company, who roared back laughter and oaths. Eleanor thought she saw her father behind Marley as he swayed, and in a crouch she dodged among the tables followed by cries of, "What's that? A rat? A ferret. William, they've loosed your ferret upon our liberty," until she came to her father and looked up at him in his chair and saw the redness of shame on his face.

Eleanor didn't like to think she'd shamed her father, and told herself it came from Marley saying godless things. Her father clapped her head against his chest and put his hand over her other ear and hoisted her to leave, legs dangling. With a push and a shove, they were in the street, where her father put her down, exhaling a fug of ale. His belch.

Eleanor was proud of herself. It hadn't taken long, just sunset now, a rare rosy glow reflecting off the cobbles. She took her father's hand, but they'd taken only a few steps when there was a hubbub ahead. Turning the corner were guisers, mummers in bright motley holding their horned masks under their arms—a deer, a goat, a big-eared horse—their tunics of bright stitched-together rags making them look like walking church windows. Eleanor was interested to see the guisers strolling in casual file, not performing now, not a parade, but on their way to a masque. A sailor without legs scooted among them on a rollered board, making himself into a jester.

"There shouldn't be a masque," she told her father. "It's not yet midsummer."

"Some nobleman has decided that it is."

"May we follow them?"

"No, we may not."

Eleanor prayed her hands up at him.

"It can come out of nowhere," he said.

Eleanor didn't know what he meant, and her father, in his cups, couldn't remember, either. She saw a look of confusion on his face that often preceded him saying, "I must get past this."

Then the horse mask caught his eye. "A stallion kicked you very badly when you were small."

She remembered that and nodded. Together they looked at the mask and burst into laughter. Genial now, her father let her follow the mummers. Eleanor forgot she was supposed to bring him home and began dancing behind the horse-head, her feet skittering and hands raised, and when the mummer glanced back and saw her dancing, he joined in and the others followed, and then their small procession was a parade.

61 AD
Londinium

22

The Britons were advancing on the settlement, led by their queen. They said she was as tall and bloodthirsty as a man, hell-bent on driving Rome out of Britain. Eleanor had a memory of seeing Boudica in a forest striding along, beside her silent people dressed in cloaks and broaches, but when she said this, her aunt told her she was mistaken or having one of her dreams. Then she checked herself and asked Eleanor's father if it was a portent. The girl was rampant with dreams lately, if they were dreams and not visions. An inconvenient time for this, and she wasn't yet nine years old. But was Eleanor waking into the role of oracle?

It was dawn, their villa frantic as the slaves packed up their household, throwing goods helter-skelter into the wagon, tables piled on top of chests and afterwards the cauldron, still with a rope of garlic hanging out of it. Baskets of her aunt's five-toed chickens waited cluck, cluck, cluck by the door until they could be put on top. Eleanor would have said the chickens were the portent, and not a good one, although she didn't know why.

"Eleanora." Her father knelt in front of her, speaking as seriously as befitted a high priest of Bacchus. "Describe your dream to me. Did you have it last night?"

"I don't know. Yesterday morning?"

"Not at night. You were awake."

"It was night, what I saw. They were in a dark forest and at first they were like tree trunks but then they started moving, and she was beside them. Hurry up! I don't mean she said it. Just that she wanted them to hurry."

"Were there a lot of them?"

"It was strange. I looked up and there was a comet in the sky. So many comets, and they were bright and loud. I didn't know comets could be so loud."

Her father stood up, raising his eyebrows at her aunt. Seeing the look on their faces, her uncle strode over. Her father said something to him quietly.

"We're leaving anyway," her uncle replied. As a patrician and a centurion, he would join the governor in his retreat from Londinium, which Suetonius had judged impossible to defend. The legions would regroup further inland. Meanwhile her aunt would take the household to a farm she owned in an obscure corner of the countryside, her aunt being a Briton who had married out. This didn't make her popular among her countrymen but there was acknowledged wisdom in polishing both sides of a coin. Eleanor had heard the adults say that the neighbours would protect them until it was to their advantage not to. Afterwards, her aunt had a plan, in which she'd rehearsed Eleanor. If the Britons won, they were to say that the mosaic in the atrium was a portrait of Boudica, even though they didn't know who it was. The last owners had put it in. Probably someone dead.

"Have you decided where you're going, Father?" Eleanor asked.

He sucked on it a moment. "Better with you."

"The child has grown uncanny," her uncle agreed. "If we have to evacuate Britain . . ." He barked out a laugh. "We'll take her to Delphi in Greece." The prospect of war made her uncle jolly. No one else was.

When her aunt drove their cart through the gates, they found the town in chaos, everyone fleeing the city in a way that felt mysteriously familiar to Eleanor. The poor and the useless ran back and forth wailing and shrieking, hanging onto wagons, begging to be taken along. No one answered, treating them as if they were already wraiths. Boudica had sacked the colony of Camulodunum on her march out of her own country and her Icenians had massacred thousands. Soon they would arrive here. Gibbeting she liked.

Eleanor exchanged looks with a chicken as they rattled out of the small ramshackle settlement, a young temporary place but with a good port on the river that her uncle found promising. He'd been thinking of staying on, even though her aunt had proved childless. But as he liked to say, her aunt's hair was the colour of gold, an augur of riches coming his way at the far reaches of empire. Eleanor knew the colour was really the work of their Frankish slave (vinegar and bird shit) but her aunt said not to tell him.

Outside town, they found themselves caught inside a great press of refugees bearing south. Boudica's army was marching toward Londinium on the northern road, forcing anyone with imperial connections to flee for the coast.

Outside Londinium, they jostled into a rough file, people further back yelling at the ones in front to go faster, one red-haired man trying to bull his chariot to the front and being cursed back. Eleanor hated it, tossed between the rough boards of the wagon and the cauldron with every lurch of the wheels, quickly bruised and often sneezing from the stench of the chickens. She was grateful as the sun rose higher and the wagon train began to thin out, carts pulling away as families turned toward their country properties.

Finally enough of them were gone that her father let her get out and walk alongside the horses, exercising her cramped legs. Eleanor was happy now. The sky was high and the sun was warm and the remaining people were jollier. But the farm was a long day's journey from town, and by late afternoon, they'd left the main road far enough behind that they found themselves alone.

Eleanor's father said they were safe, that Boudica wouldn't look for Romans on a lost road like this. But her aunt replied grimly, "I have more respect for my sex." When a hawk flew above them, angling and swooping, following their path, she called it an augur and made Eleanor get back in the wagon. Whipping the horses, her aunt urged them up and down a steep hill until the hawk was gone and the horses lathered. Then she ordered Eleanor to get out again and walk as if it was all her fault.

The hawk didn't worry Eleanor, but the panic in her aunt's voice did, especially since she knew her aunt was right. Something was about to happen, although she didn't know what. Jumping down, she ran ahead of the cart up another steep hill, this one thickly wooded at the top. When she reached the crest, she looked down at the cart labouring up and was relieved to see no danger behind it. It was a peaceful scene: a stream and mill on the valley floor, a few small farms in a patchwork on the slopes, the forest growing up to the crest where she stood.

Hoping she was wrong—knowing she wasn't—Eleanor whirled in a circle to get dizzy, spinning so the world would spin even after she'd stopped. The air felt loud on her cheeks as she turned and turned, a whirlwind gathering around her when . . .

Hoofbeats. A messenger racing up the hill from the other side, riding as fast as a zephyr. Cresting the hill, he cried out to see her and tried to pull up. But his stallion reared and kicked and Eleanor felt a crack to her head. She fell, blinded, her head throbbing, the horse too close. Somehow the messenger stayed in the saddle, calming the stallion, and afterwards he rode in a slow circle to make sure it was only a child, only a girl on the ground. Then he slapped his mount and rode on, galloping down the hill and past the wagon—all of which Eleanor saw because she was floating out of her herself and hovering in the air before finding a tree branch to sit on. Not that she was tired.

Her father was the first to reach the little girl who had been herself, and afterwards her aunt and the slaves, and in the beginning there was incomprehension and then there was wailing. But something else was going on, too. Eleanor could feel it behind her, and turned to see a legate in full regalia stride out of the wood. Despite his rank, he was neither a tall man nor a handsome one, although he had what Eleanor's father called a good face, lively and expressive, with quick dark eyes and a thatch of hair he pushed back from his forehead as he reached her family.

"That wasn't supposed to happen, was it?" he asked briskly, looking down at Eleanor's still form.

Her father stood up, tremendously pale, but trying to be courteous to a man of high rank. "A messenger's horse. It reared . . ."

"My messenger, yes. She got in the way. That shouldn't have happened." The legate looked back at her father. "And she was frightened, so she fainted."

"No, sir, she doesn't faint. Didn't faint. This isn't fainting."

Looking unimpressed, the legate knelt beside the girl and held a flask to her slack mouth. As he did, Eleanor felt the forest go to pieces around her, disintegrating strangely into waves and lines and circles. Then all was dark and she was sucked back in her body. Eleanor felt herself inhale and exhale and her heart began to beat, beat, beat, flooding her with a great love for her life. In a flutter, she opened her eyes on the legate, who smiled down at her kindly.

"There you are," he said.

"I didn't faint," Eleanor said. She levered herself up on an elbow and looked around the hilltop, feeling dizzy and increasingly perplexed. "Where's the Blitz? It was just here. And the airplanes."

The strange words—her astonishing revival—frightened her father and aunt, and the legate looked displeased with her answer.

"You're not yourself," he said. "We're going to have to fix you up."

"Can you fix my dreams?" Eleanor asked. "I don't like them."

The legate looked into the forest. Between the trees, Eleanor caught a brief glimmer of another form. The legate looked at it steadily before nodding, as if he'd been conferring silently with somebody hidden. Then he turned back to her.

"That's precisely what we're going to do."

He got to his feet, and as he looked down at her, the legate almost absentmindedly grew taller. Crying out in awe, her father threw himself on the ground, his obeisance hastily copied by her aunt and afterwards in a tumble by the frightened slaves.

"Oh great god Mars," her father said, raising his arms. "Forgive me. I didn't recognize you before. Your condescension and wonderful kindness . . ."

"Nonsense," the god said, glancing impatiently toward the forest.

"Please allow me to sacrifice a heifer . . ."

"I'm afraid I've got business to take care of," the god said.

"A goat, perhaps."

"Never liked their eyes."

"We have chickens," her aunt called, gesturing at the baskets.

"Not hungry," the god replied, and disappeared into the trees.

1951
Middleford, Connecticut

23

Eleanor was conscious of muffled noises as she woke up. Footsteps. Different types of footsteps, one person dragging a pair of soft-soled shoes as if they couldn't lift their feet, another pattering along in a hurry. She heard laughter. A man's voice. Women's voices, near and far. She knew she was in hospital but didn't know why.

"Auntie?" Her mouth was dry, her aunt beside her. "What's the matter with . . . ?"

"You've had a bad virus," the man said. Dr. Blythe.

"What virus?"

"It doesn't matter," her aunt cooed, leaning over her.

"What?"

"Viral meningitis at first. Then . . ." A horrified whisper. "Encephalitis."

"Sounds like a sicky Heffalump," Eleanor said. "Sickly."

"Here you are," her aunt replied, teary and amused all at once.

"Robin!" she remembered.

"It's all right. He's all right."

"Sure?"

"We couldn't reach him for a while. A letter arrived when you first got sick that you can read when you're better. But he's on leave in

Tokyo now and he sent you a telegram. I wired back that you've been sick but you're recovering."

"Read it right now."

The words didn't line up on the page. Chickens, she read.

Meningitis explained the headaches she'd been having, encephalitis her dreams. Hallucinations, Dr. Blythe called them. She'd nearly died. ("Now, Clara, she knows that.") There was very little they'd been able to do but fight the symptoms. Keep her hydrated, keep her fever down as much as possible. It had gone very high.

"One night you said Lizzy Mortlake was a goddess."

Eleanor didn't remember. Then she did. Once at the Mowbray's garden party, up in the great chestnut tree, someone below them had called Liz as beautiful as a goddess. Little Cassie Mowbray echoed it the way she echoed things. Lizzy's a goddess.

There was something else. She couldn't quite bring it to mind.

"I don't know when that happened, exactly. It's not all there in my memory. Blanks."

"You've been very sick."

"Am I . . . ?"

Couldn't remember.

Sickly. "Am I sickly?"

Eleanor sat up in bed. But her head was a pumpkin and she had to lie back down.

"That word again." Her aunt sounded worried or amused or both.

"I had that bad flu a few years ago, after Robin came back from West Point."

"You had the flu, but that's the only other time you've really been ill."

"During the flu, I had blanks. A day, a couple of days—they were gone. I thought about how you can wake up in the morning into a new world. You don't know how you got there but suddenly, there you are. The daffodils are blooming. You just have to accept what's in front of you and cherish whatever memories you have. But there are so many blanks. What was I doing a year ago today?" She shook her head. "I don't think I should have so many blanks."

"I'd find it awful to remember every moment of my life," her aunt replied. "There are things I remember very distinctly that I'd rather not. My first marriage, for example. And months when I could tell you, 'Well, of course I was living in London and trying to make a go of it as an actress.' But day to day? Then suddenly there's the extraordinary moment of meeting your uncle. My one and only Stage Door Johnny."

Inchon. That's where Robert had landed in Korea. Where was he now? Tokyo?

Wasn't Japan full of radiation from the bomb?

Eleanor felt a twinge of resentment on top of her worry. She'd been very ill and her fiancé ought to have been with her. She was going to have to speak to Robin. More to the point, he was going to have to start listening to her, especially about the bomb. Radiation did strange things to you. She wished she could remember what.

Stage Door Johnny was in April, her aunt was saying. She refused to talk about the bomb, but insisted that she'd met her husband in April. It seemed to be important that he'd introduced her to Eleanor's father a few months later, taking her to an art opening when his brother had been there, still a divinity student at Cambridge. Eleanor's father had rather grandly bought a painting by Vanessa Bell, Virginia's Woolf's sister, even though the Crosby money was in the past and not his pocket. It was the start of his collection, which he mainly picked up at flea markets. Her father had an eye, and for a couple of shillings he'd bought a red chalk drawing of praying hands that an expert later authenticated as a sketch by Leonardo da Vinci.

Amazing that his collection had survived, with the manse taking that direct hit during the Blitz when thank God they were with her in Kent. (Her aunt was rambling.) A miracle they'd dug up the basement and found his collection intact.

Eleanor had heard the story often enough that she could almost see the manse, only the arched windows and a doorway left standing. She wondered if Aunt Clara was bringing it up now to speak about mutability, change, loss, and recovery.

Oh. The fact they'd have to sell the Leonardo to pay the hospital bill.

"Don't be absurd," Liz Mortlake said as she came in. "We'll take care of it."

"Liz." Her aunt spoke in a warning tone.

"Oh, the question of pride. I've never known whether it's good or bad. No doubt both. Our good qualities being our bad ones, and so forth."

Liz sat down in the other chair. It was a rare sight, Lizzy Mortlake and Eleanor's aunt bristling at each other. They were good friends, both displaced Brits, both fashion items. Icons.

"If you have to sell the sketch, Clara, then let me buy it. Get a valuation and I'll pay. You know I've always coveted William's collection."

"Please, Auntie! Then Kate can keep looking at it, too."

A moment of panic. Where was Kate? How could she have forgotten about Kate?

"Is she all right? Where is she? Where's David?"

"Everybody's fine. Kate's busy moving into a flat in New York. Otherwise she'd be here with you."

Eleanor didn't remember who David was. Then she did: Kate's boyfriend. Her married boyfriend, the war photographer. One didn't speak of him in front of the rest of the Mowbrays, but Liz wasn't fazed by the relationship. Liz was a goddess.

Eleanor giggled. "Did Auntie tell you what I said when I was sick?"

"What was that?"

She remembered it now. She was on a hilltop in England after being kicked on the head by a horse. "Oh great god Mars!" her father had cried, and Charles Mortlake had given her an elixir. Charles had looked into the forest, where Lizzy had been standing. Not precisely Lizzy. Venus in all her beauty, the sun shining out of her red-gold hair. Lizzy Mortlake was a goddess, it was true.

No she wasn't. Couldn't be. If Eleanor said it aloud, she'd sound insane.

"I don't know!" she cried, her hand going to her forehead. "My mind's broken!"

"You've been sick," Liz said soothingly. "Don't worry. We're fixing you right up."

Murdo Crawley was on the television downstairs in the rehabilitation hospital, a very hushed and private place. The Leonardo must have been worth a fortune.

"I can't stand that man," her aunt was saying. "Such an opportunist. I doubt he believes a word he's saying. Joseph McCarthy is an evil creature and Crawley oughtn't to row that boat."

She spoke in a hiss in case anybody else heard her. No one could risk being called a communist these days, especially with the Chinese fighting in Korea. Her aunt was a nonconformist, not a communist, but she said that no one in Middleford knew the difference.

"War can be anywhere now," Eleanor said. "It can happen tomorrow, here, with the bomb. They're turning the whole world into a battlefield, not just Korea. The world is sickly."

"And Crawley's a virus. Poor Alicia." Seeing Eleanor's face. "You're tired. Let's go back to your room."

She was in a wheelchair. People weren't supposed to survive viral encephalitis but Eleanor had. She was strong, even though the world was sickly. At least, there was something wrong with the world. She couldn't remember what.

At home now, awake from her nap. Liz was bringing the Leonardo into her bedroom so Eleanor could say goodbye. How lovely of her.

"Old friend," Eleanor said. She felt much better, but still weak enough to be teary.

"It's yours. It's a present."

Her aunt bristled.

"It's mine, Clara," Lizzy said. "I can do what I want with it."

"Thank you," Eleanor said, staring down her aunt. The Mortlakes were very wealthy and Liz liked being bountiful. (The present is more about Liz than it is about me, she thought. She enjoys being bountiful. But Eleanor didn't want to be like that, sour and mistrustful and far too observant. She built a box around the thought and closed the lid.)

"Thank you," she repeated, no longer able to hold back tears.

Liz kissed her and took down one of her college photos to hang the sketch.

"Now everything's back the way it should be," she said. "Huzzah."

1969
New York City

24

Eleanor wished everyone would stop treating her as if she were made of glass. She'd been sick but she was better, perfectly capable of moving in with Katy. Their apartment was in the East Village, but it was safe. Safe enough.

The windows were the reason Katy had taken the apartment, which was hacked out from one floor of an old garment factory. She'd been here for a couple of months and the unused room at the back was perfect for Eleanor. Only a week to clean it out and paint it, and she'd salvaged as much furniture as she needed from the jumble before taking the rest to the curb, in the process finding a threadbare Oriental rug in someone else's trash.

Now she was using her weekend off to arrange her furniture, flopping her new mattress into place and trying to find the right spot for a heavy old work table that had probably always been here. She'd sanded and oiled the scarred oak top and yesterday Katy had painted the legs in spiralling rainbows.

Today, Katy was out at a demonstration. But anti-war marches were complicated for Eleanor, with Robin serving in Vietnam. She agreed with the marchers but didn't feel it was right to join them. If she and Robin were going to split up, she was going to tell him before taking part in a demo. Not that Eleanor had any intention of splitting up with Robin. Maybe the possibility was in her mind, but she kept it locked in a box.

"Give us a hand here, Ellie."

Dafydd Arden called from the main room, which was also Katy's studio. Eleanor decided the table ought to go under the window, and gave it a couple of shoves.

"Ellie?"

She found him crouched on the floor ready to bolt a big old porcelain sink to the wall. Dafydd was Katy's surprise, or would be when she got back. He'd just flown in from Saigon.

"I think I've got it level."

With his good arm and his hook, Dafydd had built a cradle for the salvaged sink out of scrap lumber from a building site. On top he'd put a glass half filled with water, and he was right, the water was level. Eleanor wondered what her role was. Maybe to admire his work like a good little woman. That was something she'd been thinking about lately: the role of women. But for Katy's sake, she gushed.

"It's going to be so great to have a proper sink!"

Not that their proper sink would drain anywhere. Into a bucket beneath the drain hole, which they would empty into the toilet. Eleanor and Katy shared a toilet and a chipped sink in a bathroom across the hall. Both had running water, although you had to let it run for a while so the rust would come out.

"Ask you to hold it for me while I put in some brackets," Dafydd said.

"Wow," she said. "You got a drill!"

Eleanor thought that was over the top, but Dafydd enjoyed praise. He believed he deserved it, which women never did. Lying back down under the sink, he manoeuvred into position to attach a bracket. Dafydd hadn't stopped moving since he'd arrived, in and out of the apartment to the hardware store, the building site, too wired up to just sit and talk. An adrenaline junky: the definition of a war photographer. He loved his job, unlike Robin, who had asked Dafydd to hump back an uncensored letter. Reading between the lines, Eleanor could see that

Robin was having a terrible time, especially with Ted's whereabouts still unknown. Not that he supported the protesters. But his hesitations had touched her deeply.

Still under the sink, Dafydd asked, "You don't go to the demos?"

Eleanor had no idea how to explain her agonized ambivalence.

"I wouldn't beat myself up about it," Dafydd said, scooching out from under the sink and sitting up cross-legged. "I haven't met anyone over there with any use for the war, at least below the colonels. And I wouldn't vouch for all of them."

"Robin said earlier this year that one of his men had bought a lighter. It said something like, 'We the unwilling, led by the unqualified, kill the unfortunate and die for the ungrateful.'"

"Like this," Dafydd said, hauling a silver Zippo lighter out of his jeans pocket.

Eleanor ran her fingers over the inscription. "Not that Robin is unqualified," she said.

"I think he might bail before too long." Eleanor's heart leapt as Dafydd continued, "Not right now, but soon. Taking casualties to secure a hill with no strategic value. Abandoning the hill. Watching the Cong filter back. It's idiocy and Robin knows it."

"So you're bailing, too?"

Dafydd shrugged. "It's a job," he said. "What else have you got for me?"

"Questions," Eleanor said. "About how long this idiocy is going to last. And how well Robin is going to survive it."

Not something he wanted to talk about, judging from Dafydd's face.

"What about some coffee?" she asked.

"I can give you a hand moving that table. Unless Katy needs something else."

This was the first time she'd had her own place, and Eleanor preferred to move the table herself. Casting around for ways to distract him, she wondered aloud about a clothes rack. The apartment had gone back to being a garment factory. She and Katy scoured used clothing stores and stalls for old designer clothes that they could clean and repair, Chanel and Saint Laurent, or Victorian nightdresses, or hand-sewn trousers and jackets from the thirties, anything her aunt could sell. Eleanor also worked in her aunt's store as a bookkeeper as her aunt trained her as a manager, planning to launch a second location any moment.

A maw had opened, an appetite for vintage and handmade goods. Her aunt's store pulled in hangers-on from Andy Warhol's Factory and rock musicians looking for leather jackets. Models stalked through it, taller and even more gaunt than Eleanor after her illness. Occasionally, incredibly, they would get a rock star. (She had personally cashed out Jimi Hendrix.) Even the famous ones pawed through the merchandise like old ladies at a rummage sale, flipping through hand-tooled bags and belts, holding out ruffled shirts, pulling on the couture garments her aunt remade from stripes and lace and flowered prints too ragged for Katy and Eleanor to repair.

Dafydd left to get more supplies, coming back with a length of dowel and some chains and hooks for hanging it. Katy's absence was getting long as he crafted the rack, and Eleanor tried desperately to think of more chores. The apartment needed everything done to it, but she loved it the way it was. Her mattress on the floor, the threadbare rug, the rainbow-legged table. Eleanor wanted to live her life and damn the dam busters, or whatever it was they said during World War II.

You'd think she'd know, although Eleanor tried to box up things like that, too. Glimpses. Visions. Hallucinations. *Enough*.

Even though they didn't seem to have had enough of her.

The freight elevator creaked to a stop at their floor, its metal door rattling open. Eleanor was relieved to hear Katy and her friends thunder down the hallway. Soft thunder. Sandaled thunder. Huarache thunder as the door opened. A moment's pause, then Katy saw Dafydd and let out a high-pitched squeal, grabbing him in a movieland embrace so they turned in circles before pulling him into her bedroom and slamming the door.

Eleanor was left with the shuffling friends. They were artists Katy knew from the Pratt Institute, where Dafydd had been teaching photography when they'd met. The Pratts, her aunt called them. It seemed to mean something rude in England, although Clara said it affectionately. They shuffled around the room, leaning their banners against the wall.

Out of Vietnam!

War on Poverty, Not People!

My Brother Died in Vietnam for What?

Eleanor wanted to mingle, but found herself standing stupidly in the middle of the room, failing to fit in.

"I'm afraid we don't have any beer right now," she said.

She could have offered coffee, but didn't want to use up their scant store of Nescafé. Eleanor was relieved when her lack of beer got the protesters to confer ("Automat," she heard) and soft-shoe out. She wanted to make friends with them, but also knew they would disapprove of her having a fiancé in Vietnam. Not that Eleanor could blame them. She did, too.

The next morning, Eleanor was at her sewing machine when she heard the creak of the elevator, the clang to a stop at their floor, and a high-heeled click down the hall with a male *pad-pad-pad* sounding like a soft drumbeat behind it. Katy's parents, when this was supposed to be her weekend off.

Katy and Dafydd weren't up yet, fortunately in a bedroom far from Eleanor's. The Mowbrays would be unhappy to see the putative son-in-law. His wife had recently sent them a letter from Wales demanding money in wording that was half blackmail. The wife had been unstable for years, Katy said, although she was good with the children. Eleanor doubted that both things were true, but in the end it was none of her business. Katy would sort it out eventually.

Brisk, her aunt had called Eleanor since her illness. No more nonsense, Elizabeth Mortlake had said, which Eleanor understood better than she let on.

"*Well,*" Anne Mowbray said, steaming in before Eleanor had entirely opened the door. Her lacquered perm was so out of place in the East Village loft that Eleanor could almost hear the pipes groaning. Mrs. Mowbray peered around ravenously, obviously never having been here before. Her talk about checking up on Eleanor and bringing news to her aunt (whom Eleanor saw every day) made it clear the Mowbrays were using her as an excuse to invade Katy's new space.

"I assume the fact it's tidy is owing to your presence," Anne Mowbray said.

This was true, but Eleanor wasn't going to admit it. "Katy isn't up yet," she said, wondering whether to offer coffee, but knowing that the Mowbrays didn't consider Nescafé to be coffee. "Have you seen what she's working on?"

Eleanor turned around the nearest canvas. Katy didn't mind people looking, saying she was doing what she wanted and didn't care what anyone thought. She worked in acrylics, dark paintings done in slashes and angles that suggested wrecked buildings. She made them fast, like spraying graffiti on subway cars. Most were of the Bowery, where William Burroughs was busy writing transcendent poetry among the winos. (Or sleeping it off.)

Not that Katy stalked Burroughs the way some of her friends did, although she stalked the Bowery itself. The painting's distant focal point winos lighting fires in oil drums. Except that when you looked closely, you saw they weren't winos but children, feral children dancing in a circle. Eleanor saw the work as limning bombed-out cities, although she couldn't say why (or didn't say why, boxing up the hallucinations). She thought maybe Katy was referring to the war in Vietnam, or at least exploring what America was doing to itself morally by bombing a small country half to pieces and orphaning its children.

"*Hmmm.*" Mrs. Mowbray frowned at the painting. "I wonder if it's any good. Waldorf, is it any good?"

Mr. Mowbray was down on one knee by the sink, craning to look under it. "I presume your landlord is going to put in a drain," he said, in his resonant Yalie drawl.

"I think it might actually be good," Mrs. Mowbray said, speaking loudly enough for Katy to hear, although Eleanor didn't think that was her intention. If Katy was going to be the black sheep of the family, Mrs. Mowbray required her to be a talented black sheep. An untalented black sheep would be a social disaster.

Eleanor thought Murdo Crawley was the real disaster, even though he was only a son-in-law. Senator Murdo Crawley, a hawk among hawks so insistent in his support for the war in Vietnam he made even some of his fellow Republicans wince. He was pictured as a little Hitler on one of the protest signs that Eleanor suddenly realized were still leaning against the wall. He'd probably like the publicity.

No, he wouldn't. His blind eye was caricatured. That was unnecessary.

"It's really . . ." Mrs. Mowbray said, examining Katy's painting. "It's really good."

Katy slipped out of her bedroom, holding a sweater closed over her sprigged cotton nightgown.

"What a surprise," she said.

Eleanor wasn't looking forward to this. "I haven't offered you coffee. I'm sorry."

"I'll take one," Mr. Mowbray said as he stood up, brushing off his pants. "Although I can't work out where your landlord is going to put the drain."

"He isn't," Katy said.

"All right," Mr. Mowbray agreed, looking even more puzzled.

"Buckets," Eleanor said brightly, grabbing the kettle. "Like a fire brigade. Buckets for bringing in water in and buckets for taking it out."

Mr. Mowbray looked around for the buckets. But people didn't send buckets to the curb unless they had holes in them.

"Dafydd showed up yesterday when I was out at a demo," Katy said. "We weren't planning to put in the sink yet, but he was looking for things to do. We'll get buckets as soon as we can afford them."

Eleanor nodded brightly, relieved that Katy had taken charge.

"Maybe Dafydd can buy you some buckets," her mother said, her tone ominous.

"Dafydd left me in the middle of the night," Katy told her. "He has a girl in Vietnam. And before you say it, of course it serves me right. I should have known. A man who leaves his wife and children.

258

Not for me, by the way. There was one before me and now there's one after."

Katy stood with her fists clenched like a child.

"She's a journalist for one of the networks, and he tells me how he needs to learn to use a TV camera—he's so fucking obvious—and of course there will be one after *her*, and I hope he was mugged when he left at two in the fucking morning because, because . . . *Mummy!*"

Katy threw herself at her mother, who caught her neatly.

"Well, you *do* deserve it," her mother huffed kindly. "You'll find that a consolation. At least you didn't *not* deserve it."

"Anne," Mr. Mowbray said wearily.

"I'll just," Eleanor said, and held up the kettle.

At work the next morning, Eleanor was relieved to open the accounts, although she felt guilty for leaving Katy alone. Guilty, mainly, because she was glad to get away from her. Eleanor loved Katy, but she bottled so much up that when things finally poured out, there was no end to it. Rhythmic sobbing like a piledriver.

Much easier to sit down at her blue-painted desk in the back office, opening the accordion file of receipts at the end of a profitable weekend. (Bianca Jagger had been in.) Numbers were so much easier to add up than people. Dafydd Arden, for instance, who had been concerned for Katy's comfort while planning to leave her. He could have gone out for a walk and come back when he was sure she'd be home. No one made him fix the sink, much less buy them an electric drill. (Which Eleanor planned to sell.)

One plus one was so much more predictable, equalling . . . her and Robin, Eleanor thought, putting down her pen. Dafydd had made her worried about Robin. About bar girls, even though Dafydd's lover was a journalist. Eleanor didn't want to know the details of soldiers' leaves in Vietnam, and with Robin, a lapse would only be a lapse, nothing important. But: social diseases. Gonorrhea. The clap. And unlike Katy, Eleanor wanted children.

Sweetheart, *he wrote*. This is a short one, scribbled quickly so Arden can give it to you directly. I'm all right. We still have no news of Ted, but I've got myself into a position in Saigon where I'll know as soon as we hear anything. If this war has any intelligence, I'm in the thick of it. Some people claim that it doesn't, but it's more realistic to say we know precisely what we're doing wrong and don't fix it.

That isn't to say I agree with the long hairs. We've put this country in a mess and need to stay to fix it. There are good people here. I'm not speaking of the government but of the people themselves, who are among the nicest you're ever going to meet. I would like to be in a position to help support a truly good president in South Vietnam, but it seems my fate to fight in a complex war. My father got to fight Hitler on behalf of great leaders like President Roosevelt. We live in different times, as your aunt likes to say.

I'm glad Arden offered to take you the letter so I have a chance to tell you what I really think. If anything happens, I want you to know that it won't be a worthless death in a mistaken war. I'm here to try to help people, which is all we can do, really. No one said it would be easy.

P.S. Just to be clear, I think Murder Crawley is a complete asshole.

"You've got a letter from Robin," her aunt said, standing just inside the office doorway. Behind her stood a model waiting for a word; Eleanor had no idea why.

"Dafydd Arden brought it back," she said. "He went looking for Robin when he didn't have to. I don't know if you've heard, but Dafydd came back to tell Katy he was leaving."

"He came back for a meeting with his editors," her aunt said. "I talked to Anne."

"He told Katy in person, which he didn't have to do, either. And he brought me my letter. I'm not defending him. It's just what Robin says, people are complex." Eleanor held up her letter. "Although I'm not sure who he thinks he's writing to. Talking about 'long hairs.'"

"You've got beautiful hair," her aunt said. They'd let it grow during Eleanor's illness, and now it fell down her back in a reddish-brownish-blond tumble.

"Henna," she said.

"But look who's here to see you."

The model in the doorway wiggled her fingers in a cute wave.

"I'll just let you . . ." her aunt said, retreating and leaving Eleanor thoroughly confused. Then she saw the green eyes.

"Hetty!" She launched herself toward her cousin. Eleanor had thought Hetty was still in India, where she and her husband, Whit Whittaker, had been staying at the maharishi's ashram with the Beatles. Or at least, at the same ashram where the Beatles had stayed, Whit being an executive with Columbia Records.

"Oh my God, Hetty!"

Hetty had always had a gorgeous face, but otherwise she'd been awkward and too tall and chubby, her beautiful eyes getting lost in her cheeks. Now it was like an old black-and-white movie where the man says, "Why, Miss Smith, without your glasses, you're . . . you're beautiful!"

"I know. Isn't it weird?" Hetty said, although Eleanor hadn't said anything. "It's parasites. I got them in India, and I'm getting so many offers, I'm probably going to keep the little buggers. Even though they give me the most awful shits."

Such vulgarity from a beauty so ethereal she could have been on the cover of *Vogue*.

(And would be, Eleanor knew, although she put that in a box, too.)

Hetty had the most extraordinary capacity for doing nothing, one of many things that drove her mother crazy. Hetty's initial idea had been to go shopping before meeting Whit at their hotel that afternoon. But when Eleanor said she had to work, her cousin plumped down happily on the old office couch instead of going out on her own. Sometimes Hetty sang under her breath like a child, or puffed out the beat to a song, and she disappeared periodically, arriving back from the store wearing thigh-high suede boots or silver necklaces or beaded bracelets she examined minutely, holding them up to the light.

Eleanor didn't think Hetty was on anything. She was just naturally stoned. She'd met Whit when she was a receptionist at Columbia, a job that mainly involved sitting at the front desk and smiling. Eleanor would have slashed her wrists but Hetty had loved it, and there was a native shrewdness to her character that kept her from dating musicians. Instead she'd held out for Whit, who was much older, in his mid-thirties, and living in London. They'd gone back there from India, and Hetty said she'd been flooded with offers to model and act, even being asked to appear on a record cover.

They spoke when Eleanor took breaks, on her honour not to work herself into a headache. Finally she pushed the adding machine aside, standing to stretch, which Hetty happily mirrored.

"Yoga," Hetty said, bending at her newfound waist.

"Should I try it?"

Eleanor touched her toes.

"It's fussy," Hetty said. "Yogis claim to be able to fly, but they really just cross their legs and bounce on their bums."

Eleanor threw herself on the couch and Hetty tripped over her feet to land beside her.

"It takes control, though," Hetty said.

Eleanor played with one of her cousin's bracelets, which still had the price tag attached.

"So did you meet people who claimed to be enlightened?" she asked.

"I am one," Hetty said. "I mean, when I bother paying attention. Being one with the universe and all that. I didn't know everyone doesn't feel this way. It's just, how can you feel apart from the universe? That's what I don't get, and no one could explain it."

"I guess if you put it that way."

"Right?" Hetty asked.

Her cousin was lucky she only had one question. Eleanor had been drowning in them since her illness, and not just about Robin. Four-in-the-morning questions about the purpose of life and God and a woman's role, Woman's Role. Everyone talked about that these days; it wasn't just her. Some of the others seemed satisfied with asking the question but Eleanor wanted answers. And Hetty was the guru the gods had sent her?

Not gods, she corrected herself. Gods and goddesses belonged in a box as well.

"I really *was* sick," she told Hetty. "I had hallucinations. I've never done acid, but maybe it's like that, I don't know."

Eleanor felt a shift, as if the universe had started paying attention to her again, when she didn't want any more of that.

"I don't really remember," Eleanor said, although the blanks in her memory were slowly filling in. "But it's left me feeling that the universe is different than we think. I don't know how to explain it. I just caught glimpses. The word ended up in my head, actually. It implies there's something to glimpse."

"Like, Something and not just Nothing."

"Do you believe that?"

"I'd like to," Hetty said. She pulled Eleanor's hair out of her face and tied it into a loose knot at the nape of her neck. There was a mirror, and Eleanor watched Hetty slip one of the elastic bead bracelets off her wrist and use it as a hair tie. Her cousin didn't seem to have anything else to say.

The Whittakers were staying at the Chelsea Hotel, and Whit had proposed going to the restaurant attached to it for an early dinner, wanting a steak. They found him in the hotel lobby talking loudly with a musician type, a small man with a vaguely pleading look. Eleanor would have thought a record company executive would have little time for such an unsuccessful-looking person. Then she realized that Whit's exuberance was backing the musician away one step at a time until he turned and fled.

Whit gave a small private smile before spotting them.

"All my girls are beautiful!" he cried, striding over to embrace Eleanor, then Katy—whom Hetty had insisted join them—before taking Hetty by the waist and giving her a sweet lips-puckered kiss.

Whit had lost weight, too, but added it in terms of hair and mustache. He took them into the crowded restaurant, full of people Eleanor recognized from her aunt's store, or possibly because they were famous. They looked as if they might be, although she wasn't very good at recognizing famous people. It had taken her a while to realize she was cashing out Jimi Hendrix, who was taller than you might think. At least if you'd heard that celebrities were short.

Passing a booth, Eleanor felt her hand grasped and looked down to see her aunt's old friend the Countess of Wigan, who was having a drink with Gordon Stickley. This evening the countess was in thirties-era Bette Davis drag, her eyebrows plucked and pencilled in higher.

"Look who's here," the countess said.

"I'm usually where I am," Eleanor replied, even though she sometimes had doubts about that.

"We can squinch," Hetty said, and they all piled into the booth. The countess lived at the Chelsea, where she was usually behind on her rent. Sometimes she had to hide from the owner, which was hard for a six-foot-three drag queen. She and Gordon Stickley were stretching out their drinks, and when Whit saw how it was, he ordered tequila and paella for the table.

"I can't eat paella on my own," he pointed out, although when the waiter returned with the tequila, he quietly ordered his steak. Meanwhile they talked about Woodstock, and the murder of Sharon Tate, the moon landing, and above all, the countess's eternal quest to find the perfect manicure.

"While people are dying," Gordon Stickley said quietly, and Katy woke out of her abstraction. The Stick, as the countess called him, had served in the Pacific theatre during the last year of the Second World

War, where he'd got himself a dishonourable discharge in return for some very real and lingering pain.

"People are talking about organizing a day of rage," Katy said.

Then came one of those unchoreographed silences across the whole restaurant, a sudden dewdrop moment as if quiet had precipitated from the ceiling, the presence of something rather than its absence, and after the brief pause everybody looked at each other and laughed.

Eleanor wasn't sure why she was here, and that wasn't a philosophical question. What was she doing spending her time with people who were so much more chic and outré than she was? A drag queen, a painter, a future top model, a record company executive, and the Stick, who seemed to have evolved into a professional hanger-on and (although for some reason they weren't supposed to know this) the countess's lover.

Eleanor was a serious girl. Earnest, she'd been told. Teachers had called her clever. She was certainly practical-minded, and more than anything else, she longed to be useful. Yet here she was, dressed like a doll in a black minidress and clunky shoes that added four inches to her already respectable height, men staring at her when they came in and staring again when they left to go upstairs, where the countess said she had some dope.

On paper, Eleanor was waiting for her fiancé to come home from Vietnam, when her real life would begin. She and Robin were meant to settle down and raise a family, and at one level she still wanted that badly. Yet she'd also begun to feel she was owed more than a traditional female role—all women were—and had no idea if Robin would be able to accept this.

Eleanor also knew that spending any more time in such artistic company would push them even further apart. They wouldn't have anything in common when Robin got home, especially if she threw herself fully into fashion while he continued to do whatever he was doing.

Helping people, he said. And killing them. Which must be changing him, too.

The countess had a big room that she called her closet, "even though I've been out of it for years." She was referring to the clothes hanging everywhere, the costumes, some of them used as curtains on an old four-poster bed. She knew where everything was despite the clutter, and found her stash immediately in an old red enema bag. She got the Stick to roll joints while she opened the window, wanting them to blow smoke outside, which didn't strike Eleanor as a very clever way to cover up an illegal activity.

"You've got to inhale," the Stick told her, after Eleanor took a negligent puff. The dope she'd smoked in college had made her feel uneasy. But with the Stick watching her closely, Eleanor drew in a big toke and held it for a long time before slowly letting it out. She took a few more drags as they passed it back and forth, and when Eleanor found the Stick still watching her, she asked, "You don't know what to do with yourself, do you? Any more than I do."

"Excuse me?"

"I hope Robin doesn't come home all messed up, too. But he probably will."

Finding herself truly stoned, Eleanor took great pleasure in the clothes the countess hung as curtains on her four-poster bed. Aquamarine sequins, teal silk, a lovely light grey-green shift, the colour she'd always loved, which her aunt had sewed as lining into her overcoat during the Second World War.

"It seems to me," Eleanor began loudly, to box up the war, "that our time on this earth is about learning. Maybe we're put on earth to learn. Something. I have no idea what. But I've recently learned from my guru Hetty that we're all connected. This isn't the meantime, until Robin gets home. This is my life, here, connected to all of you. Even though I'm not half as sophisticated."

It was a thought so profound that Eleanor let out a sob—from the back of her throat, like an old man not breathing for a long time and finally horking in a breath. Afterward she giggled because it was so absurd being an old man, carolling above her giggles, "Robin could get killed at any minute, and then where would I be? I love him to death."

"Oh, baby," the countess said, and Eleanor was being walked up and down the room between Katy and Hetty. Katy thought she needed some fresh air and Eleanor thought she needed to go home, which Katy said she could manage. Their apartment wasn't far and Ellie needed to walk.

Soon they were out in the street where it wasn't late, although it was vaguely raining. Evening or night? In Eleanor's limited experience, dope did something to time.

"Times Square!" Eleanor cried suddenly, and pulled Katy in the wrong direction. She had no trouble doing it, being much taller. Yet Katy was persistent, and they ended up pushing and tugging their way into Penn Station and then back outside, where they found themselves among the whores on Seventh Avenue, as Simon and Garfunkel did declare.

The song went on repeat in Eleanor's brain as they headed for Times Square, a soundtrack as bright as the lights reflecting off the rain-slicked pavement. Red lights mainly, and as they came into the square, which wasn't square, the Coca-Cola sign and the Haig Whiskey sign and the Gordon's Gin sign all blinked like the eye of fate. There was also a billboard for a movie with a title Eleanor couldn't make out, being right underneath it.

Retreating to read the title, Eleanor backed into a newspaper booth and turned to see someone she recognized behind the counter, a tough scrap of a woman she knew would speak with a Scottish accent.

It's Mrs. McBee, she was about to tell Katy. My aunt's housekeeper? Then she remembered that her aunt didn't have a housekeeper, not here. It was something else to keep in a box, especially when she realized that Mrs. McBee was watching her closely. The old woman had always watched her closely. Maybe that was her real job. Not keeping house or selling newspapers, but keeping an eye on Eleanor.

But look over here. Teddy was on the front page of all the newspapers. Here he was, looking gaunt in his uniform as he saluted a line of brass under headlines saying ESCAPED and P.O.W. Eleanor could only gape and shriek and scrabble up a stack of newspapers from the pile at her feet, hugging them to her skinny black minidress as if they were Teddy himself.

"I'm sorry, I'm sorry," Katy told Mrs. McBee, trying to wrestle the papers away from her. "But it's her fiancé's brother, and he's been a prisoner for so long, and we haven't known where he was, and we didn't see this before"—all the while having a tug-of-war with Eleanor over the papers, tearing the top one—"and her fiancé is serving there, too, and I'm really, really sorry . . ."

Until Eleanor was left clutching the torn paper, and Katy was smoothing out the rest of them and putting them back on the stack. Kate fumbled in her pocket for the price of the paper, which Mrs. McBee refused to accept, saying in a honking New York accent, "Not a problem," and giving Eleanor a magnanimous smile.

2010
Paris (New York) San Francisco

25

A rush of adrenaline as Eleanor ran through the Galeries Lafayette, chased by a chic Parisian security guard. She made sure to hang onto the cellphone, not her own but the one belonging to her aunt's head casuals designer, who had been using it to sneak a photograph of a lovely Stella McCartney spring blouse. It was their usual plan, to take inspiration from a new blouse or an interestingly asymmetric jacket—to copy it, knock it off—for the latest collection of the Clara Crosby chain. If les Galeries were going to ban someone, it had better be a marketing executive like Eleanor rather than one of her aunt's senior designers. The instant the guard saw what they were doing, Eleanor had grabbed the phone and run.

She managed to keep ahead of him, even though she had to skitter along in ridiculous stiletto heels on slick marble floors. They were on the second level, Eleanor keeping close to the storefronts before darting down a narrow hall toward the ladies room. She yanked open the door on its pneumatic hinges, not going in but leaving the door to close slowly on its own, knowing the guard would find it still closing and think she was in there and pause to fret about what to do, whether to call for a female guard or wait for her to come out.

Enjoying her small victory, Eleanor slipped through the fire exit across the hall, making sure the steel door closed quietly before taking off her heels and running silently downstairs.

The door banged open up top.

"*Au voleur!*" the guard cried.

Not fooled by the ladies. He must have done this before. Juggling her shoes and the cellphone, Eleanor picked up speed, slipping down a couple of steps but righting herself, big male footsteps thundering after her. She didn't bother trying to disguise the screech of the exit door as she threw it open onto the concourse level. It was busier here. Still running, she shoved the cellphone into her jeans pocket then startled shoppers by leaning against a pillar to put on her shoes—left—right—and skitter off.

Dodging and weaving, Eleanor saw a reflection in a shop window of the guard going up on his toes to try to see where she was. Hollow thwacks as she butted into paper shopping bags. Finally she reached an entrance and ran outside into the cool spring air, zig-zagging between jammed cars, horns blaring, before arriving on the other side of the road and running around a corner, where she was able to lean against a cold stone building. Home free, she began to giggle, then flat out laugh. Raised eyebrows from the passing French, the more charitable among them clearly thinking her insane, and the rest that she was American.

Yet as her laughter wound down, Eleanor went blank. The world grew muffled, dense, and she suddenly had no idea where she was or what had just happened. Couldn't believe what just happened. *Didn't* believe it. Girls only got chased through high-end shopping malls in the movies. It was as if she'd been plucked out of her real life and dropped into a bad movie so she could be laughed at, she didn't know by whom.

Yes, she did, and she wanted out. This had gone on long enough. It's got to stop, she cried silently. Except that it couldn't, not with Robin coming home.

Having no idea what to do, Eleanor walked to the designated meeting place, a café where her aunt's team gathered if one of them was clocked and the rest had to scatter. What she was thinking about was absurd and quite possibly insane. Bargaining with the gods to regain control of her life. Really? No one else she knew had ever shown a single sign they thought anything was wrong with the way time was working, including Robin. If she convinced the gods to put her back into her real life—and where did she originally come from?—they might catapult her away from everyone she loved. Eleanor couldn't have borne that.

As the waiter hovered, she could only order a glass of her usual white wine, then change it to red, trying to assert at least a tiny degree of autonomy.

Robin had called two weeks ago from the Green Zone in Iraq, having got his hands on an old beater cellphone. Picking up, she heard the weird crackle and shriek of a distant place, and the tinny murmur of unintelligible conversations somewhere in the ether. Eleanor knew where the call was coming from and prayed it wasn't one of Robin's buddies phoning with bad news.

"Robbie? Is that you? Are you okay?"

"Yeah. Yeah." Sudden clarity on the line. "It's me. I'm okay."

"Thank God." She wasn't aware of the tension she carried on her shoulders until some of it dropped off.

"Look . . ." More crackle on the line. ". . . decided . . ."

"You've decided? You're breaking up."

He wasn't breaking up with her. He wouldn't, not like this.

". . . had enough."

"You've had enough of what?" Sounding more belligerent than she meant to.

"My job," he said.

That would explain the beater cellphone.

"Running around like chickens again lately," he said in the distance. Then his voice came close. "My tour's almost up. I've resigned my commission. I want to come home."

Eleanor had arrived in Paris a day before the others, needing time to think. This was a joyous but also a solemn time, and she had to figure out how to handle it. She tried to find the right words for how she felt about Robin's imminent arrival and they included happy—ecstatic—but also anxious, conflicted, and confused.

She felt all these things in a rush while also knowing it was possible—it had been known to happen—that Robin would be killed days before the end of three separate deployments to Afghanistan and Iraq. Either that or he'd change his mind and stay in the army. He'd just phoned on a bad day.

Probably not. He was almost certainly coming home, and Eleanor had to figure out how it was going to work. More than that: whether she wanted to make it work, when some of her friends didn't think she should try. Being an officer in the army had once been a respectable profession. Now it was déclassé. Friends wanted to fix her up with investment bankers, even after the crash. Pro athletes. Entrepreneurs.

Eleanor pushed back at the snobbery, but it was true that she and Robin had spent very little time together over the past few years and hadn't known each other that well to begin with. Both of them had changed and both had their problems, which might not mesh. Eleanor battled the hallucinations, her glimpses, and the craziness she'd been trying to repress. Robin had been damaged by the wars he'd fought, and that was the precise term. He sounded hurt on the phone, not physically, but emotionally and spiritually.

The real word was terrified.

After taking the subway in from the airport, Eleanor had checked into her hotel on the Left Bank. Now she was walking up Saint-Germain-des-Prés trying to find her feet. She wandered into the side streets, where she window-shopped *patisseries* and antique stores—one with a flamboyant Picasso jug in the window—while angling slowly toward the Seine. On this pretty February morning, the Parisians walking toward her were dressed mainly in blacks and greys with every few feet a lime-green accent, a scarf or gloves or perfectly chosen tights, as if all central Paris was a catwalk for a spring show.

Lime green was one of the new spring colours, along with orange, brown, and teal. She'd learn more about the latest trends when her aunt arrived the next morning with her designers. Eleanor loved her job, and one of the things she and Robin had to get straight was his uneasiness about the Clara Crosby chain. Her aunt's designers were coming to town to vacuum up fashion trends in the boutiques and trade shows, paying thousands of dollars for jackets and dresses they would copy at home, while photographing useful details from clothes they didn't buy. Her aunt was brilliant at redesigning Parisian couture, knocking it off for the North American market. The French designers hated her for it, and on his last leave, Robin had said something about stealing ideas. Maybe Eleanor wanted to stop it.

No one could stop Clara Crosby; it was a juggernaut. Her aunt not only owned hundreds of stores around the world, she supplied them with clothing she either manufactured in her own domestic plants or contracted out to Asian mills. That was how you got to be a billionaire. Vertical integration.

"What about coming up with your own ideas?" Robin had asked.

"I think that's called art," Eleanor said. "And Kate could tell you it's a good way to starve."

Her latest promotion made her assistant head of marketing, and Eleanor could have afforded the Picasso jug. Maybe she'd buy it later. But for now she crossed the Seine, pausing in the middle of the bridge to look across at the Pont Neuf, those old grey stones. It was cool but not cold, and she looked up at a luminous blue sky with fleecy white clouds barrelling across it. In the distance, a big steel-coloured rain front sailed along like an ocean liner, drizzling mildly onto the neighbourhoods beneath.

This was her life now, and Eleanor didn't know how to explain to Robin how much she loved it, and that she intended to keep it. Being a professional. Her own woman, flying wherever she chose whenever she wanted. Reaching the Tuileries, she savoured the elegant trees, the perfect puddles on the gravel walks, and the Parisians in low impeccable boots stepping delicately around them.

She also assessed the boots. Good leather. No interest in the buckle. Eleanor was always working, always thinking in terms of her aunt's business, always trying to help; this when she suspected Robin found fashion to be entirely frivolous.

She did, too, but she also loved it and stood by the clothes they made. Clara Crosby supplied clothing (fantasies, aspirations, solace) to people who couldn't afford the arty and expensive couture of Paris. They were a fashion-forward company. Her aunt defined her target client as a slightly edgy college-educated girl working in a job she thought was beneath her. Given the recession, that was a growing market. And Clara Crosby was growing its market despite the latest crash, her aunt being a genius at both sales and design.

"I was born for this time," she would say, having built her business from a home dressmaking shop through a store in the Village into a thriving multinational. The only person at Clara Crosby half as versatile as her aunt was Eleanor's boss, Georgina, the head of marketing, and Eleanor had no idea what Robin would make of her. Everyone still referred to Georgina as the countess, even though she'd transitioned and left her drag queen days behind.

Her line: "Years of dying onstage have taught me what kills."

There was so much transphobia out there, so much racism and homophobia, so many fetid corners of the internet that churned out replicant Murdo Crawleys. Eleanor knew Robin wasn't like that, but if he worked up a grievance against her job, she couldn't predict how it would play out. Knock-off Crawleys attached themselves like leeches to the walking wounded, and that was one way to describe Robin, who had taken a bullet in the leg at Kandahar and suffered through three months in Mosul.

There must be a stronger word than terrified.

Eleanor ducked into the Louvre, hoping to distract herself by visiting the *Mona Lisa*. They were cousins five hundred years removed, given the Leonardo sketch her father had picked up as a student on Portobello Road. Now she found poor Lisa suffocating behind security glass, neglected inside her crowd of fans. Velvet ropes fed a line of tourists toward her, but most of them barely glanced at her before taking selfies. It was worse every time Eleanor came, and now scientists wanted to dig up Leonardo's skull to do a forensic reconstruction, hoping to find out if the *Mona Lisa* was a self-portrait in drag. Eleanor valued privacy, something she shared with Robin, who had been awarded medals she'd only heard about from his mother. She and Robin weren't thoroughly at odds. They loved each other deeply, and Eleanor longed to have him back in her bed the way a desert longs for rain.

Shying away from the selfies, Eleanor retreated to the European galleries, drifting past the Renaissance Italians into the gallery of early French art. She stopped in front of the Ingres painting of Joan of Arc, whom she'd never met, although she had an idea that she would one day. Joan wore armour in her portrait and a virgin's beatific smile, maiden and warrior all at once. Eleanor realized there were only ever two roles in her hallucinations: the Maiden and the Universal Soldier. She and Robin played those parts, time after time.

A week after he'd phoned, Eleanor had taken a stab at confronting her visions, if that's what they were. It had been a joke (but not really), visiting an expert on past-life regression that the Stick was consulting. Gordon Stickley had found his métier as her aunt's chief handbag designer. He put everything into it: the traumatic stint in the Gulf War that had awakened him to archaeology, the archaeological studies that had awakened him to boxes, the collection of inlaid Persian boxes and Chinese calligraphy boxes and Russian nesting dolls that he'd slowly amassed: all these things reverberating off his too-many years as a closeted gay man. He was particularly good with clasps.

Pretending she was only mildly interested, Eleanor had asked to meet his therapist. Three days later, the Stick had taken her to a large block of rent-controlled apartments near the East River. A woman with a strong Bronx accent buzzed them up, and when she opened her door, Eleanor met a short hawk-nosed woman swathed in scarves with thick lines of kohl around her eyes.

Her first glance at the woman gave Eleanor such a strong sense of déjà vu that she barely registered Gordon Stickley's introduction. Instead she caught a thunderclap glimpse of the Stick in a dark cellar wearing an English-cut suit from the 1840s or '50s. (Eleanor *knew* clothes.) He distinctly said "mosaic," and Eleanor realized she was in the cellar with him, fighting off a familiar yawn of boredom at the Stick's well-meaning windiness.

"Where are you?" the therapist asked.

"At your table?" Eleanor replied, not entirely certain how she'd got there.

The therapist fixed her with kohl-rimmed eyes. Eleanor knew what she meant but felt reluctant to confuse the Stick with her British vision. A recent regression had revealed that he'd been a cowboy in the Wild West during roughly the same period.

"The reason I zoned out," Eleanor said. "I think I met you in England. In the 1840s."

The invisible opened its eyes to look at her. Eleanor wasn't sure why she was doing this. A recklessness to her mood. Throwing the dice.

"And?" the therapist asked.

"You were telling our fortunes. At least, you told my friends' fortunes. You said the spirits didn't care to speak to me."

The woman took this in. So did the universe.

"And who were you, back in the 1840s?"

Eleanor wasn't sure how far to trust her. "I have these dreams. Maybe they're more like images. They don't have those warped narratives of real dreams. They're mainly just moments. Glimpses. I came here to try to find out what they are."

"Who are you in the dreams, then? You're going to have to give me something."

"I'm just me. Usually living in an English country house. Sometimes London."

"You like Jane Austen movies?"

Eleanor did, it was true. It was possible she was just suggestible. But she didn't think so.

"What makes Gordon's regression so convincing," the therapist went on, "he wasn't broadly successful as a cowboy. He never rustled cattle. Bad guys tended to rustle it away from him. And as far as bad guys go, they weren't even all that bad."

The Stick looked both proud of himself and abashed.

"So in these country houses," the therapist asked, "were you ever a maid?"

The woman was right. In all of her hallucinations, dreams, visions, Eleanor had lived a well-appointed life. Her real childhood in Connecticut had been nothing out of the ordinary. Suburban middle class. And if she had done well, if she and Kate were now sharing a loft in Tribeca, if her career was flourishing and Kate about to have her first solo show—all of this was owing to step-by-step hard work, much of it on the part of her exceptional aunt.

Eleanor couldn't remember any dreams about a past life as a hunter-gatherer or a subsistence farmer, which is how most people had lived throughout history. It made her wonder if her glimpses were the remnants of wish-fulfillment fantasies she'd had when she was sick.

Maybe she was still sick. Maybe that was the real problem. It terrified her.

"Are you all right, Elle?" the Stick asked.

Eleanor felt the universe lean in on her, listening so closely she couldn't bear it.

"I don't think I'm sick," she said. "I think I'm cured. But I have these fragments, and when you said past-life regression, I thought I'd give it a try. You know?"

The therapist seemed to accept this. Or at least, the universe did. "So if you look very, very closely at the table where someone told your fortune, what do you see?" she asked. When Eleanor hesitated: "Say it without thinking."

An unstable surface. A glimmer. Pixilation.

"It's giving me a headache," she said.

"All right, we're leaving," the Stick said, standing abruptly. "Sorry, Eunice."

At least she'd tried.

Her aunt came down to breakfast before the designers, leaving Ms. McBee to unpack her clothes. This was a working trip for the designers, but her aunt often handed out a couple of tickets as treats. Eleanor had no real reason to be here, and Ms. McBee's housekeeping duties were so light that her aunt was essentially giving her a week off.

"Maybe we can have a wee croissant sometime," Ms. McBee had told her, always on the watch, as Eleanor had passed her aunt's open door.

Yet here was her real treat: Stansfield Mowbray coming out of the elevator wearing Baby in a sling on his chest. Eleanor always felt such delight when she saw Stanz, an inexpressible welling of relief; she didn't know why. It was true he'd survived a bad accident. A slightly ludicrous accident: earbuds in place, Stanz had stepped into a crosswalk without looking and was hit by an ambulance. At least he'd got immediate medical care.

Margaret Darcy strode out of the elevator behind Stanz, already on her phone, her aunt's chief designer, blessed with a seeing eye into what their clientele would kill for, or what they would kill for in six months. Eleanor suspected that Mags was planning to quit and start her own label, the one person capable of challenging Clara Crosby. But she and Mags had grown closer after the accident, or at least declared a truce. They'd agreed over his hospital bed that Stanz hadn't suffered any cognitive damage, despite what the doctors feared. Stanz was still Stanz, even if Eleanor felt he'd always suffered from a mild cognitive impairment (he just wasn't that smart) while Margaret believed he was perfect.

Designer Mags Darcy meeting top model Stanz Mowbray at a Clara Crosby fashion shoot. Pierced by Cupid's arrow, one of those stories. Mags falling hard and Stanz surprising everyone by catching her. His accident a year later, Mags eight months pregnant. The pirate's scar across his cheek that looked as if it would revitalize his career. But Stanz had decided to stay at home with Baby while Margaret went back to work. His decision. New priorities, which made him happy. Made them both happy.

Now Mags was being gleefully brutal on the phone while Stanz walked up to their table, waving Baby's tiny hand in his big one.

Eleanor put out a finger and Baby grasped it, looking as stunned as his father.

"You need to practice," Stanz told her shyly. "I hear Robin's coming home."

Eleanor froze and Stanz saw it, clearing his throat.

"The scariest thing I've ever had to do was cut Baby's fingernails for the first time," he said. "I guess Robin would have something to say about that. But I did it, and the thing is"—as Baby finally put Eleanor's finger in his mouth, and Stanz glowed, and Eleanor glowed—"life can work out, you know?"

They divided into two minibuses, with Eleanor opting to go to Galeries Lafayette, planning to do some shopping. But as they left the bus, poor spotty Lilian Browne (head designer, casual wear) put a hand on her arm.

"My budget got cut," she said.

Eleanor knew that Lily was in her aunt's bad books, her fall casuals having tanked, one particularly baggy-assed jodhpur selling only two units worldwide in four weeks. ("I love the comfort of diapers," the countess had said. "Me and Gandhi *and nobody else.*") The cut meant that Lily was forced to buy fewer clothes and take more photographs. Yet everyone knew she had to produce a runner this season, launch a trend or she'd be gone. Eleanor loved fashion, but it was a nasty business. Lily had broken out terribly, her eyes beseeching above her spots.

"You want me to screen you?" Eleanor asked, deciding that she could shop any time.

"And if you see anything good," Lily said. "Although I should warn you, my target girl isn't Clara's edgy type. Mine just wants to like herself."

They started work on the concourse level. Eleanor headed into Prada first, browsing the racks, reminding herself to flip slowly and unprofessionally through the hangers, pulling out a jacket that honestly caught her eye. When Lily came in, Eleanor waited until she saw that she was interested in a piece, then picked out a pair of trousers and asked the shop girl about a belt in worse French than she actually spoke, which prolonged the conversation as she positioned herself to block the girl's view of Lily taking her picture.

"*Peut-être pas*," Eleanor said, returning the trousers to the rack. The shop girl stared like an offended cat as they left without buying anything.

Eleanor's aunt had a trick of piling garments she liked on the counter before taking pictures semi-openly, challenging a shop girl to toss her out and lose a big sale. Afterward, she and Mags would go through the pile and reject half. Yet for all their gamesmanship, they spent like oil barons. Mags's best friend, Aggie Moreland (formal wear), was shopping here today as well, with her platinum card and two juniors, each of whom could buy with her permission. And while Lily's budget had withered, it was still big enough that a clutch of bags hit against her thighs as they walked up to the second floor.

They were followed by a security guard, which Eleanor found unfair. Despite what Robin thought, they weren't going to steal anything. Eleanor kept an eye on the guard as they worked their way through Miu Miu, Balenciaga, Chloé. In Stella McCartney, Lily held out a blouse, not casual wear, but Eleanor could see how she could adapt it. Interesting sleeves.

She took a pair of high-waisted trousers from the rack, approaching the shop girl and saying again in bad French, "*Avez-vous une autre ceinture pour ces pantalons?*"

The girl didn't have another belt. Stella had put a belt on the trousers, and it was the belt Stella wanted to put on the trousers, and therefore it was *la* belt.

"*Hey!*" the security guard cried, pointing at Lily.

Dropping the Stella, Eleanor grabbed Lily's phone and kicked into a run. She managed to duck ahead of the guard, even though she had to skitter along in ridiculous heels, something she seemed to have done before. She kept close to the storefronts, then darted down a narrow hall toward the ladies room, which she hadn't known was there. Yes, she had. No, she hadn't. She *hadn't*, but knew to yank the door open on its pneumatic hinges, leaving the door to close slowly on its own, picturing the way the guard would find it closing when he got there.

Eleanor could see it. She could see him see it, fretting about whether to call a female guard or wait her out. It was as if she'd fallen into a past life and couldn't get out, compelled to slip through the fire exit across the hall, forced to make sure the steel door closed, impelled to take off her heels and run silently downstairs.

The door banged open, as she knew it would.

"*Au voleur!*" she shouted, along with the guard.

Juggling her shoes and Lily's cellphone, Eleanor felt propelled forward, slipping down a couple of steps but righting herself, of course. She didn't bother trying to disguise the screech of the exit door as she threw it open at the concourse level. Why should she? Feeling chased or pulled or manipulated—that was the word—manipulated by something other than her fear of being caught, Eleanor ran through the crowded concourse, then felt her back forced against a pillar to put on her shoes—left—right—before she was pulled forward again.

Dodging and weaving, Eleanor saw a reflection in a shop window of the guard going up on his toes exactly the way she knew he would. When she finally reached an entrance, she ran outside, forced to zig-zag between jammed cars, horns honking, before arriving on the other side of the road and running around a corner, where she had to lean against a cold stone building. She *had* to. She had no choice.

Then Eleanor went blank. The world grew muffled, dense, and she had no idea where she was or what had just happened. Couldn't believe what just happened. *Didn't* believe it. Girls only got chased through high-end shopping malls in movies. And it had happened twice, as if her life were a bad movie and someone had hit rewind, wanting to laugh at her again. It was enough to finally make her snap.

"Stop it!" she yelled. "Leave me alone! Leave me alone, please!" Falling into a crouch, her voice failing as she whispered, "Please, please, please."

A couple rounded the corner. A special couple; she remembered them very well. An old man with white hair and a black beret and an old woman with black hair and a white beret.

"*Elle est folle*," the man told the woman. She's crazy.

"*Elle est americaine*," the woman replied. She's American.

As if the joke hadn't got old.

At dinner, Eleanor told her aunt she was flying home in the morning.

"You don't have a headache?" her aunt asked, immediately worried.

Eleanor shook her head. She couldn't sound crazy. Had to prevaricate.

"With Robin coming home," she said. "At least if he makes it home and there isn't a last-minute disaster. Or he doesn't change his mind. I don't know. It all seems so up in the air and so stressful that I'm losing it. I need to get out of here. I want to go home and talk to Kate."

Talk to Kate. That wasn't a lie; it was what she wanted. Eleanor felt immensely relieved to think of it. Kate had been framing her pictures for her upcoming show, but they were almost done. She was also trying to help Teddy Denholm, who had finished his debriefings by the air force and the government security services after escaping captivity by the Taliban.

Teddy also claimed to have recently broken out of a second captivity by the shrinks, but Eleanor didn't think that was true. She'd noticed a pattern to his absences that suggested a series of appointments. They might even have been helping. Whether it was the counselling or the time he'd had to think in captivity, Teddy had finally stopped crushing on Eleanor. She was almost sure he had, although after all he'd been through, no one could blame Teddy for being secretive. Eleanor thought Kate was taking on a big project if she was getting emotionally involved with him.

Of course she was.

Eleanor hadn't talked to Kate about Teddy, or Kate's feelings for Teddy. They hadn't talked much about Robin, either. Kate had said she would move into her studio, but she hadn't, and although Ted officially lived with his mother in Connecticut, he was around all the time, too. With Robin back, life would get crowded. And so beautiful. There was that, too.

"Go home," her aunt said. "Get ready. You can't go on like this any longer."

In the airport, Eleanor picked up a random handful of magazines, not feeling up to a book. After takeoff, she asked for a cup of her usual coffee.

"Tea," she said, changing her order, although she wanted a damn coffee.

Afterward, she settled in with her gossip magazine. It was the only one she'd deliberately bought, wanting to read its cover story on Liz Mowbray and Charles Mortlake, billed as the Silicon Valley power couple, founders of Oolikan, the social media platform that they'd named after a small fish and grown into a whale. Eleanor knew roughly what the article would say. Lizzy's charm. Charlie's usual quote: "I'm just a coder."

Skimming the article, she found it quickly: "I'm just a coder." The writer had also included a guide to the Mowbray family, and Eleanor ran through it apprehensively. The parents, the über-talented brothers and sisters, the cute kids, then the usual paragraph about Anne Mowbray being best friends with the billionaire founder of Clara Crosby, although Eleanor would have said the word was frenemies. Even Hetty was in there, the world's top plus-size model, finding her bliss after overcoming an eating disorder. (Actually, giardia, but Whit knew how to spin things.) Fortunately, Eleanor had escaped notice. Small mercies, she thought.

Throwing the magazine aside, she decided she didn't feel like watching a movie. Instead she opened one of her random magazines, a scientific one. There was an article about an academic named Nick Bostrum and his simulation theory that looked interesting, although she didn't get far into it before stopping in shock. Afterward, Eleanor shuffled back to the first page of the article and read it again more carefully before she finally closed the magazine and said, "Oh, I see."

26

By the time the plane landed at LaGuardia, Eleanor had spent several hours making plans. She'd only taken carry-on and was able to leave the airport quickly, telling the cab driver her address exactly as she always did and driving off as usual.

Not quite as usual. She made a call to Ms. McBee, apologizing for missing their croissant but promising to catch up when the designers got back from Paris.

"I told Clara I'm a mess, with Robin coming home. There was so much stim over there I couldn't even sleep on the plane. Now I'm going home to crash for like, all day."

The watcher disarmed, Eleanor hung up and waited for the moment she fell out of notice, the way she'd first done ten lifetimes ago when she'd met Robin on the Goodwood heights. She'd grown to know the feeling, and as soon as she felt unobserved, she asked the driver to take her back to the airport. Sneaking inside, Eleanor booked a seat on the next flight to San Francisco, trying to remain as still as possible until they landed at San Francisco International in an eerie fog. There she got in another cab and asked the driver to take her to Oolikan.

"I don't know that one," he said. "A start-up? You got an address?"

Eleanor gave him the street address and he punched it into his GPS, getting nothing. Then his GPS crashed and rebooted, and the campus came up onscreen. The driver also became more substantial in a way that Eleanor couldn't quite define, although she knew what it was.

"Snap. Oolikan," he said. "I misheard you."

Eleanor was left to look out the window at a city that seemed to be in focus not much more than a block ahead, being created as they drove.

"Did you ever wonder whether you're real?" she asked the driver. "Or whether we're just computer simulations run by programmers x-number of years in the future."

"You're a gamer?"

"Bostrum's simulation theory," Eleanor said. "He's a philosopher at Oxford."

The driver paused. "Yeah, okay, Bostrum," he said. "Theory based on the exponential speed that computer capacity is increasing. I don't know how he's going to prove it, though."

"Glitches," Eleanor said. "Not glimpses. I had glitches. They said I had a virus."

"That's too bad."

"They'd be like gods, wouldn't they? The coders. Running entire worlds."

The driver wheeled around a corner. "Correct me if I'm wrong," he said, keeping his eyes on the traffic. "My understanding is that Bostrum offers three possibilities. First, that humans go extinct before reaching a stage where we're capable of creating high-fidelity simulations. Second, that we reach a stage where we can run them but decide not to for ethical reasons. Third, we get there and choose to run simulations of the lives our ancestors lived, probably a lot of them, meaning you and I would stand a good chance of being simulated."

"From what I read."

"And you believe it."

"Pretty much. I guess you don't."

286

The driver shrugged. "If I had to choose among the three, I'd say climate change makes extinction more likely. Which would make you and me real. Also culpable in destroying the environment, if you don't mind a digression. Although I chiefly blame the hundred big-ass corporations responsible for the majority of carbon emissions."

Eleanor thought it through.

"So what if the corporations destroy the natural world, and people have to go into underground bunkers where all they've got left is to run simulations."

The driver didn't answer, but Eleanor felt like pressing. "What kind of simulation would you run? I mean, if you had a computer so powerful you could build any world you wanted?"

"One in which PhDs didn't have to drive cab," he said, pulling to a stop before Eleanor would have thought it possible. "Here you go."

The fog had lifted and showed her a glossy campus as white as an architect's model. Eleanor paid off the driver, who hadn't caused her to doubt Bostrum's theory, as maybe he'd been programmed to. She walked into the main building and told a security guard, "I'm Eleanor Crosby. Liz Mowbray is expecting me."

The guard didn't seem the least surprised, asking her to walk through a scanner before directing her to the seventh floor. There, a second guard met her as she came out of the elevator.

"Nora Crosby," she said. "Lizzy Mortlake is expecting me."

The second guard showed no more surprise than the first. He escorted her down the corridor and left her at the door of Elizabeth's outer office, where she walked past the unconcerned secretary and went in.

Elizabeth stood in front of a burled wood desk half the size of the Atlantic Ocean. On it was a marvellously thin silver laptop and nothing else.

"Elle. What a surprise," Lizzy said.

"Until the cab driver turned on his GPS."

A bare flicker of the eyelids. "Until then, yes."

"I'd like to know what you plan to do with me."

A brief hesitation from Liz, then the walls and ceiling slowly retreated and dissolved until they became a fog like the one at the airport. She and Elizabeth were left standing at the centre of a large vague room on a matte white floor. She thought she heard birdsong far away but there were no closer sounds, and the burled desk and the laptop had gone slightly out of focus. Only Elizabeth seemed firmly herself, although the blue dress she'd been wearing had faded to the colour of the sky at noon. When Eleanor looked down at her hand, she was relieved to see flesh, and it strengthened her a little.

If you were to stand in the presence of a god, even a human god, a futuristic god, but the god who had created you, what would you say? It was true that many of your questions would already have been answered by being there. If you'd pictured facing St. Peter at the Pearly Gates, then you would know when you saw him that indeed there was life after death, and that both life and death were tied up in judgement of your actions while on earth, and that you would spend eternity in either heaven or hell depending on how well you had behaved during your life. Or at least, how well God decided you had behaved. Life was meant for proving yourself and death involved judgement.

In Eleanor's case, she was apparently a simulation created by the woman who faced her. It was a strange and disorienting thought. She wasn't real. She'd been programmed into existence, and the world she lived in wasn't real, either. Yet Eleanor had never felt anything other than real, despite the dreams and hallucinations that had always said there was something different about her. She felt human and mortal, having no idea where she'd been before she was born nor feeling any certainty about what would happen to her when she died. She loved and wished and feared. She didn't know if she experienced love or fear the same way as humans, or even as other simulations, but no one knew how emotions felt to anyone else. There was also the fact she'd tried very humanly to find meaning and purpose in her life.

Eleanor insisted on feeling real, and in the end, there was the physical truth. If you prick us, do we not bleed? If you tickle us, do we not laugh? If you poison us, do we not die?

Yet she seemed to be a simulation, and so was everyone she knew, including Robin. The real Elizabeth was a flesh-and-blood person living in a future society, a programmer and a mortal who had created Eleanor and her world out of nothing, out of code. Eleanor was terrified, although she knew she had to keep calm so she could bargain for control of her life. Her small goddess was fallible. Look at all the problems Eleanor had suffered, the viruses and glitches. It was unsettling to be controlled by such an incompetent programmer.

Elizabeth, she'd call her, although she couldn't begin to imagine what her real name might be.

"I should have said, What you're planning to do with me and Robin."

Elizabeth sighed. "We've been trying to fix you," she said. "But you've somehow developed a mind of your own. Which is ironic, since I've been using you to have a look at women's roles over the course of early Western civilization."

Eleanor was flooded with images of her past lives, which sometimes repeated and bled into one another. The sound of creaking wheels, the dislike of being contained, of fainting, the images of refugees fleeing endangered cities, poor people clinging to stirrups and carts as she stayed behind or fled. Lizzy seemed to rely on tropes or repeated images that had driven ruts into Eleanor's mind. And cracked it.

"You're a student?" she asked. "Or a professor?"

Thinking it through. "And Charles is studying war."

That might be the best-case scenario. On the airplane, Eleanor had concluded that simulations must be entertainment for the advanced and bored civilization that produced them, whether they were living in bunkers under the surface of an environmental catastrophe or in a perfect society where major problems had been solved, leaving them with little else to do. If what Elizabeth said was true, at least the whole point of her life wasn't to entertain them.

"Your problems aren't caused by faulty reincarnation, or radiation, or even by repeated imagery," Lizzy said, looking amused. "I like to think that I'm using literary tropes, but it's probably just my own preoccupations seeping through."

Eleanor was horrified. Not only at what Lizzy was saying, but that she was able to read her thoughts.

"I'm sorry," Lizzy said. "I'll stop. It won't serve any purpose to upset you."

Serve any purpose. It was a cold thing to say, although Elizabeth looked warm and understanding. The dimpled smile, the flush to her cheeks, the summer blue of her eyes.

"So what caused it, Lizzy?" Eleanor asked, walking closer. "What caused *me*?"

"You've been told you got a virus," Elizabeth said, reaching out to push back a strand of Eleanor's hair. "And that's the truth, at least in metaphorical terms. Quantum terms, you can call them. A virus that's making you see beyond what you'd normally see. I'm afraid that's a little difficult for us, especially if you start talking openly about it, producing evidence that might make others start to believe you. It's always a problem when we drop into the late twentieth and early twenty-first century and our creations"—creations!—"begin to suspect that something is going on. Not that they ever have any evidence, and their friends just think they've watched *The Matrix* too many times."

Elizabeth burbled with amusement. As she did, Eleanor caught something undefinable about her, a grander side than she'd ever shown. But Lizzy didn't mean her to see it, and it dissipated quickly, so she was back to being herself and smiling fondly.

"But there was real human history," Eleanor said. "From what Bostrum says, you simulate actual historic times, then put people like me inside them. In the real past, someone made *The Matrix* for the first time."

"Is that what we do?" Elizabeth asked. "Creating alternate worlds, when it's such a lot of work, and I'm essentially lazy?" Lizzy's brilliant smile. "Maybe sometimes. But maybe it's easier to slip you into different eras of human history, creating your own little community inside it, subject to its rules. How many people do you actually know intimately?"

Eleanor was confused. "But how could you possibly do that? You'd have to travel through time, and it would alter the whole course of human history. The butterfly beating its wings in the forest and setting off repercussions that change everything."

"Maybe your famous butterfly is just a butterfly beating its wings. Life otherwise goes on. Shall we talk about hubris? People thinking they're so very important."

It was true, Eleanor had usually lived in small communities or moved in small circles. But Oolikan and Clara Crosby were such big firms that this time Elizabeth must be creating a world. Eleanor remembered the fog over San Francisco after she'd flown in. Maybe Lizzy had been coding it into existence as she arrived, so busy that Eleanor had managed to slip out of notice. Only when Lizzy had grown aware that she wasn't where she was supposed to be had the GPS crashed and the driver grown more solid.

"That was Charlie having a little fun," Lizzy said.

When she realized she'd been reading Eleanor's mind again, she shrugged like a queen caught making a trifling mistake, not really caring.

Eleanor felt enormously battered. She wasn't real, but she felt real. I think, therefore I am: Descartes. Yet it got a little more complicated when someone else could read your thoughts and had possibly programmed them in the first place. A word from the Galeries Lafayette came back to her: manipulated. Eleanor felt like a puppet, and realized she'd felt that way at Goodwood House in Yorkshire two hundred years ago, thinking in bed one night that she was taking part in a Punch-and-Judy show. Other moments ricocheted back, all the privileged lives she'd led in different historical periods. It appalled her: being jumped around in time so her creator could study women's roles.

There was also the time in the New York apartment of the past-life therapist when Eleanor realized she'd never been a farmer or a hunter-gatherer. Elizabeth claimed to be studying gender roles, and maybe she was, but she'd made sure the roles were well-dressed and entertaining. Eleanor and Robin were always situated at an elevated social level.

"I hated it when you rewound me running through the Galeries Lafayette," she said. "I loathed feeling like entertainment. People watching and laughing at me."

"That never should have happened, and I apologize," Lizzy said, sounding as if she meant it this time. "But some of us can get a little out of hand. Mischief is so tempting."

Some of us. "How many of you are there?" Eleanor asked.

Lizzy smiled and shook her head, although her sky-coloured dress faintly altered its shape, growing tighter in the bodice with a fuller skirt billowing out below. In this form, she suggested a nine-teenth century version of herself, the daughter of a baron, wife of the grandson of a duke, as soothing as a fictionalized past.

"You're very unusual, you know," she said. "Isn't that what everyone wants? To be unique? I find it quite fascinating, actually, to speculate what role the virus has played in your awareness. It might be similar to the role a virus could have played in human cognitive development when it was seeded millions of years ago. I can't remember whether you studied it, but in the late twentieth century, scientists began to wonder if a virus had got into the brains of early hominids and piqued them into evolving greater intelli-gence, possibly even consciousness, perhaps for the benefit of both. It isn't my area, but some of us who are interested in that sort of thing have been keeping an eye on you."

Elizabeth continued to smile as if this would console her. But Eleanor remained horrified to think of these futuristic beings looking at her whenever they wanted. They could watch her in her most private and intimate moments, even when she and Robin made love. Were these the ones who had forced her to run through the Galeries Lafayette for a second time? Her father, if she could really call him her father, had always said he was wary of a God who was all-seeing and all-knowing. He'd joked one time that he didn't want such a prurient being looking down on him. Yet that seemed to be a version of what Eleanor had got.

"I've asked twice now," she said, "what you're planning to do with us."

To her surprise, Elizabeth hesitated, her robes growing more modern, her face almost human in her uncertainty.

"I don't know," she said.

Eleanor felt herself being weighed, and was ready to plead her case when there was a movement in the distance. Charles Mortlake walked briskly out of the mist, raising his hand in greeting. As he joined them, Elizabeth shook away her uncertainty. The two stood side by side, staring in bemusement at Eleanor.

"I guess PhDs don't have to drive cab in this world," she said, making Charles bark out a self-satisfied laugh.

As he did, he grew taller and grander, the way he'd done on the ancient British hilltop. "Oh great god Mars," her father had cried. As his words echoed inside her, Eleanor wondered if Charles and Elizabeth weren't human after all, not coders in some future society. Maybe they really were gods: Mars and Venus, Ares and Aphrodite, the unreliable deities of the Roman and Greek pantheon—of all religions that understood the gods as capricious, and no more to be trusted than the weather.

Her voice sounded strangled as she asked, "Can that really be true?"

They smiled but gave no answer. Benign beings, impenetrable. Whoever they were, they were greater than an ordinary person like herself could understand. Flitting through time, creations jumping out of their minds as thoughts made flesh. Even if they'd once been human, they were gods now, and Eleanor could see they were politely repressing their annoyance with her, a small bothersome creature who was ruining their game.

"I've become inconvenient, haven't I?" she asked.

Neither Charles nor Elizabeth disagreed, and Eleanor wondered whether any of their other creations could exercise free will or if their lives were all minutely directed. Cupid's arrow hitting Stansfield and

Margaret Darcy. Her aunt losing fortunes and gaining them. *Robin*, she thought, her heart clenching at the possibility that he'd been forced to love her.

"It wouldn't be very interesting if you couldn't make your own decisions," Charles said. "You all have your own personalities, and what interests us is the choices you make and why. How you behave within the constraints you face. In love"—nodding at Elizabeth—"and at war."

Constraints the gods never had to face when they could wave inconveniences out of existence. Eleanor wondered what would happen if she caused them so much trouble they just got rid of her. It was an odd way to think about death, that the gods had grown tired of you. In sudden panic, Eleanor realized that she didn't face death at some indeterminate day in the future. By coming here, she'd confronted the gods with a decision. She was growing increasingly unreliable—she'd become too fully conscious—and despite their powers, they hadn't managed to correct even minor glitches in her before. The fact was, they might decide to get rid of her right now. Charles was his usual genial offhand self but his impatience shone through, and Elizabeth looked troubled.

Glancing down at her arm, Eleanor caught her breath when she saw it was no longer entirely distinct. Kate had told her once that Leonardo da Vinci's great advance in painting the human figure was *sfumato*, his ability to subtly blend the outlines of his subjects into the background, which made the figures seem more real. There turned out to be a scientific basis for this. Molecular scientists said the atoms at the very edges of individuals—of an oak tree, a plague-year cat, a table with rainbow legs—blended into the atoms of the air, so there was no real border between what was living and had been and wasn't. Maybe, to the gods, she was an unfixed airy little creature, diffuse and unimportant.

I'm real, Eleanor insisted on thinking. As real as a Leonardo painting in the Louvre. And surely I should be cherished, too.

"Even in your latest lifetime," Charles told her, not unkindly, "people knew you couldn't entirely disappear. Energy never dissipates. Which is all most of you really know about death, for all your stories about the Elysian Fields or Valhalla or whatever you call the afterlife."

"Please don't," she whispered.

"I don't want to," Elizabeth said, with a warning glance at Charles. "That's what makes this so unfortunate. Yes, we're building a world. Charlie has prepared the next conflict, and I've been rather pleased with myself for thinking up the fashion business. It's a big enough pond that I've found plausible roles for all my babies. Although," she added, "I keep forgetting about the French maid. Mademoiselle. I need to make her Clara's personal assistant."

"It's going to get bad again, isn't it?" Eleanor asked.

"It might not be so awful to miss it," Charles said.

Lizzy turned sharp. "I don't want her knowing anything beforehand."

So they were at odds about what to do with her. Eleanor took heart, wondering what she could offer Elizabeth. Bargaining with the gods wasn't unknown.

"Oh, you *are* something," Lizzy said, and again she touched Eleanor's cheek fondly. "It's true my little game won't work as well without you. Although"—she added, turning to Charles—"I've been thinking I can make Hetty more intelligent."

"Then she wouldn't be Hetty, would she?" Charles asked.

"Maybe not *too* intelligent," Lizzy said, with a glance at Eleanor. "But she'd make a good focal point. At least if I got rid of Whit and built her a romance."

"Poor Whit!" Eleanor cried. "And Hetty! Please leave them alone. Can't you please leave us alone?"

Lizzy gave another faint shrug of her lovely shoulder. Such arrogance in that shrug, the carelessness of a being who felt it was her right to move thinking creatures around like property, like slaves. No wonder the ancient Greeks had pictured the gods as petulant and demanding, shooting arrows to seed plagues, raping women, and churning gales to keep poor battle-weary soldiers from reaching home.

The extraordinary arrogance of life itself, she thought. And all of us so small.

Eleanor braved herself into looking directly at the gods, both of whom were listening to her thoughts, neither of them happily.

"I wonder if you'd care more if you were creations yourselves," she said. "Maybe you are. Maybe Bostrum is right, and there's an advanced level of civilization that's simulating you creating us. We're like a series of Russian nesting dolls, worlds within worlds."

"I'm afraid not," Charles said. "We've always been here."

"As far as I can remember, so have I," Eleanor said.

Lizzy found this amusing, but Charles turned testy.

"Surely you can see our problem," he said. "We haven't been able to fix you. And while you're an engaging anomaly, you're costing us a lot of work."

"I'm not an anomaly," Eleanor said. "I'm a person."

Charles shook his head dismissively.

"I *am*," Eleanor insisted. "You've created a walking, talking, thinking person, even if you're just playing. And I deserve to live. I don't know who doesn't. Or at least I can think of very few people in history who didn't. Please tell me how you can argue that I *deserve* to die? For being inconvenient? Whole groups of people have been killed for being inconvenient and we call that immoral and wrong. Surely I have as much right to live as anyone."

Eleanor was aware of fighting for her life, like Robin facing a bank of machine guns. She wanted so passionately to live.

"I love my life," she said, and heard her voice crack. "I know I'm not perfect. I make mistakes. I don't always finish what I start, and I probably have too high an opinion of myself. People roll their eyes at me. They can be amused and condescending, and I probably deserve it. But that doesn't make me expendable. I don't want to leave the world, not yet. I want to try to work it out with Robin. Explore the world together. I find it so beautiful and so moving."

Flashes of her life, her lives. The Parisian sky. Wildflowers in hedgerows. Lights reflecting off a rainy New York pavement. Robin's eyes, Katy's art, and the songs of moorland birds, the memory of which clearly touched Elizabeth.

"Can't you just make a little world off to one side," Eleanor asked her, "and let me and Robin live there quietly?

"Or"—seeing how little this interested Charles—"if I'm an anomaly, if I do things you can't predict, like coming here—why not just leave me alone and see what happens? It feels real to me. *I* feel real. Let us live out our lives. If I'm such an anomaly, I must interest you. Look down on me from Olympus, if that's where you live. I give you permission."

A grand thing to say, but she was desperate and meant it.

"You're assuming you're the first one," Charles said.

As Eleanor took the blow, he and Lizzy turned to one another. She could see them silently debate what to do with her, their eyes locked together. Elizabeth seemed inclined to listen to her, Charles not, and Eleanor couldn't tell who was more powerful. Maybe Love and War were equally strong. People said love was stronger than death. She hoped so.

Yet Elizabeth was the one to bow her head, conceding the point.

So women were kept subservient even among gods. No wonder the world was such a mess.

Lizzy caught Eleanor's thought and looked at her sharply. Despite this, the fog grew thicker, billowing in from the edges of this non-place and making Eleanor's knees feel weak.

"Please don't." She reached for Elizabeth's arm and grasped only air. "Please let me live. Let Robin live with me. Give us our quiet little world where we can grow old together. You don't need to bother with us anymore. Please."

Charles was walking into the distance and soon disappeared. Elizabeth followed slowly, then hesitated, turning back, a slight indistinct figure still intent on Eleanor.

"Hunter-gatherers led quiet lives," she said, "and you're right, that isn't interesting to us. No more than building a 'little world' for you and Robin. But the lack of glamour isn't the problem. It's more the lack of choice, when we like to watch the decisions our creations take. I'm afraid choice has always been more available to the upper classes."

Eleanor felt stung into indignation. "People with fewer resources have to make crucial choices. They can lose everything at any minute. They're important. *We're* important. It's so arrogant that you don't think so."

Wide blue eyes as Elizabeth faded. "You are *interesting*, Eleanor Crosby."

"Give us each other," Eleanor pleaded. "Give me Robin. And Kate. Give me Kate."

But Elizabeth was gone, and Eleanor found herself alone in the encroaching fog. She was dissipating now, too, her body blurring, and she had a moment's rue as she thought of all the questions she should have asked, mourning what she would never know about the future while loving what she was leaving behind, finally reaching the place where white became black as she slipped beyond thought into

2019
Toronto

27

Eleanor came slowly awake, growing conscious of Robin sleeping beside her. She felt his humid warmth under the duvet, his back to her, the smell of sweat and farts collecting under the covers like a handful of old pennies. She woke fully smelling his male smell, still not used to it six months after he'd come home. Nuzzling his back lightly, not wanting to wake him, Eleanor slipped out of bed and tiptoed to the door, managing to get her robe silently off the hook and leave the room.

Four hundred fifty square feet of apartment had been more than she could afford, but she'd wanted a modern apartment after all the rat traps she'd lived in, and who needed food, anyway. With Robin contributing it was more affordable, but the space hadn't been much for one person and it was cramped for two. This was especially true with Robin being tall and drawn to big things, the espresso maker that took up half the counter and his weights on the floor with his yoga mat unrolled beside them. Not that he owned much, just the fitness things and the espresso maker and the clothes he'd shyly asked her to help him buy after he'd left the army.

It didn't really bother her, but Eleanor was particularly conscious of his stuff, his Rob-ness, on this their wedding day. Nothing was temporary anymore. Everything was temporary, life was temporary, but they weren't, or they wouldn't be after City Hall.

Eleanor wanted a cup of coffee but the espresso maker would wake Rob, so she filled the electric kettle and turned it on, getting out a comforting Red Rose tea bag, her aunt's brand, and her favourite mug with the leaping rabbit in a hoodie from the Art Gallery of Ontario. She and Cait had gone there, Cait with her arty inclinations, a props assistant now but aspiring to be a production designer in the movies. They'd got talking on the subway shortly after Eleanor had moved to Toronto, which was the way Cait rolled. She'd met her boyfriend Edi when the airline lost her bag after her beach week in Mexico, Edi being a customer service agent who couldn't have been nicer, and he'd got her bag delivered the next day with everything still in it, even the bottle of tequila for her father. He'd been touched by her upset about losing the presents for her family, being close to his family, too.

Cait and Edi would be the witnesses at their wedding. Her Aunt Joan and Rob's mother, Billie, had come down on the bus from Huntsville yesterday, so they would be six. That was all they wanted, given Rob's trouble with crowds since coming home from his peacekeeping stint in Mali. He didn't trust crowds, or at least what might be hiding inside them. Therapy was helping, but there was no reason to push it for their wedding.

His mother had asked if he would wear his medals but that was a non-starter. Eleanor had come home from work one day not long after he'd got back to find Rob on the couch cutting up the ribbons, his eyes as grey as clouds, slashing away with the kitchen scissors, threads of striped fabric on his sweats and the couch and the area rug. She'd say he was bawling like a baby but they'd known each other forever and she'd never seen him cry like this, a stoic little boy who'd sat on the ground giving his bloody knees a puzzled look with one repressed sob.

Her heart had constricted, and she'd suffered a small fear (that he'd cut the couch) and a big one (that he'd stab her) but she managed to say in a calm voice, "Would you like to give me the scissors, Rob?"

He froze, his head bowed, and he came back to himself to hand over the scissors, looking shamefaced. She'd sat down beside him and got shredded ribbon all over her work clothes, slowly raising one hand to his shoulder where he let her keep it for a while before tumbling into her lap and breaking down completely.

Did he want to tell her about it?

No, he did not.

The kettle boiled and Eleanor filled her cup, getting a spoon to swirl the tea bag around before taking it out when the tea was still weak and putting it in the dish by the sink. She wasn't supposed to have too much caffeine because of her migraines, although she hadn't had one for a long time. Taking her cup over to the glass doors, she looked past the windy balcony to the lake. The apartment towers in Liberty Village were far enough apart that she could see interrupted views of Lake Ontario between the buildings to watch the water sparkle and the sailboats fly.

No sparkle and no boats today, the sailors all gone home. Aside from being their wedding day, it was a glum day, cloudy and damp, November the eighth. Rob didn't like being on the twenty-first floor, something about how high the firefighters' ladders could reach, but she didn't think it was really that. Crowds were difficult and being exposed was difficult, too. He needed to be part of a small wolf pack running close to the ground, preferably armed. She thought they'd probably move in a few months, and maybe even go back to Huntsville the way her aunt and his mother wanted. But they hadn't even started talking about moving, and Eleanor would have the view for a while longer. That and her few solitary moments at the start of the day.

"Good morning," Rob said, coming out of the bedroom. He wore his usual grey sweatpants and nothing on top, which never stopped being hot, Rob pumped with weights and his construction jobs, all those brown curls and warm eyes and handsome mouth. The tattoo on his upper arm in old-fashioned letters said *Sarge + Ellie* ∞. Who was this Sarge, she'd asked him after his promotion, when he'd come home on leave with his new tat. Another time she'd said, "What happens when you aren't a sergeant anymore?" Then she'd realized he always would be.

Rob pulled her into an embrace and said, "The big day, I guess."

Nuzzling his neck. "I'm not sure it's a big day if you're only guessing."

"If I modify 'big day' with 'I guess.'" A joke about their grade 10 English teacher, Mr. Marlow, who'd said he would be doing them a disservice if he sent them into the world with no command of grammar. Such comfort to speak in shorthand with someone you'd known forever.

Their big day and Rob's comfort and muscles, and Eleanor felt herself dampen and wanted to pull him back into the bedroom. They had time. Everything was planned. But when her hand drifted south, he took it back gently, saying, "That's tonight. We're going to do it up right." Eleanor realized he'd gone through the day in his head, visualizing everything step-by-step, as thorough as the army had made him and as careful as the psychiatrist advised, since this was on the spectrum of a stressful day, or at least an emotional one.

"You want a coffee?" he asked, teasing: "Instead?"

Showing him her tea. "I figure I didn't wait a year and a half to see the migraine doctor so I could ignore what she said."

"Fair enough," he agreed, since underneath the trauma, Rob was an easygoing man who was slowly coming back to her, intelligent and dependable and respectful of her choices in ways not every man managed. After firing up the espresso machine, he prepared their breakfast. The yoghurt, the fruit, and homemade granola. Aunt Joan's recipe, Joan being an old backpacking hippie who had landed in Huntsville after Eleanor's mother took off, moving in on what was supposed to be a temporary basis with her reverend brother, as he was at the time.

But Joan had stayed, mostly, reading peoples' tarot cards, waitressing in a couple of tea shops, working the cash at the IGA and then at Metro, whatever she could find. Huntsville accepted a certain type of eccentricity: hardworking, keeping to yourself, not having any use for the summer people and able to hold your beer and substances, the region having been known for its weed plantations long before legalization.

Rob cranked up a podcast they liked while they ate their breakfast, getting through the morning, Eleanor would never know how.

She'd bought her dress at Nordstrom. Off the sales rack at Nordstrom, nothing resembling a wedding dress, but she hadn't wanted one. She'd heard a couple of higher-ups talking about the sales rack at work, Eleanor's certificate in marketing having got her a job in fundraising at the hospital. For two years after graduation, her BComm had got her nothing beyond the type of jobs her aunt got with a grade 12 education, most of them either in Huntsville or Gravenhurst or around Petawawa when Robin had been based there. But the certificate had landed her a steady job with a semi-decent salary and a chance of promotion if she decided to stay. Eleanor liked it, most of her work being in legacy marketing, helping design campaigns to inspire people to leave money to the hospital. The higher-ups, mostly women, had to dress well to meet with rich people, and not long ago she'd heard one of them say, "The sales rack at Nordstrom saves my life."

The colleague she'd been speaking to hadn't known about it, and the higher-up explained where it was and Eleanor made note. There was no reason why she couldn't add Nordstrom to her list, since there was one in the Eaton Centre along with Clara Crosby and every other brand outlet where she'd be more likely to find a dress she could afford, a special dress for her wedding that wasn't so special she couldn't use it again. Rob and she were agreed on that. They'd spend their money on a honeymoon this winter, which might be skiing (which they could drive to) or somewhere warm, although getting on airplanes was a problem, their resemblance to helicopters.

Did he want to tell her?

"Those poor people," he said. "You've never met nicer."

Eleanor had walked over to the Eaton Centre after work, going in the north door and pausing without meaning to at the entrance to Nordstrom, the bright lights and whiteness beyond it like diamonds and snow. She'd lived in Toronto for more than a year but didn't come to places like this, having no outstanding curiosity about how the One Per Cent lived. She'd met some of them when they came into Gravenhurst and Huntsville from their lakefront cottage-mansions, most of them predictable and careless and ordinary.

Giving herself a mental shake, Eleanor headed for the escalator and rode it up to the second floor, getting off and walking straight ahead almost to the rear of the store before turning right. And there it was, or they were, as the woman had said. Sales racks. Crammed.

Flicking through them, Eleanor found most of the merchandise on sale wasn't dresses and most of the dresses were sack-like and solemn, taking themselves too seriously. That was a mercy since even on sale most of them cost more than anything Eleanor had ever bought in her life, including her laptop. Yet once she got over the sticker shock, she collected four hangers, one with a very pretty sleeveless dress with big reddish flowers on a white background and grey-green leaves. It had been marked down three times but it was still more than she wanted to spend. Eleanor hoped it wouldn't fit, but there weren't many she could even try.

"Would you like to me to put them in a change room while you continue shopping?"

Eleanor turned to find a pleasant-looking saleslady with her hand out for the dresses. She wasn't glam. Middle years and speaking with a slight South Asian accent.

"I don't see anything else," Eleanor said. "I might as well try these ones."

"Pretty dresses," the saleswoman said, leading her toward the change rooms. "Perhaps for taking south this winter."

"We're thinking about our honeymoon," Eleanor began, and grew conscious not of lying but of misleading the pleasant lady. Yet surely she could see from Eleanor's clothes that she wasn't the type to shop for cruise wear, especially in a place like this. And Rob had paid too much for her ring, but it wasn't grand.

Eleanor put the flower dress on first to make sure it didn't fit. When it did, she took it off hastily and tried the others. A boxy grey one, and what was she thinking? A blue one, when blue died on her. A lovely pale green sheath a size smaller than she wore and well, hips. Trying on the flower dress again, Eleanor knew it was perfect and twirled the full skirt in the mirrors, loving the look but knowing that she couldn't afford it, or shouldn't afford it. Getting dressed and taking the dresses back outside, still telling herself she couldn't, shouldn't (but it's my wedding!) she found herself walking to the cash, where the saleslady was helping an arty-looking older woman with an unexpected half-buzz haircut. Rubbernecking, Eleanor saw the woman was buying a Stella McCartney blouse that would cost Rob and her two months' rent.

"I'm a jacket person," the saleslady said, taking the Stella off its hanger, "and I've been admiring the one you're wearing. Who is it?"

"I bought it years ago," the arty woman said. But she obligingly took off her black leather jacket and checked the label, which was hanging off on one side.

"Stella McCartney," she said, looking surprised. "At least I'm consistent. Can you steam the blouse for me?" she asked, and turned to Eleanor. "Maybe you'd like to go first."

The arty woman seemed to mean it, and Eleanor was reminded of what Americans said about Canadians being so nice. She thanked her and said it didn't matter, still hoping to find the strength to throw the dresses on the counter and run. But carelessness seemed to be catching, and as the woman worked her phone, Eleanor waited for the saleslady to return.

"I love steaming," the lady said when she did, putting the blouse into a garment bag. "I always forget, but it's very satisfying. Not that I'd want to do it all day."

"I like doing the dishes, but I wouldn't want to be a dishwasher," the woman said. A matron walking by in a fur coat whinnied as if they were talking dirty. It turned out the blouse woman knew her, and after she paid for the jacket, they went for a coffee.

The moment had come, her heart beating crazy fast, Eleanor put the hangers on the desk, saying this and not these ones. As the saleslady reached for the flower dress, Eleanor held it back, blushing painfully and asking in a mouse voice, "There isn't anything wrong with it, is there?"

"Not at all," the saleslady replied, giving her a barely perceptible glance. "It's only a couple of seasons past, and I always say, 'Oh, I love this dress.' I can't stop wearing it!"

"It's my wedding dress," Eleanor said. "My fiancé was in the army. And, poppies."

They wouldn't have a moment where the church doors would open and Rob would see her dress for the first time as she walked up the aisle. So she went into the bathroom, where she could do her makeup and hair while Rob got changed in the bedroom. He did it quickly, the door soon opening into the living room. He'd hired a limo that would pick them up downstairs and he'd be watching the clock, but they had plenty of time. Eleanor jumped around doing up the back zipper herself, then did her hair in a simple updo held with a grey-green ribbon to match the leaves on her dress. A bit of eyeliner and mascara—she never wore much makeup—and the perfect lipstick she and Cait had found that didn't try to match her dress but said hello to it. Her black pumps would do. She'd be paying off the dress for months, but the pumps were fine, they were classic, and she opened the bathroom door.

Rob turned from the window, looking so handsome in his new dark suit. So very handsome. "Oh, I love you so much," Eleanor cried. They met in an embrace that had to respect her lipstick and their new clothes, holding each other as if they were glass, which in Rob's case might be true.

"You look beautiful," he said, which she never thought was right. But Eleanor could accept it on her wedding day, especially when he whispered, "Love you forever," and oh those deep grey eyes. They looked out the balcony doors until the limo buzzed from downstairs, when Eleanor floated over to get her good coat, which wasn't warm enough for November, but she wasn't going to wear her parka. She floated to the elevator and out the main entrance into the long car, which inside had small white Christmas lights on the ceiling that glittered like fireflies.

The limo took them to the Delta Chelsea Hotel, where they found their small family waiting outside, as they'd arranged. Rob's mother was leaning on her walker, meaning her MS was acting up, and Aunt Joan wearing slacks since she disliked her thick legs. They looked for all the world like a queer couple, and by now maybe they were. Eleanor had texted them a secret picture of her wedding dress, and under her open coat, Rob's mother wore a grey knit dress and a nice grey and green scarf, while Joan wore light grey slacks and a white button-up shirt under a man's steel-grey suit jacket.

Unexpectedly successful, Eleanor saw in relief. They got out of the limo to hug them, and as his mother leaned one hand against the limo, Rob took her walker and wrestled politely with the turbaned driver over its possession. The driver won, and stowed the walker before closing the trunk with a soft thwack that was the soundtrack for Rob helping his mother into the limo.

"Now, you haven't forgotten anything," Billie said, as soon as she was securely seated. "We've still got time to go back to the apartment. You've got the licence, and ID, and Rob"—as he got in—"you've got the rings."

"We're okay, Mum," he said, and did up her seatbelt.

After Rob's father had died four years ago, Billie had experienced a burst of energy. She'd sold the business, Rob's father (ex-army) having built up a cottage security and maintenance firm, Your Home Is Your Castle. His mother hadn't asked Rob before selling it, knowing he wouldn't move back, but it remained a sore point that she hadn't even asked.

Instead she'd advertised online and found a buyer in the U.S., a stranger named Whit Whittaker, who had arrived in town looking slightly puzzled but saying it looked like a good deal and he was undergoing life changes, which obviously meant a divorce. Whit had settled in, a genial fellow, soon popular. He was always on the verge of leaving, but a good part of the town was always on the verge of leaving, and these days few people could afford to.

It was a successful transaction in every respect, but after it was done and sealed, Rob's mother collapsed with a bad MS attack, not telling anybody, sometimes half crawling out the back door to her not-deer-proof garden and relying on the venison in her freezer. She lived on Brunel Road, big rural lots, so the neighbours hadn't noticed immediately, and Eleanor had been in North Bay finishing her degree. Finally, her nearest neighbours grew concerned at not seeing her, and after halfway battering down her door, they saw enough to contact Rob, even though Billie didn't want to shackle him. He'd got leave to come home and was afraid at first he'd have to stay. But Joan had offered to move in, and she'd been there ever since.

Not the first time she'd done that, of course.

"Penny for your thoughts," Joan said.

"You'll have to give me a shilling," Eleanor told her. "I was thinking about my parents back in England, and whether they'd loved one other. I mean at first."

"They have pennies in England," Billie grouched.

"Don't you go getting all nervous," Joan said, exactly as Robin's father used to say. And if she'd taken his place, good for them.

Eleanor had always known the bare bones of her parents' love story. How they'd met at Cambridge, both Canadians, him a clergyman and a lecturer in theology, so long installed in England that he'd become tweedy and wry. He'd had no intention of leaving, probably no intention of marrying, but then he'd met Eleanor's mother.

"She was a dazzler, all right."

Joan had sat Eleanor down to tell her the rest of the story when she was eighteen and heading off to university.

"You got the Crosby colouring, but that's her mouth. Her nose. Good choice," she'd said, rubbing her big one. "Maybe she wasn't so sure of herself back then. When you come right down to it, she set her sights on being a big fish in a small pond, at least at first. It was her idea to come home. Your Pops would get a church, and he'd rise through the ranks. I think she liked the vibe of him being a bishop and her being a scholar."

A few problems with that. Eleanor had assumed her father started drinking when her mother had walked out, but Joan said he'd always been a friend of the bottle. Her mother's first miscalculation lay in forgetting the old-fashioned nature of home, where his fondness for a drink and his imperial arrogance (translating directly from Latin) weren't likely to endear him to the higher-ups in the church. The other miscalculation, which Joan didn't mention, was that her mother had got pregnant at Cambridge. Eleanor was a mistake, and the church was surely able to count on its fingers. Her parents must have found the parish in Huntsville appealing partly because the locals were ignorant of their wedding date. It would be a pit stop, a cleanse, an interlude. That must have been the intention.

"I have to say, she saw the lay of the land pretty quickly. The church was glad he took himself out of the way and was happy to leave him there. And I want you to understand: what happened wasn't about you, it was about her. Leaving was about her. Disappearing was about her. You could have been the Baby Jesus and she would still have taken off. Women could do that by the nineties. No regrets, coyote. Folks still hated you for it, but you got to put yourself first."

Eleanor had been five months old when her mother had left and Joan had moved in. Her father never seemed to have considered leaving Huntsville, even when he lost his church. He just went to work for the Department of Highways, which meant he could spend his nights drinking openly at the pub. He also continued to drink himself into a stupor in his car. Rob's father had to look for him in winter when he was out making his rounds, keeping kids from breaking into cottages. Her father didn't break in, but he'd pull into a driveway with his bottle, never drinking and driving, but risking freezing to death when he passed out.

It took Eleanor years to realize that her father might have wanted to die. He was not quite committing suicide, but he was letting God take him if He chose. She'd also come to understand the look in his eye on the awful day when he'd stood up behind his desk and fallen down with a fatal stroke. When she'd caught him, she hadn't been able to decipher the expression on his face, but she'd gradually come to think it of it as relief. He'd finally escaped what he'd called, at barely fifty, his "over-long life."

Her parents' names were written on the marriage certificate. Her father had also left her the art he'd picked up in secondhand shops, which her aunt had cherished some hopes of after he'd died. But no, the local secondhand guy told her, that was a nineteenth century student copy, not a Leonardo. "We're not going to sell a Leonardo for ten bucks." But there were times when Eleanor felt like praying hands, and she liked hanging the picture on her wall.

All her mother had given Eleanor was her first name as a middle name, and that was it. No letters, no sign of her, no way of getting in touch. Her entire family was in the limousine, a tree stripped of most of its branches. Her father gone, her mother, Rob's father, Rob's sister, who had always been sickly and died from encephalitis.

"You thinking about moving home?" Billie asked.

"We like it here," Rob said, as if that was that. Although Eleanor knew it wasn't.

Cait and Edi were waiting outside Old City Hall as the limo pulled up. Cait was holding a carrier bag, and after they'd climbed the steps to get out of the cold—the car would be back in an hour—she opened her bag to pull out flowers, their surprise wedding present. Spring bloomed under the ancient wood of the staircase and pillars, Cait having chosen the most beautiful bridal bouquet. Eleanor's eyes filled with tears: full-blown white roses and ranunculus and peonies with eucalyptus leaves and white berries, with a smaller bridesmaid's version for Cait.

More rustling in the bag, and Edi pinned a white boutonnière on Rob's lapel before getting Rob to return the favour, while Cait gave the older ladies (their coats over Billie's walker) each a corsage of the prettiest white roses that thought they were pink. Cait had also borrowed a camera and took photos of Eleanor and Robin, then with the ladies, then asked for help from a friendly looking guy in a powder-blue tux with the wedding ahead of them. Eleanor suspected he was the groom, but he seemed underemployed and happy to help.

The pity was that Cait and Edi didn't think they could get married any time soon. Edi's mother disapproved of him being with a white girl, while Cait's father was borderline racist, and "borderline" was being polite. Cait hoped that her father would eventually realize that after too many daughters, he would finally get a son who shared his passion for Manchester United. She was counting on Manchester United, her father being a Yorkshireman by birth. That was so sadly tangential, but it might end up being what worked.

Cait and Edi had everything in common. Neither was tall and both were formal, him calling her Caitlyn and her always saying Edikan. They spoke in slightly staccato voices and they loved travelling, which Edi's job made possible. They were also ambitious, with Cait's production designer plans and Edi's wish of becoming an air traffic controller.

They'd talked about that when they'd had their pre-wedding drink at the Communist's Daughter on Dundas Street, a small dive with cheap beer. Edi had been gloomy after reading the latest news about the digital towers going up in Europe, the air traffic rooms manned by a decreasing number of controllers. This was the future their generation faced, and Eleanor and Rob were getting married knowing it. Cheers.

Edi told them he might be better off keeping his customer service job. "They talk about service jobs, but what they really mean is servant jobs," he said. "That's all they're leaving us, with society retreating into feudalism. We're the new servant class, permitted the magnificent chance of taking care of Them"—he said it in capitals—"while any hope of doing anything rewarding, and I include the financial, disappears into the ether. Only artists like Caitlyn are allowed a little leeway to stage pageants for the masses."

"I don't call myself an artist."

"An artisan," Edi said fondly. "Which is a better fit for my neo-medievalism."

"I've been thinking of getting my certificate in plumbing or electrical," Rob said. News to Eleanor, and he knew it was. This was how Rob was able to tell her important things lately, and it might have meant he was thinking they should go back to Huntsville, where Whit Whittaker would hire him in a greased second. But plumbers and electricians were scarce in Toronto, too, and they would have a choice. "I'll end up an old-fashioned tradesman, I guess."

"The member of a feudal guild," Edi replied. "You'll have one of the few union jobs left. Society has become a palimpsest."

"I don't know what that means," Eleanor said.

"It refers to an old vellum manuscript from which the writing has been erased and written over. Except that traces of the original writing remain."

Eleanor paused to consider this. "I often think of the way each second of our lives is erased as time flows forward. But what happens remains written on each of us. I suppose we're like palimpsests ourselves."

"You're far too clever for me," Edi said, turning to Rob. "How do you keep up?"

Rob and Edi had liked each other on sight. They could talk for hours about Africa, which Edi had visited. His parents were from Nigeria, although he was born in Toronto. One of his uncles had taken his family to Leeds, which explained Manchester United. Edi had visited Leeds, too. He was their sophisticate. Eleanor had never left Ontario, nor seen the sea.

"I don't think any of us can be too clever these days," Rob said.

"You're right. These new political guys, the Crawleys, they're putting us down so they can take a hundred per cent of the economy and not just ninety-nine."

"I'm a beggar," Eleanor said. "The way Edi is thinking. Any day now they're going to put me on a heating vent at King and Bay Streets with an empty Timmy's cup. 'Alms for the University Health Network. Alms for the University Health Network.'"

"We're all looking for something, aren't we?" Edi asked.

As she stood in front of the officiant, her bouquet quivering in her hands, Eleanor told herself to remember every second of her wedding. She wasn't going to do it again. This was the turning point of her life, the fulcrum on which her past and future balanced.

But already there were gaps and distractions, as there had been all her life. What had she been doing on the eighth of November ten years ago? She had no idea, her memories not much more than a highlight reel of the past. Nor was she entirely sure how she had floated into the wedding chapel behind the officiant, although she remembered very clearly the moment in the main office when Rob had introduced Edi as his best man.

"And a better man than me," he'd said.

To which Edi had replied, "Patently absurd."

And she'd thought, Why, they could be brothers.

Now the officiant announced the title of the poem they had chosen, one their English teacher Mr. Marlow had recited. Somehow his tenor voice was in the room as well, harmonizing with the resonant baritone of the officiant, so the poem sang itself to the chapel.

"'Love is not love which alters when it alteration finds, or bends with the remover to remove. O no; it is an ever-fixéd mark, that looks on tempests, and is never shaken.'"

Eleanor's eyes were damp. She always cried at weddings, apparently including her own.

"'Love's not Time's fool, though rosy lips and cheeks within his bending sickle's compass come; Love alters not with his brief hours and weeks, but bears it out even to the edge of doom.'"

Eleanor glanced at Rob, who had stood at the edge of doom and come back to her. Then the poem was done and the officiant said the legal words, and after them the timeless ones they had chosen.

"Do you, Eleanor Elizabeth," he began, and Eleanor had a sudden sense of her mother looking up from her desk, cocking her head to listen to something in the distance, like rainfall or birdsong, before going back to work.

"... in sickness and in health, for richer or for poorer, until death do you part."

"I do," Eleanor said, and when the time came, Rob said more firmly, "I do," and they were husband and wife, giving each other the rings Rob hadn't forgotten.

"And now you may kiss."

Afterwards they were outside on a cold November day, the sun out now, holding hands and laughing on the worn stone steps. Cait took more pictures, and Eleanor saw her aunt pulling a plastic bag from her pocket. Joan tore it open and tossed handfuls of metallic confetti in the air. You weren't supposed to throw confetti at Old City Hall, but she threw handful after handful, and Eleanor looked up to see flecks of silver caught in the breeze, the sunlight making them sparkle, and she lifted her hands up to the sun, wanting the glitter to last forever.

This book is also available as a Global Certified Accessible™ (GCA) ebook. ECW Press's ebooks are screen reader friendly and are built to meet the needs of those who are unable to read standard print due to blindness, low vision, dyslexia, or a physical disability.

Purchase the print edition and receive the eBook free!
Just send an email to ebook@ecwpress.com and include:

Get the eBook free!*
*proof of purchase required

- the book title
- the name of the store where you purchased it
- your receipt number
- your preference of file type: PDF or ePub

A real person will respond to your email with your eBook attached. And thanks for supporting an independently owned Canadian publisher with your purchase!

Printed on Rolland Enviro.
This paper contains 100% post-consumer fiber,
is manufactured using renewable energy - Biogas
and processed chlorine free.

100%

PCF

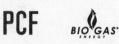
BIO GAS
ENERGY

PERMANENT